GORILLA

By the same author

Fiction

DEATH AT FLIGHT
DEATH AT THE STRIKE
DEATH IN COVERT
THE ANIMAL-CATCHERS
HAZANDA
THE COAST OF LONELINESS
THE FIGHTERS

Sport

ANGLER'S ENCYCLOPAEDIA
COME FISHING WITH ME
COME FLY-FISHING WITH ME
COARSE FISHING
THE GUN-PUNT ADVENTURE
DUCK SHOOTING

Wildlife and Travel

LOOK AT AFRICAN ANIMALS
THE ENORMOUS ZOO
AFRICA'S GREAT RIFT VALLEY

Biography

KENZIE, THE WILDGOOSE MAN

Autobiography

LANDSCAPE WITH SOLITARY FIGURE

Humour

ROD, POLE OR PERCH
DUDLEY, THE WORST DOG IN THE WORLD

GORILLA

Colin Willock

M

© Colin Willock 1977

All rights reserved. No part of this publication
may be reproduced or transmitted, in any form or
by any means, without permission.

ISBN: 0 333 21181 2

First published 1977 by
MACMILLAN LONDON LIMITED
4 Little Essex Street London WC2R 3LF
and Basingstoke
Associated Companies in Delhi, Dublin,
Hong Kong, Johannesburg, Lagos, Melbourne,
New York, Singapore and Tokyo

Typeset by
SANTYPE INTERNATIONAL LIMITED
COLDTYPE DIVISION

Printed in Great Britain by
REDWOOD BURN LTD.
Trowbridge and Esher

61021

MORAY DISTRICT
F
LIBRARY SERVICE

For Lee Lyon,
killed by an elephant,
Rwanda, June 1975

Author's Note

At this moment, mountain gorillas exist in only two African countries. Despite this sad fact, no resemblance is intended to either of these and certainly not to the political events, particularly those affecting wildlife conservation, occurring there now or in the past. Both countries have an excellent conservation record. All political figures, as well as those in the field of international conservation, were born solely in the author's mind. Anyone who has lived or worked in Africa will inevitably have met, or heard of, men dedicated to wildlife like Jean-Pierre Menant. To me, he is an amalgam of many such men. If he exists, or existed, I would have been proud to have known him. As it is, his character, deeds, opinions, adventures, both public and private, are entirely the invention of the author.

C.W.

Part One

THE HYENAS

The *Fisi* — the hyenas — were coming. There had been rumours and counter-rumours for weeks. Some of the Europeans had forecast that the revolutionary army would never bother with Kenanja Province. The Province was too small, too heavily forested, too dependant on bananas, coffee, tea and pineapples to appeal to the *Fisi*. What the self-styled hyenas liked everywhere were rich and easy pickings. The *Fisi* fed on shops, banks, office buildings, apartment houses, settlers' bungalows, rape and slaughter. Kenanja Province offered a few opportunities in the last three departments but not enough to persuade the easily disaffected *Fisi* rank and file to march for days through dark, dispiriting, lootless rain-forest. Thus had the handful of European farm managers and Kenanja businessmen reasoned. But they had overlooked the lake. They had overlooked it simply because they could not imagine a rabble of badly led revolutionaries crossing ten miles of unpredictable and often stormy water. Africans, even the terrible *Fisi*, did not like water, so they would not come.

There was, unfortunately, a flaw in this argument as the events of the last three days had proved. Not all the *Fisi* were badly led. 'General' Patrice had a reputation. It was said that the 'General' had done a year's service in an engineer regiment of the army of the former colonists where he had been considered leadership-material. Since the uprising he had justified the army's belief in him by murdering thousands of his former masters as well as many Africans who had worked for them. It was Patrice who was coming now, coming via the lake. The General had taken a strategic look at the lake and decided that, if he didn't cross it and secure Kenanja Province on the far shore, someone else soon would. He had little doubt that that someone would include the white mercenaries whom the government — no, that was the wrong word, since the *Fisi* had deposed the government — whom the former, deposed, regime were increasingly employing.

So General Patrice had acted with praiseworthy military

promptitude. With a picked *Fisi* column he had made a forced march to the north end of the lake and seized the only two steamers still in service on it. In a moment of over-enthusiasm his men had massacred the crew of one steamer by cramming them head-first into their own blazing fire-boxes. The General had been exceptionally annoyed by an act of gratuitous brutality which he might, at other times, have found amusing. To make his point he had sentenced the offenders to the same fate. The crew of the other steamer had been sufficiently impressed by this action to volunteer to sail both steamers southward down the lake for the General.

Each steamer had been built to carry fifty persons in comparative comfort. General Patrice was not interested in comfort. He wanted troops in Kenanja Province rapidly to secure his left flank. So the steamers carried 250 *Fisi* at each crossing. Some had fallen off to become food for the crocodiles, but the majority had made it. Within two days there were one thousand *Fisi* ashore and more were said to be coming. The news had been brought to the town of Baruva by a Catholic missionary, the only survivor among five priests and fifteen nuns whose mission had had the misfortune to overlook the bay where the first boatload of *Fisi* had landed. It was the priest's opinion that the *Fisi* advance guard was not more than forty-eight hours behind him.

Jean-Pierre Menant had heard the priest's tale. Now he watched his fellow-countrymen's preparations for departure. He could not honestly say he blamed them, though he himself had no intention of leaving. He had plantations in the mountains above Baruva, plantations that his father had hacked out of the living rain-forests with the strength of his Flemish character and the power of his broad Flemish hands. Menant very much doubted whether the *Fisi* would deviate far enough from the pickings of Baruva and the settlements along the lake shore to attack a solitary farm. And if they did, he was ready for them. The farmhouse was built like a fort. He had stocked it with provisions for six months' siege.

There was a well within the building itself. His father had given the house a stone tower, like a keep, eyed with weapon-slits. His father, ten years dead, could not have foretold the coming of the *Fisi* but he had known the nature of the country in which he had chosen to settle; even more, he had understood the uncertain nature of its people.

The moment, three years previously, when it had become clear that his own nation had decided suddenly and arbitrarily to grant its former colony independence, Menant had taken out additional house insurance. Explosives and weapons were easy to come by. He had bought an ex-American Army fifty-calibre machine-gun, six Stens, and a quantity of plastic explosive. He had trained three of his African trackers in the use of the Stens, since he did not rate too highly their chances of hitting anything as small as a man with a single bullet. His secondary armament included four hunting rifles, three shotguns and, most important of all, one hundred hand grenades. Stacked in the cellars, the topmost boxes opened for ready use, were thirty thousand rounds for these various small arms. The heavy machine-gun, mounted on its tripod, looked down from a weapon-slit in the tower on to the one-hundred-yard clearing in the bush he had had cut all round the house. If the *Fisi* came they would find a welcome against which even their witch doctors' magic could not protect them.

Menant sat sipping a cold Simba beer on the verandah of Baruva's Hôtel du Président. He heard the tyres of the white Peugeot squealing long before it turned the corner into the newly-named Rue du Révolution Populaire and knew that in a few seconds he could be confronted by the sallow, sweating face of Jacques Veniard, Baruva's only white doctor.

Menant's gaze, deceptively bland, innocent and youthful, met the over-heated features of the doctor with about as much cooling and pacifying effect as drops of cold water splashed on to a red hot-plate.

'You're leaving town, Jacques?' Menant pointed with his

glass towards the roof of the Peugeot piled with suitcases, bedding and what Menant recognised as Veniard's only waiting-room chair.

'Of course I'm leaving town, idiot. So should you be. I'm getting out, crossing the border while it's still open. Once the *Fisi* hit Baruva no one will get out. No whites, anyway. They'll murder their own people, too.'

'They say the Force Nationale is bringing in reinforcements any day now.'

'You surely don't believe that, Jean-Pierre?'

Menant shrugged in amusement or, possibly, resignation. 'No. But then we have our loyal resident garrison.'

'You mean those two hundred cretins down at the barracks? The FN will turn tail directly they hear the first *Fisi* shout of "*Mai*".'

'Yes. I agree.'

'Then why stay?'

'I shan't. Not in Baruva, at least.'

'Once they've taken the town they'll swarm out over the surrounding countryside. Your plantation is only forty kilos away, remember.'

'If they come, the *Fisi* won't find that *my* bullets turn to water.'

'Jean-Pierre, I beg you. When they shout "*Mai*" that's what they believe will happen.'

Three private cars and a Citroën three-ton lorry piled high with furniture were now jammed behind the doctor's car. All were hooting.

'If I can't persuade you. . . .'

'Thanks, Jacques, but you can't.'

'Then I must collect Héloïse. There isn't much time.'

As the doctor let in the clutch and shot forward, the waiting-room chair fell off the roof. Either he didn't notice or didn't wish to waste time picking it up. The three-tonner crunched it into firewood as it passed, hooting at everything or nothing.

By the time the staff of the Hôtel du Président had served

14

lunch in a manner that suggested it might be the last meal they would ever serve, the main street had become totally deserted except for a small knot of Africans. These hung around like vultures waiting for the lions to leave a kill. The carcase, or rather carcases, were almost certainly those shops which lacked steel shutters to their windows. The shops, the property of Europeans who had that morning left town, were empty of anything worth looting. This, however, would not stop the Africans from smashing their windows.

It was time for Jean-Pierre to be going. Calling for a bill struck him as being needlessly punctilious at this moment in Baruva's history. He did so with a certainty that his twenty-franc note would never succeed in making its escape from the waiter's pocket.

The vultures had taken off. This could only mean that the lions were returning. An army jeep, followed by a lorry, had stopped in the main street. As Force Nationale men in camouflaged overalls and American steel helmets jumped down, the looters ran for it. Menant guessed correctly that the FN had not come to protect European property so much as to reserve it for themselves when the situation in Baruva deteriorated further.

The occupants of the jeep, three NCOs with rifles, rattled the steel shutters on some of the shop windows speculatively while the ten men in fatigue dress began to unload material from the lorry to build a road block.

Menant's own jeep waited for him in the inner courtyard of the hotel. Even within the confines of the hotel Menant judged it unsafe to leave his vehicle unattended. His half-pygmy tracker, Mushi, lay at full length on the front seat. Mushi was named after a vine found in the forest which the little man loved to chew. Everything about the jeep except Mushi looked businesslike. Three jerricans of petrol and one of water were padlocked to a rack in front of the radiator. Welded to the frame beside the driver was a bracket that had been designed to support a Bren gun. The gun itself, together with a dozen full magazines and a box of ten grenades, lay in a locked steel container bolted to the vehicle's floor. Menant started the engine. As they turned into the main street a second military lorry began unloading empty forty-gallon drums. The fatigue party rolled the first of these into position to form a second line of defence behind the flimsy barbed-wire barrier already drawn across the street.

The sergeant at the road-block held up his hand imperiously. Menant slowed just sufficiently to make the sergeant think that he had succeeded in stopping him, then he put his foot down. The jeep shot through the gap in the barrier with an inch to apare on either side. A corporal cocked his Tommy-gun. Menant drove on without accelerating or looking back. When they had cleared the town and were speeding along the lake shore towards the distant mountains, Menant spoke to Mushi in French.

'Take the jeep home and tell Musharamena I will be back in two days.' Musharamena was his second tracker. His name meant that he always ate with his mouth open.

'I understand. Shall I come to fetch you?'

'No. I will return on foot over the mountain.'

'And if the *Fisi* come and you are not there?'

'They will not. They will go to Baruva first, but be sure to tell Pilipili to keep a guard in the tower all the time.'

'They say they can turn bullets to water.'

'Let them try.'

They had turned off the main road and were bumping up a rocky track among tall hagenia trees. After a mile of steep ascent the track ran out beside the remains of a charcoal burner's fire. Menant dismounted. From beneath the dash-board he took two full clips for the Walther .38 automatic in his belt. He slid a .306 Winchester hunting rifle out of its leather sleeve, made sure the magazine was full and eased the bolt forward over the topmost round so that it did not load into the chamber. He picked up the small pack full of provisions and put it on his back. Then he raised his hand to Mushi and set off uphill into the trees. The jeep roared away and he was alone with the mountain and the forest.

*

16

Where others found the forest occlusive and menacing, or simply did not venture into it, Menant was completely at home there. He had hunted in it since he was fourteen. He was now thirty-two. He had hunted elephant, antelope such as bushbuck and duiker as well as giant forest hog. As a boy he had once shot at but, luckily for himself, missed a young male gorilla. His father had there and then beaten the breath half out of him with a leather cartridge belt. Had he killed the gorilla he honestly believed his father might have come very close to killing his only son. Almost from that moment Jean-Pierre had developed a healthy respect for gorillas which had little to do with the beating he had received on their behalf. His father conveyed to his son his own feelings towards the great apes.

No animal, his father had told him, so closely resembled man and so reminded him of his own primeval beginnings. Far from being the aggressive creature described by hunters' tales, the mountain gorilla was a peaceful vegetarian who lived out a blameless family life, if only man would let him. He only became dangerous when threatened and then his anger was terrible indeed. But who could blame the gorilla?

Because he had a great respect for his father, Jean-Pierre listened to these views but decided to examine them for himself as opportunity occurred. So, though he hunted in the forest as often as his schooling and his father would allow, he shot at no more gorillas though he continued to stalk them. His stalking was rarely successful. He was seldom able to approach a gorilla group closely enough to obtain more than a glimpse of an arm, a face, a moving branch. They remained his tantalising familiars in the forest. Good as his fieldcraft was with other species, he made little progress in his desire to know gorillas. And so it had remained until very recently.

He had followed the trail he was climbing just over a week ago and yet the forest had closed ranks as though no one had ever passed that way. Holding a sharp clasp-knife in his right hand, Menant picked his way along at a surprisingly fast pace. He side-stepped rotting logs, ducked beneath trailing creepers

17

and, wherever a briar or giant nettle obstructed his progress, snicked it neatly with the knife. All this he did without appearing to slacken his steady upwards progress. The nature of the trail did not always permit him to continue climbing. Sometimes he was forced to follow a contour line that took him down into a ravine, formed countless centuries ago by a lava flow but now cloaked, like everything else, in clinging green. The bottom of each ravine was loud with running water though the stream itself was invariably covered by vines and creepers through which his feet slid. Even Menant found these ravines hard going. At the second one he stopped and scooped some water up in his hand. The forest was a quiet place. A stranger might have expected it to be harsh with the shriek and gibber of highly-coloured birds. The altitude was too great, the canopy too dense and lacking in blossom to attract many species. The only bird he saw was a grey hornbill plucking wild figs with its outrageously large beak. Once he heard a turaco scream. That was all. He might have been beneath the sea, drowned in the green light filtering through the trees.

When he had been climbing for an hour, the hagenia woodland began to drop away and give place to bamboo forest; not bamboo as most people think of it in terms of slender cane, but living bamboo, three or four inches thick, standing thirty or more feet high and crowned with long green leaves. A snapped bamboo with the pith gnawed out of it told him that gorillas had passed that way recently. The great apes climbed up to the bamboo thickets at the end of the dry season in search of some nutritional quality they needed at that time of year. Soon he crossed a trail made by a gorilla family on the move. They always travelled in single file. Moist dung piles told him that the apes had passed that way within the last few hours. Once, not far away, he heard an adult male's questioning bark.

After three hours he left behind the bamboos and the hypericum woodland that succeeded them and emerged on to a small plateau covered with low scrub. This was the Saddle.

Directly above, to his right, rose the bare, rounded peak of Mount Vahinga whose slopes he had been climbing all that afternoon. The Saddle connected Vahinga with the sharp, much more impressive Misoka. Misoka's Matterhorn-like summit, 2,000 feet higher than Vahinga's, was surrounded by dispersing cloud. The peak would clear by nightfall. Menant was close to his journey's end and knew that he would accomplish it now with daylight to spare. Even had darkness been half an hour away he would still have paused on the edge of the Saddle to savour the place. It was the unexpectedness of the open, marshy meadow after hours of inching one's way upwards through matted forest that was so unnerving. The Saddle had no right to be there, hung between the two volcanic peaks like a lost garden. The Saddle was a natural pass, the only pass in the volcanic massif. Yet it was a pass known by few, used by no one except the mountain gorillas and an occasional buffalo or elephant wandering at high altitude.

The track which he had used many times was more evident here. Vegetation grew so much more slowly at 12,000 feet. The vast meadow was broken by rocky outcrops and giant heath trees, a nightmarish relative of the more conventional heather. White-flowered helichrysums broke the sombre greens with the friendliness of dog daisies. He got into a swinging stride to cover the last, slightly uphill, mile to the lower slopes of Misoka's peak.

The hut had been built two years previously by the first scientist to work there. Bill Picton, US Fulbright Scholar, had used a portion of his grant to pay porters to cut and carry materials to this improbable place. The two-roomed shack, built of hardwood from the forest and carried from the timber-mill a mile below, had stood the two years well. True, the roof leaked during prolonged periods of rain, but the roof was thatched with dried bamboo and there was a limitless supply of that for the cutting and carrying.

Menant laid his rifle down on a canvas chair on the rudimentary verandah and called out softly. Everything he did, he did softly. His climb through the forest had been made softly. His progress across the meadow had been even more gentle. It was possible to feel that, had it been necessary at any point to fire his rifle, the movements that preceded the discharge of the bullet would have been softly executed. No one answered his call but he had hardly expected a response. The occupant of the hut was unlikely to return until dusk.

He pushed the door open. The small living space was divided from the sleeping area by a bamboo screen. Most of the interior was taken up by a wooden table on which lay notebooks, trays of photographic slides, cameras and lenses, specimen boxes and plastic bags containing samples of forest and montane heath vegetation. A shelf supported a row of scientific reference books. Empty wooden crates had been converted into filing cabinets. Amongst this display of order-liness there was one note of inconsistency, a bunch of helichrysum flowers stuck in a tall specimen jar. Jean-Pierre smiled, touching the blossoms with his fingertips and making a small teeth-clicking sound of approval. He took fresh meat from the pack he had carried up the mountain and began to prepare an evening meal. He seemed to know exactly where everything was stored in the tiny kitchen area, adding garlic and dried forest herbs to the steak which he pounded into edible submission with a block made from native mahogany. When the meat was ready he took fresh greenstuff from his pack and began to clean it. Last of all he produced a bottle of rough, red *ordinaire*, drew the cork and left it to settle after its long uphill journey.

When all this was done he propped his rifle against the verandah rail and sat down beside it. The sun had long gone behind Vahinga and the last of the purple light was draining from the sky when his ears caught the first crackle of trodden vegetation. Evidently he did not wish to surprise whoever was coming. Menant rose and lit the hurricane lamp on the table, swinging it gently in some pre-arranged signal of recognition before he put it down. It would not have occurred to him to call out, breaking the silence of the place. He waited just out of the circle of lamplight. The new arrival would take several minutes to reach him. His forest-tuned ears had caught the first footfalls at a good two hundred yards' range. The trail the footsteps followed traversed a steep rocky gully before it arrived at the hut.

A girl stepped into the lamp-glow. She wore stained khaki slacks and a bush shirt with binoculars housed in a special pocket across her chest. The binoculars compensated for what she lacked in inches there. Her slight figure would have won her no beauty contests, but her face more than made up for that. The blue-black hair was cropped short. She had cut it herself. The grey eyes in the bronzed face were wide-set. Helen Lawes would have stood out in any company as a young woman of striking intelligence and character. It was the combination of these two qualites that made her almost a beauty. To Jean-Pierre she *was* a beauty. He stepped out of the shadows and held out his arms. She laughed, took the binoculars out of her chest pocket and folded herself close to him.

'I gave the signal. You saw?'

'Yes. The idea of a private signal is very funny. Who else would come to see me up here?'

'No one perhaps.' He laughed and kissed her.

She became suddenly serious. 'Jean-Pierre. He's becoming much more habilitated. The whole group are. For the first time today he let me get quite close. In thick cover, too.'

'Be careful, little one. He might hug you to death. Like this.' She returned his kiss. 'That is a very unscientific attitude, Jean-Pierre.'

'I am not the scientist here. I leave that to you. I prefer the pragmatic approach. Doing what seems best at the time.'

She laughed and slipped out of his arms. 'I know where that approach leads.'

'What a shocking suggestion. I simply invited myself to dinner. I even brought it with me.' He led her into the living-room.

Half an hour later, when they were eating, Jean-Pierre said,

'I came up to tell you that I think you should leave for a while.'

Knowing that he never made a serious statement without serious purpose, she put down her glass and waited.

'The *Fisi* have landed on the west shore of the lake. They'll be in Baruva in about twenty-four hours. The Saddle is very close to the border. You could easily go down to Mitumba until we see how things are going to work out.' Mitumba was the small town across the border to which the Baruva Europeans had already made their escape.

'How long do you suggest I go for?'

He shrugged. 'Maybe a week or two, maybe a month. The mercenaries are coming. They'll soon settle General Patrice's hash. I'd rather you played it safe until then.'

She considered his suggestion carefully. After a long pause she took his hand.

'I'll be perfectly safe up here.'

'Oh? What makes you assume that?' He knew the word 'assume' would rile her.

'It's not an assumption. It's a perfectly reasonable deduction.'

Jean-Pierre enjoyed the flash of irritation. Women scientists had no business trying to be scientific all the time. He considered riling her further by pointing out that the deduction was by no means reasonable. It amused him to reflect that this would make her even more of an irritated woman and less of a scientist. It was tempting but in this case might produce exactly the opposite effect to the one he desired. She might refuse to listen to him out of sheer feminine obstinacy.

'Are you sure it's a reasonable deduction?' he asked gently.

'Well, to start with, African guerillas don't climb mountains like Europeans, just because they're there. Most of them fear the forest unless they're from forest tribes. Your General Patrice, or whatever he calls himself, almost certainly recruited his thugs from town riff-raff.'

'No one imagined Patrice would cross the lake.'

'True, but presumably he thought he had a worthwhile objective.'

'He might consider that he has one here. The Saddle is a natural pass, a good place to stop mercenaries from infiltrating over the border. I admit it's unlikely, but. . . .'

'Exactly. At twelve thousand feet! It's unlikely.'

'But an outside chance, darling.'

'A thousand to one against.'

'It's that one chance I'm concerned about.'

'It's my work I'm concerned about. Jean-Pierre, you know that I have six months left before I return to the States. I'm just beginning to make a breakthrough with two gorilla families. If I stopped even for a week or two now I might never make up the ground. It's taken me months to get this far.'

'Gorillas,' he said. 'They're headed for extinction anyway. Why take such a risk for them? They're just apes.'

She knew she had him on the run now. She lifted his hand and kissed it.

'We'll talk about it in the morning. You'll stay tomorrow?'

'Yes, and take you down with me the day after.'

'It'll be far more dangerous down below.'

'Then I'll stay here and look after you.'

'Look after me now. It'll be a cold, clear night but we'll be warm enough on the verandah.'

As she slipped into the double sleeping-bag, naked, beside him, the moon leaned on the shoulder of Misoka. The Saddle hung in the sky, remote and untroubled as the moon itself.

When they woke in the morning the Saddle was covered with thick, white mist.

'We shan't be able to start out for at least an hour,' she said.

'I wasn't thinking of doing so.' Jean-Pierre ran his finger down the ridge of her spine.

'I wish I wasn't so bony. It must be like sleeping with Misoka.'

23

He cupped one cheek of her bottom in his hand. 'Yes, but parts of the range are nicely rounded, like Vahinga here. As for Misoka, I'm not sure. The territory is certainly volcanic, but hardly extinct. I'd better do a more thorough survey.'

'Jean-Pierre, don't be so goddamn scientific.'

'Well, if I'm not allowed to be geological perhaps I'm permitted to carry out research into the mating habits of female biologists in conditions of heavy mist at twelve thousand feet?'

'Come here,' she said.

Afterwards he asked, 'Was that good for you?'

'Volcanic. My only complaint is that there's a hard rock under your side of the sleeping-bag. How you possibly slept on it. . . .' She slipped her hand under the bag and met the rectangular steel butt of the Walther automatic.

'Give me that,' he ordered.

She handed the automatic to him in silence, as if its presence was an affront to both the time and the place. The mood of after-love was broken.

'Did you really have to take that awful thing to bed?'

'I told you,' he said quietly. 'These are times of violence.'

There was nothing violent about the day that followed. Helen was anxious to show him how far her work with gorilla group Able had progressed.

Helen Lawes had been Bill Picton's most brilliant student at the University of Arizona. She had graduated with honours a few months before he had taken up his Fulbright Scholarship to pioneer the gorilla study. As a student she had worked with him on Dall sheep in the coastal mountains of Alaska. After he had left for Africa she had done some outstanding behaviourist work of her own on elephant seals on an island off the coast of Baja California. In Africa Picton had suffered from altitude sickness and had been forced to give up the gorilla project almost before he had begun to scratch the surface. Helen Lawes had kept bombarding him

24

with letters begging him to let her join him as assistant. Picton had doubts about the suitability of the place or the task for any woman biologist, with one possible exception – Helen. So, when he was forced to return home, Helen got the chance she wanted.

As soon as the mist lifted, Helen led the way to the bamboo forests on the slopes of Misoka, one thousand feet below the Saddle. Menant admired the certainty and ease with which she retraced her steps of the previous night. He could hardly have done better himself. After an hour of crouching, creeping, sometimes crawling descent, Helen held up her hand. Menant knew from the heavy smell trapped in the still air beneath the forest canopy that she had found the base-line from which they must begin their search, the place at which Able Group, as she insisted on calling this particular family, had spent the previous night.

Half-a-dozen roughly-shaped nests of crushed vines and grasses showed where the larger animals had slept. The dung on the outside of each nest was fresh. The gorillas hadn't been gone long. Perhaps they, too, had been discouraged from an early start by the mist. Above, in the hardwood trees that grew among the bamboos at this spot, were several nests of the sort that might have been made by some large and untidy bird. These were the beds occupied by the females and the young. Jean-Pierre stooped and picked some matted brown and grey hairs from the ground nest nearest to him.

'This is where your big silver-back slept.'

'Able One.'

'That's a ridiculous name for a fully-grown, silver-backed male gorilla.'

'It's not a name. It's a scientific means of identification.'

'I refuse to call him that. It's undignified.'

'O.K., give him a name then.'

'Able One? How about Absolom?' He held up the pinch of hair. 'Besides, he lost some of his hair in the forest. Yes, Absolom.'

'My son, my son?'

25

'Well hardly that.' He kissed her on the forehead. 'You biologists have a sense of humour after all.'

'Yes, and we can be very biological, too.'

'I've noticed.' He transferred his mouth to her lips.

'But not at this moment. I'm more anxious to get close to Able One.'

'Absolom,' he corrected. 'The family can't be too far ahead.'

Now that they were on the trail she gladly handed over leadership to Jean-Pierre. His knowledge of gorilla behaviour might be limited in the scientific sense but she had no doubt about his hunter's ability to track gorillas, or anything else that lived in the mountain forests. At first the spoor was simple to follow. Bill Picton had long ago described the animals' basic method of travel. When they were simply going somewhere with a purpose, to a known feeding-ground, for instance, they moved in single file, usually with the dominant male in the lead. There were fourteen animals, including babies, in Able Group. Fourteen gorillas weighing between four hundred and one hundred pounds leave a considerable impression, even on the dense ground-cover of a rain-forest. Later on, when they spread out in open order to feed, it would be more difficult to follow them, difficult not simply to know where the whole family was but to pinpoint exactly each individual. In the unlikely event that they could approach really close, it would not pay to blunder into a surprised gorilla, especially if it was a male.

As Helen had predicted, the trail led downwards into the dense bamboo thickets. At one point the girl stopped to pick up a long, stiff shoot still glistening wet with sap where it had recently been barked by a gorilla's teeth.

'*Mushi*,' Jean-Pierre said, using the native name for the vine.

'*Urera*,' she corrected.

They spoke in a whisper now.

'They're not twenty minutes ahead of us.'

'In the really thick stuff by the look of it, Jean-Pierre.'

He could sense the tension in her voice but could not judge whether it was caused by apprehension at the thought of trying to approach in such cover or disappointment that they might not make visual contact after all. He wondered, not for the first time, how she made out by herself up here on the mountain. Dall sheep and elephant seals were one thing, gorillas quite another.

She whispered, 'Once they settle down in the bamboos they're liable to stay there all day.'

They heard the gorillas long before they detected any movement. A demolition gang might have been breaking up a large, wooden building. Large beams were being smashed in two; floorboards torn up, creaking and rasping in protest; plywood doors were being crashed in. Able Group was, in fact, enjoying a light snack of bamboo.

There was little constant wind in the forest. Jean-Pierre made use of what breeze there was, climbing a steep ravine to keep, as far as possible, downwind of the family. From the top of the ravine they watched a thirty-foot-high bamboo start to bend as easily as a raspberry cane might when perched upon by a sparrow. When it had reached an angle of forty-five degrees to the ground an unseen force snapped the bamboo and it fell. It was at least four inches thick at the base.

A short, sharp bark. One of the males, Absolom perhaps, knew they were there. 'The questioning bark,' Helen whispered. 'He'll probably take them away now.'

Jean-Pierre motioned her to be quiet and to follow. For another hour he led the way in a sweaty, exhausting half-circle until they were one hundred yards below and downwind of the gorillas. During this painful crawl a male had given two more barks, less assertive than the first, as if his suspicions had partly been lulled. Jean-Pierre pointed to his right, placing a finger across his lips for silence. To the girl it now seemed as if they must be moving at right angles away from the gorillas, yet she trusted his knowledge of how animals moved in the forest. He led her up a steep bank through some giant nettles that forced them to hold their arms well above their heads. On top of the bank he motioned her to sit down with her back against a tree. He took a water-bottle and fresh fruit from his pack, offering them to her. Helen looked questioningly. He pointed to his watch — a quarter to one — and made the gesture of placing his palms together, fingertips extended, and then leaned his head in feigned sleep against his hands. Almost at once the sound of rending bamboo and the wire-brush-on-cymbal patter of cascading leaves decreased, gradually to fall away to silence, a silence punctuated by volcanic digestive rumblings. Helen Lawes knew perfectly well from her own observations that gorilla groups took a lunch break, or rather a non-lunch break, for up to two hours about this time. It was the only period throughout the day when they didn't stuff themselves continuously. What she couldn't figure out was why Jean-Pierre had chosen this particular bank, well to the side of Able Group's previous route, as their own stopping place.

After they had swallowed a little of the water and eaten some bananas they lay on their backs on the yielding, rotten-smelling ground, fingers touching, eyes half closed against the green light which washed over them, dappled and filtered by the forest canopy, reaching them as if through thirty feet of clear, tropical sea.

At two o'clock Jean-Pierre sat up, pointing first to his watch and then to the girl's Pentax camera. She nodded, understanding that he was demanding to know whether she was ready for action. Close identification pictures of Able Group were what she needed most. So far, on her own, all she had obtained were fragmentary glimpses — an arm, half a face — usually obscured by foliage. For perhaps five yards to their front, as far as the lip of the bank, the ground was clear, a perfect place for photography. Yet there seemed no earthly reason why the animals should choose to pass that way.

Able Group's siesta was over. The sounds of stirring vegetation had begun again, had not only begun but were growing nearer. The animals were still in dense ground-cover so that it was impossible to see them yet. Instead, their progress was marked by the swaying and thrashing of shrubs and bushes. Once, an arm appeared and, grasping a substantial young tree, pulled it down to ground level more or less in passing, rather as a man might heedlessly tear off a blade of tall grass as he walked. The advance was the more impressive because the gorillas remained invisible. At first Helen Lawes was positive that Jean-Pierre had misjudged Able Group's course, that they would continue on their present line some fifty yards to the left. But then came the questioning bark of a male and, a few minutes later, the bark again, much nearer. That musky smell of gorilla and then, suddenly, climbing the bank on all fours, not ten feet away, a fully-grown, though not yet silver-backed, male. Even Jean-Pierre was impressed. He had never seen a large male this close before. The sheer size and power of the animal nearly choked him. The gorilla was not disturbed, merely cautious. He stood stiffly arched on all four limbs, looking towards them with a disconcertingly anthropoid expression of near-intelligence. His brown eyes registered neither fear nor distrust. He was just totally in command of the situation. Within seconds it became clear what he was waiting for. A female who looked only half his size came up the bank, keeping the male between herself and the unknown intruders. She didn't wait but hurried by, two half-grown young, round as fur-covered beach balls, bouncing along in her wake. Jean-Pierre heard the Pentax shutter clicking and hoped to God Helen had sufficient scientific detachment to remember to use only slow movements. The male was about to move on himself when something, perhaps a sudden glint of sunlight reflected from the camera lens, caught his eye. He barked twice.

At the distance of a few feet the bark was more intimidating even than the scream of an angry elephant which, as a hunter, Jean-Pierre had heard and faced many times. The reason that it was so personally challenging was simply that the great ape was so man-like. That was what tweaked at one's fear-buds. The next instant the young male had gone. He had been knocked out of the way by something far more powerful and authoritative than himself — Absolom.

Absolom came bursting up the bank, beating the bushes and screaming at the top of his voice. He was erect on his hind feet. He looked eight feet tall, though he was more probably just under six. He came on at full tilt, leaves and branches flying like splinters. As Absolom passed Jean-Pierre the coarse hair of one gigantic leg actually brushed his forearm. There was nothing to do, nowhere to go. In any case, to move might have triggered an attack. Jean-Pierre turned and saw Helen Lawes, white-faced and shocked, pressed against the tree. Absolom's jaws were open, the yellow stumps of his teeth outlined against the red roof of his mouth. He turned and half retreated down the bank. Helen moved to aim the camera at his back. He caught the movement and came storming back, screaming and barking. This time he lashed out with his right paw, striking the camera and sending it spinning away. He seemed satisfied with the gesture, for he turned and crashed off, barking, into the bush. Within seconds the other males answered and they heard the family moving away fast in thick cover. There would be no more following them that day.

They reached the hut late in the afternoon. Helen made no pretence of maintaining scientific detachment. She was far too excited by her first really close contact. The fact that it had been far too close was something she found easy to dismiss. It had been her fault. She had, she argued, taken a ridiculous chance in using the camera at all at such close quarters. Not a chance in terms of her own safety but because the incident might well have made Absolom — she called him that now — far more difficult to approach in future. Without the confidence of Absolom there would be no possibility of getting to study the behaviour of the entire family. Absolom commanded his group absolutely. She

should have taken the sensible course of gradually habili-
tating Absolom to her presence in the forest. But the chance
to get her first positive pictures of at least five of the family
had been too much.

'At least one learns.'

'Yes,' Jean-Pierre said wryly, 'provided one survives.'

'The funny thing was, I wasn't scared by him, I just felt he
was someone I'd taken a heck of a liberty with at first
acquaintance.'

'Maybe you weren't frightened, but I most certainly was. I
thought he might kill you.'

'And not you?'

'He ignored me. Probably didn't even see me. But then I
didn't move. That camera. I shouldn't have suggested it. . . .'

'He hit the camera hard. It looks all right. Well, we'll soon
know.'

The sun was dropping towards the rounded top of Vahinga
and the mountain air was already cooling. Soon it would be
the best time of the day. He wanted to share it with her,
relaxing as they relived their adventure. A glass of wine as the
quick twilight fell, and then a meal cooked in the open on
glowing wood-ash, and then love-making; and then tomorrow
he would insist she cross over the border, keep out of harm's
way until the coming of the *Fisi* had been settled one way or
the other.

He took her hand gently to lead her towards the canvas
chairs on the verandah but she pulled away.

'You go outside and wait for me. I've got to know about
these pictures. The only way to be sure is to develop them.'

He felt himself getting angry but turned his irritation into
an amused shrug.

'Can't you ever stop being the scientist?'

'Haven't I already answered that one for you?'

'Yes, but I even wonder what you're thinking about at
those times.'

'It was you who compared my spine to a volcanic ridge.'

'Come outside and enjoy the twilight. We'll get the glow

31

off the mountain tonight.'

'After I've processed the film.'

'It'll be too late by then.'

He contemplated just picking her up and, if necessary, laying her down, but the parade-ground way she turned told him he would be wasting his time. American women: he would never understand them, especially this one who was capable of such warmth.

The sun had left Misoka's peak when he heard her moving out of the curtained space she used as a dark-room.

She called excitedly, 'Jean-Pierre. Come in here and look at these.'

She was holding up strips of negatives to the paraffin lamp. One of the strips was fogged but the rest were clear and sharp.

'Look at the young male. That's A Three. See that stiff-legged pose? That's the strutting walk. It's what they do when they want to assert themselves without being openly aggressive. A Three's got a fight scar on his shoulder. See? I never noticed that before.'

'You'll have to give him a name, too. How about Adam?'

'Look at the female in this shot. See her belly sagging? Looks as if she's pregnant but I'll bet she's not. That's food, all food. They always look like that by the end of the morning.'

'Ahitabel,' he said. 'Let's keep it biblical. Isn't there a lady in the Old Testament called something like that?'

'And the two juveniles.'

'Only a behaviourist could call those charming creatures juveniles. They're children. Ape children. But as for names! I've run out of As. I can't recall too many children's names from the bible. Hey. Wait a bit. What about Abel? The other one will just have to be Cain.'

'Impossible to sex them. They may both be female. They'll have to be J One and J Two. When I make prints I'll look for distinguishing marks.'

'Cain will have a mark, sure enough.'

She failed to react to the gentle fun he was making of her simply because she was not aware of it, possibly was barely aware of him.

'*Jeesus,*' she said, 'get these.'

'These' were seven negatives showing Absolom from the moment he came up the bank until he ended his first charge, feet away from the lens. Miraculously she had managed to stay in focus so that the last shot, on a twenty-millimetre lens, just framed his face and looked right down his open mouth.

Jean-Pierre was impressed.

'Good God, look at those teeth. Just imagine if he'd bitten you with those.' He put his arm protectively round her waist. She seemed barely to notice it.

'I should be able to get some idea of his age from those teeth. My guess is that he's in his prime. About fifteen. If he was much older the teeth would have begun to break down into stumps.'

The last few shots were blurred. One showed a huge, out-of-focus paw as it swung towards the camera. He marvelled that she had stood firm let alone continued to use the camera.

'I'll get some contact prints off.'

'Not now. You can do that tomorrow after I take you down to safety over the border.'

'Jean-Pierre. You've got to be joking. You really think I'd leave now? There's years of study up here. I've got little enough time as it is.'

'I told you, the situation in this country is going to get increasingly dangerous. Once over the border not even the *Fisi* can touch you.'

She took his hands. 'If you really want to protect me, stay up here for a bit. After all, you're a one-man arsenal. That pistol! Even in bed. Darling, I'm under no illusions why we got so close to Able Group today. It was because you did the stalking. I haven't got a hope of doing that on my own. Not yet, anyway. But I'd learn fast from you.'

'And who'd protect my plantation meanwhile?'

'If the *Fisi* attacked it in force you wouldn't have a chance. You'd lose your own life as well as the plantation. Please. Don't risk it. Stay up on the Saddle and work with me for a while.'

'You know that's impossible. Besides, if the *Fisi* did come up here we wouldn't have a chance.'

'What on earth would they come for? That's the most ridiculous part of your whole argument.'

'I don't know,' he said. 'I admit they may never bother to climb the mountain. But the Saddle is a natural pass between the volcanoes. And talking of natural passes, come here.'

She let him pull her towards him and slid her hands round under his shirt. He did the same to her, slipping his hands down the small of her back until his fingertips were driving down beneath the top of her jeans, feeling the slopes of her buttocks. She gave a cry and took her own hands from him to free her belt. He carried her out on to the verandah. She struggled at the same time, kicking off her jeans, laughing and calling him 'Absolom' as he laid her down on the herb-smelling ground. He wanted to take her then, as Absolom might have taken one of his own mates, but she held him off, laughing at him, comparing his urgency to that of the great ape himself. At first he was full of frustration and anger but then he joined in the game, beating his chest with cupped hands. She lay back, watching him, smiling at his joke. The smile stopped his clowning. He saw that the smile was tender, the smile of a woman who takes pleasure in every mood of the loved one, not least because he can find humour in making love. Jean-Pierre saw that look of tenderness and was suddenly glad that she had slowed their love-making. He lowered himself gently beside her, kissing her closed eyes. Now she was the one who was all urgency. Jean-Pierre repaid her in kind, taking his time until she could stand it no more. When they were both undressed she raised her hips so that he could remove the last flimsy obstacle.

They lay silently, side by side, afterwards, flanks touching, hands held, looking up at the sunset shadow slowly darkening first the peak and then the upper slopes of Misoka. The temperature had already fallen several degrees. Jean-Pierre turned towards Helen as if to protect her against the chill. She touched him at once and this time they made love lingeringly and tenderly. By the time they lay spent twilight had come and gone with Africa's ability to darken its ceiling at the touch of a switch.

Helen shivered. 'Darling, now I am cold. Forgive me if I go in and dress. No, please don't look at me. I'm such a mess.'

So, of course, he looked and saw only a slim, tall girl with small, firm breasts and dark, crisp hair with leaves clinging to her bottom and the marks of grasses on her back where she had lain beneath his weight.

'You're looking,' she accused.

'Surely there can't be much I haven't seen.'

When she had gone inside the hut he dressed himself slowly. Jean-Pierre had considered himself woman-proof, more than usually so in the case of Helen Lawes whom he admired and quite demonstrably desired. Her over-dedicated scientific detachment had previously guaranteed that it would be hard to involve himself beyond admiration and desire. That evening, however, something had disturbingly changed in her and, as a result, the same chemistry was even more disturbingly working within himself. Instinctively he knew that the emotional shift in Helen was an outcome of the day that they had spent together in the forest. For Helen it had been a transcending experience to make close contact with the gorillas. She was alight with the triumph which set a new key to her future study and for which she totally credited Jean-Pierre. This was the cause of her suddenly dropping the barriers and becoming for the first time a tender, loving young woman as opposed to a healthy, lustful and lonely American young woman. The cause was clear to Jean-Pierre, the effect, especially upon himself, less so.

When he had dressed he stood looking back over the

darkened forest in the direction of Baruva. A glow in the sky told him little. The town might be burning already, looted and sacked or at least fought over by the *Fisi* and the Force Nationale. Equally, the glow could be accounted for by a bush fire. There was always a bush fire somewhere, especially at this season of the year. The possibility that the flames might come from the town he had left only yesterday strengthened his determination to persuade Helen to leave, if only until the pattern of events became clearer.

He turned away towards the mountain to put the thought of what lay ahead out of his mind, for tonight at least. There was a matching red glow above Misoka's peak but this was a sight that filled him with peace. The sharp peak was really the basalt plug of an ancient volcano, lava that had welled up perhaps two million years ago. The crater around it had long since been worn away by wind and weather. The real Misoka, the one that still lived, lay half a mile beyond, a perfect crater nearly a mile wide. In the centre, guarded by the sheer, six-hundred-foot lava cliffs of the crater itself, lay a depression half this width. This was filled with a heaving lake of rose-red earth-blood, magma at a temperature of one thousand degrees and more. This molten lake glowed and flushed, darkened and glowered and threw up great jets of liquid rock high into the air. This was the living Misoka. On nights when a sheet of cloud lay above the volcano the underside of that cloud was painted cherry-red by the fires in the lake. The cloud was perfectly positioned tonight.

Jean-Pierre thought of calling Helen to share the spectacle with him but knew that it would be a waste of time. She would have returned to her dark-room to make the first contact prints from her negatives. His first reaction was resentment; his second that he could hardly blame her for her excitement. Misoka's cloud glowed suddenly and fiercely crimson. He pictured with a private, inward pleasure what was happening in that unearthly place. A huge gusher of lava had exploded from the crater lake, hurling scarlet fragments, some of them weighing half a ton, sixty feet and more into

36

the air. He had once climbed down into that crater and spent two days and nights there alone. The descent of the crater wall had called merely for normal strength and nerve. Once he was down it had taken every reserve of strength in his character to stay there. Though the molten lake was still two hundred yards distant, the crumbly lava surface shook and rumbled as though a hundred underground trains were passing directly beneath his feet. The ground smoked yellow through a thousand fissures and it was hard to find a spot cool enough on which to pitch a tent. The lake itself nearly annihilated him spiritually as well as in the flesh. Its physical manifestations wiped out personality; the ceaseless roar of the siphoning lava that appeared, at one end of the lake, to crash down a chasm into the centre of the earth only to well up in equal volume at the other; the heat that blistered the skin if you approached too closely; the lethal clouds of sulphurous gas that streamed away on the prevailing wind, a wind that had constantly to be watched for fatal vagaries. If the crater was overwhelming in daylight, when night fell its enormity became almost more than a mind, even a mind as well-disciplined as Jean-Pierre's, could bear.

By the second day he had become more adjusted to Misoka's spectacle. The second night, now that some of the initial element of terror had passed, was almost a mystical experience. It was as if he, of all people on this earth, had stood at the centre of its mysteries, shared and understood them. Just the same, in the morning he had been glad to make his escape. He doubted whether he would ever visit Misoka, alone, again. It was enough now to stand in the darkness outside the hut, look at the burning cloud and understand what took place beneath it.

Gradually the mantling cloud began to disperse. Without its help Misoka produced merely a diffused glow in the sky. He shivered and went inside to find Helen. He craved warmth but expected to discover that she had withdrawn inside the cocoon of the scientist once again. He was wrong. She was not in the dark-room as he had expected. Instead, there was a rich smell of garlic and spaghetti with bolognese sauce from a long-hoarded tin. There were flowers on the table. It touched him that she had slipped out through the back entrance of the hut and gathered the blossoms in the half-light.

That night they took the bedding outside again and made love gently until gentleness became out of the question. Before they fell asleep she asked him about the gun. She refused to sleep with a human arsenal. When he tried to laugh her anxiety aside she slid her arm under the sleeping-bag and found the hard, rectangular butt of the Walther.

'Leave it on the verandah, darling. I'm honestly terrified of it. How do I know it might not go off and kill one of us?'

'If it was going to, it would have done so in the last half-hour.' Nevertheless, he removed the gun and carried it back to the hut.

Because he never slept without weapons within easy reach he took the soft leather holster which he had specially made for such adaptations and tied it with thongs low down on his right thigh. Then he slipped on the khaki trousers and shirt in which he slept, even inside the sleeping bag, against the mountain chill.

'Where on earth have you been?'

'Answering the call of nature.'

'Snuggle close to me. It's going to be a cold night.'

As he moved against her he was careful to keep his right leg out of contact.

When Jean-Pierre woke an hour before dawn his split-second reaction was that Misoka was undergoing a violent eruption. The tops of the trees were lit with a bright red glow. Then he heard the crackle of fire and caught the uniquely acrid smell of sweaty Africans. Jean-Pierre cursed and sat up, clawing at the trouser leg that concealed the Walther automatic. An arm clamped him round the throat and dragged him backwards. As his head jerked back the leg of a second African brushed his ear. Jean-Pierre did not expect to live long enough to regret his unpreparedness. Any second would come the first slash of the panga — if he was lucky. And Helen? Was there a merciful chance that in the half-light from the fire they, whoever they were, might mistake her for a man and kill her instantly? Jean-Pierre, dragged out of his sleeping bag, lay flat on his face, a knee pressed into his kidneys. His hands, wrenched behind his back, were being bound with wire. Helen screamed. He rolled sideways, unseating the man who bound him. Jean-Pierre just had time to sit up before the African came back at him. He took in the scene lit by the flames of the burning stores hut. There were four of them. Two held Helen. A third man, who carried a Sterling gun, stood to one side. The cap this man wore was made of hyena skin. The *Fisi*! The fourth African, the man he had thrown, hit him with a wooden club.

When he came round it was nearly daylight. The stores hut was still smouldering. He judged that barely half an hour had passed since the attack. His left eye was closed with dried blood from the club wound on his head. His head itself felt as though the club was buried in his skull. He blinked, breaking the caked eyelashes free. He was lying on the verandah. From inside the hut came African voices and the crash of wood and glass. His legs were bound as securely as his hands. He tried to draw them up towards his stomach. They were tied to one of the verandah posts. By rolling half-way on to his right side he discovered what he most wished to know. They hadn't discovered the automatic.

Helen. Where was Helen? She answered his thought with a scream of protest as more glass shattered inside. The scream was cut short with a stinging blow made, he guessed, with the flat of a hand across the face. He was surprised that she was still alive. When everyone possible had raped a woman, the *Fisi* usually killed her. She kept screaming now but after a minute or so the screams stopped. The man in the hyena-skin cap came out of the hut and kicked him in the small of the back. In poor French he demanded, 'Tell me what you and the woman are doing here. The hut is full of pictures. Are you spies?'

Since Helen's pictures were all of gorillas and their food plants the question didn't seem worth answering. It wasn't worth answering it in any case. Reason, by all accounts, was not applicable to the thought processes of the *Fisi*.

The African who had hit Jean-Pierre with the club now struck him hard across the shoulder-blades with the flat of a panga. 'Kill. Kill,' he suggested.

The leader shook his head. 'The orders are for hostages.'

The panga man laughed and fingered Jean-Pierre's shirt. 'I want it. Take it off for me.'

Jean-Pierre turned his head away. The African rolled him on his back and then ran the razor-edged blade of the panga down his chest from throat to navel, cutting away the button holes and leaving behind a gleaming trench that quickly filled with blood. Jean-Pierre screamed, not from the sudden burn of the steel but in the hope that he might divert the panga from slashing the leather belt that supported his slacks. The only hope he had was to keep the automatic concealed. The blade stopped, not because of the scream but because the man wanted the shirt. So he wrenched to pull it free but forgot that the wearer's arms were tied behind his back. He kicked Jean-Pierre over on to his face again and began to pull and pull at the shirt, lifting Jean-Pierre bodily in the process. The shirt was new and the material good so that it took several minutes and the full pressure of the *Fisi*'s foot on his spine to rip the garment free. When the final seam parted the *Fisi* fell back against the hut wall, out of breath and grunting. By the time Jean-Pierre had kicked and wriggled himself on to his back again the man was proudly strutting about the verandah wearing what remained of the shirt. The sight of Jean-Pierre's blood-and-dirt-caked chest triggered something in the *Fisi*.

'*Coupez les mains!*'

Jean-Pierre had no doubt that, if the *Fisi* had thought of it at the time, that's exactly what he would have done to get the shirt off. As the man advanced at a run he realised that this was what he intended to do now. The African jerked

40

Jean-Pierre's hands hard up behind his back, lifting him to a sitting position. The panga rose to chop at the wrists. Within minutes he would bleed to death. He heard the click of the Sterling's bolt. The man in the hyena cap fired a single shot from the hip. Where his attacker's nose had been, a mushy red flower bloomed. The back of the panga man's head opened up hurling brain and bone across a hut window. As if to show him that the execution was no personal favour to himself, the leader advanced and kicked Jean-Pierre hard in the side.

The shot brought out the other two *Fisi*. Between them they pulled Helen Lawes. Her face showed a red weal. Her hands were bound in front of her. They had gagged her with a length of tightly-knotted rope to stop her screaming. Apart from a tear in her shirt she was still clothed.

They started off down the mountain almost at once, Hyena Cap ordering Jean-Pierre to lead the way.

'Where to?'

'The main road to Baruva.'

They untied his legs. He insisted that he could not possibly lead down a forest trail with his arms tied. As for the girl, she would not remain on her feet for more than a minute at a time unless she was free to hold on to vines and branches. Since the *Fisi* leader seemed to want them alive — for the moment, anyway — Jean-Pierre had a faint hope he might get away with this. With his hands free there would surely come a moment at some time during the long descent when he would catch all three off-guard. The automatic was still reassuringly there. But Hyena Cap wasn't taking any chances. He ordered their hands to be freed and then, with a six-foot length of rope, joined his prisoners, right wrist to right wrist. He placed himself immediately behind them with the Sterling gun a few feet from Helen's back. The other two *Fisi* followed.

As far as Jean-Pierre could judge, they had shown far less interest in the execution of their comrade than their wild namesakes would have done in the death of a member of their own pack. Four-footed hyenas would at least have regarded the deceased as a square meal. Given time, perhaps, this bunch would have done the same. As it was, they left the body on the verandah. No one shifted it, let alone attempted to bury it, or, as far as Jean-Pierre could tell, even commented upon it.

He had been entirely pre-occupied with his own desperate situation. Now he had time to think about Helen's. They hadn't raped her since she still wore her shirt and jeans. They'd hit her once or twice when she dared to protest at the smashing of her laboratory. The eyes, darting about above that agonising rope gag like frightened fish trapped in a small pool, were those of a woman fighting to stay within her right mind. He jerked the rope between their wrists to try to tell her that he was with her. After several tugs the rope jerked back. It was like two prisoners, condemned prisoners perhaps, tapping on the cell wall to reassure each other that one other being existed in like condition.

As soon as they cleared the Saddle and descended into the trees that reassuring length of rope became a source of torment. At first it merely snagged round fallen logs and branches. Then Helen became so weary that she blindly passed on the opposite side of a tree. Their guards hit them with the flats of their pangas until steps had been retraced and the human knot unravelled. Soon Helen began to fall down, tugging Jean-Pierre's wrist until it wore a bracelet of rope burn. Next she had missed her footing and pulled them both down a steep bank into a stream. Jean-Pierre greedily gulped water. When he had finished he saw that Helen was making no attempt to raise her face above the surface. He crawled back up the stream-bed and lifted her head. She had tried to drink but had failed because of the rope gag. She then appeared to have resigned herself to drowning.

For the first time he lost control. His thoughts had been almost totally occupied with how to kill and escape, but mainly how to kill. Now he invited the Sterling gun to kill him. The rope just allowed him to throw himself at the man's legs. The muzzle of the gun lowered to follow him but the gun did not fire. Instead, a foot caught him on the chin and threw him on to his back, half across Helen, pushing her head under once again. Hyena Cap stood over him. He hadn't even bothered to cock the Sterling.

Menant lifted the girl's head for the second time.

'Undo the rope,' he ordered. 'If she doesn't get a drink she won't be able to go on.'

Hyena Cap motioned to one of the others to cut the gag. He did so, cutting Helen's neck in the process.

The *Fisi* spoke far from perfect French. It was unlikely they understood English. 'There's still a good chance,' he told Helen. 'They obviously don't mean to kill us.' He still didn't risk telling her about his gun. 'Can you carry on?' She nodded. Her face, stained with sweat and mud, was hardly recognisable.

He said, 'We'll give these bastards a surprise yet.'

'Silence!' Hyena Cap hit him between the shoulder-blades with the butt of the Sterling. They started off again, stumbling down through the hagenia forest. Once, far off, Jean-Pierre heard the questioning bark of a gorilla.

It took six hours to reach the track where Jean-Pierre had dismissed the jeep two days previously. The sight of freshly-cut logs, sawdust and wood-chippings left by the wood-cutters and charcoal-burners appeared to give Hyena Cap a sense of orientation. Plainly, he was a man who had received some training, possibly as an NCO in the Force Nationale before the *Fisi* uprising. Unexpectedly, he now produced a marked map. Sticking it under Jean-Pierre's face he traced, fairly accurately, the route they had taken from the Saddle.

'The saw-mill,' he demanded. 'Where?' With his index finger he indicated a cross on the map. Menant saw that this was more or less correctly placed. He toyed with the idea of leading Hyena Cap in the wrong direction. Two things decided him against this. Helen, lying face-down at his feet, was not capable of going much further. If this proved to be the case, they would probably shoot her rather than be burdened with her. Second, Hyena Cap was too clued-up to be misled.

To hurry Menant's thought processes the *Fisi* leader cocked the Sterling. Jean-Pierre pointed down the trail.

'That way,' he said, 'about three kilometres.'

Whatever the stories about the chaotic organisation and leadership of the guerillas in general, this lot was plainly more than a cut above average.

The saw-mill was already occupied. A sentry, in newly acquired European shirt and recently pressed and even more recently blood-stained khaki drill trousers, lounged outside, a U.S. Army carbine held more or less at the ready.

Hyena Cap called out, '*Mai.*'

The sentry returned the shout but slid cautiously behind a stack of cut timber. Hyena Cap pushed his prisoners in front of him and halted. If anyone was going to get shot by a trigger-happy sentry it wasn't going to be him.

The sentry stepped out from behind cover and slung his carbine. There was a good deal of talk in a tribal tongue unfamiliar to Jean-Pierre. These were people from a distant province far across the lake. There were at least half-a-dozen *Fisi* outside the mill, also a parked jeep with bullet-holes through the windscreen and a wide swathe of dried blood across the bonnet.

The sentry pointed into the mill with his carbine. They were herded inside and their hands lashed once more behind their backs. The rope gag was tied cruelly tight in Helen's mouth. They were thrown on the floor against a wall. When Jean-Pierre spoke to Helen to comfort her a *Fisi* sentry sitting high up on a pile of tree-trunks fired a shot that threw up the sawdust two feet from his head. Knowing the average standard of guerilla marksmanship, Jean-Pierre counted this a fortunate escape and decided to accept the hint to remain silent.

As far as he could tell, they were the only prisoners in the place. Their guards took no more notice of them than of the piles of mahogany logs. An hour dragged by. The sawdust was soft. Helen, exhausted, had fallen asleep. Jean-Pierre decided that this was by far the best course. If an opportunity to escape came he would need every unit of energy he could store.

In late afternoon the sound of a lorry grinding its way up the track in low gear woke him. Helen was already awake. He heard her gasping and moved across to touch her. The lorry came close. Under cover of its noise he whispered, 'Lie still! Keep quiet. They haven't done anything to us yet. They're so disorganised they may forget us.' He didn't believe a word of it. Nor did she, but she stopped crying.

The lorry stopped. The sound of blows. A scream. People dismounting. The saw-mill doors slid back and about a dozen captives were driven in. Menant recognised some of them; the saw-mill manager and his wife; the bank manager from Baruva (Why hadn't he, of all people, fled the town?); his Belgian secretary, a masculine woman of about forty-five; two Roman Catholic priests; a garage proprietor. The rest, as far as he could tell from where he lay, were prosperous Africans. The *Fisi* must have hit Baruva far sooner than anyone had expected.

The guards who hustled them in appeared to be a new lot. There was no sign of Hyena Cap or of his two henchmen. Perhaps they had been sent on another mission. Hyena Cap had obviously been too useful for mere guard duty. If so, this was a help. All attention was on the new arrivals. He couldn't tell, of course, whether the man who had shot at him earlier was still up above on the log pile. The chance had to be taken. He began to wriggle, urging Helen to move ahead of him until they were almost entirely hidden between the wall and a stack of logs. From this new position he could see only part of the scene through gaps in the timber.

The prisoners were lined up against the opposite wall. They were not bound but the rifles of several *Fisi* continually jabbed them in chests and stomachs. To the left of the

45

pathetic group stood the saw-bench which cut the great mahogany trunks. From this direction he and Helen were more exposed to view. Here was the largest gap in the log pile. But the shadows were deep. Finally, the end of the mill nearest the door was, from their new position, almost completely hidden to them.

Half-an-hour passed during which the saw-mill manager's wife broke down and fell to her knees. The *Fisi* took no notice but when her husband tried to help her up the nearest *Fisi* struck him with a club. The man lay semi-conscious. Minutes dragged by. Menant had no way of judging the time but his guess was that it would soon be dark outside. During the next hour the priests twice attempted to plead with the guards to let the women sit down. On the first occasion they were merely poked with rifle muzzles. The second time they were severely thudded about the arms and shoulders with rifle butts. As to the African captives, the *Fisi* contented themselves with fingering the flowered shirts these men wore and tapping their rifles suggestively. Menant had no doubt the Africans, if not all the prisoners, would long ago have been dead had the *Fisi* not been waiting for something or someone.

Half-an-hour after the priests had received their third beating for daring to speak words of comfort to their fellow prisoners, Menant heard a jeep grinding up the forest track. There were shouts of challenge outside as the jeep's head-lights searched for and found chinks in the mill walls. The guards struck what they imagined to be alert and military attitudes, parodies of drill once taught or perhaps only seen. The very absurdity of their poses somehow only made them seem more dangerous. The mill doors slid back and the jeep drove in, its headlights full on the prisoners.

Menant could only see the wheels and lower part of the jeep's body, also the legs of the man who dismounted from it. The legs, unusually long and thin, were encased in khaki puttees and ended in brown boots. They gave the impression of belonging to an extremely tall man. The man's right hand carried a swagger-stick with an embossed silver knob of the type used by under-officers in the Force Nationale. No sooner had the tall man alighted than a second vehicle drew up and stopped. From the babble that arose it was plainly loaded with Africans. A shot was fired. The voices ceased instantly to be followed by a low keening and moaning. Beyond the jeep Menant saw a confusion of black legs. The African occupants of the truck were being herded in and made to stand apart from the earlier prisoners.

The swagger-stick began to beat a rhythm against the owner's puttee'd legs. The rhythm emphasised a staccato tirade spoken in French and delivered in a strange, high-pitched voice.

'The forces of the People's Democratic Revolution are in complete command of the province and the town of Baruva. Nevertheless, you have dared to organise resistance against us. You have been brought here to answer for that. When you have been taught your lesson, these people' — the swagger-stick swept round out of Menant's vision to indicate the Africans who had just arrived — 'will be released to tell their fellow-citizens what to expect if they do not obey us.' He repeated this in a tribal tongue. This time, strangely, he had a pronounced stammer.

'The People's Democratic Revolution does not sentence people without trial. You will be given a chance to co-operate and to serve us by telling me what I want to know.'

The stick shot out, indicating the garage proprietor. The man was dragged forward.

A second voice from the direction of the jeep read out his name and occupation. The tall man shouted, 'We know that you have vast supplies of petrol hidden in the forest. The People's Democratic Revolution needs that petrol. Where is it?'

'I have nothing,' the man pleaded. 'Perhaps two hundred gallons. All that is left in the pumps in my garage. You are welcome to take that.'

'We shall do so. Where is the one thousand gallons in

barrels you have hidden?'

'I implore you to believe me. There is no more.'

'Show him,' shrieked the man with the stutter, 'what petrol is.'

Menant, who had heard of the ways of the *Fisi*, now knew that he was about to witness something very terrible. He heard the sounds of liquid being poured from a can.

'Drink this.'

'No. No. For God's sake, no.' The garage proprietor shrieked and then choked as the petrol was forced between his lips.

'Set him alight.'

The man cannot have lived long. The petrol that had reached his stomach exploded inside him. Flame choked his scream before he was flung outside so that his burning body should not endanger the sawdust and timber all around.

Menant thanked God that Helen was gagged, otherwise she must have screamed as the other two women now screamed.

'The bank manager next. Our forces have searched your bank but there is little money, even inside the safe. You have five seconds to tell us where the money is hidden.' That halting voice again.

'All the money is there in the bank. You have it all. The rest was flown out to head office a week ago. Look,' — desperately — 'I will give you the keys to the safe. My secretary has them.'

'Search her.'

The masculine woman was dragged out. Two of the *Fisi* began to tear off her clothes.

'Search the other one, too.'

The guards had already begun to strip the saw-mill manager's wife as her husband shouted, 'Stop. She has nothing. Oh, please stop.'

The masculine woman stood there naked, pendulous breasts hanging, knowing what was going to happen to her but no more capable of making a protest than a cow in a slaughter-house. The saw-mill manager's young wife fought all the way before they stretched her over a forty-gallon oil-drum alongside the secretary and raped them both until half-a-dozen *Fisi* had had their turn. Then they shot them both in the head.

The African audience swayed and sang in a slow rhythm that was part terror, part lament, but mostly terrible excitement.

Jean-Pierre felt Helen's body against him, trembling and straining as if in fever. All he could do for her was to try to block her view of the things that were taking place.

The tall man knew where he was going. Though the Africans he had dragged in to witness these murders might be scared half to death themselves, he knew that he had connected them with a flow of power as dark and hidden as the history of Africa itself. The swagger-stick swept towards the little group of prosperous African tradesmen in their fancy shirts.

'What shall we do with these countrymen of yours who have made themselves rich at your expense?'

'Kill! Kill!' shouted the audience.

The stick gestured towards the quaking men.

'Stop,' shouted the tall man. 'It would be a pity to spoil those European shirts.'

A *Fisi* with a revolver advanced and shot each of the men through both knee-caps. As each African fell to the ground a second *Fisi* pulled his shirt over his head. When all three had been stripped a *Fisi* with a Tommy-gun sprayed their prostrate bodies, scarcely taking aim and not caring whether he killed or not.

The priests had long dropped to their knees in prayer. One stretched out his hand to give a blessing to a dying African and as he did so a *Fisi* with a panga lopped that hand off. The blow became a general signal for the pangas to begin slashing at the other priest. Mercifully both were soon dead. There remained now only the saw-mill manager and the banker.

The stammering man, still hidden to Menant from the waist upwards, held up his stick and shouted for silence.

'I still haven't discovered what I came here to find out. Where you have hidden arms and money. This is your last chance to tell us. You. . . .' The cane shot out towards the saw-mill manager, who stared blankly back.

On the wall behind the two remaining prisoners was a switch-box with a red and green button. The tip of the cane touched the red button and pressed. At once the mill was filled with the high, singing sound of the circular blade gathering speed in the saw-bench.

'Seize him.'

The saw-mill manager started to scream as he realised what they intended to do with him. The screams continued as they laid him on the saw-bench and fed him head-first towards the rotating blade. At first they allowed the teeth merely to carve a narrow groove in the skull, While chips of bone flew from the blade. Then suddenly, as if bored, they pushed the travelling table of the saw-bench home so that the great whirling saw threw out flecks of brain. They kept up the pressure until they had severed the saw-mill manager to the groin as neatly as a split carcase of beef. A great groan went up from the African watchers.

The tall man's final question was as much an empty formality as a defence counsel's speech at a Soviet state trial for treason.

'You have a last chance to tell us where you have hidden the bank's money.'

The bank manager never heard the question. He had collapsed on the floor as the blade bit into the saw-mill man's head. They carried the fat bundle that was the banker to the saw-bench. There they spread his legs so that his genitals made the first contact with the blade. They meant to emasculate him slowly but at the first terrible bite of the saw he knocked one of the *Fisi* holding him sideways. He was lucky that the immediate response of his torturers was to press him hard against the saw so that it ploughed into his stomach as far as the navel. They stopped there and hurled him among the other corpses in the reddened sawdust. Even so, the bank manager did not die for a full minute. Jean-Pierre could see one leg flailing about, though he made no sound.

Jean-Pierre's only thought was to get one good look at the owner of the matchstick legs and halting speech. If he lived, he would sometime, somewhere, settle with him. But the logs still obscured his view.

The swagger-stick swished towards the trembling Africans. The stammer was prominent again.

'Take them back in the lorry and release them. Shoot any that give trouble.' To the Africans he said, 'Go and tell everyone you meet that you have seen the justice awarded by the People's Revolution. See that they understand what will happen to them, and to you, if they resist.'

The jeep started. The tall man's legs disappeared as he climbed aboard. The lights swung across the empty wall where the prisoners had stood. A wheel bumped across the headless body of one of the priests. Within five minutes the saw-mill was silent and empty except for the chatter of the two guards they had left behind.

Only one thing mattered now. They had been overlooked. Menant tried to reassure Helen by touching her. He found that she had somehow managed partially to bury herself in a drift of sawdust by wriggling into it. He dared not turn over to look at her. She made no response to his touch. She felt rigid. Had she suffocated? It might be best, he thought, if she had done so. Impossible to know how much of the execution she had actually seen. Simply to hear would have been enough to turn most women's minds, even a mind as logical and detached as hers. He kept his leg against her. After some time he sensed a slight movement. There was nothing more to be done.

Jean-Pierre Menant had become accustomed to being told he was a hard, cold man. Though the verdict did not entirely accord with his own self-analysis, he found himself wondering now just what kind of a specimen he was. Even the revolting nature of the murders had not made him want to throw up. He had known this was what the *Fisi* could do, almost certainly would do. When they raped and shot the two women he had known that this, or worse, was what they would do to Helen if they discovered her. This did not get to him in the way it would have got to most other men. Nor did the thought that, if found, he was likely to end up, testicles first, on a circular saw. His mind concentrated entirely on killing in return and in particular on killing the unknown stammering man who had conducted the massacre.

He began to work on his wrists. The wire was well tied and there was no hope, without a cutting aid, of escaping from it. The one favourable thing was that the bindings round the wrists were not sufficiently tight to stop the circulation.

The saw-mill remained quiet apart from the occasional movement of one of the guards outside. He was reasonably sure that there were only two men on duty and that one of them was probably asleep. The information was little use, though, so long as his hands remained bound.

In the early hours of the morning a jeep drew up. Menant's heart jumped. Was this to be a repeat performance? Someone shouted orders and abuse. Menant's guess was that this tirade was prompted by lack of alertness on the part of the sentry. If so, this argued that the newcomer was someone in authority. Was there something familiar in the angry tones of the voice?

Two men entered the saw-mill. One, cowering before a stream of fury, was plainly the unlucky sentry. The man who ranted at him was the most unwelcome sight Jean-Pierre could think of — Hyena Cap. From his restricted viewpoint Jean-Pierre saw that Hyena Cap had been busy since he left the saw-mill. He wore a police sergeant's uniform jacket and he was three parts drunk on *pombe*. The shouting had awakened the other African left to guard the mill. This unfortunate now came in for Hyena Cap's fury, an anger all the more lethal since it was accompanied by a great deal of threatening gesture with the Sterling gun which had already killed at least one comrade in arms that day.

Menant pushed against Helen's leg, willing her to accept his reassurance and remain still, but there was no response. The main hope was that Hyena Cap was too drunk to remember the earlier happenings of that long, terrible day. But now a frightening thing happened. With the instinctive obsession of his kind with carrion, Hyena Cap began to turn over with his foot the results of the tall man's massacre. Not many hours had passed but already, aided by heat and humidity, the processes of putrefaction had set in. As his foot turfed and turned the air became thick with the sweet stench of dried and drying blood, mixed with the resinous tang of cut timber and sawdust. It was only when he came upon the two violated and head-shot women that Hyena Cap sensed there was something missing from the scene: his own personal contribution to it.

'Where are they?' he shouted. 'Find them. I brought them for questioning. Find them or I will shoot you both. Find them.'

If Hyena Cap was going to do the searching, there was still a chance. Menant was certain he was too drunk to look far or see much. Hyena Cap, however, appreciated as much for himself and had no intention of tottering round the ill-lit ramifications of the mill so long as there were two subordinates to do the job for him. Menant wriggled as far as he could beneath the nearest log. What use was this so long as Helen remained exposed?

One of the guards shouted as he spotted Helen. Seconds later, Menant was jerked from his hiding place by the legs and dragged out into the open.

Hyena Cap said, 'They haven't been questioned. It was intended. They have been overlooked. Bring the man here.'

Jean-Pierre was pulled, face downward, through the stinking sawdust. Hyena Cap's boot cracked him in the ribs.

'What were you doing on the mountain?'

The boot kicked again, forcing the breath out of him so that he could not answer even had there been a sensible answer to make.

'Throw him against the wall. Now, sit him up so that he can see.'

Menant felt something hard, cold and jagged at his back, one of the spare blades for the saw.

'Bring the woman forward. Strip her. . . .' The boot connected with the shins of the guard who had made a move to take the rope gag from her torn mouth.

Menant felt for the saw teeth of the blade and began to rub away at the wire, except that his first movement missed the wire and drove a tooth deep into his wrist.

They had laid Helen across the saw-bench and the first *Fisi* had begun to operate on her. Like a bloody baboon, was Menant's reaction. As the *Fisi* prepared to enter she came to life and lashed out with a knee, catching the man in the crutch. The *Fisi* fell back, howling like a hyena that Jean-Pierre had once seen cruelly and deliberately shot in the genitals by a Belgian farmer. At once, just as a baboon might have done, the second guard took over. Menant sawed away, cutting himself as much as the wire. By the time the second *Fisi* had spent himself he had succeeded in cutting one strand of flex. Helen lay without resistance, her head thrown back over the edge of the saw-bench, her eyes wide open, the edges of the rope gag white with saliva. The man she had kneed now took up where he had left off, grunting and growling with pain.

The second strand of wire parted: one more to go. When the second *Fisi* had finished — and, as a result of the knee in the groin, it took him a long time — Hyena Cap laid down his Sterling gun and unhooked his belt. Evidently he had regained sufficient command of his *pombe*-clouded mind to feel that he could exact his share of the white woman. He took his time to reach the required degree of tumescence. In this respect he was a disagreeably impressive man, even without his full potential realised.

The third strand of wire snapped as Hyena Cap began his unsteady advance on Helen. Despite the fact that she was barely conscious she was held spread-eagled by the other two

54

men as tightly as if she was fighting for her life.

Jean-Pierre waited all the time he could afford to make sure he had sufficient feeling in his wrist and fingers. The last thing the *Fisi* were doing was looking in his direction. Hyena Cap still had six feet to go to reach Helen. Jean-Pierre slid his right hand down inside his slacks and found the butt of the Walther. He drew it and, resting the automatic on his knees, took careful aim and shot Hyena Cap deliberately at the root of the penis, the bullet passing on and upward into the lower abdomen. Before the *Fisi* on the left could react, Jean-Pierre shot him through the kidneys. The third man started for the Sterling gun but didn't make more than a yard before a bullet took him between the shoulder blades.

Jean-Pierre crawled forward behind the logs, watching the entrance and waiting to see if there were any more about, but all he heard were the screams of Hyena Cap. It was unlikely that one more shot would attract any attention but he wasn't going to risk it. Hyena Cap would undoubtedly bleed to death, but it might take a long time. Jean-Pierre had never seen so much blood leave a man's body or travel such a distance in such a short time. But then, it had no doubt been under considerable pressure when the bullet struck. He picked up a panga and, putting a foot on the man's face, cut his throat.

Helen had not moved. Her face was swollen and her eyes closed. Blood ran down her thighs. He picked up the Sterling gun and a spare magazine. Then he picked her up. Outside was Hyena Cap's jeep. It would be light in an hour. He laid Helen on the front seat and covered her with a tarpaulin. Then he drove off down the forest track without lights.

The lower slopes of the mountain were well supplied with tracks, tracks that linked farms with banana groves, tea and quinine plantations. Some were well used as regular thoroughfares by farmers' lorries and cars; others were travelled only when workers needed to plant, tend or harvest a certain crop; yet others were barely used at all. It was these that Menant now sought out, often turning and doubling back on himself like a forest antelope fleeing down a maze of tunnels and runs known only to himself. Overgrown branches slashed and whipped at his windscreen. Grass loomed like a tall, green wave to break and smash against front axle and radiator. Not once did he use his lights, nor did he need to. Several times when in momentary doubt he stopped, took the Sterling gun and made a reconnaissance on foot. Each time he did so he checked on Helen's condition. She was still, as far as he could tell, in a state of comatose shock. He covered her and drove on.

After an hour of jolting, rackety progress he turned the jeep downhill towards the lake. He had reached the point which had been on his mind ever since leaving the saw-mill. Here the mountain tracks ran out. He had no choice but to hit the metalled main road that ran along the lake shore. After two miles he would reach the turn-off to his own plantation. If the *Fisi* had fanned out beyond Baruva the lake road would be their natural route westwards.

The sky to the east had that watered-down look with which approaching day prematurely dilutes night. In three-quarters of an hour it would be full daylight. Jean-Pierre laid the Walther on the seat beside him and checked that the magazine was fully home in the Sterling. Then he eased the jeep down a steep grass bank on to the main road and started westwards at a steady fifty, a speed that gave him the option of stopping to open fire if necessary or putting his foot flat down for outright escape.

The road-block, built of five-gallon petrol cans, was just where he expected it to be, beyond a sharp left-hand bend where a cliff overhung the lake edge. Two *Fisi* leant against it. He had about five seconds in which to assess the situation. In this time he saw that the cans on which the men had put their weight had been pushed back from the general line of the wall by several inches. Therefore, they were not filled with earth or anything more solid than air. The chances were that the lower layers of the wall were in the same condition.

56

The gap in the road-block was not nearly wide enough to allow the jeep to pass. He put his foot flat on the accelerator pedal and hit the gap dead centre, hurling aside cans and sentries on either side. It was then that he saw the second wall of cans fifty yards further on. There was no gap at all in this wall. The jeep had lost impetus as the result of its first use as a battering-ram. This time when it struck it only broke the wall. As Jean-Pierre backed off to complete his break-through, the *Fisi* guarding this second element of the road-block came to life. There were five of them, only three of whom carried rifles. He shot the nearest of these with the Walther as the man fired wildly from the hip. The second *Fisi* had hardly unslung his carbine when the bullet took him in the chest. The third armed man Jean-Pierre ran down with the jeep so that he was thrown across the bonnet. Jean-Pierre did not waste time shooting him then and there but drove on, crushing his legs against the scattered and now yielding cans. With his last strength the spread-eagled *Fisi* managed to throw a grenade on to the jeep's front seat. But he had failed to pull the pin.

Through the road-block now, Jean-Pierre paused long enough to pick up the grenade, remove the pin and drop it as he drove away. He had only gone thirty yards when the grenade exploded, detonating the happily responsive mixture of air and petrol vapour still trapped in many of the empty petrol cans. Almost casually Jean-Pierre shot the moaning *Fisi* lying on his bonnet in the top of the head. Then he stopped and opened up on the blazing road-block with the Sterling. At first there were one or two rifle shots in reply. By the time he had emptied a whole magazine there was nothing. He pushed the dead man off the bonnet and drove away, conscious of the fact that he had relished every cold, calculating, deadly minute of it.

He drove as fast as possible now, knowing that several bullets had hit the jeep but not knowing whether one had penetrated the petrol tank. Though he expected no further opposition beyond the road-block — the *Fisi* would be reluctant to move on in darkness – he did not wish to run out of fuel on the mile and half of main road still ahead of him. Once he made the turn-off to his plantation his chances of getting away with a break-down would be far higher, even handicapped by a still unconscious Helen.

He met no one on the road and the jeep behaved perfectly. The sky was fast growing light by the time he reached the track leading to his farm. He could detect no recent tyre marks. Nevertheless, when he got within two hundred yards of the house he drove the jeep into an eight-foot-high thicket of scrub, switched off and listened. The only sound was that of a grey hornbill, disturbed into unwonted early rising. Jean-Pierre had no way of knowing whether the farm was still occupied by his African staff; whether they had run for it (which seemed most likely); or, if still in residence, what would be their reaction to the arrival of an unannounced jeep – provided they were awake and alert enough to detect its approach. Mushi might not be the greatest marksman in the world but even he could cause unexpected damage with a fifty-calibre machine-gun at thirty yards' range. So Jean-Pierre made a reconnaissance on foot, calling out softly, 'Mushi. It's me, Jean-Pierre Menant.'

To his surprise he saw the muzzle of the fifty-calibre depress slightly and feel out the bush in his vicinity. Jean-Pierre flattened himself behind a tree. 'Mushi, I'm back, safe and sound. Is Kamuji there? I'll want some breakfast.'

The mention of the cook's name did it. Mushi's face appeared above the gun. 'Come out and show yourself, master.'

Jean-Pierre stepped out from behind the tree quickly, knowing that a sudden movement might be dangerous but calculating that Mushi would recognise him long before he could get back behind the gun and fire a burst in panic.

'It's you, master.'

'Yes. It's me. I'll go back and fetch the jeep. Stay where you are. Don't fire. It's only me.'

He noticed with approval that, when he finally drove up,

the machine-gun depressed its muzzle to follow him until Mushi was perfectly certain that the master actually sat in the driving seat.

When the African servants had taken down the beams closing the teak doors into the courtyard, he drove inside.

'Tell Kamuji's wife I want her to look after the mam'selle. Put her to bed. Bathe her wounds. Give her hot soup if she will take it. Understand? Now, Mushi, you have done well. Come with me. I want to make sure we are ready for them.'

'Will they come, master?'

'Soon, Mushi. They are barely two miles down the road. Get the best men and place them where I have taught you to place them.'

'They will kill us all, master.'

'No, Mushi. We will kill all of them.'

Jean-Pierre stationed himself behind the fifty-calibre in the tower and laid his hunting rifle, a twin to the one he had lost up on the Saddle, beside him. He put a magazine on the Bren that commanded the rear of the house from the tower. He had checked the weapons of the four Africans who, in addition to Mushi, he had partly trained for defence of the farm. They were frightened, as they had every right to be. But, he reflected, they were probably even more frightened of him if they disobeyed orders. Those orders were simple: not to fire until he gave the signal with a whistle blast.

The first *Fisi* appeared one hour later. They gave the appearance of being a highly disorganised reconnaissance party. A fat *Fisi* in a camouflaged jacket seemed to be in command. When he first appeared on the track up which Jean-Pierre had lately driven he stood still for some time in the middle of it, staring at the house as if uncertain what to make of it. Jean-Pierre was sorely tempted to shoot him where he stood but resisted the urge, sure that there must be others nearby. After two or three minutes the fat *Fisi* waved his arm. Immediately three more appeared from the bush on either side and joined him. Jean-Pierre made savage gestures to Mushi and the other four defenders not to fire. The *Fisi* separated now, stringing out in a line, and began to walk towards the house. At thirty yards Jean-Pierre shot the fat man in the forehead. Then, working the bolt smoothly between each shot and never once taking the rifle from his shoulder, he cut down the other three. The last man had run back scarcely ten yards by the time the last bullet smashed his spine. Jean-Pierre licked his lips with pleasure. It had been like breaking clay-pipes in a shooting gallery.

'Well done,' he called to Mushi. 'You did quite right not to waste bullets. Next time there will be more of them. Then, when I blow the whistle, you may fire.'

'But if our bullets turn to water as they say?'

'Did mine?'

'No, master, but they did not use their magic. Not one shouted "*Mai*".'

'Next time they will do so, but the result will be the same.'

No doubt because the *Fisi* had other properties to examine, they did not miss their recce party for a further hour. It was mid-day when the lorry drove up and stopped out of sight down the track.

This time they came out of the bushes in bunches, firing wildly at the brickwork. They shouted, '*Mai, Mai*', 'water, water'. Jean-Pierre blew his whistle at once, before the magic word the *Fisi* witchdoctors had assured their followers would turn their enemies' bullets to water got a chance to turn the defenders' hearts to water instead.

Jean-Pierre opened up with the fifty-calibre, firing short, well-aimed bursts. On either side of him he was aware of his Africans firing their Stens. Most of the damage he caused himself. Not a single *Fisi* got within twenty yards of the house but still the Africans fired at the heaps of bodies. Knowing it would be useless to try to stop them, he let them shoot their magazines out. Then he leapt up blowing his whistle.

'Well done, well done. You see now. Their magic does not work. You have killed them all.'

On the cleared ground in front of the house Jean-Pierre counted eighteen dead. He knew they would come again, but not immediately.

The African women house servants had put Helen into his own large bed. She was conscious though she stared, wide-eyed, at the wall. He sensed that she had heard the firing and that this had driven her further back into a state of terror. He held her hands, talking, talking, talking softly all the time. At first her hands lay limply in his as if she did not recognise him, but gradually she began to grip him so tightly that he winced.

After an hour, Mushi came down from the tower.

'The men are frightened without you. Their courage is disappearing like the early rains into parched ground.'

'Are all their weapons reloaded?'

'Yes, master.'

'And is there sight or sound of the enemy?'

'No, master.'

'Then go back and tell them there is nothing to worry about.'

Jean-Pierre rightly judged that such encouragement would only last a very short time. Ten minutes later, therefore, he was back on the battlements. He inspected each man's weapons, congratulating each marksman on his valour. Before he climbed up into the master position in the tower, from which he commanded 360 degrees of fire, he moved Mushi to the one weapon-slit facing the rear. The next attack might come from that direction, though the ground there was more open and less favourable for surprise. Mushi was the only one he could trust to stand firm in the isolation of that position. Though it was only fifteen yards away it was separated by the physical void of the central courtyard. The other four would need the proximity of their companions if they were not to succumb to terror of the *Fisi*. Jean-Pierre checked the tripod of the rearward-facing Bren and traversed it once or twice to show Mushi that he was well supported should the *Fisi* decide on a suicide assault from the back of the house.

The second attack, just after two o'clock, took exactly the same form as the first, except that there were now more of them. This time they left ten dead on the ground.

The afternoon passed uneasily but without incident, save for the arrival of four white-backed vultures and a griffon who, with the prescience of their kind, knew a bad thing when they smelt it. Prompted by the sun, the odour of decay was, by mid-afternoon, readily detectable even to human nostrils. The vultures sat huddled in a tree for a respectful period, the respect being paid to caution rather than to the dead, and then descended to begin feeding on the nearest of the corpses, the last man of the group of four first killed by Jean-Pierre.

It was fruitless to try to guess the *Fisi*'s future tactics. The most likely answer was they didn't have any. From time to time there was a sputter of distant firing and something that sounded unpleasantly like mortar bombs. At least someone else was opposing them somewhere. To show they were still around the *Fisi* put in sporadic bursts of automatic fire and single rifle shots from the cover of the forest, but the bullets flattened harmlessly against the walls. Jean-Pierre gave orders that no one was to return the fire unless the enemy showed themselves in the open.

About four o'clock he sent Mushi and two of the Africans down below to get some sleep in the house. He did not expect the *Fisi* to attack in darkness but, nevertheless, he wanted at least half his force to be awake if anything developed. Around five he visited Helen again. He was certain her eyes showed that she recognised him but as soon as he spoke to her her mind retreated behind barricades of shock. She now had a high fever, so he told his house-girl to bathe her face and wrists in cold water. He tried to persuade her to drink some orange juice but she resisted the glass with clamped lips.

Just before dusk he started the generator and tested the spotlight in the tower. At seven he woke Mushi and posted him in the tower with orders to sweep the surrounding bush with the light at irregular intervals and to fire short bursts of the Sten into the trees to accompany his illuminations. Mushi was to call him in two hours' time, after which he would do watch and watch about with him, two hours on, two hours off. He changed the other two Africans over and lay down beside the off-duty pair on mattresses carried up from the house.

As he had hoped, the night passed peacefully but dawn brought an unpleasant surprise. A familiar popping thud made him look upward in time to see a small, possibly a two-inch, mortar bomb at the peak of its trajectory against the pink of the eastern sky. The bomb passed high overhead and fell on open ground one hundred yards behind. Accuracy was plainly not going to be this mortar crew's strong point. But, in time, even they must get the range. They tried again several minutes later. This time the bomb fell fifty yards to the left flank. After the third bomb had fallen harmlessly into the bush he thought he had the mortar fixed. It was barely one hundred yards away along the track leading to the house. He guessed correctly that they had set it up on the open space he had cleared and laid with hardcore as a turn-round for plantation vehicles in the rainy season. Directly above this turn-round was a fault scarp, a cliff some fifty feet high. The top of the cliff was heavily bushed, as was the approach to it from the direction of the house. Only the first thirty yards were open where he had cleared the ground as a defensive precaution for the house. However, this precaution would be of little assistance if that mortar ever succeeded in getting the range.

A fourth bomb burst on the open ground in front. To the right of the house, in the direction of the mortar, half the distance to the trees lay in dead ground, provided one crawled. After that there were three large rocks with gaps of a yard or more between. Jean-Pierre had little doubt that he could cross the vital thirty yards without being hit, but was less certain that he could do so without being spotted. He called Mushi to the tower and gave him detailed instructions.

He made him repeat these.

'When you get to the rocks, master, we give them absolute bloody hell with all we've got.'

'Good. What next?'

'When we know you are safely across, we cease firing until your grenades go off, then we start firing again and continue until you are back in the house.'

'You will make the others obey?'

'I swear it.'

'If you do not I will be killed and you will be on your own to face the *Fisi*.'

'I have already thought of that, master.'

Jean-Pierre put four hand-grenades in his haversack, checked that the Walther was fully loaded and also the Sterling. He placed three spare magazines for this with the grenades in the haversack. He let himself out of the side door into the area of dead ground and began to crawl. When the dead ground ran out he was within six feet of the first large rock. He lay on his back in the gully looking up at Mushi. The little African was, thank God, paying attention. Jean-Pierre gathered himself for take-off, raised his hand and dropped it sharply. The fifty-calibre opened up first, scything and slashing the banana leaves on the far side of the clearing. Almost at once it was joined by the Stens. Crouching double, Jean-Pierre got up and ran for the trees behind the rocks. The firing continued for a further ten seconds, then stopped. Jean-Pierre made sure the grenades were readily to hand and began to dodge fast between the trees. The mortar crew had dropped flat at the first burst of automatic fire. As he reached the cliff top they had regrouped round the mortar, preparatory to firing another round at the house. Jean-Pierre crawled through the low scrub to within three feet of the cliff edge. During this approach he heard the plop of the mortar firing once again, the burst of the bomb, followed by a scream of triumph from high ground further along the cliff. Of course! An observation post. Someone must oversee the whole scene, observing the fall of shot. Then, obviously, that someone had overlooked him. Jean-Pierre cocked and laid the Sterling down beside him. He took two grenades from the haversack, placing one beside the Sterling.

Below the cliff the crew were bunched, ready to load again. Jean-Pierre pulled the pin from the first of the three-second grenades, let the firing lever go, delayed one second, and lobbed the grenade over the cliff edge. It burst three feet above the ground, cutting down every man in the mortar crew. At the explosion of the grenade the spotter stood up to see what had happened. Jean-Pierre shot him in the chest with a two-second burst from the Sterling. He waited briefly to see if more than one *Fisi* manned the observation post, pulled the pin from the second grenade and dropped it in the middle of the stacked mortar bombs beneath him. A satisfactory detonation suggested that this particular weapon would give no further trouble. He ran back between the trees. Good for Mushi. Automatic fire had opened up from the house again. He paused momentarily at the edge of the trees and, scarcely bothering to bend double, ran behind the rocks until he reached the dead ground without, as far as he could tell, a single shot being fired at him. When he reached the foot of the tower he saw that he had dealt with the mortar only just in time. Its last bomb had burst on the battlements, disembowelling one of the African Sten-gunners and wounding a second in the calf. With one lucky hit he had lost almost half his effective defensive strength. However, the *Fisi* did not know this.

The loss of the mortar and its crew had evidently discouraged the *Fisi* greatly. They did not attack again, apart from taking occasional pot shots at the walls. Shortly before ten o'clock two Dakotas flew over in the direction of Baruva. A quarter of an hour later there came sustained firing from the direction of the airfield, including the bursts of heavy mortar bombs. Shortly afterwards the *Fisi* stopped firing at the house. Jean-Pierre heard confused shouting followed by the sound of a truck driving away fast. The siege seemed to be over.

Helen Lawes was conscious. He told her very slowly and repeatedly that she was safe. The fighting around the house was over. There was no way of knowing whether she understood this message. She continued to stare fixedly at him.

'Safe, Helen. You're quite safe now.' He didn't know whether he believed this himself. 'As soon as I can,' he told his house servant, 'I will send a doctor to her.' This he believed even less. Where could he possibly find a doctor? He had seen Jacques Veniard leave Baruva.

After a time the sound of fighting had died down in the direction of the airfield. It appeared now to have moved into the outskirts of the town. Two Dakotas flew low overhead, back in the direction from which they had originally come. This could only mean that the airfield was secured. The planes were going back for reinforcements.

Jean-Pierre slipped out of the side door once more and made a brief, cautious reconnaissance of the grounds. The dead mortar crew lay where the grenade had slaughtered them. Otherwise, as he had suspected, nothing. Sensing themselves cut off, the *Fisi* had retreated, almost certainly in the direction of the town.

Jean-Pierre now had only one ambition — to be in at the death, and at the death of one man in particular: the tall, thin, stammering man who had ordered the massacre in the saw-mill. Though during the intense action of the last twenty-four hours he had had little time to think of the tall man consciously, he now realised that he had been in his thoughts all the time; every time he had looked at Helen; every time he had killed, first the four *Fisi* scouts and, later, the mortar crew and their observer. Each time he had killed he had done so with a detached joy — pleasure was too mild a word — making his victim stand proxy for the tall man whose face he had never actually seen.

His jeep stood in the courtyard. He ordered Mushi to unlock the metal container on its floor, remove the Bren gun and place it on the side mount to the left of the driving seat. He considered whether he should take Mushi with him but finally decided he should remain to take charge of the house. At the last minute the little African again proved his resourcefulness and reliability by rushing out with a national flag which he lashed to the right side of the windscreen. If his master was suddenly to run into friendly forces it was as well that he had some means of identity. He was right. Mercenaries were hardly likely, in the circumstances, to see if the target had a white skin before they opened up. Another reason for leaving Mushi behind.

Jean-Pierre met the first mercenaries at the road-block he had shot up the day before. He stopped two hundred yards short and extended his flag. A burst of automatic fire ripped over his head but he stood his ground, fluttering the flag. An officer in a para smock inspected him through binoculars. In a few seconds an arm beckoned him to approach. He drove slowly forward, keeping his eye on the barrel of a heavy machine-gun which followed his progress. At ten yards' range he stopped and called out, 'Jean-Pierre Menant. I've been holding out in my farmhouse two miles up the road.'

The lieutenant in the para smock walked out at that, carrying a Luger in his hand.

'Any *Fisi* up front?' The voice was South African.

'I don't think so. They pulled out soon after the planes brought you fellows in.'

'Glad to be of service.' The South African held his nose, pointing to the shallows of the lake where three burned and bloated *Fisi* corpses rocked in the slight swell against the reeds.

'Someone got here before us.'

'Yes, I did. Thirty-six hours ago.'

'Christ, man, you're a bit of a one-man army, aren't you?'

'I was lucky. I surprised them.'

'Anyone killed up at your place?'

'A whole pile of *Fisi*!'

67

'I meant your people.'

'One African killed, one wounded. There's an American girl I'm very worried about. Multiple rape case. She's nearly shocked out of her mind.'

'Bastards!' The South African spat in the direction of the corpses. 'Only doctor we've got dropped with the paras on the airfield. You'd better come into town with me. The boys are cleaning up there now. Perhaps the C.O. will spare a car for your casualties. Sure there are no *Fisi* operating up the lake shore still? O.K., we'll pull back into Baruva, then. More use there, I guess.'

The mercenaries had done a good job for everyone save the town of Baruva. The Hôtel du Président where Menant had eaten lunch — was it only four days before? — had been struck by a bazooka bomb square in its entrance porch. The rather pretentious balcony, formerly supported by two Doric columns, hung down in a tangle of shattered concrete and twisted steel reinforcement. Bullet-holes pocked almost every building. A Chevrolet three-tonner burned itself out before the bank. The bank had already burned. It had been one of the first buildings the *Fisi* had demolished in an attempt to open its strong-room. The sweet smell of human carrion mixed nauseatingly with the stench of burning. There must have been three hundred bodies in the two-hundred-yard length of the main street. Most were those of African townsfolk the *Fisi* had murdered. They had made no attempt to move or bury their victims. The rest were *Fisi* caught in the murderously professional crossfire of the mercenaries. Among them were several whose hyena-skin caps or outrageously decorated uniforms — they wore pips, crowns, bars, stripes, epaulettes, any badge of rank they had been able to wrench from a former victim — proclaimed them as officers. Jean-Pierre searched for one man and one man alone and half hoped he would not find him.

They found the colonel in charge of the mercenary force at his command post, a badly shot up police station at the north end of the town. A Belgian in his early forties, he wore a breastful of ribbons that included a *Croix de Guerre* and an M.C. If a human being could have mated with an armoured car, the colonel might just have been the result. You got the impression, helped by numerous scars on such flesh as was visible, that bullets bounced off him. His stocky body was topped by a crew-cut head that was more of a turret than a skull. Shakespeare might have had Colonel Jules Dalan in mind when he wrote, 'Let [the eye] pry through the portage of the head. . .'.

The South African lieutenant saluted smartly.

'Hullo, Janny,' said the colonel.

'Brought in a civilian from north lake sector.'

'Anything happening up there?'

'Not much. My friend here seems to have done very well without us. The *Fisi* got no further than his farm. By the time we dropped on the airfield he'd discouraged them so much that they fell back on the town.'

'How many attacked your place?' the colonel asked.

'Twenty or thirty. There must be about ten left.'

'He knocked off eight himself, sir. Oh, and a road-block.'

The colonel looked at Jean-Pierre with interest. 'Sounds as though you should join us.'

Heavy firing a hundred yards away drowned the rest of the sentence. A bullet passed through the rafters and, deflected by a beam, flattened itself against the opposite wall. The colonel took no notice.

'That was meant for "A" Company. They've got the rest of the bastards penned up in the bus station. For once the *Fisi* are putting up quite a show. They seem to have someone reasonable in command.'

'The so-called General Patrice?' Menant asked.

'That's the rumour. It's certainly someone who can organise them better than usual.'

'Anyone seen him?'

'No, but they say he's a tall, thin fellow. But I'll tell you when we get a smell of his corpse. Come on, Janny, let's have a first-hand look at this situation. It ought to be over by now.

69

Maybe we'll need your company to help out.' The colonel turned to Jean-Pierre. 'You've done enough, you'd better stay here.'

'I'll come, too.'

The colonel looked at Jean-Pierre and what he saw persuaded him not to argue.

'A' Company was pinned down by light automatic fire among the wrecked buses parked outside the bus station. The *Fisi* shot with more than their usual inaccuracy at anything that moved. 'A' Company had already taken four casualties, a sergeant dead and three privates wounded. Bazookas and rocket-launchers had made little impression on the solid concrete of the bus station. The *Fisi* also held the high ground behind, leading directly into the forest. The bus station lay on the very outskirts of town. To outflank it would mean a savage and possibly costly house-to-house battle up a narrow street on either side.

Crouching behind an empty petrol tanker, into which bullets periodically whanged, Colonel Dalan held conference with the commander of 'A' Company, a young Rhodesian.

'What do you propose to do, Mick?'

'I'm waiting for the heavy mortars to come up from the airfield, then I'm going to stonk the place hard. I don't want any more casualties.'

'Quite right. Not worth it. Sorry about MacIntyre.' MacIntyre had been the sergeant.

'Yes, we could lose a few more like him if we try to rush them.'

'Agreed. Use the mortars then. If that doesn't shift them, we'll just have to hit them at night.'

A burst of bullets tore the air open overhead and kicked up the dust three feet from the colonel.

'That's a new one, colonel. They've somehow got a light machine-gun into a house on the right of the bus station. Whoever's in charge knows what he's doing for once.'

The walkie-talkie in the Rhodesian's hand clicked and a nasal voice said, 'O.K., Sunray. Mortars in position. Any particular target?'

'Sunray answering. Flat-topped house five degrees east of bus station. Got a Simba beer advert on one wall. There's a machine-gun on the roof.'

'O.K., Sunray. Got it. Will commence firing immediately.'

Ten seconds later they heard the thump of the mortar and watched the heavy, finned bomb arc in apparent slow motion overhead. The dirty brown cloud of smoke and debris rose twenty yards beyond the house.

'Down twenty,' said the Rhodesian.

As the smoke drifted about the house, Menant saw a man move on the roof. He was a tall man, for he found it hard to remain totally hidden when moving behind the shallow parapet of the house. The man from the saw-mill?

'Quick,' the Rhodesian ordered, 'they're moving the bloody gun.'

The mortar thudded almost at once. The bomb's flight took perhaps twenty seconds. In that time Menant saw the machine-gun's crew of two run from the back of the house for the shelter of the bus station. This time he had no doubt. The third man directing the fire was the tall, puttee'd man of the saw-mill. Menant snapped off a shot from his hunting rifle but knew that he was behind as he squeezed. As the gun crew reached shelter the house they had recently occupied collapsed like a sandbag under a ten-ton lorry. The yellow dust that had been its brickwork clouded the air.

'How's that?' asked the walkie-talkie.

'Great, but you were too late.'

The wind drifted the dust of the demolished house across the front of the bus station and with it came something else — smoke. The mortar had set the next house in the street on fire. Under cover of the smoke the Rhodesian lieutenant began to move elements of his company out on to the right flank. Soon, to the irregular fire of the heavy mortar was added the explosions caused by 'A' Company's bazooka artist who had established himself, with light machine-gun support, in the region of the burning house.

Colonel Dalan crawled happily around among the abandoned and bullet-riddled buses, chatting to the men dug in there. Every concussion from an exploding heavy mortar bomb not only made the bus station rock but seemed to lift Jean-Pierre, sitting behind his petrol tanker, several inches off the ground. He sat there with his rifle propped on his knees, not particularly relishing the situation. This was not his kind of fighting. The forces were too impersonal, too remote from his own control. He was sure that the tall, stammering man was in command of the twenty or thirty *Fisi* holding the bus station. He had had a chance at him and missed. It was late afternoon. There would not be many more chances. He had just made up his mind to take off on a solitary sniper's expedition in an attempt to reach the trees behind the station building when Jules Dalan crawled back. The colonel looked quite happy.

'We're going in as soon as it gets dark. They're never any good at night. Shit-scared of evil spirits, I suppose. "B" Company on the left have got a flame-thrower. They won't use it until they're in really close. "A" will work round behind to give covering fire. Zero is 1920 hours. Might as well have a sleep until then. Sorry if the mortar boys woke you up. From 1830 we'll be doubling the rate of fire. Have to go easy on ammo until then. Have a drink. . . .' The colonel passed Jean-Pierre a half-bottle of local cognac.

' "B" Company found some in the hotel cellars. By the way, I reckon you're right. Got a glimpse of your tall, thin, man. It must be Patrice. He's in command all right. Anyway, we'll soon know. Even if the flame-thrower fries them all, I reckon he'll still be recognisable.'

A stray bullet hit the empty tanker above their heads but Colonel Dalan was by then already practically asleep.

By 1845 it was becoming dark. There was no longer any question of sleep, even for the turret-faced colonel. The mortar was now lobbing them over every minute or so. Beneath this barrage, fire from the *Fisi* had slackened. Just after 1900 hours it sputtered away altogether. At 1915 the

72

mortar began to fire as fast as its crew could load it, this time dropping smoke among the high explosives.

Dalan shouted, 'No need for you to stick your neck out. Stay here . . . oh well, if you insist.' He looked at his watch. Together they walked out into the smoke. A few seconds later 'A' Company's automatics opened up in covering fire. They crossed the open ground at a run. The colonel tossed a grenade through the nearest window at the same instant as the hiss and roar of 'B' Company's flame-thrower scorched the left side of the building. The grenade exploded. Dalan and Menant jumped over the window-sill into what had been the booking office. It was at that moment that they realised that not a single shot had been fired in return. What remained of the bus station was manned by dead and wounded.

The mercenaries combed the place carefully, suspecting a trap. At the end of ten minutes they had counted eighteen dead, mostly killed by the blast of the big mortar or by fragments from its bombs. Six wounded *Fisi* still lived, but not for long. Dalan's men did not bother with prisoners. They shot them where they lay. Twenty-four accounted for, but piles of cartridge cases suggested that there had been at least eight more men.

Jean-Pierre inspected the *Fisi* dead. The tall man with the stammer and the puttees was not among them. He had slipped away with the unwounded survivors in the twenty minutes between full darkness and the start of the attack.

Colonel Dalan held an orders group with his company commanders.

'Well done all. No casualties? Good! As far as we can tell about eight men, including the commander, escaped. "C" Company has already moved to mop up along the *Fisi*'s lines of communication back to the lake. The point at which they landed will already have been secured by our Special Boat Unit. The survivors, including their commander, are bound to get caught in the net somewhere. Tomorrow at first light we'll move out to reinforce "C" Company. Any questions?'

Jean-Pierre spoke up. 'With respect, colonel, I don't think

the tall man will get out the way he came in.'

'Oh! What then?'

'I believe he'll try to escape over the Saddle.'

'Saddle? It's not on the map.'

'It's on the tall man's map. It's where they caught me. The pass between the volcanoes.'

'Supposing you're right, Menant. I can't spare a company to chase one man through the clouds. There's a hell of a lot of mopping up still to do.'

'Fine, colonel. Then I'll go after him. Just give me two or three men used to mountains.'

'Menant, I can't really afford them. You know that.'

'You can't afford to let this one escape, colonel. Apart from that, I want him. If necessary I'll go alone with my tracker, Mushi.'

'He's got seven or more with him.'

'All the easier to find him. I know the mountain.'

'O.K. You can have two men. Anyone from mountain country here?'

Two men stepped forward. Both were in their early twenties. Both struck Menant as seasoned and fit. The first held out his hand. 'Corporal Van der Meer. My old man farms in the Drakensberg.' Menant took the red-haired South African's hand. 'Used to moving fast at high altitude?'

'You name a climb in the Drakensberg, I've done it.'

'Christian name?'

'Carl.'

Jean-Pierre turned to the second man. He was lighter, fairer, perhaps a year or two younger than the South African.

'Corporal Stringer. Peter. Rock climber. Climbed with Joe Brown. Peak District. Alps. Dolomites. Ex-Royal Tank Regiment.'

'You're both on. Start at first light. The *Fisi* won't get far during the night.'

The colonel was giving his orders for securing the town during the night. When he'd finished he said, 'Menant, you'd better come and have a meal with us. I'm setting up my HQ in the Hôtel du Président. Perhaps they've left something for us in the cellars.'

'I'd like a doctor first, colonel.'

'Impossible. We've only got one. He'll be dealing with our own casualties.'

'Colonel. I have a casualty at my house, a very serious one. An American woman scientist. Multiple rape case. I believe she'll die if we don't get her help soon.'

'Sounds from what you say that she'll need more than an emergency field-dressing station. The Dakotas will be here as soon as it's light. I'll see she goes out on the first flight.'

'One other thing. I'd like to have my tracker, Mushi, tomorrow.'

'O.K. We'll be sending out a routine patrol to north lake sector. They'll bring him in before dawn.'

Mushi woke Jean-Pierre on the floor of the bridal suite of the Hôtel du Président at five o'clock. Dalan was sleeping on the bridal bed with a Luger beside him.

'Master! In one hour we must go to the mountain.'

Jean-Pierre regretted now that they had discovered an intact crate of Montrachet in the cellars. He fanned the wine fumes out of his mind by sheer will-power and asked, 'Mam'selle. How is she?'

Mushi closed his eyes and then flickered the eyelids, turning his pupils upward, leaving only the bloodshot yellows showing, miming troubled sleep. Then he held his hand to his heart, tapping it in irregular rhythm.

Jean-Pierre looked on Mushi with affection tempered with despair. Half pygmy, half forest tribesman, the little man was utterly loyal and dependable when sober, utterly unreliable when high on native beer or the pot which he grew and harvested himself. At the moment he was remote from the source of both. Mushi was therefore at his best. He had already wakened Van der Meer and Stringer.

Waking was all that had been necessary. Trained in the hard school of Colonel Dalan, they had turned in ready to turn

75

out. Jean-Pierre noted with approval the arms they had chosen. Each carried a carbine and revolver. Van der Meer had a Schmeisser machine-pistol. Stringer had opted for a similar weighting of grenades. Neither had bothered with water-bottles. Water in plenty they would find in the mountains. Each had a light haversack of chocolate and emergency rations. The rest of their load was spare ammunition. Jean-Pierre took his Winchester .306 hunting rifle and his Walther, nothing else.

For a start, Jean-Pierre led. There was only one possible trail out of town and he was certain his man would have taken it. Confirmation came just before it became light. Flattened grasses and the still-warm and covered ashes of a fire showed where the *Fisi* had slept. It was still too dark to see much.

Mushi did not need sight. He had a nose. 'One of them bleeds,' he said.

'How many, Mushi?'

'Eight including the badly-wounded one. They are two hours ahead. The thin one you speak of made them move in the night. There is a moon.'

Jean-Pierre's respect for the *Fisi* leader rose. Anyone who could make superstitious African guerillas march through forest by night had truly remarkable powers.

'Let's keep going.'

When daylight came, Jean-Pierre put Mushi in the lead. Good as were his own powers, he had no illusions when it came to measuring them against the fieldcraft of the half-pygmy. He watched the little man moving with the sure spring of a duiker through the lower canopy of the forest. In his right hand he wielded a panga with which he constantly chopped away at the obstructing vegetation held in his left. Occasionally the sharp blade sliced a sliver off a calloused fingertip. Mushi did not appear to notice this but then, he was a partially burned-out case of leprosy. The disease, rooted in his diminutive body, could permanently have been arrested long since. Jean-Pierre had persuaded the little man

76

to undergo several years of injections. But Mushi drank so much native-brewed alcohol and smoked so much home-grown hemp that the good effects of medication were all but cancelled out. His proudest possession was a piece of sticking-plaster or soiled bandage with which to cover the extremities of his sorely used digits.

Mushi stopped and pointed at a nettle-leaf. On it was a dark splash of recently dried blood. He held his mutilated fingers to his lips. Jean-Pierre signalled him to stay where he was. He fanned the two mercenaries out into open order and advanced carefully. After two hundred yards they came to a large fig tree. A *Fisi*, shot through the left lung, was propped against the trunk, dead. Jean-Pierre heard the Schmeisser being cocked but Mushi came up and said, 'Not here. They are still far ahead.'

They climbed steadily throughout the morning. As Jean-Pierre had predicted, the trail lead directly to the Saddle. He was surprised to find how much he dreaded seeing Helen's hut and the burned-out store. The horror of their night capture was still far too fresh. He was grateful when Mushi lead them straight through the middle ground of the Saddle, leaving the hut high above them on their left. Soon they reached the southern limit of the Saddle. Ahead the pass led down towards the far-distant lake, the direction from which Hyena Cap and his companions must have come that night. Mushi pointed to the ground and turned, unexpectedly, away eastward, round the shoulder of Misoka. Jean-Pierre didn't query his judgement. The *Fisi* were making not for the lake but for the border of the neighbouring state.

They hurried on throughout the mid-day heat, losing altitude gradually across country that became increasingly heart-breaking. In past ages streams of lava had run down from Misoka's crater. These had been eroded into black, razor-backed ridges, dragon's backs on whose scales their feet slid and slithered raising an obnoxious grey dust.

Jean-Pierre noticed the signs a few seconds before Mushi. The *Fisi* were not the only game they tracked. A family of gorillas had passed this way recently. A dropping, only a few hours old, bore the impression of a boot heel. The gorillas had passed this way first.

Jean-Pierre stopped for the first real break just after two in the afternoon. Stringer and Van der Meer confessed that they were out-classed at this kind of tracking. Stringer asked, 'How far do you reckon we are behind them?'

'A mile maybe.'

Van der Meer said, 'They can't have any idea we're on to them.'

'I agree. There's no way of knowing in this sort of country.'

'Then we've got them, Menant?'

'Not necessarily. We're within five miles of the border.'

'Then let's press on,' Van der Meer said. 'I haven't come all this way just to let them escape.'

'When we get close, take your orders from me,' Menant said. 'They're two to one. We'll need to surprise them.'

Surprise of a quite unforeseen sort came one hour later. They had descended a long, V-shaped wall between two lava ridges when firing broke out four hundred yards below them. When Jean-Pierre clapped his glasses on a slope of scrub-covered hillside he saw brown blobs moving there. Gorillas! A dozen or more animals were bounding and crashing through the bush. Then, in the ravine below, his binoculars picked out an incredible sight. A silver-backed male stood at bay, covering the retreat of his terrified family. Jean-Pierre shifted his field of view slightly and saw the object of the big male's fury. A tall, khaki-dressed figure stood on the track ten yards away. Patrice!

The silver-back charged. Jean-Pierre heard the gorilla's angry bark a second before the shot. The gorilla paused and then carried his charge past the *Fisi* leader and on into the bush. There were two more shots but the silver-back kept going. It was all over in less than thirty seconds.

'What the hell was that all about?' Van der Meer demanded.

'Our friends the *Fisi* are terrified of gorillas. They've been pushing that group ahead of them for some time. The gorillas felt trapped in that narrow ravine and decided to break out.'

'That tall chap shot at one with his pistol. Did he hit it?' asked Stringer.

'Could hardly bloody well miss,' Van der Meer said. 'Even from here the brute looked about six feet across the shoulders.'

Below them now was no sign of *Fisi* or of gorillas. 'Come on,' Jean-Pierre ordered. 'We're wasting valuable time. We should catch them now.'

The track led downwards at an increasingly steep angle. In the next quarter of a mile they lost so much height that Jean-Pierre's ears popped. 'Eight and a half thousand,' he registered automatically. When they reached the place where the *Fisi* leader had shot at the silver-back they found three empty nine-millimetre cartridge cases and several large drops of barely dried blood. The last of these lay on a leaf where the silver-back had turned his charge away into the bush.

Jean-Pierre led now, Mushi next, then Van der Meer, with Stringer in the rear with orders to watch from above and behind for signs of an ambush. There was something about the young English corporal that suggested unusual alertness combined with a sense of at-oneness with the forest. Van der Meer might be used to the bare crags of the Drakensberg but he stuck out in the forest like a zebra in a herd of horses. Because they needed to achieve surprise, and to avoid being surprised themselves, their pace inevitably slowed. If anything, that of the *Fisi* increased, perhaps because their encounter with the gorillas had badly scared them but more likely because they sensed that they were nearly across the border.

By late afternoon Menant's party had dropped four thousand feet. Misoka towered above them. They were in open woodland, open because the trees could find little to root upon in the weathered remains of the old lava floes. Wherever there was soil, a tree grew. The going was brittle, cutting even to leather boots. In places their feet broke through the lava crust. Grey dust stuck in dry throats, thickly sulphurous. The place was all too plainly Misoka's ill-used backyard, a volcanic dumping ground. Jean-Pierre had never been this side of the mountain before yet he was familiar with similar terrain on its lower western slopes. Something he had been told about such country troubled him. In his present state of physical and mental exhaustion, he couldn't remember precisely what.

They came at last to a patch of intensely bright green vegetation. The area, perhaps a hundred yards long and thirty yards wide, lay below them, half a mile ahead in a forest clearing, flanked with steep, rocky walls. Something shone white and clean, like piles of stones, among the emerald grass. As they watched, half-a-dozen figures emerged from the forest and began to cross the clearing. A tall man ran fifteen yards ahead. The *Fisi* disappeared into the long grass. Jean-Pierre watched through the glasses, anxious to catch a glimpse of that tall man, hoping to satisfy himself that it was the man who had organised the saw-mill massacre. He saw none of the *Fisi* emerge, but this didn't surprise him since the grass that ran right up to the trees on the far side was five feet high.

'Come on,' he shouted. 'We've got to catch them in the next few miles. After that it will be dark and they'll be across the border.'

They reached the edge of the green patch where the *Fisi* had disappeared. The place was incredibly still. Ahead, on the edge of the lush grass, lay a pile of scattered elephant bones and beyond again bones of hyena and jackal. The horns and boss of a buffalo skull poked out of the grass beside them. Jean-Pierre held up his hand for his party to halt. He sniffed the air like an antelope sensing lion on the wind. Above, on either side, rose the steep walls of two fault scarps. There was no way forward except the way the *Fisi* had taken.

'For Christ's sake,' Van der Meer yelled. 'What are we waiting for?'

'There's something that worries me. I can't exactly tell you what.'

'The *Fisi* won't try to ambush us here. There are plenty of better places.'

'It's not ambush I'm thinking of. Something else. I can't quite place it.'

'Time's running out,' Van der Meer said gruffly. 'If you won't press on, I will.'

'Wait!'

'I'm not under your command.'

Van der Meer cocked his Schmeisser and started to run. They could see his head and shoulders above the tall grass. He had run about twenty-five yards into the reeds when he slowed down and almost immediately swayed and fell.

'Stay here!' Jean-Pierre filled his lungs and ran into the reeds towards the place at which Van der Meer had disappeared. He was aware of a faint susurration in the ground at his feet. It was as if the crevices in the lava were actually breathing, exhaling. The grasses above some of these cracks stirred, though there was no wind to move them. As he ran he dodged between piles of bleached animal bones — elephant, a small herd of elephant, buffalo, giraffe, numerous hyenas and the skull of a single lion.

By the time he spotted the South African's camouflage jacket in the grass his lungs were nearly bursting. He would soon have to breathe, but a puff of yellow vapour in the air beside Van der Meer's body warned him not to do so. One look at Van der Meer's upturned face left no doubt that the man was already dead. Jean-Pierre turned and ran back, letting out the stale air in his lungs in a last relieving spasm just before he reached Stringer and Mushi.

Stringer bent over him. 'What the hell!'

'It's a *musuku*.'

'A *what*?'

Jean-Pierre pumped air in and out of his lungs. 'I should have guessed. All that greenery.'

Mushi rubbed Jean-Pierre's back with his crab-like claw.

Slowly the stabs of light behind Jean-Pierre's eyes vanished.

'All those animal bones. I've never seen a *musuku* until now. Those elephants and the rest just wandered in there and died, like Van der Meer.'

'Like the *Fisi*, too. But what the hell killed them?'

'The *musuku*. It's a vent for volcanic gases. Usually almost pure carbon dioxide. Maybe that's why the grass is so green. It gets regular doses of the stuff. That and the fact that no animals ever survive to graze on it. A herd of elephants ambles in to get at the grass. The vent suddenly starts to breath out. They keel over almost at once. Later, some hyenas catch the scent of their carrion. The same thing happens to them. Just occasionally there's an even more toxic vent, perhaps hydrochloric acid or sulphuric acid gas. I'm afraid poor Van der Meer ran into one of those.'

'The *Fisi* must all have bought it, then, in exactly the same way?'

'Maybe.' Jean-Pierre sounded reluctant. 'There was one bastard I wanted to kill myself.'

'The tall one. The one who shot the gorilla?'

'The tall one.'

'Could anyone have got through the *musuku* alive?'

'Just possible. I've been told that the vents aren't at full blast all the time. Come on, let's find a safe place to get a look at it from the top.'

Leaving Mushi at the bottom, Stringer and Jean-Pierre climbed the crumbly scarp on the upwind side of the *musuku*. When they looked down into that green valley of death they could just see the huddle of *Fisi* corpses partly hidden in the grass. It was impossible to tell exactly how many lay there amid the elephant bones or whether there was a pair of thin, puttee'd legs among them.

After a time Jean-Pierre stood up and cursed long and fluently in his native French. Then he made what was for him a totally irrational and useless gesture. He fired his automatic down into the pile of *Fisi* bodies until the magazine was empty.

Part Two

THE GORILLAS

The big silver-back, Absolom, had been hurt many times before. The play-fights with other young males in his youth had accustomed him to numbing blows, though these were seldom intended to wound, let alone to maim, merely to establish respective places in the male-dominated gorilla hierarchy. At the age of nine he had misjudged the strength of a vine clinging to a *bwamba* tree. The vine had snapped twenty feet above the ground and he had fallen on his shoulder. The bruised arm had been unusable for weeks, yet so thick was the muscle that had taken the blow that he had eventually recovered the full power of the damaged limb.

Absolom was therefore no stranger to pain. But none of these earlier hurts compared with the agony caused by the thing from the tall man's outflung, flashing hand that had struck him in the pectoral muscle. It had hummed like a bee, but a bee with a sting like nothing encountered in the rain-forest.

Absolom had met men several times before. Little black men whom he feared and hated. These little men of the forest — the pygmies — were the traditional enemies of his kind. He did not need to be told this. He knew it from experience and from his blood. It was these puny, agile dwarfs who eight years before had killed his mother, wrapping her about with nets cunningly suspended from trees and then hacking and stabbing her to death so that they could afterwards eat her flesh. He had learned from experience that these pygmy hunters were to be charged and, if necessary, attacked on sight. On the two occasions he had been forced to do so his instincts told him that his object was to intimidate rather than kill. He knew himself to be a peaceful being whose great strength was not intended for rending bones and flesh.

There were also taller black men who lived on the edge of the forest. These resembled Absolom in one respect. They often appeared to tear at vines, leaves and fruits, though he never saw them transfer the vegetation they gathered directly to their mouths. He had no way of knowing it, but these were African farmers.

Lately there had been a strange, lightly built man-person, perhaps a female of the species, who lived in a hut high on the mountain. This one seemed to imagine it was one of them, for it followed his group of gorillas continually.

Absolom and his family had known the *Fisi* were behind them long before the eight fleeing guerrillas, led by the tall, thin man, had any idea of the great apes' presence.

Absolom's last contact with the man-people had disturbed him to an unusual degree. It had occurred less than six nest-buildings previously. Time meant very little to Absolom but he was dimly aware that he had made several nights' halts since the encounter had taken place. On that day he had taken the family below the Saddle to feed on the bamboo forest. Two man-people had followed them all the morning but they had moved so skilfully that only occasionally had he been aware of their presence. No scent reached him on the wind as it invariably did when the one who lived a solitary life in the hut followed them alone. That one had a peculiarly sweet and pungent smell. So it had been a complete surprise after the mid-day siesta to find the two waiting on the bank in his family's path. Even when he had discovered their presence, Absolom had not been particularly alarmed. Their attitude did not resemble that of hunters. The upright shape of a man was what he had learned to fear. These two were crouched, in a submissive attitude, against a tree. Nevertheless, he watched guardedly as his Number Two male, the one later called Adam, a fully grown black-back not yet wearing the silvery covering of the adult male, climbed the bank to place himself between the two man-people and one of Absolom's females.

Absolom was further reassured to recognise the scent of the smaller of the two. It belonged to the one who lived in the hut and appeared to think it was a gorilla. But then, quite suddenly, the young male, Adam, had shown alarm. He had barked twice. A flash of light and a sudden movement had scared him. As leader, Absolom felt bound to give Adam some support. He did so by false-charging up the bank towards the two crouching figures. He would have left it at that had not one of the figures moved a hand in a way which reminded him of a pygmy's first movement in throwing a spear. So he charged again, screaming, striking out and knocking a hard, heavy object from his possible enemy's hand. This was how Helen Lawes had temporarily lost her camera. Absolom had lost something, too. Though satisfying the requirements of leadership, the episode had cost him some of his own confidence. Thus it was that, when four days later he discovered the eight *Fisi* following him, his nerves were still on edge from his recent encounter.

At first Absolom was puzzled. The gorilla group's pursuers were not moving in the usual way of men. Experience had taught Absolom that these strange animals had only two basic paces of travel in the forest. The first was the one to beware of. This approach was silent and secretive. It was the approach that the gorillas had come to associate with hunters. Such men either approached stealthily, head on, or else tried to encircle. The counter-move was to shift the family away quickly to dense cover. If cornered or caught unexpectedly, then the females had to be given a chance to escape behind the diversion caused by the most terrifying charges the fully-grown males could command.

The other method of travel was the one most commonly seen among the tall, timid men who lived in the plantations at the edges of the forest. When confronted with gorillas, even those going about their lawful occasions, these men almost invariably took to their heels and ran.

The approaching *Fisi* fitted neither of these well-known behaviour patterns. They appeared to be fleeing *towards* Absolom's family at great speed and with no attempt at stealth or concealment. When Absolom caught the first, far-distant sounds of their approach, his immediate reaction was that the noise was made by another gorilla group demolishing a banana tree. Within seconds his acutely sensitive early-warning system had dismissed this explanation. The sound of tearing and trampling was too continuous and irregular to come from one source. It could only originate from a sizeable party of individuals crashing through the forest. Gorillas simply did not move in that way. Nor, in Absolom's experience, did men. The unfamiliar called for extreme caution. With a series of short, sharp barks, Absolom drew the attention of his family. Then, by body gesture and the direction of his gaze, he made it clear that he wished them to retreat down the mountain side at a pace that would give little scope for opportunist feeding.

Still the sound of the other party's advance gained on them. Absolom sensed the unease that ran through his family. The younger males barked continuously and one of the more nervous females repeatedly beat her breast. The pursuers were very close now. At this point even Absolom felt panic. His nostrils were sharply aware of the musky fear-smell of the other males. He had led the family into a part of the mountain forest comparatively unfamiliar to him. They had entered a winding ravine between old lava floes. To his right the wall rose steeply. To the left the lava had been worn into a rounded shoulder, covered with low scrub. He barked again and turned away left-handed, urging the females and their young to hurry.

When the intruders appeared round the bend in the trail, the gorilla group began to fan out as he desired, though they were moving far too slowly. He screamed and the tall, thin man in the lead stopped and pointed. He appeared not to see Absolom. The man's attention was held by the rest of the family bounding away through the scrub. Absolom knew the response that the situation demanded. He rose on his feet and came, flailing the bushes with his arms, his mouth open in a scream. Somehow, perhaps because of the unusual manner of their approach, he sensed that the pursuers were particularly dangerous. A smell of fear hung about them. He made his first charge at full speed and might even have made body contact. His experience four days previously had shown him that it was possible to take such extreme action and

88

remain unscathed.

When he was still some distance away, the tall man raised his hand in a quick movement that finally decided Absolom to press his charge all the way home.

The object in the man's hand flashed, just as the object in the slender man-person's hand had emitted a stab of light. But with a difference. This time there was a crack like a stout branch breaking. Absolom weighed over 450 pounds. Travelling at ten miles per hour this weight produced a great deal of energy. So, apparently, did the invisible thing that struck Absolom in the thick muscle of his right shoulder. The impact swung his body through ten degrees. There was no stopping the momentum of his charge and his newly-aligned course took him past the tall man and on into the scrub where the rest of his family lay hidden.

The shock of impact was by now replaced by the pain of awakened nerves and ruptured flesh. Absolom had no wish to return to the attack but simply to escape further onslaught by the hornet that stung with such bemusing power. So he kept going, barking and screaming in rage and terror, a combination of sounds that at last woke the family to action and drove them faster and further into the thick bush. Absolom, in great pain, called more and more stridently for them to stop, but his cries only had the effect of urging them on in greater panic. At last even Absolom was forced to slow down. Weakened by his wound, he sank into a thick bed of nettles and cautiously examined the blood oozing from his shoulder.

The family did not travel far beyond the point at which Absolom had collapsed. Not long after the eight *Fisi* had disappeared, four more men appeared briefly on the track through the ravine. These men stopped to inspect the place at which the tall, thin man had released at Absolom the hornet that made a noise like a breaking bough. Then they had hurried on at great pace.

Peace returned to the forest. The family gathered round Absolom, staring at him with bloodshot, brown eyes, nervously touching him. Abel, the young black-backed male, even dabbed his finger in the viscous blood matting the hairs on Absolom's chest. He sniffed at this and recoiled, yelping with fright. For an hour or more Absolom rested to recover his strength. The family continued feeding around him. As the afternoon passed he grew more and more aware of their restiveness. They were looking to him for a lead. Adam, especially, became increasingly agitated. An hour before dusk Absolom summoned his great reserves of strength and led the fourteen animals uphill towards a hagenia grove. His shoulder had stiffened. Each step drove spearheads of pain into his body but at last he reached an acceptable nesting site and indicated that this was where the family would spend the night.

Absolom had no way of knowing what caused the searing agony in his shoulder muscle. He slept little but lay for the most part in silent misery, curled on his left side in a nest he had hardly bothered to make. Once, just after midnight, the pain became too much for him. He rose to his feet and dashed barking and screaming a few yards through the forest. But the moon was five nights past full and the upper canopy of the trees shut out most of its light so that he soon bumped into a tree. The pain caused by the collision forced him to lie down again without bothering to return to his nest.

When morning came his body felt hot. The female whom Jean-Pierre had christened Ahitabel climbed down from the nest she had made fifteen feet up on a stout branch and came to look for him. Ahitabel was a senior female and had borne one of Absolom's children, Cain. Cain had nested higher up in the same tree as his mother. He followed her to the ground, swinging his way down with youthful flourish by means of a vine and ignoring the easier route down the trunk. Ahitabel looked for Absolom where she knew he had built his ground nest. The big males were far too heavy to trust their weight to the trees. When she failed to find him there, he coughed in greeting and then barked a warning as she advanced to greet him. She smelt the blood and sat a little apart. By and by, other females and their young approached. They sat round, curiously, in a circle, sniffing and peering at him.

The sun rose through the lower branches of the trees. All round, bellies began to rumble. Soon hunger would put the family on the move in its daily search for food. Absolom knew that a lead was demanded of him but his limbs were too weighed down and his brain and vision too clouded to make the effort. After half an hour the inquisitive group of females and young started to disperse, apparently without purpose. One or two began to feed on the leaves and vines in their immediate vicinity but their effort was spiritless and disorganised. It was then that Adam, the young, fully-grown black-back, made his move, barking with newfound purpose and chest-slapping with newly-sensed importance. Without perhaps meaning to do so, he had stepped into a vacuum. At last he plucked up courage and moved off into the hagenia woodland. To his surprise, perhaps, the rest of the family followed. After a while Absolom dragged his huge frame in their wake. He did not feel much like feeding but a raging thirst drove him to scoop some bitter pulp with his good hand from the core of a wild banana tree. Like all gorillas he did not drink water directly, even when he found some. He derived all the moisture he needed from the vegetation on which he fed. In his present condition he craved fluid but the natural means of obtaining it turned his stomach.

The family's reaction to Absolom's wound would, to human eyes, have appeared extremely callous. Once they had established that there was some frightening, inexplicable change in him, they seemed totally to ignore him. This was because they needed a leader to take them through their day and Absolom was no longer able to fulfil this need. Yet the group slowed down its rate of feeding progress through the forest as if to allow Absolom to keep up. There was almost certainly no conscious effort involved in this. It was simply that the family was veering like a scattering of iron filings between two magnets of varying power. The stronger was

91

Adam, whose youth and vigour by no means fully compensated for his lack of authority. Occasionally the old, accustomed pull of the wounded silver-back's presence would cause the females and young to hang back longer than they would normally have done, especially when Absolom barked or groaned in pain, which he did more and more as the day wore on.

As the sun rose, the flies found Absolom's wound. He was used to the buzzing clouds of small, two-winged flies that invariably surround gorillas like clouds of mosquitoes. The flies which sought out his wound in order to lay their yellow clusters of egges were large and irritating, with fat bodies of metallic green that glinted in the sun. By evening Absolom was two hundred yards behind the rest of the group. His body burned with heat he did not understand. He felt desperately weary, yet when he heard his companions breaking branches and flattening grass to make their nests he dragged himself onward to join them. They looked at him with curiosity as he limped into the nesting site. Not a single animal examined him at close quarters. Absolom settled down twenty yards beyond the boundaries of the family circle as if he sensed that, though by no means an outcast, he was merely tolerated as he himself had tolerated the old male he had long ago deposed to take over leadership of the family. He had neither the strength nor spirit to contest this group verdict. He was wrapped in bewildering pain.

All that week he managed to keep up with the group although now, as the pull of his former authority weakened daily, the family moved through the forest at a faster pace in their insatiable search for food. As always, the gorillas paused frequently as they came upon some particularly appetising vine or herb and these pauses, together with the mid-day halt for digestion, enabled Absolom to catch up.

The little, pale fly-eggs had now given birth to little, pale, wriggling maggots that fed on the matter round the edge of the wound. In a short while these had cleaned up much of the extraneous mess. Absolom hardly noticed them while they did this but when they moved out into the coarse hair surrounding the bullet hole he scratched them out with fingers that looked surprisingly like human digits encased in a soft, brown leather glove. With opposing thumb and fore-finger he even picked out individual maggots that escaped the scratching process. Absolom did not realise it but the activity was a turning point. He had begun to see over the horizon of shock, fever and pain into a more normal world beyond.

Then, days after Absolom had received his wound, the family's continuous treks in search of food had led them back on to the higher slopes of Misoka overlooking the Saddle. They were heading for the bamboo forest. To reach their feeding grounds they had had to pass through the narrow ravine where the tall man had shot Absolom. Adam, now grown in stature and confidence, led the group through the defile without fear or apparent memory of what had taken place there. It was just as well that he displayed this unawareness. The older females, Ahitabel and Abigail particu-larly, were troubled by the associations of the place, at first hanging back and then growling and barking to show their unease. But Adam forged fearlessly ahead. When they reached the spot where Absolom's blood had splashed the grass Ahitabel shrieked and darted sideways into the bush and Abigail followed.

Absolom saw all this from well to the rear and higher up the slope. He was puzzled by the brashness and inexperience of Adam. Nothing would have persuaded the wounded silver-back to lead the family through that place with its so-recent association of pain and danger. Nothing would persuade him to make the narrow passage on his own. The alternative was one he did not care to face, yet face it he must. To avoid the pass he must make a long, steep climb up the mountainside. At the speed his wound allowed him to travel, the detour would take several hours. During this time he would certainly lose touch with the family.

When the family awoke next morning, Absolom was not with them. Not a single member appeared to notice, or to be

93

disturbed by, his absence. Adam had assumed leadership completely and no one now thought to question his decisions.

Ahitabel was nervous. A large, dark female with a belly that perpetually sagged with food, giving the impression that she was far gone in pregnancy, she was the oldest and most experienced of the group. She had borne a child by Absolom's predecessor. Cain, her latest, was Absolom's. When she rose from her nest an hour after dawn her belly was empty of everything but wind, which she broke in the stentorian manner of her kind. She had voided in the night several times, taking care the solid, three-lobed droppings fell well clear of her own door-step. But her sharp old ears had caught sounds far off in the forest that the others either failed to detect or else did not connect with danger, man-danger. In her youth Ahitabel had been hunted by the little black men of the forests. The pygmies were delicate and skilful hunters whose movements blended with the ripple of a stream, the cadences of wind-stirred leaves. These distant sounds were not made by pygmies. They were far too lacking in subtlety. She moved clear of the nest and defecated once again. This time the movement of her bowels said plainly that she was afraid of something.

When Adam set off, his eyes fixed steadily ahead on a downhill route towards the hypericum blossoms that grew on the Saddle, Ahitabel hung back, persuading her offspring Cain to do likewise. But, in the end, the discipline of the group was too much for her. When Adam barked, she reluctantly followed.

After an hour of desultory feeding they came out in a clear patch among wild blackberries. These grew on brambles that would have looked familiar to any European. So would the fruit they bore, except for one thing. These ripe mountain blackberries were bright red. Two youngsters, Cain and Abel, tentatively picked up one or two and popped them into their mouths. Cain looked at his mother Ahitabel, as if for a reaction. She often indicated to him what was right to eat at any given moment. But his mother was not paying any attention to him. Nor was she feeding herself. She was tensed up and listening, as were the other adult members of the group. Cain was disturbed by her unfamiliar reaction. To relieve the tension he felt, he beat his breast with cupped hands. Abel immediately followed suit. The hollow sound of their chest drumming was at once echoed by a different, distant percussive noise, a series of pops following in continuous stream, so fast that no gorilla could have made them. A series of single pops followed, nearer this time.

Adam was learning discretion fast. He turned and faced uphill, indicating that he intended leading the group to cover in that direction. After half an hour of fast climbing, he reached a position which he considered safe. Only then, on a steep, forested slope overlooking the open valley they had just forsaken, did he allow the family to pause and feed. They were hungry by now and fell upon the available vegetation with far less discrimination than usual. The meal was soon interrupted. The sharp reports that had troubled the group earlier were more insistent and very close.

Three men appeared in the clearing far below, making Adam dash back into the scrub. His brown eyes remained uncomprehendingly fixed on the scene below. His experience of men was far more limited than that of his vanished leader, Absolom. His in-built caution told him there were things about this group that were familiar, dangerously and recently familiar. They were black and tall, unlike the little forest hunters. Yet they did not behave timidly like the tall, black men who lived on the borders of the forest. He associated their general ragged appearance, the fur caps that two of them wore, with the sharp sounds heard earlier in the morning. His brain, half as large in capacity as a man's, did not incorporate the sophisticated data-collating system known as human memory. Rather, that part concerned with retaining and evaluating experience resembled a coarse-meshed net in which only experiences most essential to survival were caught and held.

Adam stared fixedly at the scene below. The last of the three men moved far more slowly than his fellows. As vegetarians the gorillas were not particularly familiar with blood, except that which flowed from the minor wounds they themselves incurred through falls and the rare bites and clawings that sometimes resulted, usually by accident, from dominance fights. Blood in quantity was largely outside their experience. The man who now stumbled and eventually fell as he tried to catch up with his companions was red with blood. The entire left side of his chest was covered with it. The sight tugged at a thread of the memory net in Adam's brain. Absolom had looked much as this man looked. The blood had flowed down his body in much the same way.

Adam drew back his lips and grunted, crouching lower and holding an arm in fear in front of his face. When he lowered his arm the two leading men had run back to their wounded companion. The prostrate man stretched out an arm to them. The two turned away, talking together. The injured man cried out in a high-pitched scream, more like an ape's cry than any sound Adam had heard a man use before. One of the two standing men kicked his prone companion flat with his foot and then, pointing the stick he carried at the small of his back, made the stick produce the popping sound and flashing light that had caused Absolom to halt his charge and stumble away into the bush, eventually to vanish from the family for ever. Unlike Absolom, the man did not move again except when the other two turned him over with their feet and took his possessions, including yet another banging stick of different shape. They even pulled at the dead man's legs until the feet seemed to come away, and then one of the men put these feet, which were light brown and hung about with two slim trailing sinews, on to his own feet, which were darker brown and bare like Adam's own. Finally, without looking back at the corpse, the two *Fisi* survivors hurried on into the forest.

Half an hour later, when the gorillas had climbed further along the slope to feed on a wild banana tree, another party

96

of men appeared in the clearing. These were twice as numerous as the *Fisi* and their appearance was quite different from anything the gorillas had seen before. They were white-faced and the outward appearance of all but one resembled the leaf pattern of trees in the forest. The exception was light-brown coloured except for his face, which was white. To both Adam and Ahitabel he was familiar. He wore a red head-covering, like the man who had sometimes accompanied the thin man-person who had lived in the hut on the Saddle. This man turned over the dead one with his foot and then signalled the leaf-coloured men to follow him in the direction taken by the *Fisi*.

For the next two weeks the gorillas occasionally heard distant, snapping reports that caused Adam to pause and curl his lips back in fear. But then the mountain forests fell silent again. The last *Fisi* had been rounded up and even the hut on the Saddle was now deserted.

It was six weeks later when Adah's time came, thirty-eight weeks after Absolom, taking his pick from the females in season, had coupled with her. Their mating had been brief and not entirely without tenderness. At first she had resisted the big silver-back until at last she had lain and allowed him to take her from behind. The coupling had been over in less than a minute. She had experienced no great pleasure from the mating. It merely appeased a need slightly more impera- tive than the easing of her bowels. The carrying of the young that had resulted from the union had caused her no dis- cernible inconvenience. Adah was one of the youngest fe- males in the group. She was barely seven. Outwardly there was nothing to show for her pregnancy. By mid-day her belly sagged no more and no less than that of the other females after they had spent the morning cramming their stomachs with vegetation. Towards the end of her carrying time there had been a difference, however. When she arose, empty- bellied, from her nest shortly after dawn, her stomach was considerably more distended than that of Ahitabel or Abigail.

Moreover, she had begun to cast maternal looks at Aaron, the six-month-old baby which now often rode on Aquila's back.

That morning the group seemed to sense that Adah was being delayed by forces far beyond her control. In the end even Adam acceded to her requirements and walked round, stiff-legged, to see for himself what this woman's business was all about. Once she had started, Adah gave birth effortlessly and in less than five minutes beneath a helichrysum bush. The baby, black and almost immediately lively, resembled, with its long, spindly arms and legs, a large and active spider. It was practically bald. Its eyes were huge, appealing and black, like moist grapes. Almost from birth it could reach out and cling to its mother for warmth, protection and milk. Had there been a human on hand to witness the event, he or she could only have said, with the arrogance of the race, that it was surprisingly 'human'.

The other females inspected the infant with a kind of blunt curiosity. They made no attempt to touch or fondle it but stared at Adah as she fed it. Not knowing how to react, the young apes Cain and Abel clapped their chests with hollowed hands and then, taking advantage of the unusually early halt in the day's march, fell into a rough and tumble. Abraham, a young black-back, marked the occasion with the full ritual of breast-beating, beginning the routine by throwing a piece of vegetation into the air. He then turned his head away and charged off sideways into the bush — all signs of a highly disconcerted gorilla. Births did not happen every day and, when they did, were apt to disturb the established order of things. Order and recognisable routine were important to the stability of Abraham's young life. He had recently adjusted to Absolom's disappearance and the assumption of command by Adam, whose back was only just showing hints of silver, the sign of full sexual maturity in a male.

In fact, the arrival of Adah's baby made little difference to the status of the young males in the group. The shift, although a relatively minor one, was felt by the females. Normally there was little evidence of marked hierarchy

98

among the adult females. Age appeared to make little difference as to who got the best parts of a banana tree, who moved first along a narrow trail, or even who became the dominant male's temporary favourite. A difference of opinion was generally settled by a brief vocal squabble or making of faces. Quarrelling of any sort was rare within the group. When it took place it was almost invariably among the females. Now, the addition of a baby had given Adah a new standing among her fellows. When they moved off to feed, Abigail and Ahitabel no longer assumed she must bring up the rear. Just as Aquila, with the six-month-old Aaron at her breast, was treated as an equal, so Adah now found herself admitted to the favoured society of senior matrons. The fact that she had a newborn infant temporarily put her in the front rank of females.

Once he found himself alone, Absolom's chances of recovery from his bullet-wound began to improve. There was no longer the compulsion to keep up with the group. He had found this an intolerable drain on his energies. Worse still, the knowledge that he was no longer the dominant male in charge of the family's destiny had started to eat away at the core of his being. At first he had resembled an old-age pensioner, doddering out his last days. But soon he settled down to feed with a relish he hadn't felt since the tall man had hurt him. He could feel the herbs that he plucked and stuffed into his mouth with his good left hand putting some power back into his body. Instinctively, he selected the vines and leaves with the most nourishment in them. His right arm still hung useless at his side yet externally, at least, the wound was healing and closing. The maggots had done him a good turn, cleansing away the dried blood and suppuration from the hole of entry. A large, healthy scab formed over the bullet-hole. Under this the lips of the wound were closing, though the nickel-clad automatic bullet still lay an inch below the surface, encased in muscle so hard that it had flattened and distorted the slug and prevented it from penetrating further.

Even in his depleted state Absolom feared no natural enemies. He was too big to be troubled by leopards and there were plenty of those in the forest. The elephants he met working round the shoulder of Misoka in the woodlands at eight thousand feet did not even give him a second glance, though the old cows raised their trunks curiously to catch his scent on the wind. A small herd of forest buffalo munched their way past within feet of him. Their small, suspicious eyes did not waste more than a second on identifying him as harmless. Absolom likewise. This was the world to which he had been born, a world that did not contain that form of life he had come to fear — man.

Unknown to himself, Absolom had instinctively followed much the same feeding route as the family. So it was not surprising that he eventually arrived at the clearing where the wounded *Fisi* had been slaughtered by his comrades for his boots and his machine-pistol. Absolom's highly sensitive nose told him that there was something alien and calling for caution just ahead of him. When the ravens rose in clamour he ducked and put an arm across his face. Sudden movements by large birds often disconcerted him. The breeze was not in his favour and he almost blundered on to the corpse of the murdered *Fisi*. Since Absolom was a good forty-eight hours behind the family's line of march, the corpse was in an advanced state of decomposition. Absolom had no way of knowing that it had recently been a man, let alone of knowing the fate this man had received at the hands of his companions, a fate so unlike the treatment Absolom had been accorded by the gorillas of his own group. They had merely acknowledged there was nothing they could do about his plight, so had ignored it. There had been nothing savage, let alone murderous, about their actions.

Absolom was now cast out into the wilderness, in exile, an accidentally deposed and self-banished king. Perhaps because his huge body had received such a shock, he was in no condition to resent this, to turn into what men sometimes call a 'rogue'. During the first six months that he travelled about the mountains alone, he became aware that there were several other silver-backs on their own, too. There were always too many mature males about for the number of family groups available to them for dominance and for mating. Sexual drive, given no outlet, sometimes produced in these loners highly aggressive temperaments. This did not inevitably follow. The characters of gorillas, just like those of their distant relatives higher up the evolutionary scale, differ greatly from individual to individual. During those six months of solitary convalescence, Absolom's path quite frequently crossed that of other gorilla groups. He made no attempt to intrude on them, nor did they show any signs of resentment or aggression towards him. He generally kept his distance, ignoring the questioning barks and occasional uneasy hoots of the males escorting them. Once he came very close to his own family, feeding in deep cover along a stream bed. He recognised them by their distinctive smell long before he saw them. Once they had detected *his* presence Adam became extremely restless, going through the complete ritual of agitated breast-beating.

Absolom stared him hard in the face. Then he showed his teeth and gums with lips curled back, alternately opening and closing his mouth and giving out a deep roar. Adam retreated and began his display all over again. After a while, Absolom got bored and moved away on all fours or, more accurately, on all threes. He still could not bear to load his damaged right arm with its fair share of his 450 pounds' weight. As he withdrew he heard the questioning barks of Ahitabel and Abigail but the pull of the old family ties was not yet sufficiently strong to make him want to join hem. He barked once in reply and moved on.

Adah's baby was four months old. In those first four months it had progressed physically at a far faster rate than a human baby of similar age. It could crawl, swing and climb. At first Adah had carried it clutched to her breast with one hand. At four months it occasionally still travelled in this way though mainly when it demanded to be fed. Often it dropped to the forest floor and followed Adah for short distances, glancing continually to her for reassurance and guidance. When it met something strange and frightening, like a three-horned chameleon stilting its slow-coach way on jerklegged gait among the leaves, the baby rushed back to its mother and clung. As its confidence grew it increasingly rode jockey-fasion on Adah's back. The youngster was so light that she scarcely noticed its weight, though she was quick to appreciate that its presence added to her own status.

One morning, shortly after dawn, they had left their nests and were starting to move off in single file in the direction Adam had indicated for the start of the day's foraging. Adah was sitting quietly on the narrow track kept open by the day-to-day passage of forest antelope. She was allowing her baby to warm himself on her back in the first pale rays of the sun. Ahitabel and Abigail were some way down the track behind her; Aquila with the now ten-month-old infant, Aaron, just in front. Normally both these senior matrons would have waited, allowing Aquila and herself to move off first with their young. Suddenly Adah felt herself violently shoved by a gorilla rushing headlong past her on all fours. The baby went flying into the scrub. The next second Aquila, too, had been buffeted sideways. Adah's first thought was to recover the baby. She'd hardly had time to pick herself up when a second hurtling form caught her off balance. She recognised Abigail and, just disappearing into a thick bush ahead of her, Ahitabel. Almost at once came the quite distinctive sound, softer than in the male, of Ahitabel beating her breast. Something had scared the two experienced females badly. All that mattered to Adah now was that she should recover her child and seek a hiding place herself.

She found the infant buried deep in some briars. The baby was crying and making a surprisingly loud job of it. Adah felt fear. Fear now travelled from Adah, Ahitabel and Abigail to Adam. Adam's scent-glands reacted by loading the still morning air with a heavy, musky smell of insecurity. Some-

102

where out on one flank Abraham, the six-year-old male, responded with his own immature scent. The family crouched, aware now of the sound that had first alerted Ahitabel and Abigail to danger. They were being hunted — hunted, what was more, with stealth.

Abraham coughed nervously. The tension communicated by the adults was too much for Cain and Abel. Their bellies rumbled and they broke wind noisily. As leader, Adam stood listening until he caught and placed the direction of a snapping twig. He barked to let the family know he had come to a decision and led off towards the thick woodlands above the Saddle. Up there it was difficult for anyone to follow. Yet the pursuit persisted though the pursuers themselves never came in sight. Within an hour Adam had become aware that more than one hunter was following them. The ape's hearing was possibly no more acute than that of man, but it was far more sharply tuned to the wave-lengths of the forest. By turning his head slightly he could detect that the sounds of those following his family came from fractionally different directions, though the actual distances separating them may not have been more than a few yards. Mostly, though, the men appeared to progress in single file, exactly like the gorillas themselves when moving to a feeding ground. Even when they moved, Adam was still able to tell that there was more than one man. His ears were sharp enough to spot that, when one man stopped, another one, or possibly two, behind him still continued to move a pace or two.

Then a very strange thing happened. Just when the pursuers were getting within a range that demanded that Adam lead the group on again, the men halted. For several minutes Adam stood stiff-legged on all fours, listening keenly. There was no doubt: the men had stopped also. This was not the behaviour of hunters.

Twice more that morning he stopped. Each time the men did the same. The performance was repeated throughout the afternoon and then, two hours before dusk, the pursuit ended and the pursuers vanished without once showing themselves.

When the gorillas built their nests that night they were still hungry. Their bellies rolled in a thunderstorm of indigestion. Throughout the night they woke constantly and shifted to relieve their tortured bowels well clear of the nest. When they started out next morning the family was both irritable and hungry. Adam, recognising the demands they made on him as leader, allowed them to begin feeding almost as soon as they had left the nesting site. Nevertheless, he remained tense and alert, straining every sense to detect the close presence of the followers in the forest. After the first nervous hour he became more and more certain that the strange hunters were not on the mountain to trouble them that day.

In the next two months they all became aware that a new dimension had been added to their day-to-day living. They were constantly being followed. Adam managed to get a good look at their pursuers on several occasions. The leader he had seen before. He wore a red head-covering — a beret — and moved with the sureness of a hunter. Adam remembered Jean-Pierre Menant from a time long back when he had squatted on top of a bank with the thin man-person who smelt of wild herbs. He had seemed to mean the group no harm then and Adam doubted if he meant them harm now. That first time, Absolom had been there to deal with the situation. Adam recalled that when he had barked in alarm at a sudden movement, Absolom had charged without hesitation, knocking some hard, weapon-like implement out of the thin one's hand. Absolom had had age and confidence on his side. Adam preferred caution. Thus he did not acknowledge their almost daily observer's presence, but led the family cunningly away each time so that they faded like wood-cutter's smoke among the trees. Because of this, the red-capped man seldom caught more than a glimpse of a swaying branch, a furry hand, a bright brown eye peering between leafy branches.

Not once in those first two months did Jean-Pierre succeed

in meeting the gorilla family in the open. Part of Adam's reluctance to allow contact to be made was due to the others who accompanied the white man. They were small, brown and wrinkled, not unlike gorillas themselves. They were pygmies and, from a gorilla's point of view, there was no more dangerous animal in the forest.

The way in which the members of Adam's family reacted to the new situation was an indication of their highly individual characters. Adam, with his steady brown eyes stuck on his flat face like two large raisins on a rich brown cake, remained true to his nature — calm, cautious and seldom hysterical. Abraham, the six-year-old black-back who usually brought up the rear of the troupe, did most of the barking, screaming and breast-beating whenever he felt that the intruders were too close for comfort. The other members of the group were not impressed by Abraham's tantrums. Accordingly, he found outlet for his aggressions by inter-vening from time to time in the play-fights of the two five-year-olds, Cain and Abel.

It was the season of the *bwambas*, those hard, lobed, nut-like fruits that grew on the gigantic, smooth-trunked trees at the edge of the forest. In the year that had passed since his wounding, Absolom had lost his appetite for many things, including sex, but not his taste for *bwambas*. However much he might have desired these succulent fruits when they had last been in season, he had been in no condition then to climb up to gather them. Now, after a year, his shoulder had healed amazingly well. The bullet was still encysted in the hard pack of muscle there. His right arm would never be quite as mobile as before but he commanded almost full use of it provided he bent and flexed it more slowly than he would normally have done. To crop the *bwamba* harvest he would need the full strength of both arms as well as the thrust of his powerful legs to hoist himself into the topmost branches.

That he at last felt himself capable of this was demonstrated by the fact that he was making a journey of over five miles, at the forced-march pace of a mile and a half a day, to reach the *bwamba* area at the moment when memory and instinct told him the fruits would just be turning ripe.

When he reached what he remembered as the edge of the forest, Absolom received a shock. Several of the trees, including the biggest and best of all, had been cut down. A large area had been clear-felled. As he watched from a thicket of nettles, he saw men moving about among a scattering of thatched huts. Smoke rose and there were stange, alien smells of cooking. A tall black man hacked with a long-handled implement at the soil where the *bwamba* trees had once stood. Absolom sensed that these men were not hunters. What he could not sense was that they were a breed that, in the long run, would prove even more dangerous to his own race — farmers.

He back-tracked into the forest to explore other areas along its perimeter that had traditionally been famous for their *bwamba* trees. In each case the story was the same. Trees had been felled. The soil was being dug. The smoke of charcoal-burners' fires stung his nostrils. In one place the sound of axes announced the imminent fall of a tree in which Absolom had gathered his first *bwambas* as a young black-back. All this disturbed Absolom badly. His wound had made him frightened of man. His first impulse was to avoid contact with the species, especially with the black variety. He had been imprinted with the figure and outline of the tall black man who had struck him with the stinging bee that made a loud singing sound just over a year ago in the ravine. He would never forget that man. He knew that none of those who now cut trees and tilled the soil where the trees had once stood was he. Just the same, he wished for no close contact with them.

After a little while he slunk back into the forest and, quite by chance, happened on medium-sized *bwamba* tree of whose presence he had been totally unaware. For the first ten minutes he scuffled around on the open forest floor at its foot, gathering such fallen fruits as had not already been discovered by other forest-dwellers. There were few left. The tree had only recently come to ripeness and the *bwambas* had barely begun to fall. The trunk of the tree was smooth and without brances for its first eight feet. Absolom encircled it with his good left arm and, hanging backwards from this support, applied the soles of his feet to the bark, pressing them hard against it. In this way he virtually walked up the first few feet. Then, by reaching upwards with his right hand, he was able to grasp the first bunch. It was the first time he had placed such severe strain on the damaged shoulder muscles and he felt a sharp needle of pain as he pulled. Involuntarily he gave a short, angry scream but the pain passed almost as soon as his left arm was raised to share the load. He sat in the lowest notch of the tree, annoyed at the itchy, tingling feeling the effort had left in his shoulder. The delicious bitter-sweet taste of the first *bwamba* submerged all other considerations. He started to climb with a confidence that conceded nothing to the nagging pain.

His long arms reached out and made the most of the *bwamba* harvest all round him. For ten minutes he picked, stuffed and munched until suddenly he became aware of a small movement on the edge of the trees below, thirty yards away. He stiffened with a *bwamba* lodged between his teeth. His eyes searched. Had he been at ground level he would not have picked out the white man in the red beret so easily. The man stood as still as the bush he had chosen as his background. From high above, however, Absolom had the advantage of a different angle for which the observer had made no allowance. Thus when the man signalled with his hand held low down for someone following him to stop, Absolom was able to see this movement. He could not, of course, interpret it, but his eyes followed the direction of the man's gesture in time to see the bush ten yards behind him temble. There were other members of the man's group there. He concentrated on the spot and finally made out a face staring up at him. It was the face of one of the little dark forest hunters whom he had learned to fear. Absolom glared at this face and had the satisfaction of seeing it look away. Its owner had thus shown his inferiority, was perhaps even afraid of him. The white man had hidden himself well. Slowly it came to him that the man seemed familiar. Had he seen him before somewhere in the forest? He could not be sure. The shock of being severely wounded by a human being — he would never lose the image of that particular man — had confused his total memories of the species and of the few close contacts he had had with them.

From time to time the man below him moved, holding a bright metal object in front of his face. Each of these movements was followed by a mechanical click. This, too, stirred something in Absolom's brain. Though he could not clearly recollect the experience, he had encountered both Jean-Pierre and a camera before in his life.

A half-hour passed. Absolom exhausted the *bwambas* within easy grasp and decided that it was safe to make a move to the branch below him. His descent drew a series of clicks from the watcher on the ground. Absolom stopped with his feet balanced on the lower branch and gave a roar to indicate that he had not entirely accepted the situation down below. The roar, which was one of the louder noises in his repertoire of twenty-seven sounds, brought an immediate reaction. A second small, dark figure, seated behind the one he had already placed, jumped to his feet and ran back several paces into the bush. Far from being satisfied by the result of his small demonstration, Absolom became uneasy. Sudden movement troubled him. He ate the remaining *bwambas* within range and then descended in a series of swift, unhurried movements, each one so perfectly co-ordinated that it might have been worked out, almost choreographed, in advance.

Absolom hit the ground like a gymnast, springingly, with both feet at once. He glared at the place where the white man stood. He was harder to locate from ground level. He barked once. To the watchers the sound was far louder and more frightening than when made from the tree. It was too much for the pygmy squatting immediately behind the white man. The little black man immediately jumped to his feet and ran in wild panic back into the scrub.

His flight triggered off instant reaction in Absolom. Standing upright, he measured five feet ten-and-a-half inches. Upright, he charged screaming at the white man, lashing out at the bushes with his arms as he came. The scream was all the more remarkable because he held a *bwamba* firmly clenched between his teeth. To his surprise, the man did not turn and run, but stood there as rooted to the ground as the *bwamba* tree that Absolom had recently vacated.

Absolom retreated and tried again, putting on one of the most terrifying demonstrations of hostility in all of wild nature. The man still did not move. Nor did he make any movement to cause Absolom injury or pain. Not knowing what to do, Absolom stood and screamed, showing the man the red roof of his open mouth and the intimidating display of teeth contained therein, and all this at a distance of perhaps six feet.

At heart, Absolom wished for no trouble. His demonstration had evoked none. The situation was deadlocked and the deadlock had to be broken somehow. Absolom broke it by rushing sideways, away from the man and into the bush. As he ran he struck out with his arms and screamed, feeling better every second he did so and at every yard he put between himself and the intruders. Even Jean-Pierre's heart was beating unusually fast as he reloaded his camera.

After the season of the *bwambas* it was the season of the bamboos. Adam knew it. The whole family knew it. After the rains the bamboos began to put out new, appetising shoots. To reach the bamboo forests called for a considerable effort since they only began at 8,000 feet. Once they'd made the long climb it was as if the gorillas had been let out of school or had at last reached the scene of a long anticipated holiday. They attacked the tall, swaying columns of the

109

bamboo as though this was the last meal they'd ever get.

Ahitabel, who had enjoyed many previous bamboo seasons, was the first to shin up one of the slender green masts. Up, up she climbed, toes gripping the four-inch bole of the tree, powerful arms pulling her upwards. The conclusion was foregone. Two hundred pounds of gorilla perched fifty feet above the ground on a single shaft as slender as a flag-pole was bound eventually to become insupportable. Ahitabel appeared to relish the situation, climbing until the bamboo bent to her weight and continued bending at an accelerating rate that seemed to doom Ahitabel to a bone-shattering crash on the forest floor. With the aplomb of a high-wire artiste, the female gorilla allowed the swaying stem to carry her through an arc of forty-five degrees. When still twenty feet above the ground and gathering speed, Ahitabel deftly transferred herself from the doomed bamboo to a still-upright neighbour whose skyward path it had crossed. But the damage was done to the first tree. Even with Ahitabel's weight removed, it remained leaning tipsily at thirty degrees to the ground. She slid quickly down the trunk of her new refuge and, raising one enormous arm, seized her first victim and hung all her weight on it. The four-inch-thick bamboo split two feet above the ground, a perfect greenstick fracture. Ahitabel seized a length of the tree between her hands and bit savagely into it as if the tubular trunk of the plant had been no more substantial than a stick of candy.

For some reason the gorillas felt themselves vulnerable in the bamboo thickets and were often unusually aggressive in consequence. Perhaps this was due to the nature of the woodland. The trees themselves gave sparse shelter, though the ground-cover was thick. Thus they could be surprised at ground level while remaining unusually exposed once they were up in the trees. Directly Abraham discovered that the white man and his pygmy companions were once again watching them, he indulged his irritable young nature by mounting a series of threat charges. His last and most daring one took him to within ten feet of the red-headed one who remained unmoved, looking him steadfastly in the eye. Abraham, disconcerted, eventually turned and shambled off into the bamboos.

The man had now introduced an entirely new element into his relationship with the gorillas. He began to make sounds at them, sounds not unlike those they made themselves. Adam, who had watched Abraham's display with interest, construed these noises as unfamiliar but certainly not aggressive. He laid his head on one side and listened attentively, declining to become alarmed and to lead his family away. One noise in particular intrigued him, a most gorrilla-like cough. It was the sort of subdued cough gorillas themselves used to announce their presence to each other when on the move and hidden in dense undergrowth. Adam saw no reason to make the single coughing sound in return since he and the man were perfectly visible to each other in open country. Nevertheless, he listened and wondered. For the first time it dimly occurred to him that this creature who followed his own family so harmlessly and meaninglessly might be something very like himself.

The man coughed again and now, attached to the cough, was another, quite unfamiliar, sound which was, though Adam could not possibly know it, his own name, the one word 'Adam'.

They stayed feeding along the shoulder of Misoka, where the best bamboos grew, for over a fortnight. During this time the man was often close to them. Some nights he and his two small, black companions slept in the forest. The man made a strange nest of his own, usually under a tree from which he draped a white cocoon-like substance not unlike the web of some of the larger forest spiders. Abraham still charged him whenever he got too close. Adam only once became concerned for the group's safety, when the man advanced step by step until he was within ten yards of Adah and her baby. Then Adam gave him the full, silver-back treatment, hooting, screaming, barking and flailing the vegetation with his threat-charge until he was within arms' length of the man. This

111

time, too, the man did not run, did not even move. Instead, he called out softly with sounds Adam did not comprehend. These certainly did not sound aggressive, however. Again they included those two syllables with which the young silver-back leader was becoming more and more acquainted — 'Ad-am'.

Because the feeding was so rich, the family moved slowly through the bamboo forest. At the end of the fortnight, though, they had travelled to the far side of the tree'd slope two thousand feet below Misoka's cone. They were all now becoming a little tired of an almost unrelieved menu of bamboo. Moreover, the young shoots were getting past their best. It was time for a change of diet and of scene. Adam had no clear picture of what to do or where to lead the family next. Memory, instinct, some pattern maybe imprinted in youth, led his footsteps downwards into unfamiliar country. He had been taken there before by Absolom and by the old silver-back who led the family before him, yet he did not remember the trail clearly. He just followed it and the family followed him.

In one sense this was neither miraculous nor hard to explain. The gullied slopes above the bamboo forests consisted of razor-ridged lava scree. There was nothing for a gorilla in that direction. In fact, the whole of this face of Misoka was decidedly unfriendly. It was drier, harsher, pock-marked, pitted and plastered with the after-effects of recent eruptions. For the gorillas there was no incentive to trail back through the bamboo. There was little to eat where they stood. The only possible route was down. Thus it was probably no conscious, or even subconscious, decision on Adam's part that guided his footsteps steeply downhill. Nor was it coincidence that he was reacting to a given situation and circumstances in the precise manner of generations of gorilla leaders before him. They had had little choice either. Yet the strange thing was that the area for which the family was heading would provide exactly the kind of vegetation they needed to balance their prolonged feasting on bamboo. They were headed for the cyperus swamp three thousand feet below them, a marsh whose reeds and cyperus sedges were an excellent dietary change from unlimited bamboo.

It was a long descent to the cyperus swamp but they covered the ground in two days. Feeding on the way was poor in both quantity and quality. Thus Adam hurried them along in search of more or better forage. The babies, Aaron and Adah's infant, the New Arrival, became fractious and clung increasingly to their mothers' breasts.

Early on the second day of the descent, the gorillas heard the sound of rushing water. It was a sound they were accustomed to. Many small streams ran down narrow ravines in the forest, often hidden beneath a matting of vines and fallen leaves. These made no impact on the gorillas' lives. They did not utilise this water for drinking as did other animals. Nor were the forest streams a hindrance. They were too narrow to trouble the gorillas who were perfectly happy to splash through them, ankle-deep, when the need arose. The stream they now came upon was something far more formidable. The rainy season that had just passed had been exceptionally heavy. Much of the water that had fallen on the mountain had run straight off. Some, however, had soaked down into the porous beds of old lava and was only now finding its way to the surface through a series of springs that gushed out at intervals on Misoka's precipitous upper slopes. This spring water, added to the overflow from a small crater lake filled to brimming by the rain, fed the stream in question. Hidden by banks of fern growing along the lip of the lava gulley which channelled it, the stream leapt and roared, twenty feet wide, deep in places, boulder-scattered, cold, pure and whipped to white by the urgency of its determination to reach the lower ground.

It was no place for a gorilla and Adam knew as much directly he set eyes on it. He also knew that the marsh which the stream fed lay mainly on its far side. This was where he wanted to be, yet the last thing he intended to do was to venture into that terrifying smother of water. Like all of his kind, Adam was either unable or unwilling to swim. It was this lack that, to a large extent, limited the range of his species. Large rivers proved insurmountable barriers to expansion of territory. This was not a large river. At other seasons the family might have crossed it virtually dry-shod. But not at the moment. Dimly, Adam knew that he wished to cross it. Disconcerted and unsure of himself, he led off downstream, topping the bank at regular intervals to discover whether the rushing river had become any more reasonable. It had not. Adam continued downwards alongside the torrent for an hour or more. Now the gradient was beginning to ease and the river to slow. But as it did so it also became gradually wider. The enticing green world of reeds and rushes on the far side was rapidly coming into view.

As Adam rounded the last bend before the stream widened out to enter the marsh, he spotted the fallen tree, its trunk greyed by the years yet still sound, its roots caught and held by the lava rocks on one side, its broken branches jammed by the boulders on the other. The top surface of the trunk was grooved by the claw marks of generations of gorillas who had crossed this way before. Adam had made the journey himself at the age of three, though he had no recollection of it.

Adam took the decision expected of a leader. Carefully he moved out on all fours on to the trunk. Then, more out of fright than confidence, he bounded across. Once safely on the far bank he tore off a handful of sedges and began to eat, watching with curiosity to see what the rest made of the bridge. However, he knew that, where he had led, they would eventually follow.

Much of the area fed by the river was too marshy for the heavy animals to travel over in comfort. As they moved further into the wilderness of reeds and sedges, the ground dried out. Still, even in the firmest parts it was spongy underfoot. At first they found this mildly disconcerting but the reeds, often five feet tall, more than compensated for this. They gave a feeling of security. This, however, was to prove an illusion.

Once deep in the swamp, a perpetual problem for the

114

mothers was the ease with which their babies became lost. Three or four times each day Adah and Aquila found themselves trailing back behind the line of march to rescue Aaron or the New Arrival who had wandered off into a dense clump of reeds and was unable to find the way back. Usually the babies were easy to detect because they kicked up such a row out of sheer fright. The New Arrival lived up to the reputation for devilment he was rapidly gaining by straying further and more often than Aaron. So now Adah carried the infant whenever they were on the move, at least when it allowed her to do so. The year-old gorilla was adept at sliding quickly off his mother's back so that often she failed to notice that he'd gone. Then, inevitably, came the hysterical crying that meant that her offspring was lost once again.

If the dense reed-beds gave the adults a feeling of security, they plainly did not do the same for the young. Even Cain and Abel, Ahab and Abednego confined their play-fights to recognised halts between feeding. Cain, the most adventurous of the four juveniles, got a bad fright the one time he allowed himself to become separated from the group. They had all sensed that there were other inhabitants in the marsh. Now Cain proved it by blundering into a crouching, light-brown form that jumped to its feet, stood tall above the young gorilla, stamped a leg and then crashed away through the reeds at tremendous speed. The marsh antelope, a sitatunga, had heard the gorillas coming from far off and, not knowing what they were, had decided to freeze against a clump of dried sedges that exactly matched the colour of its coat. Thoroughly scared, it bounded away through the reed-beds, its elongated hooves, specially adapted for movement over boggy ground, leaving only the shallowest of slot marks in the soft soil. Cain was a good deal more frightened than the sitatunga.

Others moved in the vast area of the marsh and these were not sitatunga nor were they gorillas, though they somewhat resembled the latter. Six small, black hunters had found the

115

gorillas' trail where they had entered the cyperus marsh by the river. They had known the gorillas would come, if not Adam's group then another family. Each year, following the season of the *bwambas*, the bamboos and the rains, at least one large party came to feed on the cyperus sedges in the marsh.

For three days one of the pygmies followed the trail — it needed very little of his considerable tracking skill to find it — through the reeds. Early on the third day he was sure by which route the gorillas would leave the marsh, and when. The great apes, whom he both feared as enemies and loved as delicious meat, seldom spent less than a week, rarely more than ten days, in the marsh. After that their appetite for its delicacies appeared to wane. They never returned the way they had come. Once deep inside the cyperus beds, a series of widening streams dictated which exit they would take. Having satisfied himself of these facts, the solitary pygmy swallowed the last of the maize meal and roots he had brought to sustain himself and headed back to his companions, consoling himself that soon there would be something far better to eat.

The six pygmies set off at once. They had far to go. They would circle the outside of the marsh rather than attempt to cut a path through its matted centre. It was far longer by the circumferential route but they would travel much faster and, if the reckoning of the pygmy who had done the tracking was correct, they had three days in which to cover the distance.

As full strength returned to Absolom he began to feel lonely. Most of all, now that his shoulder had ceased to draw away his strength, he felt the need for a mate. Perhaps it was this that pulled him back to the former home-range and that of his family, the country around the Saddle on the western slopes of Misoka. Possibly he hoped to make contact with his group there. He could not know that they had made the long pilgrimage to the other side of the volcano, to the marsh.

On the same day that the pygmy hunters started their long

journey around the perimeter of the swamp, Absolom browsed his way through the hypericum belt above the Saddle. He had always liked the area. It was open and caught the sun from just before mid-day until sunset. It offered a wide variety of food within a very short distance. The sun had not yet climbed above the old volcanic plug that was the false peak of Misoka. It was still cold and mist, or perhaps cloud, sat firmly in the Saddle.

It was just past mid-day when he came out five hundred feet above the Saddle. The sun had looked over Misoka's shoulder a good hour and had given the mists a glare that told them it was time to be moving. They were particularly obstinate this morning and hung around like a crowd starting to thin but reluctant to disperse. Gaps appeared among the grey streamers only to close up again.

It was Absolom's intention to descend to feed on the Saddle meadow. He was unwilling to do so until visibility improved, and for a good reason. His sense of direction told him that he was in the immediate region of the dwelling where the thin, sweet-smelling man-person had once lived. He had always given the hut a wide berth and encouraged members of his group to do the same. The hut was an alien and unknown quantity and best left completely alone. Even though the hut had been empty for over a year, he still felt exactly the same about it.

Just when it seemed that the sun was winning and the mist finally dispersing, a new element crept into the scene below him. The thinning white vapour took on a yellowish tinge. Absolom's flattened nostrils twitched. He had detected an acrid smell and one he knew quite well, that of burning vegetation, familiar from the many small bush fires that started on the mountain in the dry season. This was no spontaneous bush fire, though. The hut was still far below him, but a breeze had sprung up and this breeze brought faint sounds of men's voices and the *clack* of pangas falling on wood. Absolom crouched low. Two tall, black men were piling recently-cleared scrub on to the flames. The familiar

117

figure of the white man in the red head-covering was directing them to fell a number of small bushes that had grown up in front of the hut.

Absolom watched suspiciously for several minutes. Then, deciding the hut was still a place to be avoided, he moved on round the shoulder to find a safer feeding point at which to descend to the meadow.

Absolom was not the only gorilla to smell smoke that day, and with it fear. At first Adam was not alarmed when he saw the brown plume rise behind his family as, in the early morning, they fed their way towards the far edge of the cyperus marsh. Dry clumps of reeds were as liable to fire, probably more so, than much of the more familiar forest vegetation. There was little breeze. Even had there been a fairly strong wind, Adam knew that his group could quite easily outstrip the progress of the flames. Large wild animals are not often perturbed by fire. They live too much with it. The victims are always the small creatures who receive no warning and cannot escape even if they do. Insects, lizards, snakes, small burrowing mammals such as mole-rats, these are the ones who become trapped and burn to death like the occupants of some ancient and overcrowded tenement building, ill-provided with warning systems and escape routes.

In Africa there are opportunists who know these facts and are perpetually ready to take advantage of them. Already, a party of white storks, resting in the marsh on their migration north, had spotted the smoke and were planning to enjoy the feast they knew it would provide. The firstcomers patrolled like sentries along the fifty-yard front of the fire, picking off the frogs who tried to hop out of its path, the beetles, spiders, centipedes, many of them already half burned, who writhed and wriggled at the feet of the flames.

When a second strip of reeds to his right and a further clump, fifty yards to the left, caught fire, Adam began to take notice. The smoke drifted across the feeding family. In a very short time it would be difficult to communicate with the various members, let alone keep them together. He barked several times and heard the other males answer. It was time to be moving on. Adam waited until Ahitabel and Aquila had caught up with him. Then, taking this as a sign that the females had got the message, he set off for the far boundary of the swamp. As he loped rapidly along on all fours, barking and coughing to keep the family in touch, a disconcerting thing took place. For the first time he realised that a stream lay on either side and that these watercourses were rapidly drawing together, narrowing the funnel of land in between. He was leading the group into the apex of this triangle. The thickening smoke confused things further. Adam drew a deep draught of the acrid stuff into his lungs that made him splutter and cough. His reaction was to increase speed even more. Behind him he could hear the crash of the rest of the family as they blundered blindly through the reeds.

Adam did not even see the net stretched across the narrow neck of land between the two streams. He hit it at full tilt, tearing it down from the poles that held it. One foot caught momentarily in the coarse sisal meshes but tore free, barely checking him in his stride.

The pygmy crouching in the reeds on the river-bank flung his spear. But he had expected the gorilla to be held fast in the net and so the spear passed harmlessly behind. Adam kept the impetus of his charge going, clawing down the second tiny, naked figure who stood in his path, jabbing with a second spear. The blade cut a superficial groove in Adam's left flank, releasing the bright red blood below the rib cage to course down to his hip.

Adam felt the hot sting of pain and, catching the pygmy in the throat with a wild swing of his right paw, hurled him into the reed-beds. The diminutive hunter lay there, bleeding and gasping, with his wind-pipe exposed to the air. Adam kept going and behind him, through the gap he had made, came Ahitabel and Abigail, Aquila and Aaron, Ahab and Abednego, Cain and Abel, and lastly the young black-back,

Abraham.

The third pygmy, who stood in the centre of the net, held his ground, aiming his spear at Abraham. Abraham saw him and charged, screaming wildly, knocking the spear out of the little man's hand and raking the length of his naked chest with his hand. Abraham ran on to join Adam and the others who had already broken through on that side of the ambush.

Adah was not so lucky. She was out on the right flank. From the moment panic had begun to spread Adah had become confused, confused by the smoke, the continual barking of the males, the sudden urgency of the family's rush through the thick clumps of sedge. Most of all she was confused as to the whereabouts of her infant, who had chosen this moment, of all moments, to stray from her side once again. The infant's absence blocked her mind to everything else. She turned back to look for her child and immediately ran into Cain. The five-year-old cannoned off her, the collision deflecting Cain's path to the left so that the young gorilla ran safely through the section of the net which Adam had already knocked down. Close on Cain's heels came Abel. He, too, escaped by the same route, treading on the pygmy with the torn wind-pipe as he did so. Adah waited a fatal second or two in the swirling smoke, still hoping to find her child. Finally, drawn by the screaming and hooting of the males ahead, she ran straight forward, hitting the right hand section of the net where it still stood firm and upright between its poles. The net collapsed round Adah as it was intended to do.

This time the two pygmies waiting with spears did not miss. The first spear took her between the breasts, the blood that rushed out mixing with a white dribble of the last of her milk. She clutched at the shaft much as a man might have done and roared once; but the roar was cut off by a rush of blood in her throat. The second pygmy finished her by driving a long, thrusting spear into her kidneys. Adah toppled forward on her chest, breaking short the shaft of the throwing-spear that had lodged there. The third and last pygmy appeared from the reeds on the right-hand river-bank. Chattering excitedly, the four unharmed survivors of the ambush began to untangle the dead Adah from the net. They did not, apparently, think it worth while to walk ten yards to see how their companions had fared. There was more important work on hand.

Adam kept running until he was clear of the smoke and a good hundred yards past the point of ambush. Then he stopped, hooting and screaming, more uncertain of himself than at any time since Absolom had disappeared. He crouched, waiting for the others to come up. First to appear, within seconds, was Ahitabel, followed a yard behind by Abigail. Next Aquila with Aaron crying and demanding a ride on her back, a demand which the badly-scared Aquila ignored. A longish pause until Ahab and Abednego with Cain and Abel arrived in a growling, hooting heap. Abraham, who had been early through the gap in the net, arrived surprisingly late. Abraham had stopped, mainly out of terror but also because of his naturally belligerent nature, to make several false charges in the general direction of the pygmies. It was during the last of these demonstrations that Adah's baby, the New Arrival, had found Abraham and attached itself to him.

Possibly the baby was the only member of the group even remotely aware that his mother had been killed. If Adam recognised that the pygmies had speared one of their number, he gave no sign of it. Adam set his gaze resolutely towards the border of the cyperus swamp, now only one hundred yards away. As always, the group followed the signs given by their leader. Each gorilla wanted to put behind it, as rapidly as possible, the unexpected, unforeseen terror of the last five minutes.

The cyperus sedge gradually thinned. There came a capillary network of shallow waterways to splash through and then Adam cautiously poked his head out on the world of the mountain once again.

The cyperus swamp, many square miles in extent, lay cupped in a gigantic hollow on Misoka's shoulder. Ahead, and beyond the swamp, the slope rose again to hagenia forest, and above that to bamboo and above again to the world of giant heather, groundsels and lobelias. The family did not stop until it was securely beneath the hagenia trees. Only then did the group sense hazily and collectively that one of their number was missing. The only one who felt the loss closely and personally was the New Arrival, who huddled against Aaron, who in turn huddled against his mother, Aquila, for warmth.

The moment they were sure that the gorillas had retreated, the three unwounded pygmies, joined by the one who had missed Adam with the first spear, fell on Adah, rolled the corpse on its back and began to skin it. They had no use for the skin and so they did not trouble to make a neat job of it. To them it was of no more account than is the peel of an orange to a man about to eat it. They hacked and slit with their knives, tugging at the loosened skin as if trying to pull a tight, wet jersey off an unconscious man. When some part of Adah, in the first instance a hand, obstructed them they simply lopped it off. Theirs was a very different performance from that of a trophy-hunter, who skins out his victim with the delicacy of a surgeon. The four pygmies wanted only one thing from the dead gorilla — meat. In their effort to get at it they were soon as red as the corpse itself. At last they came to the head from which the mild, maternal eyes of the young female had minutes before looked out with something close to mother-love on the New Arrival. The leader of the pygmy hunting party fetched his spear. Then, sawing and jabbing at the heavy spinal column, he at last severed the head. He did not throw this away into the reeds as the others had done the hands and feet. There were brains in that squat skull. If the skull were carried to a place where there were rocks, it could be broken open to release this rare delicacy.

Bloody as they were after their work of butchery, the pygmies did not immediately wash themselves in one of the nearby streams. First, hunger had to be assuaged and hunger

122

was what the whole long, exhausting, dangerous work of the last five or six days had been about. These little pot-bellied hunters of the forests were starved of protein. To them the gorilla was just so much conveniently-packed animal protein on the hoof. The meat from one gorilla would support them for some days to come, its memory and sustenance temporarily blotting out the dreary, debilitating, daily diet of roots, berries and meal made from poor quality millet or sorghum. They had no pity for the gorilla they had killed but even less for each other. The only pity in their sight was the fact that just one gorilla had been caught in the nets and speared. They had hoped for two at least. Now there was little chance that they would find another gorilla group in the cyperus swamp. It seemed likely that they would have to return to their village, three days' march away, with the meat they had, little enough to offer their wives and children.

Not until the skinning was complete did the four survivors even appear to take notice of the hunting party's casualties. The man whom Abraham had clawed in the chest had crawled to a small, muddy pool. There he had lain with his chest immersed until the tea-coloured water had changed to the shade of strong coffee as the blood staunched into it. When the bleeding eased he plastered the wound with clean mud. Then, supporting himself on the remains of his spear, he staggered over to the group.

The pygmy whose wind-pipe had been raked open by Adam lay for some time, semi-conscious, in the reed-beds. At last, with his breath coming in gasps, he dragged himself a foot at a time towards Adah's corpse.

The pygmy leader took his hunting-knife and, making a long slit in the belly, eviscerated the dead Adah. Red to the biceps, the pygmy pulled out coil after coil of intestines packed with the waste products of the first meal of the day. The stomach walls bulged with pounds of undigested young cyperus leaves. Finally, the hunter's hands found what they sought, a thick, blackish lozenge of liver and two kidneys packed in a surround of rich, white fat. The little man

123

grunted with satisfaction, groping under the rib cage until he reached the heart. So thick were the connecting arteries that it took him at least a minute to cut through them. He held the heart up triumphantly, displaying it to his comrades. He cut it into six more or less equal portions and gave one to each of the hunters.

The man with the chest wound sucked cautiously on his share, but the others, including the pygmy with the terrible throat laceration, began to champ and chew at the meat.

The glistening, rubbery flesh slowly disappeared. Only the man with the throat injury had trouble until, in the end, hunger for the long-awaited meat overcame his pain. The pygmy crammed the entire piece of heart into his mouth and pushed with his fingers until it was forced into his throat. Perhaps he believed that, if the meat could only reach his stomach intact, it would give him the strength necessary to make the long journey back to his village. The meat would have had a difficult enough passage at the best of times. Now, with the throat partly closed by the wound and the muscles contracting with pain, the meat had no chance. Nor, as it turned out, had the pygmy. He began to choke, retching and jerking in a desperate effort to dislodge the obstruction. His companions watched him almost with curiosity, making no attempt to help, as if they regarded his death as inevitable in any case. Finally, when his spasms became too much even for his fellows to bear, one of them turned him over on his face. Almost at once, blood flooded out from under him. An artery, already damaged by Adam's blow, had ruptured. Within minutes the little hunter was dead.

The man who had turned him on his face moved away, the whole group neither touching, nor even looking at, the dead pygmy again.

One day, when the orphaned New Arrival was eighteen months old, Adam's group became the victims of a successful take-over bid. Adam, who had been depressed and far less active since he received his spear-wound in the cyperus

124

swamp, had at last recovered his normal strength and vigour. It had taken him a full six months to do so. Nothing much had changed in the family during that time. Adah was long forgotten, even by her offspring, who had developed a violent attachment to Aaron and therefore tended to treat Aquila as its own mother.

As his wound healed, Adam had gradually led the family back to its old home-range in the hagenia woodlands below the Saddle. The journey had taken a long time. There was much to eat on the way. At last they were back among the tall trees through whose canopy enough light and warmth filtered to make the living not only easy in terms of gathering herbs and vines but also extremely comfortable. As might have been expected, there was a fair amount of competition for such desirable residences. During their first week back in their home-range they bumped into two other gorilla families, both bigger than their own. But the area of the hagenia woodlands was immense, reaching all the way round, and for at least two thousand feet down, the mountain. Sensibly and without stress, the three gorilla groups drew apart. Beyond a hoot and a growl or two, and some prolonged spasms of breast-beating, there was never any danger of a serious clash.

The Intruder, however, was a different proposition. The Intruder was one of those mature, free-ranging, swash-buckling silver-backs who wandered the mountains in a buccaneering, opportunist kind of way, looking for a group of females to take over.

Adam and Abraham had been aware of his presence for some days. At first he contented himself with far-off demonstrations of hooting and barking. Then one day he presented himself to Adam, standing tall, barking and staring the young leader scornfully in the eye. It was then that Adam saw that the Intruder had two mature females with him.

True to form, Abraham was inclined to make some demonstration in return. He charged half-heartedly several paces towards the obviously senior silver-back, who treated this impudence with complete scorn, merely curling back his

125

lips and exposing his teeth. Abraham, recognising ritual revelation of superior fire-power, backed down at once, withdrawing to sulk while continuing to grunt and growl. Surprisingly, Adam did nothing, allowing the silver-back with his two attendant females to move into the family circle. Without fuss or bloodshed, Adam had simply relinquished command. For several days the existing close-knit group remained aloof, then very gradually the two strange females were permitted by Ahitabel and Abigail to approach within several feet of them and even to build their nests ten yards from their own chosen positions. Squabbling only broke out if the two newcomers tried to touch Aaron or the New Arrival. When this happened, it was Aquila who made the counter-demonstration, hooting and barking and rushing up and down in a hysterical manner between the two infants and the strangers.

From this display of maternal temperament Adam, Abraham and the Intruder stayed loftily remote, the two former having their own problems of adjustment to make. As far as the Intruder was concerned, there were none. Like a robber baron, or perhaps a Chicago gangster of the Prohibition era, he had moved in on a new territory. Everything in it was, as a natural outcome of this physical fact, his. Everything, including women and the best places to nest and feed, was his — just so long as he could exert his dominance. Beyond an occasional stare, snarl and show of teeth, he apparently had to do very little to establish this. His presence and bearing were enough for the other two males.

Adam seemed to take the view that leadership so unexpectedly assumed could equally unexpectedly be lost. During the first week of the Intruder's rule he only once forgot his new role of second-in-command. This was on a morning when Adam rose from his bed of leaves earlier than the Intruder, who had, this morning, decided on a few minutes' extra lie-in. Adam, finding the majority of the family expectantly grouped around him, had given an indication of the direction in which they were to move off in search of food. This was too much for the Intruder, who came bounding, stiff-legged, from his nest and chased Adam for twenty yards while unleashing an impressive vocabulary of abuse.

Demonstration completed, the Intruder sauntered back and indicated to the family the direction in which *he* desired them to march. The fact that it was precisely the same as the one selected by Adam made no difference. The point had been made. Only one gorilla gave the orders and that was the dominant male, a post the Intruder did not intend to see usurped by mere striplings just acquiring the first touch of silver on their backs.

Abraham's adjustment to the new balance of power within the group was the most surprising of all. He appeared to realise that he was no longer second-in-command. The arrival of the Intruder, impressive in his rich saddlery of silver, had relegated him to third place. The steam almost immediately went out of him. No longer did he brag and bluster at all and sundry. Instead, he slipped back an age-group, finding it within himself to join in the play-fights of Cain and Abel, Ahab and Abednego, though always in a bullying kind of way. These fights were now almost the only outlet for his aggression.

Thus the males adapted to the change in hierarchy. The two females the Intruder had brought with him took longer to find their place in the group. Both were young and without children of their own. But it did not seem as if one of the two new additions to the group would remain childless for much longer. One day, when the family was reclining on a sunny slope digesting the morning's feeding, Adam rose casually from his couch in a bed of nettles and lay down beside the smaller of the two. The Intruder, barely ten yards away and higher up the slope, watched him with lazy disinterest. Adam lay stretched out beside the smaller female — a gorilla who might reasonably have been reckoned the Intruder's property since he had brought her with him — and threw an arm round her. The female shifted away a foot or so, whereupon Adam repeated the gesture. This ploy and counterplay continued for a minute or more, during which time the female, without seeming to do so, gradually turned her back on Adam. The young silver-back now began to emit a loud, almost plaintive yoo-hooing noise unlike any sound made by the males at other times. At last Adam sat up and, grasping the female round the hips, pulled her backwards on to his lap. Calling out more urgently he began to thrust vigorously. At this the Intruder propped himself up briefly on one elbow and, seemingly satisfied that all was proceeding according to natural plan, lay down again. Far from exhibiting rage, possessiveness and jealousy, he showed no further interest in the proceedings.

Later that month Abigail came in season. The Intruder coupled with her two or three times. On each of these occasions Adam took even less notice of the mating than the Intruder had done in his own case.

By the time the results of these couplings had materialised in the shapes of two hairless and nearly helpless gorilla babies, Jean-Pierre had become the group's almost daily companion. The Intruder resented him bitterly but, then, he had not yet become used to his presence in the forest. The Intruder, so easy-going in matters of internal discipline and inter-group sex, reacted totally differently to the attendance of the white man and his two small, black companions.

It was nearly three years since Jean-Pierre had taken upon himself the almost daily study of the Misoka gorillas. He had made enormous strides in gaining this family's confidence. The arrival of the Intruder had almost taken him back to square one. Whenever he sensed the man was close to him, the Intruder hurried the family away. Sometimes he had great difficulty in asserting his authority. Adam, Abraham, Abigail and the rest had long since accepted the fact that, given a reasonably wide berth, the man was no great threat to them. They resented the Intruder constantly urging them away from delicious patches of herbs just because Jean-Pierre was somewhere close by. They could not begin to fathom why their new leader considered the situation so disturbing.

As deposed dominant male, Adam found outlet for his energies in waging increasing war on the two black, forest dwarfs who invariably crouched to the rear of the man when he stood silently, sometimes without moving for half an hour, making his observations. The man still uttered strange sounds and Adam sometimes answered the low cough that told him that the man was somewhere nearby in the thick undergrowth. However, these days the man's sounds were more often directed at the Intruder, who ignored all such blandishments and charged the hell out of the man whenever he got too close.

The Intruder was an absolute specialist in threat charges. He employed the whole range of intimidation at a mature silver-back's disposal. His barks and screams were more resonant, more piercing even than Absolom's had been. Before he made his final charge, which often only stopped less than a yard short of the man's chest, he rushed around flailing the bushes with his arms until the branches and twigs flew as if from an explosion. In the face of the worst that the Intruder could do, the man managed to stand firm, though once or twice even his resolution nearly failed him. On the one occasion, early on, when he involuntarily took a pace backwards, he immediately realised his mistake. The Intruder followed his charge through and struck him a glancing blow on the chest. The silver-back then turned aside into the bush only to make a fresh charge. This time the man stood still and the Intruder stopped, mouth open and screaming, at the usual distance of a yard or more.

While all this was going on up front, Adam amused himself by enfilading the two pygmies. It seldom failed. Usually the little black trackers were too riveted by what the Intruder was doing ahead of them to give much thought to what Adam might be doing behind. Thus, when he came bursting out on them from the rear, surprise was total. What had started out of genuine fear and hatred, as a result of the spear-wound he had received in the marsh, had now, on Adam's side at least, turned into something of a game. After his one and only success in catching and throwing a pygmy, it was enough for Adam to see them run panic-stricken through the bush.

If the Intruder had been a human being he would not have been considered a good marital risk. During the next six months he twice wandered off on unpremeditated sprees. The Intruder was one of life's natural bachelors. Easy come, easy go appeared to be his motto. The first time he disappeared into the blue he went alone and was away on who knows what kind of a binge for ten days. When he returned he brought with him a strange female who had a four-year-old juvenile at foot. During his absence Adam had uneasily and uncertainly resumed command. Now Adam was seriously disturbed to find that his role had shifted once again. He expressed his displeasure by barking inhospitably at the foreign female. The Intruder looked on this display tolerantly while helping himself to the moist pith at the heart of a wild banana tree which he was casually dismembering. His exertions out there in the forest had made him both hungry and thirsty.

Three weeks later the Intruder took off once again. It was almost as if domesticity bored him. He was intensely intolerant of the young, particularly the New Arrival. The orphan had become more adventurous and boisterous than ever. Moreover, the Intruder's normal imperturbability was tried to its limit by the juvenile that his latest concubine had introduced to the group. At mid-day siesta when Aaron, the New Arrival and his concubine's bumptious infant had been play-fighting all too vigorously close to his chosen reclining place, he simply rose to his feet, barked to attract attention and set off into the trees without looking back. At his bark his concubine obediently rose and followed, closely accompanied by her offspring who, taken off guard, received a parting shove from the New Arrival as a farewell gift. Farewell

130

it was. This time the Intruder was gone for a fortnight. When at last he returned, looking a shade less paunchy than when last seen and bearing a small but unmistakable fight scar on his left shoulder, he was alone. Somewhere, somehow, he had rid himself of his concubine and her noisome offspring, presumably shedding the load on to some other family, perhaps even her original one.

Absolom was back on his home-range, close to the Saddle. His powers had fully returned to him. He had formed one or two brief attachments to two other gorilla groups in his recent wanderings. In the manner of his species he had been tolerated and even allowed to mate with a female who was in season during one of these visits. But Absolom had never felt entirely at home in these other families, nor had the dominant silver-backs concerned ever quite settled to Absolom. There was something almost too commanding about him. All silver-backs are impressive but Absolom in his full glory of adulthood was positively majestic.

Jean-Pierre, who now lived a large part of his time in the refurbished hut on the Saddle, knew that Absolom was back on his former home-range. He had met him in the hagenia woods several times lately. Once, when he had surprised Absolom resting, the great silver-back had charged him ferociously. Nevertheless, he had the feeling that Absolom recognised him and had only put on a maximum show of aggression because he had been caught unawares. Jean-Pierre was also well aware that Absolom's former group, under the Intruder's leadership, was in the area and he was curious to see what, if anything, would happen.

When it did happen, Jean-Pierre was not there to see it. Early that morning one of the small, black men arrived at the hut on the Saddle bearing a message. He had been climbing since late the previous afternoon and had slept, as a gorilla might have slept, in a kind of nest on the ground, but under an improvised shelter of leaves.

This messenger brought fresh meat and some vegetables.

131

The white man was not so much interested in these as in the letters he carried. One long, yellowish envelope with an official crest on it he tore open eagerly. Then, when he had read the contents, he threw his red cap in the air. The messenger grinned, delighted at such an unaccustomed demonstration, though not knowing of, or caring about, its cause. Within half-an-hour Jean-Pierre had stuck a few provisions in a rucksack and, with one of his trackers at his heels, set off down the mountain at a great pace.

That morning he was not in a mood to look at gorillas, even though he could not help noticing their signs all around him. As a matter of routine he interpreted those signs. A large group had crossed his track in open order, undoubtedly feeding as they moved, about thirteen animals all told, with four or five infants and juveniles, up to five adult females, a large young male and possibly two silver-backs. Two hundred yards down the track he encountered the indisputable and fresh tracks of a solitary, very heavy animal, almost certainly a large silver-back. The urge to investigate the situation and its possible implications was almost overwhelming. But then, so was the news that he carried in the opened letter in his rucksack. Turning temptation aside he hurried onwards and downwards.

From higher up the slope Absolom watched him go. When the two figures were out of sight and the sound of their progress through the forest had died away, Absolom continued on his own chosen path. He knew perfectly well where it was leading him. Before the man came on the scene he, Absolom, had been doing some following on his own account.

He came out an hour later above the clearing where the family were relaxing for their mid-morning period of supine digestion.

He coughed twice. The second time Adam answered him confidently. Abigail sat up and Ahitabel paused in mid-chew. Even Abraham stopped annoying Ahab and Abednego. The New Arrival did something now quite out of character.

Sensing that something was up, it scampered back to Aquila. Only the Intruder took absolutely no notice, lying indolently on his back playing with one huge foot which he held aloft.

Absolom strode into the middle of the group. His mouth was open. He screamed twice and advanced, barking, towards the recumbent Intruder. Too late the Intruder realised that Absolom meant business. He scrambled to his feet and was automatically at a disadvantage. He never actually managed to stand upright but compromised with a stiff-legged, four-footed pose. In this position he was rather like someone sitting in a chair who is being intimidated by a man standing up.

Absolom made no further directly aggressive move. Instead, he stared the Intruder steadily in the eye, mouth wide open and screaming.

If a gorilla can ever be said to shrug, the Intruder gave the impression of doing exactly that. Almost nonchalantly, he turned away into the bush as if loss of face was of no consequence and, having turned, kept going. The Intruder was not seen again that day, nor did he make any attempt thereafter to return to the family he had so casually adopted.

As for the family, they made no overt demonstration at Absolom's return. They settled down almost immediately. In a few days it was as if Absolom had never been away.

Bwamba time had come round again.

It was nearly a week later when Absolom led the group towards the promised land at the edge of the forest. Since he had last visited the area several more *bwamba* trees had been felled.

The tree where Absolom had fed only a year previously had been chopped down and the ground cultivated around it. Just beyond the place where the tree had stood, on the new forest edge, was a strange growth which Absolom did not recognise. Its wood was newly cut and at the top of a single stem was a large, white board which smelt of some totally strange substance. There were black marks on the white

133

board and, though Absolom did not recognise it, a poor likeness of a gorilla.

The board had been erected a week before by the man who had hurried down the mountain. In fact, that board was part of the reason for that hurry. The writing on the board said:

Parc National du Misoka:
Sanctuaire des Gorilles.

Part Three

MEN AND GORILLAS

Jean-Pierre Menant winced at the squeal of the Peugeot's tyres as it rounded the corner into the main street. Only one European in Baruva perpetually drove like that. The car braked violently, scraping the kerb as it stopped. Jean-Pierre heard the door slam and looked up to welcome his visitor. Jacques Veniard, Baruva's only European doctor, walked in.

'I came to christen your office on its opening day. Christ, it's hot.'

Jean-Pierre smiled, saying, 'It's in the fridge.'

Apart from a table, an old wooden filing-cabinet and a sign which said: *Parc National du Misoka*, the fridge was the office's only furniture. The doctor helped himself to a beer, sat down and propped his feet on the table.

'Been busy today? Lots of customers?'

'I could ask the same of you.'

'And I could truly answer, "yes". Let me see. Two childbirths, three malarias, one suspected case of mumps, one V.D. and the usual lot of hypochondriac white women. Well, at least *they* won't be here much longer. I doubt whether any of us pale-faces will be. Except, maybe, you.'

'Why me?' Jean-Pierre asked.

'You're well-connected.'

'Thanks. I wish I shared your optimism.'

'Optimistic or not, what the hell do you want with an office in this dreary town? You'll admit you're hardly at home behind a desk. You still haven't answered my question: how many visitors have you had today?'

'You're the first.'

'Exactly. Then why bother?'

'Because the president of this fantastic new country has been graciously pleased to recognise my humble efforts of the last three years by gazetting Misoka and Vahinga as a national park.'

'Bullshit.'

'I don't intend it to be.'

'What's this office then?'

'As you say: bullshit.'

'Precisely.'

'But necessary bullshit. You should be the first to realise that the park won't exist unless it is seen to exist. Right here in the centre of Baruva for a start.'

'For a man of action, you're a great romantic, Jean-Pierre.'

'Maybe. I'm also a realist.'

Veniard raised the nearly empty beer-can. 'Here's to your first visitor, then. Meantime, as a realist I must go and distribute a few aspirin tablets.'

Veniard lobbed the empty beer-can into the waste-paper basket and sniffed appreciatively. From a half-open door at the back of the little office flowed an appetising, airborne slick of garlic. The doctor leant back in his chair and extended a leg with which to kick the door open. An African girl in her late teens, dressed in a loose, traditionally-patterned cotton, stirred a large saucepan simmering on a butane gas stove.

'*Bonjour, madame*,' Veniard said gravely.

The girl cast down her eyes and smiled.

'*Bonjour, m'sieur le médecin.*'

'Delicious,' the doctor said. 'Quite delicious. The cooking, I mean. As I said: you're very well connected.'

Jean-Pierre shrugged. 'We have known each other since my schooldays. Her parents worked for my parents. Such things do not make one any more secure of tenure in this brave new world. Perhaps rather the opposite.'

'Quite,' Veniard said. 'Well, I mustn't take any more of your time. There is probably a long queue of people in the outer office waiting to see you. By the way, Jean-Pierre. Is what I hear true, that you have added your own farmlands to your new national park?'

'Perfectly true.'

'Then, my friend, if you should ever need a doctor, do not send for me. You are in need of a psychiatrist. The state will undoubtedly take your farms away from you eventually but, if you had held on, they might at least have paid you something by way of compensation.'

'By that time there might be none of my forest friends left. They need the space more than I do. At the rate they're chopping down trees, they'll all be driven out of a home in a year or so.'

'Ah, you mean your gorillas. Now I truly know you are touched in the head. Thanks for the beer anyway — and don't work too hard.'

Veniard paused at the door. 'I'll bet you a good dinner at the Hôtel du Président that you don't get a single business visitor today.'

Ten minutes later the doctor lost his bet. A white Mercedes saloon pulled up outside and a large, paunchy African in a creased, purple, light-weight suit got out. Jean-Pierre had arranged his desk so that he could see between the slats of the window-blinds any visitors approaching from the street. When he realised it was Kama Chiribanda he slipped out into the kitchen and spent some minutes tasting the dishes the African girl was preparing. Without a word she stood aside to let him do so. Soon he heard the caged-lion pacing of Chiribanda in the office outside.

He touched the African girl's cheek. 'Excellent soup.'

She smiled in pleasure. 'You have a visitor.'

'I know. That rogue Kama Chiribanda. It will do him good to wait a while.'

'*Monsieur le Conservateur*,' Chiribanda shouted.

'Very correct, you see.'

'Would you not expect him to be? He is the *Commissaire du Sous-Région*.'

'He's a crook.'

The African's voice had a more peremptory tone now. 'Monsieur Menant. I am waiting to see you.'

'Give me a plate of stew, please.'

The girl filled a plate, placed it on a tray and handed it to Jean-Pierre with a hint of a bow. The sounds of vexation and impatience from the office increased.

'*Monsieur le Conservateur*. If this is the way you run your office I must tell you I cannot afford to wait all day.'

139

Jean-Pierre thoughtfully swallowed a mouthful of stew, then he opened the door, placed the tray on his desk and sat down in his chair. For the first time he appeared to notice his visitor. With the utmost outward courtesy he said, 'Good day, *Citoyen Commissaire du Sous-Région* Chiribanda. What can I do for you?'

The African had been about to shout at him but was mollified by the correctness of the European's approach.

'I did not realise you were having your lunch.' A gold front tooth sparkled when he spoke. One had the feeling it had been put in his mouth simply for show.

'Quite all right, *Commissaire*. The office of the National Park remains open at all times. What can I do for you? Sit down, please. Can I invite you to share some food?'

'No, thank you. I came on business.'

Jean-Pierre broke a piece of bread and waited.

'You are aware that I own the farming concessions on the lower south-west slopes of Mount Misoka?'

'I noticed that someone had been felling trees there very recently.'

'On my express orders. I intend to plant quinine there to aid our splendid state medical services.'

Jean-Pierre ground some black pepper from a wooden mill on to his stew. It was as if the spicy dust thus released had got up the African's nostrils. He snorted and suddenly burst out, 'Someone has had the impudence to put signs on my land declaring it to be part of the National Park.'

'There must be some misunderstanding, *Commissaire*.'

'There most certainly is. Those signs claim the area which my men are, at this very moment, clear-felling for the quinine plantations.'

Jean-Pierre rose and unrolled a six-inches-to-the-mile map.

'Perhaps you would like to show me the exact place where you are felling trees?'

'No trouble about that, I assure you. Here, give me the map.'

Chiribanda jumped to his feet, jabbing the map with a

140

sweaty finger. He took a felt-tipped pen from his breast-pocket and drew a long, positive line across its middle. Then he hatched in crude shading on one side of the line.

'All the land I have marked, more than half the map and much more besides on other maps belongs to me. It has been awarded to me by the central government in recognition of the gallant part that I played in putting down the regrettable *Fisi* insurrection.'

'You have documents from the central government to back up your claim, of course?'

'Documents? I don't need documents. I am the *Commissaire*.'

'Of course. I realise your position, but in the absence of documents—'

Chiribanda thumped the table. 'I suppose *you* have documents?' The gold tooth winked like a warning light.

From behind his desk Jean-Pierre took a transparent overlay on which he had drawn in red chinagraph pencil the outline of the entire park boundary.

'I was about to put this over the map and place both on the wall so that anyone could call in at my office to make sure he wasn't intruding on the park — like yourself, by mistake. Since this is only the first day the office has been open, you'll have to excuse the map not being on display, *Citoyen Commissaire....*'

Chiribanda struck the table-top with his fist so that the plate leapt on the tray, spilling its contents. 'It's you who've made the mistake. One you're going to regret.'

Jean-Pierre regarded his visitor with bland innocence. 'Excuse me, *Citoyen Commissaire.*' He opened the door and called softly, 'Marie. If you please. We're going to get your good food spilt all over these maps unless we're very careful.'

The girl slid quietly into the office, saying *'Bonjour, Citoyen Commissaire,*' and removed the tray.

'Now,' said Jean-Pierre pleasantly. 'If I unroll this overlay and place it on the map you've already marked, you will see that all the area which you claim is yours falls well within the

141

park boundary.'

'That's all a fake. You can draw that line anywhere you like and that's just what you've done. Now it's my turn to ask you. What kind of documents can you produce to justify stealing my land?'

'Ah. I'm glad you raised that point.'

Jean-Pierre took a letter from the desk-drawer. At the head there was a crest, a martial eagle, the national insignia recently chosen by the central government. Menant read the letter slowly, emphasising the paragraphs which described geographical boundaries, contour lines and spot heights that defined the newly-gazetted Misoka Park. Finally, he read out the signature for the President of the Republic himself.

Kama Chiribanda snatched the letter. 'I don't believe a word. Where is the president's signature? This is just a forgery by some underling you've bribed.'

Jean-Pierre said gravely, 'You should know that you cannot bribe officials of the state. You yourself, a *Sous-Commissaire*!'

'Give me that!' Chiribanda snatched the letter and crumpled it. 'That's all the notice I take of fakes.'

'Don't worry, *Commissaire*, it's only a copy. Here, take another copy with you and read it carefully.'

Chiribanda stuffed the letter in his pocket.

'Is that all you've got to say?'

'What else should I say?'

'You'll soon see what *I've* got to say.'

'Good day, *Citoyen Commissaire*. Since you're a regional official, I know I can rely on you to see the law enforced.'

The door slammed. A few seconds later the Mercedes shot away with a squeal of tyres.

'Marie. I will take my lunch now.'

Later that afternoon, when both the map and a framed copy of the letter had been fixed to the wall, the doctor looked in on the way back from his rounds. He pointed at the map.

'Well, at least you've filled in the time by making the place

142

look prettier.'

'Jacques. You owe me a good dinner.'

'You've had a visitor? I don't believe it.'

'Marie will bear witness.'

'Take care that's all she bears! I'm busy enough as it is.'

'Keep your ribaldry for your bored white women patients.'

'O.K. Who was your first visitor then?'

'Kama Chiribanda.'

'That bush pig. Then you're going to need a good dinner. He's such a bastard, I'll even throw in a bottle of wine.'

Marie Maputa was nineteen. She had been brought up as a Catholic in the mission-school along the lake shore north of Baruva, close to the fortress-home built by Jean-Pierre's father. Her parents had worked there as house servants for the Menant family. Her schooling had ended abruptly with the departure of the colonists and the civil war that had followed. Her missionary teachers had been among those slaughtered by the *Fisi*. In the three and a half years that had passed since the mission-school had been destroyed, such roots of Catholicism as had taken hold had withered away. She had retained an affection for some of the outward trappings of the True Faith, however. She sometimes wore a crucifix attached to a rosary of African beads and she kept a small, plaster effigy of the Virgin which she appeared to treat as some kind of charm. She was a bright girl. If Catholicism had failed to take a lasting hold, education had done much better. She could read and write fluently and cope with practical, everyday arithmetic. It had been natural that, after the *Fisi* rebellion had been put down in Kenanja Province, she should come to work, as her parents had done before her, at the Menant plantation. Jean-Pierre had been aware early on that she was a well-mannered, well-proportioned girl, proportions that had begun to make their impression on the outside world in her very early teens. By the time she had returned to Menant's service she had become a rare beauty, coffee-coloured of skin with the finer kind of Bantu features coupled with a body and carriage that would have drawn attention in a Paris fashion house, or any other Paris house, for that matter.

There was no question of droit du seigneur. Such liaisons frequently came about by mutual consent and were seldom frowned upon in either white or black community. Many were even sanctified by marriage. Jean-Pierre's and Marie Maputa's was not, partly because neither had a formal, or even common, religious background. The Menants, with their Flemish origins, had never veered towards the almost universal Catholicism of colonial days. As for the Maputas, they had only recently emerged from the bush. In Marie's case, once the white fathers had died under *Fisi* pangas and bullets, the tribal beliefs of the bush had taken over just as surely as the actual and literal bush had taken over the burned-out ruins of the mission itself.

Jean-Pierre and Marie could have undergone a civil ceremony but they had never got round to it. He had simply given her a ring and the understanding that he would care for her. The union had been precipitated by the fact that the old fortress farm which he had defended during the *Fisi* troubles had been burned to the ground during one of his long absences in the forest studying the gorillas. This had happened a full eighteen months after peace had finally been restored to the country. No one had ever arrived at the truth concerning the fire. He would never know whether it had been carelessness on the part of the servants or a typical act of local revenge or local avarice. There was plenty of motivation in either case in the period of semi-anarchy that followed the civil war. All he knew was that, when he returned to find the farm house burned out, only three of his servants remained, living in the huts nearby. Among them was Marie.

Jean-Pierre was not a poor man. He had money back home in Europe which he was allowed to bring into the country. The plantation had ceased to interest him financially or as a way of life. He there and then decided that his own lands were to be a private sanctuary for mountain gorillas. It was not much, but it was a start, something to build on, above all a gesture which might later persuade the government to set up a national park. If that happened he would give his land to the park. With money from Europe he bought himself a house on the outskirts of Baruva. He needed someone to look after it. When he moved there, Marie moved with him.

The morning after Chiribanda's visit he woke early expecting to find Marie beside him. He stretched out his arm, hoping to persuade her into the act of love. One of the things he admired was that she could be as capricious as any European woman. There was nothing totally submissive about her. He had discovered that she was frequently responsive in the early morning. But this morning she had risen silently before he awakened, leaving behind her the faint, acrid taint of her sweat mingled with the harsh, floral tang of the oil she rubbed into her body. The mixture was particularly arousing. It reminded him faintly of crushed scents with which he was familiar in the forest.

She came into the room wearing a flowered kekoy that left her naked from the waist up. She set down a tray on the bed. On this she'd laid sliced paw-paws, pineapple and lemon tea.

'You're going to the forest today.'

He'd hardly been aware that this was his intention, though this undoubtedly had been his first, no, his second, waking thought.

'But the office,' he protested. 'It's only the second day.'

'I can look after it.'

Chiribanda's visit had already decided him that the office was not the place to be today, but how did she know this?

'Supposing someone important calls?'

'I can take a message. Your rucksack is already packed. I've woken Mushi and told him to be ready.'

Jean-Pierre dressed quickly. Then he took his rifle and panga and put them into the jeep. Mushi and his fellow half-pygmy tracker, Musharamena, were already in the vehicle.

145

When Jean-Pierre went back to the house to say adieu, Marie did not ask him whether he would return that night or how long he would be away. She merely kissed him on the brow. He often wondered how many white women would have accepted so unquestioningly and completely his unpredictable comings and goings and long absences in the forest.

Jean-Pierre did not know exactly what to expect. He only knew that he expected something and that the something was not likely to be good. It wasn't. Chiribanda had given him a sign, quite literally a sign. An arrow was sticking from the main notice-board. He had set this up only a few days previously on the track leading to the burned-out shell of his old home which served temporarily as park headquarters. Later, maybe, there would be time and money to rebuild at least part of the plantation house. The walls had defied the fire just as they had defied the *Fisi*. The arrow, which was sticking in the chest of the crudely-painted gorilla, might have been laughed off as a childish act of vandalism except for one thing. The tip was coated with the black, resinous pitch of arrow-poison. Its message was only too clear.

The arrow had not penetrated deeply. Indeed, in a living victim it would only have needed to break the skin to produce paralysis of the muscles controlling, among other vital functions, the breathing. Taking care to hold the arrow well up the shaft, Jean-Pierre pulled it free and laid it inside the hinged, metal pocket beneath the jeep's windshield. He had intended to drive straight on to headquarters, if only to see that his embryonic ranger force of four former plantation workers was on the alert: perhaps, also, to put them through some elementary rifle drill, a heart-breaking task, as he had lately discovered. Instead, he swung left-handed away into the forest, climbing the rutted track at a pace that threw the two pygmies in the back around like dice in a box. Surprisingly, this produced squeals of laughter, the little men balancing at a position of full knees' bend, arms extended to grip either side of the bouncing metal body, so that the vulnerable parts of their anatomies seldom made contact with the leaping floor and sides of the vehicle. Even above the roar of the labouring jeep's engine another, higher-pitched engine note soon intruded. This stopped suddenly, to be followed by a great creaking and groaning. Up ahead a cloud of red dust rose, followed, a split-second later, by the sound of a falling tree.

Two hundred yards from the forest edge, Jean-Pierre stopped the jeep, signalling the pygmies to stay where they were. He picked up his rifle and set off. The tree-felling had advanced twenty yards since he had put up the park boundary signs just over a week previously. The signs of which Chiribanda had complained were nowhere to be seen. Further down the slope a bulldozer was working, clearing away the undergrowth from a recently-felled area. Without being immediately aware of it, Jean-Pierre stepped on the remains of the first of his boundary signs. The bulldozer's tyre marks were still newly-printed where the machine had run over the sign and smashed it into firewood. A second sign had been uprooted and stuck defiantly on the front of the bulldozer, like a captured battle flag.

Beyond the bulldozer stood Chiribanda's Mercedes saloon, its gleaming white paintwork lightly powdered with red dust from the newly-churned soil. Beside it was Chiribanda himself. Jean-Pierre caught the flash of sunlight on the gold front tooth.

Jean-Pierre stepped out of the trees and advanced over the torn earth. It is doubtful whether at this point he had made up his mind on his precise course of action. Yet decisive action there had to be. When he was fifty yards away, Chiribanda spotted and recognised him. His reaction was immediate. Running to the front of the bulldozer, he tore down the park sign lodged there and laid it with insulting deliberation in the vehicle's path. Chiribanda leapt aside and watched with folded arms while this second signboard was reduced to matchwood.

147

Jean-Pierre slid a round into the breech, fighting the urge to shoot Chiribanda smack on his gold tooth. Instead, he fired the moment the butt touched his shoulder at the offside front tyre of the bulldozer. Reloading at the shoulder he deflated its nearside fellow. The machine slewed, momentarily out of control, offering him a quartering shot at one rear tyre. By this time the driver had baled out and was running for cover. Jean-Pierre sent a fourth bullet to kick up the earth a yard behind his fleeing heels.

Chiribanda had meantime legged it back to the Mercedes. Jean-Pierre toyed with the idea of putting his last bullet through the saloon's radiator. He fought temptation and slammed the bullet into the cylinder block of the wounded bulldozer where it would do more permanent harm or maybe good.

The Mercedes had gone. The clearing where, a few minutes ago, half-a-dozen Africans had been busily working under Chiribanda's eye was deserted. The only sound, apart from the *churring* of cicadas and the repetitive moaning of mourning doves, was the drip of hot oil pouring from a mortal wound in the stranded bulldozer's engine. There was nothing more to be done. When he got back to the jeep Mushi was hopping around anxiously.

'You didn't send for us, master.'

'There was no need.'

'You killed someone?' Mushi sounded hopeful.

'No. Just something.'

'We find gorillas today?'

'Not today. Today we paint more signs and teach guards to shoot.'

'Good,' said Mushi, who was neither a painter nor a marksman. He foresaw a long, blissful day ahead lying on the ground and smoking his best home-grown marijuana.

For the next hour and a half, more in desperation than hope, Jean-Pierre drilled his four retainers. Loti, Marema, Ndungu and Jahazi: they had all worked moderately hard and

148

sporadically faithfully on the Menant plantation. Now, for want of a plantation — it was all rapidly reverting to bush — and for want of more promising material, he was attempting at short notice to turn them into some kind of ranger force. A national park, particularly a newly-gazetted one whose only hold on a wild and isolated region was a sheet of presidential note-paper, needed a ranger force. Jean-Pierre expected little practical and no financial support from the capital, which lay 1,500 miles away across country that was largely rain-forest and lacked any communicating roads. Such tracks as there were became totally unusable during the rainy season. In the dry, they merely connected one lonely village with another. As for the airlines, there was supposed to be a regular, weekly, internal flight between Baruva and the capital. This, however, only rarely turned up on the appointed day and more often than not did not turn up at all. As one American pilot, who had nursed his tired DC3 into the strip at Baruva only one day late, had remarked almost proudly to Jean-Pierre, 'We're the only airline in the world they can't hijack. Nobody knows our goddamn schedule.'

The miracle, in Jean-Pierre's view, was that Misoka Park had received even paper recognition. He had met the president just once, at a military parade and reception held in Baruva to celebrate the re-establishment of peace and order in Kenanja Province after the civil war. The president had struck Jean-Pierre as a lively, nervous and intelligent man. After Menant had been introduced to him as a civilian leader in the fight against the *Fisi* rebels, the president had asked him what he intended to do now that peace had returned.

Jean-Pierre had explained that he was studying the mountain gorilla with a view to protecting one of the nation's priceless natural heritages. He had piled it on thick, making it plain not only how much the outside world envied this natural heritage but also how much the Western world would respect a determination to preserve it. He himself was prepared to give over his own lands immediately as a reserve for the gorillas in the hope that in the not-too-distant future

149

the president would see fit to make the volcanoes, Misoka and Vahinga, into a national park.

Jean-Pierre had not expected to hold the president's attention for more than a minute. In fact, the great man listened attentively for at least three minutes, giving an order to his aide to take notes. He asked only two questions, 'Is my country the only one in the world to have a significant population of these animals?'

'Most definitely, *Monsieur le Président.*'

'We are therefore world leaders in this respect?'

'Undoubtedly.'

'Let me hear your plans in detail. Write to me in person.'

Jean-Pierre had done so within a week of the president's invitation. He had sent maps and plans of the proposed park. As he had anticipated, he had heard nothing in return. He had followed this with monthly reports based on his continuous study of the gorillas in the forest, his estimates of the total numbers remaining on the mountains, the problems affecting their survival. He had kept this up for over three years. No word of encouragement had come from the capital. The president undoubtedly had plenty of other problems on his mind. Such had become Jean-Pierre's involvement with the gorillas that he could conceive of no national problem more urgent, though even in the midst of his obsession he was aware that he might be losing his sense of objectivity. He told himself that, where the survival of the Misoka gorillas was concerned, he could not afford the luxury of objectivity.

Just over a year ago had come a lucky break — and from a totally unlooked-for direction. An American girl photographer and journalist had turned up in Baruva. Her assignment: to write a series of articles about the country two years after the civil war. Jean-Pierre's reclusive nature had told him to avoid an encounter with the lady at all costs.

One afternoon, on returning to the burned-out shell of his farm, he had found a tall, sinewy blonde who recalled not a little the young Katherine Hepburn, in manner if not in looks and voice. She was busy clicking away at the ruins with a

150

Nikon. Jean-Pierre's immediate reaction had been to play Spencer Tracy to her Hepburn and pitch her into the nearest giant nettlebed by the seat of her jeans. In the event, something in the spirit of the lady struck a sympathetic chord. He had ended by dining her at the Hôtel du Président, telling her as much of his *Fisi* experience as he thought was good for her — which was almost nothing — and steering the conversation throughout almost the whole evening to his work with the gorillas. Nancy Genova was not disturbed by this. She had already learned almost all there was to learn about his *Fisi* period from other sources. His sudden switch from efficient destroyer of life to preserver of life, albeit animal life, was what she found totally fascinating. He was not an easy man to interview. The story lay more in what he failed to say than what he was actually prepared to tell.

'How do you reconcile killing men — all right, savages, if you like — who were prepared to kill you with the gentleness you obviously feel for these great apes of yours?'

'As you say: I had to kill to stay alive.'

'But one cannot escape the feeling that you did so with considerable pride in your efficiency.'

'I did not tell you that. You must have been talking to some very fanciful informants.'

'You're a bit of a legend around here. A legend at thirty-five. Legends have no business to look so young.'

'Nor have lady journalists who write articles for *Life*. Besides, I'm thirty-six.'

Miss Genova smiled. At least she'd got one personal fact out of him.

'Why did you decide to give up your farms, then?'

'I didn't need them. Anyway, I wanted to do something really constructive.'

She was on to this quickly but without seeming to pounce. 'Perhaps as an antidote to all that killing?'

'Maybe. I never thought of it like that.'

'But you enjoyed the civil war.'

'When you are about to be stuck, testicles first, through a

151

circular saw, I doubt if you have much time to consider whether the situation is exhilarating.'

'So that particular story was true?'

'There were many such stories. Most did not have such a fortunate ending.'

'For you?'

'For whom else?'

'Wasn't there some girl or other? You rescued her?'

'Many girls,' he smiled, 'but none so persistent as you.'

'Some scientist?' she urged.

'Yes. She had a terrible time. She went back to the States to get over it.'

'Did you hear from her?'

'Not for some time. After her experiences, I doubt whether Africa is her favourite country.'

The blonde Miss Genova consulted her notebook. 'Helen Lawes. Berkeley University, California. Multiple rape case.' She saw him withdrawing behind the stockade of his private face. 'Sorry. I guess that's all history.'

He nodded. She was aware that she had blundered, lost the contact with him which she had gradually established throughout the evening. 'Look, you have my word that I won't follow the story up as far as she's concerned when I get back to the States. Truly. I mean it. Let's get back to the gorillas. Your work with them is what I'm really interested in.'

It took a good hour and a lot of brandy and coffee before she was sure enough of her position to ask what had been in her mind all the evening. 'If I did exactly as you told me, is there just the faintest chance that you would take me out to see your gorillas?'

At the end of the evening, after he had kissed her hand very formally, he told her, 'Be ready at 0730. Wear slacks and comfortable shoes. I will call for you here.'

They had been lucky that day. Adam and the family were feeding within an hour's march of the park headquarters. Mushi picked up the trail quickly. They came up with the

152

group in a clearing an hour before the mid-day siesta. Abraham obligingly charged the pygmies from the rear and Nancy Genova had got the sort of stills, first time out, it might with normal luck have taken her three months to obtain.

That night she bought *him* dinner at the Président.

'If you think I'm going to sensationalise, I'd rather not write about you at all. But even you should consider whether your cause couldn't do with some publicity.'

'Publicity, no. Recognition, maybe. Even then, it depends on who's doing the recognising.'

'I meant recognition by scientists, world figures in conservation.'

'Such as?'

'I was thinking of a man like John Redfern.'

'The great American primatologist? He's getting on now.'

'In his sixties but still bright-eyed and bushy-tailed. He'd be mighty interested in your gorillas. He did his famous early work on chimpanzees. Now he spends every second he's got on persuading emergent nations to protect their wild resources.'

'You know him?'

'Know him? I travelled around with Redfern for six weeks while I was researching a *New Yorker* profile about him. One of the most exhausting times I've ever spent and that includes covering a couple of minor wars. If I could get hold of him, persuade him to come out to see you, maybe he might be able to use some good old American muscle with the president of this country to get your park set up the way you want it.'

Jean-Pierre was sceptical. 'The last thing they'll listen to is outside pressure.'

'Redfern knows how to wrap it up. He'll make it seem as though the president himself thought up the idea. Besides, there's always something these guys want from the decadent West. A new power station, maybe. A squadron of Phantoms.'

'That doesn't sound like Redfern's line.'

'Anything's Redfern's line so long as it gets him his own way. I'll try and persuade the great man to come and see what you're doing here. Mind you, I can't guarantee to get Redfern all wound up.'

'I accept that.'

Accept it he did and thought no more about it until, three months later, he received a cable saying: 'Hope to arrive Baruva earliest flight end of month stop Considerably interested in your fight establish gorilla preserve Redfern'

Nancy Genova had not exaggerated when she had described the grand old man of conservation as bright-eyed and bushy-tailed. Six feet tall, sixty-three years old, white-haired, lean, straight as a bamboo, he had demanded to be taken into the forest within hours of stepping off the plane. Despite the fact that the altitude obviously tired him considerably, he had crawled and crept for two hours until Jean-Pierre could show him Adam and his family. The old man had kept this up for two more days. After that he had rested for three days in Baruva, during which time he continually probed Jean-Pierre's knowledge of the Misoka gorillas. Even more important, he questioned him about his plans for their survival. Jean-Pierre resented none of this because he realised that he was being interrogated by a world authority on primates and their ecology.

The shy, Flemish-extracted ex-colonial and the elderly, charming and sometimes caustic Californian formed an instant liking for each other. At the end of his stay John Redfern said, 'Jean-Pierre Menant, I am not sure that I can bring any influence to bear on your president but I'm sure as hell going to try.'

Six months later had come the presidential letter that had brought Menant rushing down from the Saddle to set up the notices proclaiming his National Park. John Redfern's name did not figure in the president's correspondence, but Jean-Pierre had little doubt whose hand had been at work. About

154

the same time Nancy Genova sent him a copy of her *Life* article, which began: 'Directly the civil war ended, Jean-Pierre Menant, ruthless civilian leader in the fight against the *Fisi* rebels, switched his life-style from taking life to preserving life. Almost every day for three years, rain or shine, he walked in the forest, learning the ways of the mountain gorillas who live on and around his family plantations. For the first six months the gorillas were so shy he caught barely more than an occasional glimpse of them. Gradually, one gorilla family, at least, came to accept him as if he was one of their number. . . .'

Apart from the use of adjectives like 'ruthless', at which he frowned, Miss Genova had not sensationalised. The piece referred to a daring escape from captivity in the local saw-mill where many people, including missionaries, nuns and local businessmen, had already been murdered. But it did not mention Helen Lawes. Not surprisingly, it did not refer to the tall, thin *Fisi* leader who had organised the massacre. This was a secret known only to Jean-Pierre, Helen and the mercenary patrol with whom Menant had operated in the mountains in the campaign to exterminate the last of the *Fisi*. Jean-Pierre's desire for personal revenge on this man had made an impression even on the handful of hard-bitten South Africans, British and Belgians with whom he had fought. There had been no chance of the industrious Miss Genova contacting any of them later even if they remained alive. No, that secret was still his and Helen's.

Since the arrival of the presidential letter and the six-month-old copy of *Life*, Jean-Pierre had received no word from either of his American sponsors. He was on his own in the fight to get his park established; on his own, that is, except for people like Loti, Marema, Ndungu and Jahazi.

On the flattened patch of bare earth he used as a parade ground, Jean-Pierre regarded Loti, Marema, Ndungu and Jahazi with resignation that was almost African in its depth. On being ordered to take aim Marema, the small, thin tractor-driver, held his rifle as if it was a crocodile about to bite him, leaving a three-inch gap between butt-plate and shoulder. His finger was convulsively curled round the trigger in a grip approaching that of rigor mortis. By some merciful accident the safety catch remained on. The rifle was fully loaded with a round in the breech, for it was Jean-Pierre's intention, in view of the events of that morning, to let his ranger force discharge one shot in practice at a tea-chest twenty yards to their front. He was doubtful if they would hit this but reasonably confident that the fifty-foot cliff immediately behind the target would collect most of their bullets. However, there could now be no question of giving the order to fire. Had he done so, Marema's rifle must inevitably have crashed excruciatingly back on to his collar-bone, perhaps extinguishing his military ardour for ever. Wearily, he told his troops to unload, remaining well to the rear while they did so. He inspected the empty weapons with some relief and settled for ten minutes' more arms drill. At this they rather excelled themselves, swinging their arms exaggeratedly and crashing down their bare feet to raise enough dust for a platoon of booted regulars. Perhaps there was some hope after all, though he doubted whether their performance would ever reach a standard to impress such as Kama Chiribanda, enraged by the death of his bulldozer.

High above these military preparations, Absolom wavered between a last forage of the vines that were still lush along the forest edge and moving the family direct to the bamboos. In the end the bamboos won. The deciding factor for Absolom was the amount of noise and man-activity that was taking place along the boundary. Trees he had known since he was an infant were crashing down daily. So he led the family upwards, where the clouds hung low and all was silent except for the rustle of the bamboo leaves.

The Intruder, however, pursued his usual solitary course, a loner by instinct and inclination. Besides, he was exceptionally partial to bedstraw and there was plenty of that weed a safe distance from the place at which the men uprooted trees with strange roaring machines.

He was so busy rolling up the sticky bedstraw fronds so that he could stuff them into his mouth that he did not hear anyone approach above the distant growling of the machines.

As soon as he reached the park headquarters next morning, Menant knew there was more trouble. Mushi was three-parts drunk, always a bad sign. Native banana beer did not make the little man incapable, merely excitable. Now he hopped around like a mole-cricket on the hot ground left behind by a bush fire. Jean-Pierre knew better than to question him. Mushi, especially when drunk — drink and marijuana were his insulations against the hard knocks of life — was practically incoherent. There was nothing for it but to follow where he led.

The pygmy's state of inebriation did not detract from his ability to find his way like a snake through the thick matting of forest undergrowth. The only sign that he was the worse for alcohol was his more than normal carelessness with his panga. Twice he took large slices of skin off his leprosy-deadened fingers as he hacked away at vines and creepers blocking his path. They kept going for an hour, at a speed and in a manner that told Jean-Pierre that, whatever it was that Mushi insisted on showing him, it was not a gorilla. No living ape would have stood for the noise with which Mushi organised their march.

No living ape was involved in the occasion.

When at last the pygmy stopped, they were looking down into a small clearing close to the edge of the forest. Supported by one of the park notice-boards, arms outstretched and bound to a cross-member of bamboo in an attitude of crucifixion, was the corpse of an adult male gorilla whom Jean-Pierre recognised instantly as the Intruder. In his great, now sagging chest were the ragged tear marks of a dozen bullet-holes made by large shot, probably SSG discharged at short range from a shotgun.

Jean-Pierre's first reaction was that he should collect his sadly inadequate ranger force, mount the Bren gun on the jeep for the first time since he had shot up the last canoe-full of *Fisi* trying to escape across the lake, and go down to have it out, if necessary shoot it out, with Chiribanda. He was angry in a manner totally strange to himself. Nothing he had seen in the civil war had produced this kind of fury, not even the horror of the saw-mill, not even the rape of Helen Lawes. Those terrible events had taken place between human beings. They were what he had come to expect from the species. They had produced only a cold and calculated wish to repay in kind, to behave as a better co-ordinated savage than those around him. Even his hatred of the tall, thin *Fisi* officer had been and still was, in large part, a symptom of this deadly one-upmanship. Nancy Genova had been right on one score. He *had* enjoyed the fighting, perhaps almost in the same way that the mercenaries had enjoyed it, though they had killed and fought for money as well. The mercenaries had, he guessed, felt fulfilled by their prowess. They belonged to the breed that was only at its best in war. Was he the same?

At the war's end he had feared that this was his true and only nature. Then he began to walk in the forest with the gorillas. At first the determination to get to know the great apes by becoming their daily companion was both a harking back to his affair with Helen and a return to the guiltless days of hunting in his boyhood — except that now he no longer had the urge to hunt. Soon, studying the gorillas became an end in itself, an occupation that was utterly satisfying, one whose hold grew on him the more the gorillas accepted him, the more he learned about the apes. One kind of challenge had replaced another. It was the challenge that was the common factor. But he had at least satisfied himself that he was not just a killer, a hunter, an efficient survivor. He was capable of protecting something worthwhile and feeling deep involvement with the life-form concerned. Perhaps the only question about himself he had not succeeded in answering was why he experienced this deep rapport with gorillas more easily than with people.

Had it been a dead man lashed to the notice-board, Jean-Pierre might have registered disgust, revulsion, even compassion. Any of these reactions could have been followed by a decision to take violent action. In a dead man's case — depending on the dead man — he might even have turned away unmoved and taken no action at all. The sight of the butchered silver-back catalysed a brain chemistry that scared him badly. Because it was a gorilla that hung there, one of the gorillas given to his charge, he wanted to seize Mushi's panga and hack Chiribanda, whose work he had no doubt this was, to bits.

Even in his fury he remembered that evidence might be needed. The Pentax was housed in the metal box lined with foam rubber behind his seat. Standing on the bonnet, he took shots with standard, wide-angle and close-up lenses. He moved the vehicle and repeated the process from several positions until he had used up a whole roll of film.

Mushi was gesturing at the Intruder's corpse, grinning and making unmistakable gestures of eating. Jean-Pierre recognised the logic of the demand. Dead, the Intruder was of no further service to his own species. Dead, he was over 400 pounds of valuable protein to Mushi and the other pygmy trackers and their families. Gorilla was traditionally one of their favourite foods. The Bantu park staff would not touch the meat. He nodded his agreement to Mushi.

Together they lugged and tugged at the massive body until they had levered and heaved it over the tailboard of the jeep. The physical effort had given Jean-Pierre time to find his mental balance. The thought of killing Chiribanda or even beating him up had been wild fantasy. This was an African country and Chiribanda a municipal official of that country, albeit a junior one. Isolated from the capital by 1,500 miles of rain-forest and savannah, Jean-Pierre could expect little protection from local justice on the strength of a presidential letter setting up a park with which no one sympathised. Chiribanda had to be taught a lesson quickly and that lesson must be within the law. How much law had he got on his side? Chiribanda would certainly have got someone else to do his dirty work for him.

Without any clear motive, he drove the jeep down towards the forest edge. Perhaps he partly hoped for a confrontation with Chiribanda. The African's plantation lay half-a-mile through the trees in the direction he was taking. The cool side of his mind told him such an encounter might prove disastrous. He was still not sufficiently in command of himself to control the violence in him. As it turned out, events provided him with a violent solution but one within the law.

Heaving and bucking through the heavy undergrowth like an open boat in a full gale, the jeep rose on the crest of one gully only to crash down into the trough of the next. As it took a fresh cascade of vegetation in a breaker of green over its bonnet, it nearly collided with a large horned animal. At first Jean-Pierre thought he had run into a sleeping buffalo. The solitary old bulls sometimes lay up for the day in such places. Then he realised that what he had dislodged was a domestic bull. Native scrub cattle were forbidden to enter the park. The browsings, grazings and tramplings of what could potentially add up to hundreds of beasts could do enormous damage to habitat badly needed by the gorillas.

The animal stopped, turned and looked with dumb enmity at the jeep, as if making up its mind whether to charge or not. This was no scrawny specimen of scrub cattle. This was a brute of considerable breeding and pedigree. Only one person in this neck of the woods owned such a herd — Kama Chiribanda. No confirmation of actual ownership was strictly necessary. Nevertheless, within minutes Jean-Pierre got it. After he had driven a further hundred yards he had established beyond doubt that the beast was not an accidental stray. Upwards of fifty sleek, fat and beautiful head were brutalising his precious forest within easy counting range. God knows how many more there were hidden by the trees. If further evidence were needed, it soon appeared in human form. Jean-Pierre recognised one of Chiribanda's herd boys. The boy was whacking the backside of a cow that seemed inclined to turn back towards her owner's plantations. The boy waved good-humouredly at the jeep. Equally good-humouredly, Jean-Pierre waved back. He had no intention of doing anything to frighten the lad.

If Mushi had been alarmed at the rate of his master's progress downhill, he was utterly terrified at the speed of his uphill return. The pygmy solved the problem of how to stay aboard without breaking bones by clinging to the body of the dead gorilla and using its vast chest as a shock-absorber. Having arrived at this solution, he grinned happily. He had seldom before been so close to so much meat. Already he had worked out that, as he had brought the meat in, he would be entitled to certain prior claims, perhaps the liver or the heart. He knew Jean-Pierre well enough to guess that he wouldn't interfere with his legitimate aspirations.

Jean-Pierre had other things on his mind. When he reached the park headquarters he leapt out almost before the jeep had stopped and ran to one of the downstairs rooms that had only partly been gutted by the fire. The room was now a store. Against one wall stood a stock of notice-boards made by Loti to replace the ones Chiribanda had smashed. Loti had already started to letter one of these, copying the outlines Jean-Pierre had sketched on the white paint. Despite these outlines, Loti had once again managed to turn the 's' in 'Gorilles' upside down. Another time Jean-Pierre might have reflected sadly on the drawbacks of a little learning, which is precisely what Loti had received during his one year at missionary school. He was in too much of a hurry, now, to register either amusement or resignation. All he wanted was the lettering brush and some black paint.

He took down two of the plain boards and wrote on them in bold, crude capitals: MISOKA NATIONAL PARK — CATTLE FORBIDDEN BY ORDER OF THE STATE. From his bush-jacket he took the photocopy of the president's letter. He carried this at all times as his authority but also as a

161

talisman. There was the all-important sentence: 'The conservator is hereby given authority to deal as he thinks fit with all domestic stock entering the National Park, having first given the appropriate warning.'

All right, he was going to give the appropriate warning. Outside Mushi and Musharamena, aided by the rangers, were carrying away the body of the Intruder. Once the feast started he could forget the two pygmies' further services for at least twenty-four hours. Anyway, they weren't right for the job. This had to seem official.

Loti was changing a wheel on the park's only other transport, an old Chevy lorry that looked as though vultures capable of digesting metal had already dined on it. Jean-Pierre seldom raised his voice. When he wanted to, he could make a whisper sound like a command.

'Loti, get your rifle and uniform. Fetch the other three. Tell them to be ready to start in five minutes.'

If Loti did not actually jump to it, he moved at what, for him, was a lightning pace, a pace which might be described as a medium-fast walk. Jean-Pierre carried the notice-boards to the jeep. The black paint had run slightly but it would serve. He collected a heavy wooden mawl from the stores. Everything else he needed was in the padlocked metal box riveted to the floor of the jeep.

The urgency or perhaps excitement of the moment had at last got through to Loti. Closer to ten minutes than the ordained five, he arrived at the double, rifle at the trail. Behind him, in a state of more or less good order if not military discipline, followed Ndungu, Marema and Jahazi. Loti crashed to a halt, stamping his bare feet down in a perfect parody of the parade ground. The other three fell in, two on his left but Jahazi, for some reason known to no infantry training manual, on his right. Jean-Pierre decided to let well alone and was about to order them aboard the jeep when Loti, still holding his rifle in his right hand, gave him a sweeping salute with his left. Jean-Pierre returned it gravely and saw that something more was expected of him. Reflec-

162

tion told him that Loti was quite right. He had called a parade. He had got one. However raw they might be, he was taking his ranger force on a mission, their first mission. They had every right to be taken seriously.

Jean-Pierre moved Jahazi to his correct place on the left of the file. Next he inspected their dress, correcting the angles of their berets, telling Ndungu to do up two buttons on his jacket. Lastly he ordered them to port arms for inspection. When he had assured himself that all the weapons were empty, he told them the purpose of their mission. 'There are cattle in the park where the president of our country forbids them to be. We are going to see that their owners do not repeat their offence. Loti. . . .' He felt that the tall African's performance during the last few minutes entitled him to being put in charge of the detail. 'Loti, you will ensure that the men sit upright in the jeep in a military fashion. We must impress outsiders by our bearing.' Loti saluted again and they drove off.

This time Jean-Pierre took the track along the open edge of the forest. When he reached the point at which he judged Chiribanda's herds had been driven into the park, he stopped and ordered Loti to erect the two warning boards two hundred yards apart. Loti himself did not wield the heavy wooden mawl to bash home the stakes. At other times he would have relished doing so. He liked showing off his height and strength. Now Loti ordered Jahazi and the diminutive Marema to do the work. Loti was definitely showing that he was potential NCO material.

Once the boards were in position, Jean-Pierre drove slowly along Chiribanda's entire frontier. Whenever he came across parties of plantation workers he stopped or circled round slowly, letting them get a good look at his four smartly-dressed and armed rangers. As he came in sight of the notices for the last time, Chiribanda's foreman was sitting at the wheel of a battered pick-up truck. Reading the nearer one, he spurted away, trailing a red smoke cloud of dust, no doubt to tell his employer of this latest effrontery. Jean-Pierre recalled the phrasing of the president's letter '. . . deal as he thinks fit . . . after appropriate warning has been given. . . .' Well, the warning was undoubtedly appropriate and, now that the foreman had seen it, there could be no denying that it had been given. Nevertheless, he would allow a further hour to elapse. It would take over half that time to climb up through the forest to the point at which he had met the marauding cattle. When at last he stopped there was a quarter of an hour to go.

Jean-Pierre unlocked the padlocked arms locker on the floor of the jeep, taking out one clip of five cartridges for each of the rangers and a box of twenty-five .306s for his own hunting rifle. At five minutes to zero hour, he fell his men in.

'You saw what was written on the notice-board. No one is allowed to drive cattle into the National Park, especially if those same people have shot one of our gorillas. We shall now shoot exactly ten head of cattle to make this point clear. I shall issue each of you with five rounds. You will kill one cow each. You will aim at the heart, here. . . .' Jean-Pierre drew the outline of a cow in the soil, running his stick up the front leg until he came to the vital spot and placing a cross where a bullet would do the fatal damage. Surely not even marksmen such as these could miss so large a target at so short a range?

He saw the fear in Loti's eyes at the enormity of the action he was being ordered to perform. The smoulder of fear suddenly burst into the flame of excitement at the prospect of using his rifle in anger. Jean-Pierre was warned by that wild look and said sternly, 'You will each only fire when I order. You will be in serious trouble if you injure the herd boy or anyone else.'

He handed out the ammunition and ordered, 'Load!' He was surprised to see that the operation was carried out reasonably smoothly and safely. Only the tiny Marema forgot to put on his safety catch afterwards. This was one force Jean-Pierre preferred to lead from behind. He showed them how to carry their rifles at the high port so that their muzzles threatened only the oblivious sky. He strung them out in open order five yards apart and advanced them downwards through the forest. Almost at once a heifer broke out of a thicket on the right flank with the speed and agility of a bongo. Jean-Pierre snap-shot it. The beast's front legs folded and it somersaulted forward on to its horns.

'One,' he shouted and, seeing Ndungu's rifle sweeping dangerously round, added, 'As you were, Ndungu. You will be told when to shoot. You will shoot only cows that are standing still.'

The heifer Jean-Pierre had killed had leapt into action, like the bull earlier in the day, simply because it had been surprised at rest. The next six cows, all handsome specimens, were browsing in a clearing. They stood and looked at the intruders.

'Loti. Take aim at the right-hand cow.'

Jean-Pierre watched Loti's wavering muzzle until it had stopped prescribing small circles in the general region of the target area and, figuring it was now or never, ordered 'Fire.' The bullet took the beast high in the shoulder muscle. Before it could stampede and frighten the rest, Jean-Pierre shot it dead.

'Well aimed, Loti!' Loti was so busy wrestling with his bolt to reload that he hadn't heard the second shot. The remaining five cows stood considering their fallen companion irresolutely.

'Ndungu, the one next in line.'

Forgetting all instructions, Ndungu aimed directly at the boss of the cow's horns and by some miracle missed his target. The bullet whined harmlessly away. 'Reload, Ndungu.' Ndungu struggled with the bolt in time to fire a second shot at the animal as it bounded off. This second shot hit the cow who had been standing next in line, unbelievably killing it instantly. The surviving cattle fled.

'Excellent, Ndungu. That's three.'

Only Marema and Jahazi remained to be blooded.

'Marema. You shoot next.' Marema was the one who never put the butt of his rifle into his shoulder. So, when they came upon a solitary young bull, Jean-Pierre stood behind the little man, positioning and virtually aiming his rifle for him. Having made reasonably sure that Marema was not going to be stunned by his weapon, Jean-Pierre stepped to one side and brought up his own rifle, timing his order 'Fire' with the squeezing of his own trigger. He never knew where Marema's bullet went, though Marema was so certain that it had found its mark that he later composed a special hunting song to celebrate the occasion.

Jean-Pierre found it impossible to predict what Jahazi's performance would bring forth. Everything about Jahazi was unpredictable. As his name suggested, he had Arab blood from somewhere centuries back. The slave-traders had come this way from the coast at Zanzibar, two thousand miles to the east. From time to time they had put new stock back into the country. Jahazi owed his fine-drawn features and fiery temperament to one of these long-forgotten encounters. Jean-Pierre had thought several times about the wisdom of equipping Jahazi with a rifle. On this occasion, Jahazi ran true to form. On finding himself unexpectedly broadside on to a cow at thirty yards' range, he at once opened fire without orders and continued firing with extraordinary facility until his magazine was empty. The fact that not one of the bullets reached its mark depressed him not in the least. Jean-Pierre shot the cow for him, making number five.

Each of the Africans now believed he had done his duty with accuracy and dispatch. Without taking the rifle from his shoulder, Jean-Pierre shot the next group of four in about the time it took him to reload and fire. One more to go. A violent thrashing in the bushes only a few seconds later had the rifle leaping to his shoulder. His thumb pushed the safety catch, his index finger crooked the trigger but didn't take up the pressure. Instinct warned him this wasn't a cow. Chiribanda's herd boy came crashing in panic out of the undergrowth. He saw the rifle and his eyes rolled.

'Stand still. No harm is going to come to you.'

'The master. His beloved cows.' The herd boy plainly thought that if Jean-Pierre didn't kill him, Chiribanda would.

'The big bull. Where's the big bull? Tell me or I will arrest you for driving your cows into the forest.'

Jean-Pierre saw the boy's eyes flicker to his right and knew that the bull was somewhere close by, probably tethered.

'Take me to him.' The muzzle of the rifle moved fractionally towards the youth. The herd boy led off through the trees at a trot. Within fifty yards he stopped. Tied to a large hagenia tree was a magnificent breeding bull. Jean-Pierre walked up to him and almost casually place the muzzle of his rifle against the bull's brain. The animal dropped instantly, like a puppet, all of whose strings have been simultaneously cut. When Jean-Pierre looked round, the herd boy had run for his life. The message would not be long in reaching Chiribanda.

Loti and the others were waiting by the jeep.

'Loti, take Marema. He will drive the jeep. Then bring the lorry, with as much help as you can get, to the edge of the forest. Be as quick as possible.'

Loti's eyes flashed. 'We are going to take all this meat, master?'

'No, just two cows as a fine. The rest belongs to Kama Chiribanda, if he cares to fetch it. Ndungu and Jahazi, show me that your rifles are empty. There will be no more shooting. Now, both of you, follow me.'

Jean-Pierre led the way through the trees to the farmland. On the way he passed the last group of slaughtered cows. He pointed to the youngest and fattest. 'When the lorry comes we will take these two.'

Jahazi prodded one of the beasts with his rifle and made appreciative eating gestures. Ndungu rubbed his belly. Perhaps there was something to being a park ranger after all.

During the next hour Ndungu had reason to wonder about that. Jean-Pierre made both of them stand properly at ease, on sentry duty, fifty yards apart in the full blaze of the sun.

Moreover, they were facing the possible enemy. Satisfied that his sentries were maintaining a reasonably military pose, Jean-Pierre withdrew to the cover of the trees to watch and, if necessary, to back up his extremely thin black line. Sure enough, someone did come to look. First to approach was the pick-up truck. It stopped three hundred yards away. A promising sign. Through the miniature Zeiss glasses which he carried folded in his breast pocket, Jean-Pierre saw that the driver was Chiribanda's foreman and that he, too, was cautiously examining the situation through glasses. The pick-up drove away. Ten minutes later it returned, followed by the white Mercedes. If Chiribanda was going to make an open show of force it would come shortly.

Jean-Pierre could see the herd boy making wild gestures. He guessed from the movement of Chiribanda's binoculars that he was first examining the sentries and then sweeping the forest edge. The African was getting back into his limousine when he spied the dust cloud made by the approaching Chevrolet lorry. Chiribanda climbed out of his car once more. He and the foreman stayed watching while half-a-dozen willing helpers from the park headquarters dragged the two dead cows out of the forest and loaded them aboard. They were still watching when Jean-Pierre picked up the sweating sentries and gave the order to withdraw.

Jean-Pierre did not for a moment consider that Chiribanda was finished, yet he knew that the park had won this particular battle. Strength, he told himself, was the one thing Chiribanda respected. Chiribanda would go nearly out of his mind with fury at the death of his cattle. But then, he would certainly have read and reread the copy of the president's letter he had stuffed in his pocket in the park's office in Baruva. The vital phrase about keeping domestic stock out of the park must have convinced him that not even Menant would have dared to shoot a *Sous-Commissaire*'s cattle without the backing of some extremely high authority — the president's!

Chiribanda would surely make a counter-attack. Where,

when and how? First the park would get an outrageous bill for the dead stock. This, as Chiribanda must know, would be ignored. Chiribanda might try killing more gorillas. This was a very real possibility. Fortunately, at this season most of the groups were away up in the bamboos. True to character, the unfortunate Intruder must, as usual, have been doing his own thing. The pygmies reported no other gorillas within a couple of hours of the forest edge.

For a while Mushi and the rangers would have to maintain constant patrols to keep the animals away from the plantations. An attempt on his own life? Possible, especially if it could be made to look like an accident. Jean-Pierre felt more than a match for anything Chiribanda or his minions might try in that line. Destruction of property? The park headquarters had already been destroyed by fire, but there was still the hut up on the Saddle. There was already one man living on the Saddle. Jean-Pierre could only spare one more in case Chiribanda decided to burn the place down. Jahazi was mad enough to frighten anyone, especially if he maintained the rate of fire he had directed at the cow. So Jahazi it had to be.

Instinct told Jean-Pierre that his opponent was unlikely to make any open reprisal, at least not immediately. He only hoped he was right. With all that beef and gorilla meat available, the entire park force was going to be incapacitated for at least the next twenty-four hours. All things considered, he decided to go back to town.

But the thing that depressed him most was that, though he had stopped Chiribanda for the moment, the African was only one symptom of a much wider environmental disease, one that threatened the entire existence of the mountain gorilla. All around the borders of their present range on Mounts Misoka and Vahinga, other farmers, other developers, would be constantly threatening, perpetually encroaching. If he eventually succeeded in stopping Chiribanda, it would only be a local success and one that came within the limited sphere of his authority as director of a newly-formed national park. Real power would be needed to stop the timber concessionaires, the mining engineers, the agriculturalists and the ranchers who would, he knew, continually nibble away at the vital habitat. To stem that tide one would need power at a national level. Fat chance of that. All he could hope to do for the present was to concentrate on Chiribanda.

Jacques Veniard was drinking a beer in the office.

'Hello. I hear the famous one-man army has been in action again.'

'Meaning me?'

'Who else? News travels fast when you have a practice like mine, half black, half white and quite a lot khaki. You're sticking your neck out a bit, aren't you?'

'I doubt it. To show weakness would have been fatal. Next time I'll shoot twenty damn cows.'

'Aren't you forgetting that you're living in their country?'

'The president's black, too.'

'As the ace of spades, but he's also a long way away.'

'Then I'll go to the capital to see him if I need to.'

'Fat chance. He's got too many other problems.'

'Judging by his letter, he obviously thinks my park's important.'

'The possessive pronoun still! If you want the president's patronage, you'd better start thinking of the park as something temporarily entrusted to your care.'

'Jacques. You're right, but by God I'll need help — rangers, vehicles, scientists, a deputy warden. Where am I going to get those from and, supposing I do get them, how do I pay for them?'

'This country's broke. You've got to get the outside world interested in your problems.'

'Diplomacy isn't my strongest point.'

'I've noticed that much, but you pulled it off once before. Where's your venerable Yankee patron?'

'John Redfern? He's done all he can for the moment.'

'Nonsense. Why don't you fly to the States and twist his

arm?'

'I need to watch friend Chiribanda for a bit.'

'Sooner or later you're going to have to give up fighting him.'

Jean-Pierre shrugged. 'Over my dead body. One of his minions, probably that young son of his, Francis, filled one of my finest silver-backs with buckshot.'

The doctor put down his beer and stared at Menant. 'Oh, so *that*'s what your slaughter of the innocents was all about! I didn't hear that bit. I thought you were just exercising your gratuitous passion for shooting off guns.'

'I told you. I finished with that when the war ended.'

'Got any evidence to prove this gorilla was shot by Chiribanda?'

'Christ. I almost forgot the camera. Jacques, can you run a film through your bath for me?'

'Tonight if you like. I've got some snaps of my own to process.'

Veniard was a keen amateur photographer, though 'snaps' usually meant case-history pictures for a book he was compiling on tropical medicine from a general practitioner's standpoint.

'What's on the film that's so urgent?'

'The dead gorilla.'

'Hm. But even that doesn't prove Chiribanda's men did the deed.'

'I don't need proof, I know.'

'Watch it, my friend. Time to demobilise that one-man army of yours. I'll drop the pictures round in the morning.'

Veniard made the park's office his first call of the day. He flung an envelope down on Jean-Pierre's desk.

'You're quite a photographer.'

Inside the envelope were two ten-by-eight glossy blow-ups of one of the pictures and a sheet of contact prints, half-a-dozen marked with red crosses. The single enlargement was, by any standards, a sensational picture. The slumped

171

body of the Intruder filled the frame. Every hair on this corpse was pin-sharp. The way the light caught them, the buckshot wounds showed up like tiny shell-craters. A trickle of dried blood ran down the left breast. The likeness to a crucified human form was powerful.

In Jean-Pierre's 'Christ!' it was just possible to read more than an exclamation. A trick of light helped the illusion. Jean-Pierre had not noticed it at the time, but a single shaft of sunlight lancing down through the forest canopy caught the dead gorilla's face like a spotlight.

'What are the rest like?'

'Good, but none approaching that. Good close-ups of face, hands, wounds, etc. That's the picture of a lifetime. What more do you want?'

'Live gorillas.'

'Of course. That picture could help to ensure they stay alive.'

'I don't see how.'

'Every newspaper and magazine in the world will want to publish it. Properly handled, it could enlist enormous sympathy for what you're trying to do here. Sympathy means money and money means vehicles, rangers, scientists — all the things you say you need. All we've got to do is to get your picture published. I tell you, it's worth your flying to New York.'

Jean-Pierre said, 'Nancy Genova.'

'Come again?'

'The *Time-Life* girl. The one who got to Redfern.'

'Now you're talking.'

'Redfern, too.'

'Important, but not so vital in the first instance.'

'I'll mail the pictures to them both straight away.'

'The mail's too unreliable. Things get stolen or at best held up for weeks. I've got a better suggestion. An internal flight landed last night. Young American captain. He's staying at the Président. Ask him to take the pictures out and put them on a New York flight. They've all got friends flying inter-

172

national routes. It can be mailed directly the crew reached New York.'

'When's he leaving?'

'Today, I guess. I'll call in and find out. Meantime, sit down at the typewriter and put the facts as you see them on paper. Everything you can think of. No, not everything. Better leave the monstrous Chiribanda's name out of it. Here, give me the negs. You keep one of the blow-ups.'

'I don't want to part with the negs.'

'Don't be bloody stupid. My printing isn't bad but I don't imagine it will be good enough for the art editor of *Time* or *Life*. Now get cracking, Jean-Pierre.'

Jean-Pierre did exactly as the doctor ordered. He took a copy of his notes to Nancy Genova and put them in a second envelope with the contact print of the vital picture and addressed it to John Redfern in California. One enlargement he kept for himself. He wrote Redfern a covering letter explaining that the negatives had gone to Nancy at *Life*.

The young American was the same pilot who had boasted about the impossibility of his airline being hijacked. He was in no hurry to leave. Even if he had been, it would have made little difference. The freight he was supposed to pick up hadn't even arrived at the airstrip. He whistled appreciatively at the picture and gladly agreed to take negatives and information out with him. If he ever got out, that was. He knew a friendly Pan-Am stewardess who would certainly post the package on arrival at Kennedy airport.

At mid-day, to his total amazement, the airstrip called to say his freight was being loaded. At two-thirty Jean-Pierre heard the DC3 labouring its way over the town with just enough time to find its way through the mountains before the afternoon banks of cumulus closed in completely.

The time had inevitably come when Adam was feeling his oats just like any other young male. For several days he dutifully followed Absolom's lead further and further into the bamboo forest. Then, one morning, quietly and without

173

fuss, he slipped away, taking Aquila and Hepzibah with him. He had sensed that Hepzibah was ready for such an adventure. She was, after all, a fairly recent arrival, brought by the Intruder and abandoned when he went his own blithe way to eventual death. So her attachment to the family was still not strong. Hepzibah had given birth to a small memento of his brief reign, an active baby whom Jean-Pierre had christened Toto, Swahili for 'little one'. Toto was now three months old.

Aquila was probably swayed because she was young and had formed an association with Hepzibah. Adam could have done without the orphaned New Arrival who was still attached to her. Her own Aaron was old enough to start trying his luck with the other juveniles. He stayed with the main family when Adam and the two females broke away.

The little group travelled fast. It was inevitable that Adam should want to put as much distance as possible, as soon as possible, between himself and the family he had just left. Not that he needed to fear retribution from Absolom but, like any young man striking out into the world for the first time, he wished to be free of family influences. Though he was not a territorial animal, he recognised the vague concept of home-range. He aimed to get out of Absolom's home-range for his first attempt at going it alone.

Over the next few days he led the females into totally unfamiliar country on the lower slopes of Misoka. Adam could not know it but this was country normally shunned by gorillas. It was border country with the neighbouring state, an area much troubled by poaching. Not poaching or, rather, hunting to live as practised by the pygmies, the kind which had caused Adah's death, but organised poaching for meat, hides and ivory, strictly for commercial gain.

Musharamena, the park's number two tracker, had followed Adam's trail because he was curious to see how the young male would make out and knew Jean-Pierre would want a full report when he returned to the forest. Just before dusk on the third day he came across the remains of a

174

temporary hut, recent ashes and newly-cut stakes on which meat or hides had been pegged out to dry. The work was not that of pygmies. It was professional, though, and revealed to Musharamena that a gang of about eight poachers was operating in the area.

Early next morning, Adam rose from his nest and led his little group down a lava gulley covered with low scrub. There was no wind in the gulley to bring him scent. All was silent. When he was over half-way along the defile, two men rose from the undergrowth on either side, shouting and waving their arms. They were well above Adam's level so there was little chance of charging them. He turned to find another man with a spear running down the track behind him. A keen pricking in his flank reminded him of that other ambush in the swamp. Nevertheless, he made a half-hearted false charge in the direction of the spearman, roaring and screaming out of rage and fear.

Adam felt the bodies of Aquila and Hepzibah brush by him before the spear took him full in the chest. Blind with pain and anger he rushed towards the man who had wounded him, but the butt of the spear struck the ground, checking his charge and allowing the man to dodge past to one side. The grounding of the spear drove the double-edged blade even more deeply into his chest. His toppling fall broke the spear, leaving a foot of the shaft protruding from his wound. Adam tottered on, not knowing where he was going or why.

Without Adam to lead them, the two females and young panicked forward towards the hidden net. Aquila hit it and went down. Hepzibah stumbled over her body, momentarily caught a foot in the net, wrenched free and kept going. The baby Toto made use of the moment to leap on her back and thus escape with her. The New Arrival had hit the net to the left of Aquila. The men piled the net on top of both of them, stabbing and clubbing Aquila until the life went out of her.

The New Arrival they seized and put in a sack. He was the booty they had been after though they had hoped to capture both the infants. The New Arrival was a fine prize, however.

175

He was four years old, old enough to feed himself, and had a good chance of surviving to be sold to an unscrupulous collector for a large price. Since these men did not eat gorilla flesh, they left Aquila where she lay.

When, an hour later, Musharamena followed the gorillas' trail towards the scene of the ambush, it was Adam's corpse that he found first. Adam had travelled a quarter of a mile before dying. Shortly after he found Aquila and read the signs of the struggle that had taken place.

When Jean-Pierre got the news of the decimation of Adam's break-away group his first thought was that this was the hand of Chiribanda. Musharamena's description of the style and methods used by the poachers soon convinced him that his local enemy had nothing to do with it. This was the work of a well-organised poaching gang who knew what they were after and how to get it. Ten to one they had come in from over the border, though there was always the chance they were residents. Musharamena had made the journey back in one day and night. If he moved fast, Jean-Pierre could be on the scene within eighteen hours. The poachers had no reason to suppose they had been spotted. There was just a chance, therefore, that they still had a camp somewhere in the area. Frankly, he thought the chances were slim. The fact that Musharamena had come upon a recently abandoned camp suggested they were constantly moving. His finding the untouched corpse of Aquila told Jean-Pierre what the poachers had been after — the infants. He reasoned that, with one or more captured young, their main anxiety would be to get the babies to a secure place as soon as possible.

The news that he had to set off again at once would not surprise or dismay Musharamena. Jean-Pierre toyed with the idea of taking Loti or one of the others but dismissed it. Loti would only slow them up. The value of his extra rifle if it came to a showdown was more than extremely doubtful.

He called Marie Maputa.

'I'm going off into the forest for two or three days.'

'I will prepare some food. Do you leave at once?'

He looked at this extraordinary girl, who calmly accepted everything he did and said, and felt a sudden, overwhelming flush of tenderness for her. By European standards he took every advantage of her acquiescence. Yet she was African and African women had a totally different outlook. He provided status and protection. She, in return, provided what was expected of a wife.

He caught a glimpse of the statue of the Virgin on the shelf. He knew she would take this down and decorate it once he had left. As protection for herself? No, the ritual surrounding this magic talisman was mainly for him!

She still stood there. She hadn't asked: '*Must* you leave at once?' but '*Do* you leave at once?'

His answer came long after the question.

'Not at once. Not for a little while anyway.'

His hand went to the knot that tied the African cotton behind her shoulder. The cloth slid away and he was glad to see that she had been hoping for this. Her nipples were as hard and full as black cherries. She stepped out of the complete garment and lay back on the edge of the bed, her feet still placed on the floor. He entered her standing and she closed her legs round his hips in a way that he had taught her.

Fifteen minutes later, when he drove away with Musharamena, he saw her removing the statue of the Virgin from the shelf.

John Redfern was well pleased with the result of his foreign tour. Three conferences and a dozen meetings with European businessmen, all within a fortnight, would have taxed most men in their forties or fifties. In his sixties Redfern was still generating enough steam at the end of his tour to drive a locomotive. It had long been his view that the United States needed a conservation organisation that could tap the immense wealth of his country; not only that, but plug in to the respect and goodwill the U.S.A. commanded in European industry. He also had the strong feeling that the emergent nations to which the U.S.A. had given foreign aid would listen to an American spokesman where they might suspect Britain and other European nations of neo-colonialism. Not that this was entirely borne out by the facts. Redfern was the first to admit this. The World Wildlife Fund had done a tremendous job. It was his private opinion that European organisations hadn't cut as much ice in the U.S.A. as was lying around for the right kind of iceman, the native-born variety, to collect. Redfern proposed to set up a body that would fulfil that role. He had succeeded in persuading the many, often rival, conservation bodies in America to agree to accept his leadership on an international front. This in itself was a diplomatic feat of which Bismarck might have been proud. He didn't see any need to clash with the World Wildlife Fund or anyone else. It was simply a question of dividing areas of interest and fund-raising. He had already had talks in Europe on this basis. World Wildlife and his own Ark International would prove complementary to each other. At all times he would keep his opposite numbers informed.

Redfern was a controversial scientist, which is another way of saying that an unusually high percentage of other scientists didn't approve of him. Some even called him a commercial scientist. His early work on primates had been of unchallengeable stature. In his fifties he had suddenly decided to popularise it, writing a series of witty, perceptive and, his enemies said, scientifically questionable books comparing human behaviour with that of animals. *Who's Aping Who?* had unfavourably matched the goings-on in a New Jersey commuter community with those among a troupe of Botswana baboons that Redfern had once studied. *The Bad Behaviourists* had taken a smart wedding and the events leading up to it and sought to explain them in animal behaviourists' terms. *Manhattan Zoo* was a study of commercial New York with jungle parallels. The books had made big paperback deals and a lot of money, some of which Redfern had wisely diverted to chosen research projects. Nevertheless, he had emerged comfortably well-off and this was particularly unforgivable. What the purists could forgive even less was John Redfern's undoubted panache. They found this superficial and self-seeking.

Redfern himself was amused by this jealousy. As a behaviourist he explained this element of flash in his personality as a form of display necessary to catch the attention of those he wished to woo in one way or another. He rightly saw this display as being crucial in the promotion of Ark International. His only regret was that he had a limited number of years left to devote to his new project. He started making the most of those years at 9 o'clock sharp the day after he returned to California.

Grace Yardley, his secretary, had a regular and ardent boyfriend of her own. A pneumatic brunette of twenty-eight, she also had traces of whatever does a girl for an Oedipus complex. She had often fantasised about being made love to by her own boss. Not that he had ever suggested such a thing. For any woman who liked older men, John Redfern was first-class fantasy material. The trouble was that he did not look his age and, if rumours around the campus were to be taken seriously, certainly didn't act it. Many a girl student had been willing to put the matter to the test. Dr Redfern, however, had very definite and prudent views concerning the activities to be indulged in on one's own doorstep.

Grace watched her boss walking spring-heeled across the grass and felt the usual tremor. She quickly gave a rearranging flutter to the bunch of tulips she had placed in the crystal vase on his desk. A zoology graduate herself, she immediately recognised this nervous reaction as a displacement activity. Redfern wore Bedford cord trousers, very English; a hound's-tooth sports jacket, even more so; a polka dot bow tie.

They began to open the mail. When she came to Jean-Pierre's letter she slit the creased brown envelope and pulled out the slightly crumpled ten-by-eight of the crucified Intruder. Redfern heard her suck in her breath.

'May I see?'

She handed it over. 'Isn't this shocking, and magnificent,

179

too, in a way? It sums up all you're trying to do, Dr Redfern.'

Redfern looked at the picture in silence for a good ten seconds. Then he said just what Jean-Pierre had said and in much the same tone. 'Christ! Whoever killed that marvellous animal even got the pose right.'

'There's a letter with it, doctor. It's from Jean-Pierre Menant in Baruva.'

After Hepzibah, with her baby, Toto, clinging to her back, broke out over the net, the terrified female kept going until the baby screamed to be allowed to get down. Hepzibah continued at a lope until all sounds of the tumult behind her had long died. At last she stopped, bewildered and exhausted, the baby whimpering at the jouncing it received during the rough ride through the bush. Once it was able to descend and feed, it quietened down immediately.

Hepzibah had never been on her own before. First there had been the secure juvenile and sub-adult life with her own family, one of the Vahinga groups; then the adventure with the Intruder, who had, typically, abandoned her to Absolom's family; recently, the ill-fated break-away with Adam. And now this leaderless solitude.

Despite her apparent flightiness, Hepzibah was a remarkably sensible animal. Indeed, her flightiness which is, after all, a purely human and therefore totally irrelevant concept, may in gorilla terms simply have equated with independence. Once she had calmed down and satisfied herself that she was no longer pursued, she had one uppermost urge: to return to the only anchor she now knew, her home-range. Though this was still a long way distant, she had a good sense of direction and oriented herself correctly, who knows by what means. The sun? Distant glimpses of Misoka's peak? Or merely by a bump of locality, which even human beings are said to possess to some measure?

In this endeavour she had one stroke of luck. On the third day of her solitary journey her trail crossed that of Jean-

Pierre and Musharamena. They had followed the poachers beyond the site of the ambush and found, as Jean-Pierre had expected, that the gang had crossed the border a good twenty-four hours before with the captured New Arrival. Menant had followed into the neighbouring state's territory for several miles in the hope that the poachers had decided to rest there for a while in the belief that they were safe, perhaps before returning to plunder afresh. If they had done so, Jean-Pierre would have had no hesitation in taking the law into his own hands. No such luck. Once the forest across the border started to thin out, he knew that the situation was hopeless. Men and gorilla would simply have vanished into the villages of a highly populated area.

They were many hours past the scene of the ambush on their return journey when Musharamena pointed to the fresh tracks of a single female and baby in soft ground. The gorillas were plainly still badly scared. It soon became clear that they were moving at an unnaturally fast pace. Jean-Pierre had little doubt who the female was. The tracks were those of a very small baby, obviously Toto. He immediately slowed down his own pace in order not to panic the fugitives. He hoped that, if he moved cautiously, he might be able to drive them in a direction in which they had a chance of eventually meeting up with their own family. At the very least he'd be steering them away from immediate danger from poachers. So, for two days, he moved cautiously and was rewarded by the fact that the female and infant were moving in the safest direction. On the third day, just before he left Musharamena to complete the task, he had the satisfaction of knowing that the familiar hagenia forests of Misoka lay ahead.

Directly he reached the terminal building at La Guardia, John Redfern rang Nancy Genova's apartment. He was delighted to find her there. When he had left that same apartment just over forty-eight hours previously she had been uncertain whether she might not have to leave shortly on a magazine assignment to Baja California. He'd fed her a lot of background lately about how the proposed new Baja highway might lead to the Sea of Cortez becoming seriously polluted and the rich marine life there disturbed or destroyed.

'Nancy? You're still around. Glad to hear me?'

'That's not a very deductive question for a distinguished scientist. Surprised and glad. I'm always glad. You know that, John.'

'I wish I was younger.'

'You're young enough from what I remember.'

'Most of the time.'

'You didn't fly back from the west coast just to sing me your version of "September Song".'

Redfern laughed, a shade bitterly.

'Done any work for *Life* recently?'

'Not in the last month or two. Too many staff men kicking their heels up there.'

'Still on good terms with them?'

'Yes. Why not?'

'Could you place a picture story with them?'

'You know some of the answers to that, John. Depends on the story, the space they have, the editorial mood they're in, whether they've run anything like it lately. Most of all, it depends on the pictures.'

'Picture. One picture. I can guarantee the quality of the picture.'

'Don't be so mysterious, John.'

'I'll come round.'

'No, don't do that. Bee's here.'

'Oh!' Disappointment. Bee was a girl photographer who shared the apartment. More often than not she was away on an assignment. 'I don't care about Bee.'

'I do. I'm old-fashioned about you.'

It was true, and one of the things Redfern found most endearing about this apparent hard-case from whose company he got both pleasure and solace. Nancy Genova had certainly had her share of love affairs but she was totally unwilling to compromise Redfern.

182

'Bee's a goddamn intrusion on our privacy.' On the rare occasions his infrequent visits to New York coincided with the photographer's residence there, he had had to book a hotel room for Nancy and himself. This, at his age, was something he deeply resented. A widower for fifteen years, he sought the feeling of being part of a woman's home, of being among her clothes, her books, her possessions. He heard her laugh.

'Meet me at the Algonquin.'

Nancy Genova was a shade too tall, more than a shade too thin. She had style, though, the kind that doesn't demand an entrance. She entered the Algonquin as she might have entered a news-room, confidently but with no deliberate attempt to make an impression. When she found Redfern he waved at her extravagantly and joyously. She sat down and gave him no more than a decorous, filial peck on the cheek. Beneath the table he squeezed her hand.

'Nice to see you back, John, and unexpected.'

'I had to register here. That damn photographer friend of yours.'

'Bee? You didn't give me a chance to tell you. She's booked out to Europe on an 1830 flight.'

'Then I've wasted my reservation.'

'Aren't you assuming, Dr Redfern, I'll ask you back to my apartment?'

'Won't you?'

'That depends on what you've brought me. Let's have a look at it.'

Redfern took the envelope from his brief-case. He waited for her to examine the photograph.

'*Kee-ryst!*' was all she said.

'Well?'

'*Kee-ryist* again.'

'Think you could make something of that?'

Nancy Genova said, 'It *is* a fantastic picture. Yet you can never tell with *Life*. What I do know is that it's one hell of a picture. Tied to the launching of Ark International, it could become a great story. Then Ark can use the picture afterwards as a reprint from *Life*.'

'Are you sure *Life* will do it?'

'It's impossible to be certain. But if they don't, then *Paris-Match, Der Stern*, someone will. . . . It's a great picture by any standards. Are there any more?'

'Menant's note says he sent all the negatives to you at *Life*.'

'Then I'd better get round there straight away. Look, you go straight to the apartment. Bee will have left by now. Make yourself at home.'

'What about my room here?'

'Even famous scientists go on the town occasionally.'

Directly Jean-Pierre walked through the office into the kitchen he smelt the evil. Evil in this instance stank of decaying food and rank drains. He had been away less than a week but food had gone off in his absence through neglect. She had simply not been there to attend to it. This event also had its specially evil smell. The smell was that of Chiribanda. He called out for Marie and then hurried into the bedroom, disturbing a large agama lizard that had found its way in to pilfer the rotting scraps. The bed had not been slept in.

Then he saw it. The statue of the Virgin had been beheaded. The face of the babe was streaked with red dye to resemble blood. The flowers she placed in front of the image as an offering during his absence had vanished. In their place were some dark, plaited roots. He recognised these as having magical meaning connected with death among some of the forest tribes. Marie Maputa came from such a tribe. He had no doubt now where he must look for her. She would have returned to her own people.

Eventually, he found Marie in a broken-down reed hut close to her family's compound on the edge of the lake. The hut had been abandoned two rainy seasons ago when the lake level had risen and flooded it. No one had bothered to rebuild it since.

Marie lay on her face on the floor on a pile of dried reeds. Jean-Pierre turned her over carefully. Her features had already shrunk. It was likely that she hadn't eaten for several days. Her eyes were as blank as if coins had been laid in the sockets. He shook her and called her name, knowing he would get no answer.

Jean-Pierre stormed outside. An old man watched him from a safe distance.

'Come here at once.'

The old man shook his head.

'You a relative of hers?'

The old man turned fearfully, as if to run. Jean-Pierre caught him by his torn khaki shirt.

'How long has she been here?'

The grey-beard shook his head.

'Come and look at her then. Maybe it'll help you remember.'

'No, master. She has been cursed.'

'I know she's bloody well been cursed. Who's responsible? Who's the witch-doctor? You must know. Everyone here must know. Unless you tell me, she's going to die.'

'She will die,' the old man agreed gravely.

'I'll see that you die, too, unless you tell me.'

'There is nothing you can do. It is a very powerful spell. A week perhaps. She will die.'

Jean-Pierre pushed the old man away so that he fell to the ground. Then, discovering he was not hurt, the ancient gathered himself together and ran as fast and far as his matchstick legs would take him.

Jean-Pierre gathered up Marie Maputa in his arms. It was like carrying a roll of carpet, a very soiled and stinking roll of carpet. She hadn't moved from the hut to relieve herself, perhaps not even from the bed. He sat her in the jeep, passing a length of cord round her lolling body to stop her falling out. He drove back to town. When he had carried her into the house, he stripped Marie, washed her and laid her in the bed.

185

Already those firm breasts were sagging. The smooth stomach wall was slack. All this time she gave him no more reaction than a corpse. She stared — no, 'stared' was a word that implied conscious effort; she presented eyes in his direction that knew neither him nor the surroundings in which she lay. He covered her and walked lifelessly, as if unconsciously imitating Marie's trance, into the office. The shutters were down against the sun. The place had probably been closed since he had left for the forest, certainly since Marie had found the beheaded statue of the Virgin and, reading its message, returned to her own people to die as she knew she had been ordered to die.

A fixing had fallen out of the map he had so confidently placed on the wall that first day. The map hung slant-wise. Jean-Pierre's immediate reaction was to tear it down and screw it up.

It was as if the whole great, steaming, stinking, unfeeling continent of Africa had fallen into that small office, point-first, and buried him and his national park under its weight. The very idea that he could set up such a park had been, right from the start, a ridiculous fantasy. It was all based on one letter from the president's office. A letter that had probably been forgotten as soon as written, had almost certainly only been written quite cynically in the first instance to please some white pundit like Redfern and gain an easy propaganda point in the outside world. Had he really imagined that, by putting up a few notices, by shooting a few cows, by trying to strong-arm a petty local crook, he could beat the system? Some day, a park might be set up. But they, the so-called rightful owners, would have to be the ones to do it. They'd have to bring in their own strong-arm men, maybe even troops. The capital would need to install a *Chef du Région* who had orders to see that the park existed and was respected. He might have to shoot a few people, dispossess others, throw Chiribanda, or whatever local racketeer then existed, into jail but, in the end, the park would become a fact, on paper at least. By that time, of course, the gorillas that the

186

park was intended to protect would almost certainly have disappeared — at least if these past few weeks were anything to go by. First the Intruder and then virtually a whole sub-family. The process would go on and on and he was powerless to stop it. Chiribanda had outflanked him in a uniquely African manner. As to the poachers from across the border, they had got away with it unpunished, mainly because he had no way of detecting their presence. To spot them he needed aircraft, which at the moment he did not even know how to fly. It was completely hopeless. Not even he, who had thought himself self-sufficient, could hope to overcome the odds.

The office felt and smelt dead and musty. The only activity he could detect was that of a paper-wasp who had found a way in through a chink between window frame and brickwork and was building a nest in the angle so formed. No one else had found a use for the office. Probably no one else ever would. He yearned more than anything else to be back in the forest and most of all to be back in the hut on the Saddle.

At last he remembered his main reason for entering the office at that moment. He had intended to phone his friend Jacques Veniard. By some unexplained, probably unexplainable, miracle, the operator got him the doctor's house within five minutes. When Jean-Pierre had described the situation, the doctor said, 'Doesn't sound as though you should be sending for me.' Then, 'I'll be round in an hour.'

While he waited, Jean-Pierre opened first the shutters, then the windows. He didn't care what annoyances, heat, flies or noise this allowed to enter. All these were symptoms of life. Above all he wanted to let in life. When he had liberated the office he did the same with the kitchen and bedroom, hurling the rotten fruit and festering meat into the bin outside, sluicing the floors with strong disinfectant. The decapitated statue and the sinister twisted roots he placed in an outhouse. Marie Maputa had changed her position on the bed to the cramped crouch of an embryo. She had given no sign that she

187

was aware of his presence or of his activities.

Veniard arrived within forty minutes. He turned the unprotesting girl on her back and examined her eyes, felt her pulse and listened to her heart.

'Who did it?'

'Who else but Chiribanda?'

'Probably.'

'What sort of shape is she in, Jacques?'

'Physically not bad. Heartbeat is strong and regular but slowed right down. Any civilised doctor would say she's in some kind of trance. Hypnotic, possibly, except the symptoms are exaggerated. Not quite a coma but getting on that way.'

'You've seen them like this before?'

'Often. Usually,' Veniard added sardonically, 'the patient hasn't been on my list.'

'Meaning?'

'You know my meaning as well as I do. The only doctor who can cure her is a witch-doctor, the one who did the damage in the first place!'

'You believe in that kind of thing?'

'Of course! So do you. You know you do.'

'Suppose I do. What can you do for her?'

'One of her problems is that she hasn't eaten or had a drink for a long time. She's badly dehydrated. I can try to keep her going on a drip but she'll probably tear it out. Might have to tie her down and then there's no guarantee it will help.'

'You must try, Jacques.'

'Of course I'll try, but you know Africans. Once they've made up their minds they're going to die, or believe they've been told they're going to die. . . . Oh well, let's see the blessed or rather cursed Virgin, not that cleaning it up and sticking it together will help.'

When Jean-Pierre showed him the twisted skein of roots, Veniard said, 'If only our sort of medicine knew how to do as much by sheer suggestion. I recognise that stuff and, I tell you, it's not good news.'

'Get busy, Jacques. Marie's got to be saved.'

'I'm no witch-doctor, my friend, but I'll do what I can.'

Marie did not struggle when he taped her wrists and ankles firmly to the bed-frame. Jean-Pierre's telephone call had told Veniard what he might expect to find so he had brought with him all the apparatus necessary for a drip-feed. When it was done he asked for a large Pernod and insisted Jean-Pierre take one with him.

'Will it work, Jacques?'

'Frankly, I don't expect it to help very much and I don't think you do either. Whether you like it or not, I'm going to give you some advice — as your doctor. You can do one of two things. Both are unpalatable. The first is: make a deal with Chiribanda.'

'Impossible.'

'Is it? You're going to have to make one sooner or later. If not with him, then with someone just like him. So far you've done everything with your trigger finger. It's a useful digit for many purposes, but it never did much for diplomacy. Diplomacy is what you're going to have to learn now. African politics. Crooked politics, if you like. Nothing gets done in this country without that sort of politics. So my first considered medical opinion is that you should do a deal with the odious Chiribanda. Let him have a few acres of forest if he wants them.'

'Thanks. And your second piece of advice?'

'Play Chiribanda at his own game. Either find the witch-doctor who put the hex on Marie and buy him off; or find another one and do the same by Chiribanda, or to his near and dear ones.'

'You don't believe. . .?'

'Ah, we aren't talking about your or my beliefs but about Chiribanda's. Since he obviously believed he could do this to Marie he must be vulnerable to the same sort of suggestion himself.'

Jean-Pierre shrugged. 'It's ridiculous. Even if there were

189

any sense in it, I wouldn't know how to find the right man.'

Veniard was on his third large Pernod. 'My own medical acquaintance in this district is a large and catholic one. Chiribanda has a twenty-one-year-old son of whom he is very proud. I know, because I attended the boy after a minor accident when driving a tractor. There, you have my advice.'

'And your fee?'

'Ask me when I have applied the treatment. Meantime, try to keep that drip-feed going but if it comes away I wouldn't worry too much.'

After Veniard had left, Jean-Pierre finished what remained of the Pernod. By then he was in no state to tell whether the doctor had been serious, joking or just drunk. With the cynical Veniard it was often hard to say.

Life turned the story down. They felt there weren't enough other pictures to back it up. Redfern returned to the west coast but a week later Nancy's agent phoned to say *Paris-Match* wanted to run the Intruder's picture on the cover as soon as possible and use Menant's story, with Nancy's earlier pictures, inside. They would tie the cover up with a piece they were about to run on the launching of Ark International — provided the Misoka gorillas became Ark's first adopted project.

For the present, Chiribanda's bulldozers felled no more trees. Nor did cattle invade the forest. On the surface, it looked as though Jean-Pierre Menant had won. Marie Maputa, however, was still slowly sliding downhill. Most of the time she accepted the drip-feed as she accepted everything else around her, without being aware of it. Occasionally Jean-Pierre found the tube detached from the needle in her arm. He was certain this was not a deliberate action on her part. She did not have the will to perform anything so positive. It was just that a movement of her body, and even slight movements were rare, had dislodged the apparatus. Veniard visited her each day, drank some Pernod, shook his head and went away.

When she had lain inert at the house for five days, Mushi arrived with a message that Hepzibah and Toto were back in the vicinity of the Saddle.

Jean-Pierre had to get back to the forest. Even his reserves of self-sufficiency were running low. But Marie could not be left. No African would risk close contact with her in order to look after her. Once again, Veniard came to his rescue by arranging for a young American Peace Corps nurse to visit her three times a day.

Jean-Pierre left for the forest at once, feeling guilty but released from an overwhelming burden. Directly he and Mushi started to climb through the trees the sense of oppression fell away. They reached the hut on the Saddle in four hours. Jean-Pierre was pleased and surprised to find that Loti and Musharamena were alert and had kept the place clean and in good order. The pygmy reported that he had seen Hepzibah and Toto the previous afternoon. They were about two hours' march away on the upper slopes of Misoka, on the edge of the hagenia woodlands, in bad country streaked by the razor-backs of recent lava floes.

Since it was mid-afternoon, Jean-Pierre decided to make a start early next morning. He had brought no fresh meat with him so he took the rifle and went to look for forest hog. He hadn't hunted for a long time. The fact that he was about to do so inside his own newly-created national park troubled him not in the least. Game animals were a resource to be used wisely. The park's primary purpose was to protect gorillas, not so much other animals which were not only in no danger but in plentiful supply. There were no tourists to be disturbed or outraged by the sound of a shot. He smiled to himself at the mere thought of tourists following the path he and Mushi had scaled to the Saddle. He hoped there never would be tourists here and yet his intellect accepted the contradiction. National parks were for tourists and their purpose was largely to attract tourist revenue. Maybe one day the tourists would come to see his gorillas. He shuddered at the idea of his private paradise being invaded. Well, if they came, they'd have to come on their two flat feet. There'd be no zebra-striped minibuses up here.

He crossed the Saddle meadow until he reached the upward gradient of Vahinga. Then he climbed away southwards. Because it had been extinct for a long time, or anyway dormant, the mountain was much softer scenically than Misoka. Strangely enough the gorillas did not appear to use it as much as they did its twin, the active peak. Possibly the vegetation did not suit them quite so well. It was certainly not so varied.

As so often, Jean-Pierre felt the inadequacy of his own knowledge. He was no scientist. He thought for the first time for some weeks of Helen Lawes. The last time he had hunted forest hog had been to provide meat for her, a few weeks before the *Fisi* came in the night. If the park was to succeed in becoming a true gorilla sanctuary, if it was allowed to succeed, it would need a resident scientist, preferably a scientific unit with visiting students. This gave him a jolt, as the thought of visiting tourists had done. He had heard from friends in East Africa what happened once a park became established. The hoteliers moved in. The wardens became glorified guides, their lives taken up with quarter-mastering and para-military administration. The day that Misoka–Vahinga looked like going that way, he was finished with it. He hadn't given up his own lands for that. But what if such a course proved the only way to protect the gorilla population?

He angled away round a buttress of Vahinga. Almost at once he noticed that a group of gorillas had passed this way within the past twenty-four hours, their tracks heading towards the cloud-covered peak. All very well, he reflected, to say that the apes didn't patronise Vahinga very extensively but was this really true? No one knew the answer. Least of all himself. He had a superficial knowledge of some of the groups whose home-range appeared to be on the part of Vahinga that lay within the park. But the mountain was vast. The far side was heavily forested and uninhabited except possibly for pygmies. Helen had always believed that there

192

were more gorillas than anyone knew, or even suspected, on Vahinga. A scientific survey would have to be carried out before anyone could make a half-way accurate estimate. If the apes were present in numbers, then would be the time to consider trying to get the area of the park enlarged. The prospect of this seemed absolutely nil when one considered that at present it was impossible to secure the existing limited frontiers against poachers and crooks like Chiribanda.

Giant forest hog were shy and difficult creatures to come up with even when one knew their haunts and habits intimately. On Vahinga they were remarkably conservative. One narrow valley, filled with low scrub, had always been a particular favourite of theirs and his. Even at the height of the dry season a trickle of water ran down it. Where this stream levelled out lay a small, boggy pool, half the size of a tennis court. Many animals came to drink there, forest hogs included. The place was so secret and secluded that they sometimes did not wait for evening but ventured to drink during the heat of the late afternoon.

As he approached the pool he stopped to feel the wind on his face. This afternoon the walls of the valley effectively shut off any breeze, at least any breeze detectable to a man. He took from his bush-jacket the small linen bag, the size of an apple, that he carried when hunting. The fine linen was filled with even finer wood-ash. He held the bag clear of his body and shook it. A light-grey cloud dispersed, hung hesitantly on the air and then slowly started to drift away from the water one hundred yards distant. He made the test twice more to make sure that the breeze was consistent. Closer to the pool he examined the soft ground. Hog had been there as recently as this morning, a whole family with piglets. They'd be coming again for a drink before nightfall. If they didn't the chances were that something else edible would. The almost undetectable breeze was still steady. He climbed up on to a lava pile and sat down to wait, screened by some tall grass.

There was no cover from the sun and the sharp pumice cut

into his backside. It was mortification of the flesh in the extreme, yet in a strange, masochistic way he enjoyed it. A branch cracked. At once his senses became concentrated in his eyes and ears. For five minutes nothing moved. Then he caught it, the sound of subdued grunting. The hogs were somewhere close by. Ten minutes passed during which the unrelieved pressure of his body on the lava cut him through the seat of his khaki slacks and sweat dripped from the end of his nose. The bushes on the far side of the pool parted a few inches. He could see the wet snout and one glinting piggy eye of a monstrous shaggy sow. He did not want her. She'd be far too big for him to carry home more than a fraction of the meat. She'd probably be as tough as a pigskin boot into the bargain. Most important, if he had judged things correctly, she almost certainly had a family of young with her. That was why she was being ultra cautious. She grunted again. This time Jean-Pierre grunted back. Her head cocked and the snout emerged a little further. Behind her he could now glimpse movement, the impatient milling of the young. He called her again. This time she brought half her immense bulk into the open and stood with ears pricked and snout twitching.

No matter how many times he saw them, he never quite got used to the appearance of giant forest hog. To a warthog or even a large European wild boar they compared as a mammoth to an elephant. The hair-covered sow had decided it was all right. She trotted confidently out to the muddy edge of the pool. Behind her came a jostling convoy of six large piglets. Jean-Pierre could have shot any one of them. He held his fire for two reasons. He wanted to watch them to see how they behaved at the water-hole. The opportunity to observe forest hog was fairly rare. Also, he wanted, if possible, to pick out a young male.

The family lined up alongside the mother, two on one side, four on the other. They started to drink at once. For young animals they were unusually cautious, lifting their heads from time to time to listen. The sow paused continually in her drinking. Maybe she was worried about that other unidentified grunt, the one Jean-Pierre had given. Amused, he grunted again just to see what would happen. What happened was an instant explosion of pigs throwing up snouts in a cascade of muddy droplets, pigs kicking up clods of mud and pigs spurting dust as they accelerated for cover. The sow and the two piglets on her right flank had crashed back into the scrub almost before he could react. Two of the other group escaped through some reeds. The last two collided flank to flank. He shot at the one that sprawled, knocked off balance, proving once more, as if proving were necessary, that the predator picks out the least efficient, the least apparently fitted to survive. The bullet took it through the neck, smashing the spinal column. A turaco screamed in answer to the shot.

He bathed his face, dipping his entire head beneath the surface where the stream trickled clear into the top of the pool. Then he cleaned the pig, noting with pleasure that it was, after all, a young boar. He slit it neatly from rib-cage to genitals with his hunting knife. He spilled out the spiral ribbons of intestines in which the reflexes of digestion still twitched the little boar's last meal of roots and grass along a conveyor belt, whose end-product, energy, would no longer be needed by the owner. Instead, the pig would become a source of energy for himself and the pygmies. It was all of a piece. Well-meaning people who decried hunting came nowhere near to understanding this. Even the pig's guts would find a place in the energy equation. He cut them loose, nicking round the genitals and pulling them free, laying the steaming, odorous result on the ground. He knew that he would not have left the waterside more than a few minutes before a white-necked raven, a lizard, a foraging party of red forest ants, would have found the remains and begun to make use of them. Within an hour barely the stain would be left on the ground. He pierced a tendon on one front and one rear leg, sticking the lower joint of the opposite legs through the slit. He slid the carcase, back first, into the empty rucksack he had brought with him for the meat. Emptied of stomach contents, it folded compactly, just the four feet, now bunched together, sticking out. When he had washed knife and hands he started back the way he had come. All tension had fallen away. The forest was heavy with perfume, like a woman evening-scented for love. The forest had no need to make a special overture on his behalf. He was permanently in love with it and never more than at this hour of promise.

The sun was well down behind Vahinga when he at last reached the Saddle. Far away, across the meadow, a red light flickered. The Africans had already lit a fire, anticipating that he would bring meat. He was more content at that moment than for a long time past. Looking towards the hut he half expected to see a Tilley lamp swinging as a signal. The Africans, even Loti, would not bother to light a lamp. He was thinking of Helen again. A few letters had come after she returned to the States and then nothing. The mountain chill struck him now that the sun had gone. He longed to reach the warmth of the fire or perhaps the warmth of the hut and what it had once meant. For the first time for months he recalled the agony of that last night and the sadism of the tall, thin *Fisi*.

Loti and the pygmies were ecstatic when they saw the bunched feet of the young forest hog sticking out of his rucksack. He told them to cut off two legs and roast them over the fire. The rest of the meat could be dried and salted down in the morning.

When they had eaten the juice-oozing, dark, thick-fibred meat, they turned in. At first he had thought of sleeping in the hut but the hut was, in his present mood, too easily peopled with Helen. So he dragged his sleeping-bag out by the fire and, watching the flames, fell asleep. It was a troubled sleep and he woke once out of a dream in which another fire lit the clearing, the fire the *Fisi* had made four years before.

The cold woke him just before sun-up. The sky already had that pale, watered-down look that meant the sun was shouldering its way up towards the rim of the earth. Misoka's

196

false peak delayed the sun's entrance upon the scene. The milkiness of the light told him that Misoka's summit was well covered in cloud. In a few seconds the base of that cloud would be dyed flamingo pink. He had no need to look at his watch. Many nights of sleeping out on the mountain told him it was half-past-six.

He rose and stirred the ashes of the fire with a stick. Sparks flew from a half-burned branch. He gathered some dried grass, laid it over the smouldering wood and blew steadily. The fire had retreated inside the heavy rain-forest timber to die. His breath was the kiss of life, reviving the fire, bringing it back cherry-red and glowing.

Soon a small flame appeared, leaping to engulf the grass. Mushi materialised, grinning happily, his tiny arms loaded with dried sticks. Jean-Pierre hung the kettle in the smoke. He fetched a loaf of bread made from maize flour and cut the remains of the cold, roasted leg of hog into four. His own piece he laid between slices of the coarse native bread. Mushi crammed his share wholesale into his mouth and, when he found he couldn't swallow it all, took his panga and cut it off short just beyond his lips and nose. When the water was boiled Jean-Pierre made himself a strong mugful of instant coffee. The flamingo light had gone. In its place a solution of gold had been poured over the clouds. No man, he felt, had the right to enjoy such a breakfast in such company in such a place. This was for the gods.

Mushi performed a gluttonous eating mime. Jean-Pierre shook his head severely. 'Leaving in three minutes,' he said.

Hepzibah was lost. At first she had felt confident that she was heading in a direction which would shortly enclose her in the security of a gorilla group. The attachment of the infant Toto was a constant distraction. When the couple hit a bad area of recent lava interspersed with low scrub she became increasingly uneasy and less tolerant of her baby's demands on her.

About the time Jean-Pierre started back to the hut with

197

the dead forest hog, she made a ground nest, with Toto beside her, among some bushes on top of a mound of weathered lava. She rose next morning to the sound of the baby crying. Two hours' journey away, Jean-Pierre and Mushi were eating forest hog for breakfast.

Hepzibah knew from its whining cry that the baby was hungry. She could not help that. Her main concern was to move out of the lava zone as quickly as possible. The place was foreign to her and made her feel thoroughly insecure. She set off downhill at a fast pace which did not allow for the fact that the infant found many of the lava fissures far more difficult to cross than she did.

Hepzibah could now smell the herbal scent of the richer feeding area ahead. Impelled by the belief that she was nearly out of the wood, or, rather, nearly *into* it, and that the baby would soon catch up with her, she doubled her speed.

Toto was, by now, in a panic. She could hear the sounds of her mother's slipping and slithering progress far ahead. The deep crevasse in the lava looked no wider or deeper than any she had crossed so far. The shadow of a bush deceptively concealed the true width of the chasm. The baby never even considered the depth. It leapt, falling short by two feet. It fell and fell, coming to rest eight feet down at the bottom of a deep, V-shaped cleft. At first, it lay there. Then it began to whimper and to try to extricate itself from the cutting apex in which it was jammed. When it did so, it screamed in pain, not so much from the multiple cuts and abrasions but because its right arm was broken at the elbow.

When the baby did not join her at the edge of the lava flow, Hepzibah waited anxiously. After a time she began to search, barking and screaming. Toto heard her once and cried in answer. But the walls of lava swallowed its cry. After two hours during which she became more and more desperate, Hepzibah gave up the search. All she wanted now was a feeling of security. She pushed on alone, faster and faster, knowing that her home-range once again lay ahead.

*

Mushi led the way round the top of the lava area. He found the old nest-site easily. The signs indicated that the two animals had headed onwards into the centre of the lava. Mushi tried to track them. At first he was lucky. He found one or two stale droppings. But the hard, gritty surface of the lava offered little help. Vegetation was too sparse to provide the usual clues in the form of broken twigs and branches. Jean-Pierre stopped him after the first hundred yards and pointed down the slope. Mushi nodded with pleasure. He'd had more than enough of the lava. He never put laces in his boots, which were several sizes too big. The crumbly pumice was already powdering into them. Soon he'd have to take them off and track in bare feet, as he sometimes did in the forest. Even Mushi's hardened feet were not looking forward to close contact with that lava.

They back-tracked to the point at which they had entered the flow. There they headed downhill on good ground until they reached the bottom edge of the lava. Jean-Pierre's plan now was to follow the margin of the floe until they found the point at which the two gorillas had emerged. This should have proved relatively easy, provided the animals weren't still in the lava-field itself. This seemed against all the odds of normal gorilla behaviour. When they reached the place at which the lava thinned out and the trees began, Mushi stopped and pointed at the ground. Barely detectable in a soft patch were the impressions of four large toes. Like a hound on the scent, Mushi hit a line and took off. Within forty yards he triumphantly held up a stripped vine and then some fresh droppings. The little man looked puzzled. He held up *one*.

Jean-Pierre had come to the same conclusion. The signs were those of a single adult. Only one gorilla had emerged from the lava. The baby was missing. Had the poachers returned? Perhaps a leopard had its lair in one of the volcanic overhangs. It was just the sort of place. There was only one way to find out; to retrace the path by which the single female had left the lava. One encouraging sign: there were no ravens or vultures in the air. But then, if the baby had been killed the tiny carcase wouldn't keep the smallest pack of scavengers happy for very long.

They moved slowly, Mushi in the lead. Seldom did the little man seem seriously in doubt. Jean-Pierre's fieldcraft was good but he knew that he would have made little sense of this problem. Mushi paused once or twice to point out recently dislodged pumice, where Hepzibah had slid on the shaly surface. Jean-Pierre had almost ceased to believe that Mushi knew where he was going when he himself spotted a leaf unmistakably torn by gorilla's teeth. They had gone two hundred yards into this horrible country when Mushi stopped. Ten yards away a small branch had been snapped from its parent bush, as if someone had grabbed at it. Mushi cocked his head on one side. Jean-Pierre heard it too, a faint whimpering. But for the broken branch they might easily have passed by. Mushi climbed a ridge and stood looking down, grinning widely.

The little gorilla lay in a huddle at the bottom of a steep-sided, narrow fissure. It lay, apparently trapped, feeble and exhausted. Nothing moved except the moist black grapes that were its eyes. When Jean-Pierre climbed down into the dark, sulphur-smelling crack the baby tried to draw away in terror and bared its teeth in a pathetic attempt at ferocity. Jean-Pierre covered it with his open rucksack and, while it was momentarily quietened by the darkness, slid his hands beneath its body, freeing it and shovelling it upwards into the rucksack. It was when his hands touched the arm beneath the trapped body that he felt the bone broken below the elbow. There was nothing to be done now about that. He turned the rucksack upright, pulling the drawstrings tight. For several seconds the baby inside used its depleted strength to fight, then it gave up. He made sure there was enough space at the top of the rucksack for air to circulate and handed the bag up to Mushi. Then they set out to reach the hut as quickly as possible.

He recalled that Helen had kept a well-stocked first-aid kit.

200

That had been nearly four years ago. Perhaps the *Fisi* had smashed and looted it that night. It was equally likely that Loti or one of the trackers had sampled its contents, either for pleasure or in pain. Mushi was always hacking the leprous tips off his fingers and there was nothing he liked more than the status that a bandage gave him.

Jean-Pierre was in luck. He found the first-aid box under a pile of old blankets. Even more incredible, its contents were virtually untouched. His problem was to take some action that would immobilise the baby's arm before it died of shock.

He closed the door of the living-room and eased the baby out of the haversack. At first it lay there but, when he tried to touch the arm, the little gorilla thrashed about wildly. Jean-Pierre looked at the morphia and syringe in the first-aid kit. How much morphia did one give a baby gorilla without killing it? He knew how much to give a wounded man, but that didn't help very much. Mushi came in from the verandah grinning happily. He carried some wild banana leaves and a banana-tree stem split so that the moist pith showed. The baby regarded these with interest. Mushi scooped out some of the pulp and held it out on the handle of his panga. The baby licked with his tongue and then, with its undamaged arm, covered his fingers with the pith and sucked them. Mushi's eyes shone and darted like Toto's. Not for the first time, Jean-Pierre found himself making the obvious comparison. Where baby gorillas were concerned, Mushi was a natural nurse.

The infant must have been badly dehydrated after lying in that stifling crevasse. She scooped up banana pith greedily though she seemed disinclined to eat the leaves. It was then that Jean-Pierre found the small bottle of chloroform at the bottom of the box. There was also a crêpe bandage and a splint. He cut and divided the splint until he had two sections to fit the baby's forearm.

Mushi had less to lose in the way of bitten fingertips than either Loti or himself. He told the little man to hold the baby down by the shoulders. Then he poured some chloroform on to a pad of lint and dabbed it quickly over the gorilla's face. At first the baby struggled, using its feet as an extra pair of hands. Mushi clung on gallantly and, gradually, the infant relaxed. Jean-Pierre held the pad in position a second or two longer. He felt the parted bones delicately with his fingers, laying them together in what seemed a natural way. He laid the shortened splints on either side of the break and bound the crêpe bandage around them as tightly as he dared. The baby was still unconscious. Had he given it an overdose of chloroform? There was nothing to be done now. He placed the tiny creature on the safari bed and closed the door. Loti was watching curiously through the window.

'Make a boma,' he told him. 'The wired-in enclosure where you keep the paraffin will do. Get a big crate. That tea-chest. Saw open the front and fill it with leaves like a real gorilla's nest. Just for the night. Tomorrow I'll take the baby down the mountain so that we can get some proper attention for that broken arm.'

The novelty of the situation appealed to Loti's sense of the dramatic and he began to help Jean-Pierre with an enthusiasm that was as touching as it was often misguided. At last they had everything ready for the injured infant's overnight stay. Jean-Pierre went back into the hut to fetch an unconscious baby. Toto was no longer the only one under the influence of chloroform. Mushi, always a slave to his senses, had been greatly attracted by the smell of the anaesthetic. After Jean-Pierre had left the hut, he had sniffed a good deal of it himself — straight from the bottle. Now he lay snoring and unconscious on the floor. On the bed Toto was just beginning to come round. Mushi was dead to the world, fortunately unaware of the splitting headache that lay ahead when he awoke.

Paris-Match did not waste any time. The Intruder's picture appeared on the cover just before the Easter week-end with the title 'Le Crucifixion d'un Gorille'. There were a few who

202

found the caption offensive. Nancy Genova was not among them. Nor was Dr John Redfern. She had already announced in the article that she had asked *Match* to give her fee to Ark International. Within three days a French aircraft firm, known to be worried about its image as polluters of the international air, had contacted John Redfern in California and offered him 20,000 dollars a year to be devoted to the protection of gorillas in Misoka Park. Other, smaller, bequests were already rolling in as the result of the canvassing Redfern had done during his last European tour. Redfern phoned Walther Werz, the smooth young German he had appointed as Ark's European organiser, and told him the glad news that he could now assume that his salary would be paid. This had never been in doubt. Redfern had long ago conned his university into making a grant to cover Werz. Nancy Genova's literary agent called her to say that the picture and piece were being widely syndicated and that in Italy *Oggi* wanted her to write an article attacking the Italians as the least conservation-minded people in Europe. All Nancy knew at that moment was that they had one alpine national park and ate thrushes. She agreed to leave for Rome, expenses paid, at once. She called Redfern back and told him.

'Why don't you come and work for me full time?'

'I'm probably doing more good the way I am. Independent. Anyway, aren't I pretty well full-time?'

Redfern laughed. 'I've got a new idea for Ark's logo. A dove flying in carrying a one-thousand-dollar bill.'

'Now I know why you're so unpopular with all those stuff-shirt professors. You're such a cynic — and commercial with it. *Ciao.*'

'*Arrivederci Roma.*'

When she had rung off, Redfern picked up the receiver again and dialled Tufts University. He knew just the biologist he wanted for Misoka National Park.

Toto rode down the mountain in style, carried in a kind of litter formed of a tea-chest with chicken mesh stapled across the open top. Loti had wired a long bamboo to each side. Jean-Pierre carried the forward ends of these, Loti brought up the rear. The infant seemed completely to have accepted the fact that her arm was immobilised. Curled up on a bed of grass inside the box, she moved around very little. Possibly this was due to the fact that Mushi had secretly sprinkled some of his best home-grown pot on to her food plants. He had not thought it politic to tell Jean-Pierre of this simple though drastic medication. Mushi had not even considered the possible effect on the baby's digestive system or brain. He had simply asked himself how he might have felt in similar circumstances and, having got an answer from himself, had acted accordingly. In the event, the infant swallowed little of the dose. Shock accounted for its docility more than anything else. Toto was asleep when the jeep finally drew up in front of Jean-Pierre's office in Baruva.

The sense of freedom and elation which he had experienced during the last two days dispersed in direct proportion to the rate at which he descended the mountain. By the time he reached the jeep it was at zero. On the short drive into Baruva his temperamental mercury measured a minus quantity. Marie was increasingly on his mind. He was surprised and relieved to see Jacques Veniard's car outside the national park office. He had been dreading walking into that house on his own, seeing that sightless, mindless, living corpse, or perhaps finding a corpse in fact. He shrank from smelling the staleness and human dirt. Who knew whether the Peace Corps nurse had attended or how often. Jean-Pierre had felt guilty when he left for the mountain. Now he experienced double guilt. He knew that he'd hoped that it would be all over with Marie by the time he returned. He who had seen death so many times was not willing or able to face this death. Marie's bewitched state was nothing he could alter or affect in any way. But was even that true? He could have gone to Chiribanda, as the doctor had suggested, and bartered with him. A few acres of trees for a life. Veniard's car at least meant that he didn't have to face it alone.

The office exuded a hospital tang of disinfectant. Veniard called out.

'Hullo. Who is it? Oh, it's you. The boy from the backwoods.'

'How is she?'

'Alive.'

'Coming out of it?'

'I didn't say that. What I do say is that you owe me two goats. Chiribanda's beloved eldest son cut himself badly with a mechanical saw when felling some of your precious trees the day before yesterday.'

'Serve him bloody well right.'

'At two goats, such an accident is ridiculously cheap. My dusky medical colleague likes payment on results. I've already given the old bastard one goat on account. I didn't specify what sort of accident I wanted, just said something I could treat and cure, if necessary. But I forgot. You don't believe in such things. You're such a realist.'

Jean-Pierre pointed at Marie. The flesh had fallen away round the eyes and cheek-bones. The skin that had once had the high gloss of a well-handled wood-carving was a dirty grey.

'I have to believe in *that*.'

'Yes. Chiribanda has sent for me again. The first call reached my surgery yesterday. I didn't go. He sent a messenger today. The envelope contained a father's appeal to save his favourite son's life — and quite a lot of money in notes.'

'And?'

'I sent the cash back. My fee is to be paid in kind. I think Chiribanda's getting the message.'

'You'll let the boy die?'

'He's not got to that point yet. A heavy course of antibiotics could fix him up quickly.'

'To hell with young Chiribanda. What about Marie?'

'A heavy dose from the same kind of doctor who caused her present state could still fix her up, too, but we're getting close to a point of no return now. See if there's a cold beer left in the fridge, there's a good lad. It's very dusty on the track leading up to Chiribanda's place.'

On the way out the doctor passed Loti carrying the bandaged and splinted baby gorilla to an improvised cage in the yard.

'I suppose I'm expected to attend to that as well,' he said. 'This is one hell of a practice I've got.'

Jean-Pierre put up a camp-bed in the office. He couldn't face sharing his own bed with a zombie. But he got up in the night to look at her. He did not know what he expected to find, an improvement perhaps. He had trouble detecting her breathing even when he held a mirror to her lips. Her pulse was so feeble that he thought at first her heart had stopped altogether. He wet her lips. Drip-feeds had long ago been given up as a bad job. The American nurse had promised to look in during the morning. Knowing this, he shrank from cleaning her and was ashamed of his reaction.

It was daylight and one of the few times in his life he had overslept. Someone was banging on the street door. At first he thought it was the nurse. Then he heard the doctor's voice.

'Open up. I've come to look at the patient.'

'She's the same. No change at all. She's sliding away fast.'

'Not her. I've come to see the one with the broken arm.'

'What about Marie?'

'I'll tell you what to do with her in a moment. Wake your ideas up. I haven't got all day.'

Toto regarded the doctor with friendly curiosity.

'Age?'

'A few months.'

'Sex?'

'Female. Good God, Jacques, what is all this rigmarole?'

The doctor continued his examination. 'Any previous illnesses?'

'How the hell should I know?'

'You should know enough about doctors by now to realise

that all this talk is supposed to calm the patient. In this case, it seems to be you who needs calming.'

Veniard had by now removed the bandages and splint. He felt the break. 'Not too bad a job for an amateur. I could leave it, but the arm would probably be fairly stiff and useless when it mended. What do you aim to do with her?'

'Do? Return her to the wild some day, of course.'

'So. She'll need all her faculties to survive, then? That joint needs resetting and pinning. Since she's a minor, I'll need the parent or guardian's permission to operate. Which are you, by the way?'

For the first time that morning Jean-Pierre smiled. 'Mushi says I'm the father.'

'Hm. Wouldn't surprise me. All those nights up there in the forest. A lusty young chap like you, hob-nobbing with apes all the time. What you see in the beastly creatures beats me.'

Veniard had slipped a hypodermic needle neatly into the little gorilla's backside while he was speaking. Toto yelped and struggled for a second but Veniard had given many African children, who found the needle strange and terrifying, their shots in exactly the same way. He pressed firmly in the small of the baby's back for a few seconds, the time it took for the drug to take effect. Jean-Pierre watched the long, nicotine-stained fingers exploring the nature of the fracture and then decisively parting the bones in order to reunite them correctly.

It was an hour before the pin was finally in place and the arm encased in a plaster cast. The baby snored throughout.

'She'll come round in about an hour. Nothing we can do now. Pity we haven't got an infra-red lamp but it's not exactly chilly here. Give her warm bedding and keep her out of draughts. Now, about the other patient. She's got to be moved.'

So absorbed had he been in watching Veniard's operation on the baby gorilla that he had almost forgotten Marie.

'Moved? Where? There's no hospital worth talking about for miles.'

'I wasn't talking about hospital. She's got to be moved back to the hut where you found her. To her own people.'

'They won't do anything for her.'

'They will now. They'll understand things have changed where she's concerned.'

'She'll recover?'

'It's the one chance she's got. I'd put it at least as high as young Chiribanda's chances. That arm really was a mess. Blood-poisoning setting in. I practically used up my supply of penicillin. By the way, when *he* recovers you've got to do something for the Chiribanda clan. It's part of the bargain.'

'I can't be held to anything like that, Jacques.'

'No? Well, let's get on with it. Put the girl in your jeep and take her back to the hut where you found her.'

'What do I do then?'

'Just leave her there. It's all you can do.'

The cable from Redfern came three days later.

'Delighted to tell you Misoka Park first fully adopted Ark International project stop Funds raised largely result publication your picture of dead gorilla enable Ark make grants sufficient pay six rangers and establish research programme you urgently require stop Have approval central government send you highly qualified gorilla biologist stop Details and date of arrival follow Redfern.'

Jean-Pierre sat down in the office and stared at the cable for fully two minutes. His immediate reaction was that the help he badly needed was on the way. Beneath this was a nagging unease, the sensation he often got when there was something troublesome and hard to isolate in an apparently satisfactory situation. It was like biting on something generally appetising in whose complex flavour there was an element of bitterness that could not at once be identified. He ought to be pleased. The cable promised him much of what he wanted: money and assistance. Was it the unknown personality of the biologist whom Redfern had selected that troubled him? Only in part. Jean-Pierre needed the man's brains and talents if the gorillas were to survive. He could cope with almost any personality difference and, anyway, he didn't have to live on top of the fellow. The factor that disturbed him went deeper than that. The truth was that he sensed that things would never be quite the same again. Misoka—Vahinga Park would cease to be entirely his private world. He could see ahead into a time of tourists and lodges and he did not care for the picture one little bit. He told himself sternly that whether he liked such a development or not was largely immaterial if it was clear that putting the park on the map, even eventually making it a tourist attraction, was the only realistic way of protecting the gorillas' habitat.

He went into the yard and inspected the baby gorilla for the tenth time that morning. Toto had completely recovered from her operation. After some experimental gnawings at the strange white growth that encased her arm, she had decided that plaster wasn't edible and had resigned herself to the fact that she had a limb which, if it no longer pained her, was totally useless for all normal gorilla purposes. The plaster was grubby and chipped but so far intact. Veniard called in each evening on his way back to his bungalow by the lake. He referred to the baby gorilla as his favourite patient and appeared even more besotted with her than was Jean-Pierre, letting the small creature climb all over him and cling to him like a large, friendly, black spider.

On the second visit Jean-Pierre asked what he should do about Marie Maputa.

Veniard said, 'I'll probably have to put some more plaster on in a day or two.'

'I was asking about Marie.'

'Oh, so you were. Well there's absolutely nothing to be done, of that I assure you.'

'Shouldn't I visit her?'

'That would be the worst thing you could do.'

'She may be dying.'

'If she is, do you think you could save her? It's out of your hands — and mine.'

'You're supposed to be a modern doctor.'

'Perhaps you haven't noticed that where medicine is concerned I have my primitive side. With some primitives whom I know, it's different. A few even prefer gorillas to humans.'

Veniard prised the fingers of Toto's good hand loose from the lobe of his left ear. 'I'm not sure that I don't myself. As for you, why all this sudden devotion to a member of the human race? Can it be a sign that Menant, man-of-action, gorilla-lover and ice-cold killer of *Fisi* and bulldozers, is thinking of including humans in his personal cosmos?'

'Marie has been very good to me. She supplied everything I wanted.'

'Oh, I see. It isn't affection or anything effete like that, just loyalty to a good comrade.'

'Shut up, Jacques. I'm not in the mood for your more acidulous pleasantries.'

There was nothing he could usefully do in the house or office. If Redfern did send a biologist immediately, the fellow would need somewhere to live. It hurt him to think of it. Helen had been the last scientist to occupy the place, but the hut on the Saddle was the natural and obvious base for any field worker. He decided to climb up there once more to see that the hut was inhabitable and to issue directions for stocking and supplying it. Toto was in good enough shape to be left for forty-eight hours. Loti could feed the baby and the doctor would be round as usual. He could bet on that. Lack of news of any sort about Marie had further depressed him. As always, he needed the calm of the forest.

Hepzibah had been travelling confusedly ever since she lost the baby nearly a week previously. She was already dis-oriented when she emerged from the lava floe. She had not consciously made an effort to find the baby. However, the tug of maternalism was sufficiently strong to make her feel that something had gone out of her day-to-day existence. Possibly, too, it was a sense of loneliness that made her wander aimlessly in circles in the same general area for nearly three whole days. The gravitational fields that governed her life eventually established their own balance. The orbit of her vague searchings became elliptical, the ellipse constantly extending in the direction of her home-range. As the pull of the missing infant weakened, so the pull of her vanished family and their home territory increasingly exerted itself. On the day Jean-Pierre and Mushi climbed to the hut she had, without being aware of it, forgotten about the infant. She was going home once more. Mushi picked up her tracks and fresh droppings close to the topmost edge of the hagenia forest. Her path had crossed theirs an hour or two previously.

'Could be a lone male but the tracks look too small,' Jean-Pierre said.

'Female who lost baby,' Mushi pronounced.

'Maybe.'

'I tell you for certain. Mother of your child.' The pygmy fell apart laughing at his own joke, his face wrinkled with glee like some fiendish little black Pan.

Jean-Pierre wanted nothing more than to follow the tracks, to discover if Hepzibah had found her family and was accepted by them. He discovered with a shock that he knew nothing about the present composition of Absolom's group, or of any other group for that matter. Since the setting up of the park his days had been filled with drilling Loti, Ndungu, Marema and Jahazi and with putting up notice-boards, sitting in an office, fighting Chiribanda, worrying about Marie. He had even acquired a tame gorilla, or, anyway, one well on the way towards becoming tame. He was following the classic pattern of all park wardens he had ever heard about. Meantime, the real job, the study and protection of the very animals the park had been set up to protect, wasn't getting done. It was time he had a full-time biologist, and a deputy if he could find one, who would allow him to get back into the forest himself.

The hut came into sight across the Saddle. He no longer felt such a pang at the thought of it being occupied again. It was high time.

When he got down to Baruva two days later there was a cable lying on his office desk together with a note from Veniard.

'Shan't be in for a couple of nights. Some idiot thinks they've got a case of cholera up the lake. The young invalid is doing fine. Chiribanda junior will live, you will be glad to hear. By the way, the captain of the DC3 that came in yesterday brought this cable. Looks as though things are working out for you.'

Veniard had opened the cable in case it was urgent. If not exactly urgent, the news it brought was immediate. 'Biologist you requested arriving next internal flight due 2 May all formalities for three year stay cleared Redfern'

Tomorrow was 2 May.

The weekly internal flight was due in at 9 a.m. The airline scheduled its arrival early because the pilots hoped to fly out early. There were always unscheduled delays on the ground. Cloud built up viciously around the peaks shortly after mid-day. If they came in at nine there was at least some chance of getting out by eleven. In fact, the whole scheduling exercise was relatively academic. More often than not, the DC3 did not come on the right day, let alone at the right time. Sometimes it did not come at all. Nevertheless, the faithful went to meet it. Those with sufficient bribe money to guarantee them a seat often waited until they heard its distant hum as it flew up the lake. Then they drove flat out to the strip nine miles out of town and hoped that no one had meantime outbid them. Those who could not raise the top bribe money, or had to walk or catch the sporadic local bus — when it had not broken down — took the precaution of setting out at first light. A few anxious souls preferred to sleep in the insanitary tin hut that served as airport arrival

212

and departure hall.

When Jean-Pierre drove up at half-past-nine, a queue composed of the hopeful and the faithful had formed outside the hut in the already broiling sun. Some clutched their belongings. Most preferred to travel light. That way there was a better chance of escaping extortion at the hands of the two large airport officials who sold the tickets under the protection of an even larger airport policeman. He was doubtless getting his cut, too. There were no Europeans in the queue this morning, not that they could have expected preferential or even fairer treatment: quite the contrary. If the aircraft was full with on-going passengers, the usual system was to let those who already held tickets on board and then sell any remaining seats to the highest bidders. If there was plenty of room the 'authorities' confined themselves to levying an unofficial airport tax or charging absurd excess amounts for quite insignificant items of baggage. Since the airport staff was rarely paid, or anyway rarely paid in full, they simply saw this as an equitable method of making up the difference. The only way they could lose was if the aircraft did not come at all. This morning it looked as though they might be on a loser.

Jean-Pierre was just about to drive back to Baruva when, at eleven-forty-five, his ears caught the beat of engines. Either the pilot was trying to make up lost time by slipping in through the peaks, an unscheduled approach that was only possible before cloud built up, or this wasn't the DC3 at all. At last, Jean-Pierre detected a flash of blue and white against the shoulder of Vahinga. The DC3 was a dirty, oil-streaked silver marked with the hot orange and yellow colours of the republic.

Momentarily the plane had vanished behind a foothill. Then, when barely half-a-mile away, it revealed its deception to the disappointed assembly. A blue-and-white charter Aztec, it passed once over the strip at around six hundred feet, the pilot satisfying himself that there were no cows, petrol drums, antelope or other typical African bush strip impedimenta to render his touch-down hazardous. A mile out over the lake the plane banked, its raised wing a shark's fin slicing through the blue water of the sky. The pilot lined up, apparently high, putting his undercarriage down with the slow grace of a heron dropping its legs to alight. Jean-Pierre, who yearned to fly, marvelled at the steepness of the final approach that ended in the merest kiss between rubber and concrete. The Aztec shot past, the white-shirted figure of the pilot masking whoever it was who sat on his right in the front passenger's seat.

Jean-Pierre was down to earth also. The Aztec might not have brought his man but he could not imagine who else would have come by such an expensive form of travel. Ark International must learn to watch its money. His mouth felt dry and he told himself that he must be pleased he had got the help he had demanded. In saying hello to his colleague he knew that he was saying goodbye to a measure of freedom.

The little plane was bellowing as if in fury at being confined to the ground once more. The pilot opened one throttle to turn, threw open his side window panel to let some air into a cabin that was already absorbing the tarmac's heat. He taxied up to the apron, the propellers making no more fuss than large electric fans. Jean-Pierre still could not see the passenger's features through the plexiglass.

The pilot, a Dutchman whom he'd seen several times in the Président, stepped out on the wing with his documents, helping out the single passenger inside. From his attitude of professional gallantry, Jean-Pierre suddenly realised that the passenger was a woman. Were there perhaps other passengers? The Aztec could carry six.

There were two large, sweating African businessmen and a single, tall European. That must be the one. The whole group had now disappeared round the far side of the plane. When they came into view again Jean-Pierre saw that the tall European wore a crucifix. A Catholic priest. At last the pilot and the woman emerged from behind the tail. The pilot had waited to carry the lady's bags. Evidently Jean-Pierre's man

214

wasn't on the chartered Aztec. The woman took off her dark glasses for a moment and he saw that he was both right and wrong. His man hadn't come. Helen Lawes had.

He was so taken by surprise that for once he lost his famous cool, so much so that he almost pressed the starter with the idea of driving away, not really away, but far enough away to reorganise himself. She looked older, but four years multiplied by what she had been through does not exactly add up to a dip in the fountain of eternal youth. What a bastard Redfern had been not to warn him. But then, he had detected an element of mischief, of love of drama, in the old man, even in the brief time they had spent together.

By the time his hand had moved half-way towards the starter button he had regained control of himself. He let the hand continue on its course but, when the engine fired, he drove forward smoothly towards Helen. She saw him and waved.

'Jean-Pierre!'

He jumped down and kissed her hand. The face was as full of character as he remembered. But where it had once been like his own forest, wild, where flowers opened almost instantly and unexpectedly, it was now a garden, tended, disciplined, walled-in. The fragrance and beauty were there but it was organised and protected.

'How wonderful to see you, Jean-Pierre.'

'Well, I can see I've done all I can for the moment,' said the pilot. 'I get used to this sort of thing. You win one, you lose one. Mostly I lose them all.'

Helen squeezed his hand. 'You've been very kind and very sweet.'

It was like listening to any Californian hostess. What the hell did he expect, then?

'John Redfern didn't tell me it was you.'

'Didn't he?' She seemed genuinely surprised. 'What would you have said if you'd known?'

'I don't know,' he said quite truthfully. 'For one thing, I never imagined you'd want to come back to this part of

Africa.'

'Well, here I am, back.'

'What a marvellous surprise, Helen. I never dreamed. . . .'
Such polite conversation.

The pilot had gone to lodge his flight-plan in what passed
for a control tower. The heat and confinement of being
earth-bound were stupefying him. He wanted to be up and
away again.

'I'd forgotten how hot it could get.' More Californian
small-talk. Surely she couldn't have forgotten the heat?

'It'll be cool in the mountains.'

'Is that where you live and work?'

'No. The farm was burned down. I wrote to tell you.'

She didn't offer to explain why, after the first few months,
she had never written back.

'There are a couple of suitcases in the luggage compartment
of the plane.'

'O.K., let's find the pilot, then.'

The Dutchman had lodged his return flight-plan. He was
canvassing the waiting passengers, telling them the DC3
wouldn't be coming that day, cajoling them to pool their
resources and charter the Aztec. He was going back empty
anyway. Almost any offer would be acceptable. Two Indians
and an African tea-plantation manager argued the toss,
working out how much they could jointly afford to offer,
allowing for the bribe money they stood to lose on the
delinquent Dakota.

The pilot waved his hand at the arguing group. 'They'll
need a computer to work that one out. . . . Tell you what,' he
shouted at them, 'I'll take the lot of you for five hundred
U.S. dollars. . . . They'll do it. Sorry. Your bags. You two
know each other? Lucky fellow. All I get is fat ministers'
wives. The ministers are usually fat, too. Christ, I hope they
make their minds up soon. Bloody clouds are banking up. If I
have to fly round that lot I'll use five hundred dollars' worth
of fuel.' You could see he was loving every second of it.

'I've booked you in at the Président for a couple of nights

until you get sorted out.'

'So the hotel's still standing?'

'A few bullet-holes here and there, but they repaired most of the damage within a year of the end of the fighting. Pretty good going for these parts.'

They were rushing down the red dirt road between quinine and tea plantations. She shouted, 'I'd forgotten the smell. It's quite different from anywhere else on earth. Like snuff without the sneeze. Lovely!'

He smiled. She recalled that he seldom laughed outright. He had different depths of smile for different degrees of amusement. This smile meant real pleasure at her remark, far more pleasure than he would have shown to a stranger. She was not sure that she wanted to be treated other than as a stranger, for a time, anyway. Coming back was more of a shock to the system than she had supposed. To put the conversation back where she wanted it, she said, 'The place doesn't seem to have changed a great deal.'

'It's changing, all right. Faster than most of us want.'

They joined the lakeside road.

'Isn't that the track up to the plantation?'

'Yes. We're going into town first. I'll show you the Misoka Park office. It's not grand, but at least it puts us officially on the map. It's really part of my house.'

'You live in Baruva?'

'I have to have a base somewhere. I'm in the forest as much as I can manage. I imagine you'll want to go back and work on the Saddle. . . .' He had to make an effort to say this. 'I've had the hut all renovated and cleaned up. . . .' The sentence tailed away since he couldn't guess at her response.

'Of course,' she said. 'It's the ideal place.'

He stopped outside the office rather than drive round to the house entrance in the yard. He had a childish desire to impress her. Modest as the office was, it was a way of saying how things had altered. She took in the map on the wall, saying, 'Very impressive. So those are the boundaries!'

'Yes, but we have some local problems here.' He indicated

the Chiribanda plantations. 'And there's so much to be surveyed outside the park, land we ought to bring in once we've established there are gorillas living there. That's one of the first things I hope you're going to help us to do.'

'It's certainly *one* of the things,' she agreed. He noted that she was making clear that it was up to her to establish which were the scientific priorities.

'Come through and see the house. I'll get you a Fanta orange out of the fridge.' He remembered that this had been her favourite drink.

'I'd rather have a bitter lemon if you've got one.'

'Of course. Tastes change.' Quickly he added, 'When you've had a cool drink there's someone very special I want you to meet.' He was curious to see what Helen's reaction would be to Toto.

The moment he had said this he realised his remark was about to be misconstrued. There was a familiar floral tang in the kitchen. The smell had not been there when he left that morning. The first thing he saw was the Virgin and Child. It was back in its accustomed place, the statuette cleaned, its head temporarily stuck back on its shoulders with flour paste. Marie was standing by the bed, neatly folding the counterpane, just as if she had never been away. It was a thin, wasted Marie but her eyes were alive once again. She bowed to him.

'Marie, my dear. When did you come back? It's wonderful to see you. You look thin and so frail.' He took her hand and kissed it warmly.

Helen said, smiling, 'Is this who you wanted me to meet? Well, I can understand it. . . .'

'Marie, this is Dr Helen Lawes. She's a scientist. She's come to study the gorillas for us and to help the park.'

To Helen, who was holding out her hand politely, Jean-Pierre explained, 'Marie has been very ill. She's been away with her people while she recovered. I'll tell you all about it later. It's a wonderful surprise to see her back. In fact, it's a day of wonderful surprises. Marie, you must not work too

218

hard. You oughtn't to be working at all. Sit in the sun.' He was amazed to hear himself gabbling on. 'I must just show Dr Lawes round, then you must tell me everything.'

Marie said, 'There is nothing to tell, Jean-Pierre. I have been away on a long journey. Now I have returned.'

Jean-Pierre said, 'I want to show Dr Lawes our new house guest. Have you met her, by the way, Marie?'

'Yes, Mushi showed me.'

'What do you think of her?'

'I like her very much.'

'I'm glad, because you're going to have to help educate her.'

'You must show Dr Lawes.'

'Of course. Come on, Helen.'

Outside, Helen asked, 'Is Marie your wife, Jean-Pierre?'

'No. Not officially. Do you object?'

Helen laughed. 'Me object? Good God, Jean-Pierre. Why should I? It's four years since I was here.'

He was embarrassed. 'I didn't mean object in that way. I meant. . . .'

'The fact that she's African. American universities tend to give people, even their lecturers, a pretty liberal outlook. Besides, aren't you forgetting that I know this part of Africa and its customs?'

'Yes, I apologise. Finding Marie back here — she's been at death's door, some kind of African spell — was rather confusing for me, especially on top of your own unexpected arrival.'

'Confusing? You always were a master of understatement, Jean-Pierre.'

She said everything pleasantly but there was a cutting edge to her sentences that had not been there in the old days.

Toto was lying on her back, playing with her toes just as a human baby might have done. Helen sucked in her breath.

'Oh, isn't she marvellous! Can I handle her? Where did you get her? Her arm's broken. What are you going to do with her? Wouldn't it be stupendous if we could eventually return her to the wild? What did you say she was called? It is a she, isn't it?'

'You're losing your scientific detachment, Helen. Now which question do you want answered first?'

'Can I handle her?'

Jean-Pierre reached inside her enclosure with one hand. The baby gorilla seized it and swung upwards with her good arm. She hung on Jean-Pierre's hand while she gravely inspected Helen, then, presuming her to be friendly, grasped one of Helen's hands with her foot.

'There you are. She likes you.'

Toto had now transferred herself completely to Helen, clinging round her neck.

'She's adorable.'

'Yes, and she was a wild gorilla until a week or so ago.'

'Who'd ever want a human baby after her?'

'Ah. Now you *are* losing your scientific cool. Better put her back while you can still think straight.'

'Tell me her history. How you got her. How she broke her arm. Who mended it? He did a very skilful job by the look of it.'

'Lots of time for all that. Let's get you to your hotel. You look as though you're nearly out on your feet.'

She prised Toto gently free.

'Yes. I have been travelling for rather a long time. All this, too. Coming back is rather overwhelming.'

Veniard was in the office when he returned.

'You've seen Marie?'

'Yes. It's incredible.'

'You could call it that. Two goats and a good dinner, please. You owe me one more thing or, rather, you owe it to yourself.'

'Name it. It's yours. I can't believe that she's back.'

'She'll need some looking after, but she'll be all right now. I hear someone else is back, too.'

'This bloody place. The locals aren't the only ones with a bush telegraph. How did you hear?'

'Never mind. Will you be taking up where you left off?'

'Why don't you try minding your own bloody business, doctor?'

'Because lately I've been too bloody busy minding yours.'

It was hard to get angry with Veniard. Jean-Pierre smiled. 'The beer is in the fridge or would you prefer a Pernod? Now what's this other thing I owe you, or, rather, myself?'

'A visit to Chiribanda.'

'That bastard. You've got to be joking.'

'I may be. The point is that he's not. His son's making a good recovery, by the way. A good strong lad.'

'Chiribanda can come and see me if he wants to, though tell him not to bother if he's thinking of presenting a bill for that bulldozer.'

'He's not. It's about his son. And fifty hectares of clear-felled land, I gather.'

'He stole that from the park.'

'Exactly. He wants to give it back.'

'It's not much good to the park without trees.'

'You should meet him just the same.'

'Why? Tell me one good reason why.'

'I can give you several. First, this is Africa. Second, you don't want any more trouble for Marie or anyone else. He's a powerful man locally is our Kama Chiribanda. Third — no, I'll leave you to find out the third.'

'I'm damned if I'll go to his house.'

'I'm pretty sure he'll see you damned before he comes here. Why not neutral territory? My house. I'll arrange it.'

'If you think it's necessary.'

'I do, if you want any peace to get on with your job.'

'I'll make no promises, then.'

Marie made Jean-Pierre's dinner just as if she had never been away. The pleasure he felt at having her well again and back home amazed him. Her fine features were sharpened and made angular by the wastage caused by her long illness so that her full beauty was hidden. But it was there beneath the skin and would return. He took her hand, feeling the bones more prominent than usual in her slim fingers. She let him hold her hand but remained passive. Jean-Pierre desperately wanted to make love to her. The feeling was more than an old, accustomed desire, enhanced by absence and excited by sudden opportunity. It was stronger than ever before. This was most simply explained by weeks of deprivation, but only partly so. Possibly the shock of seeing Helen again had increased his longing for sex. None of these explanations interpreted his feelings precisely. The truly wonderful thing with Marie was that he had never found it necessary to force himself on her. Indeed, it was not in his nature to do so. Marie Maputa would have made a great mistress in any country, in any language, at any period of history. It was usually she who apparently and artlessly gave the signals.

So tonight, when he went to their bedroom, he waited expectantly for her to enter as she so often had in the past, her wood-carver's mahogany breasts bare above the flowered kekoy wound round her waist. He turned when she entered, arms held out towards her, and saw that her breasts were covered. Of course! They would have wasted like the rest of her body during the weeks of starvation. She did not want him to see her like that. He must let her know that it made no difference. He walked towards her and touched her face gently. She remained with her head covered.

'Marie. It's so wonderful to have you back with me. . . . You mustn't worry if. . . .'

There were tears in her eyes. 'Jean-Pierre, you're so gentle with me. Only you would understand. . . .'

'Please don't cover yourself. You mustn't worry if your figure has lost. . . .' He saw from her look that he hadn't understood after all. She had merely thought that he had.

'Why are you covered then, Marie?'

'The wise one, the one who brought me back to you, has forbidden me to make love with a man not of my own race. He tells me that if I disobey I will fall sick again, like before.'

'How long is this to continue?'

'He did not tell me.'

'I see,' Jean-Pierre said grimly.

Chiribanda was still at work.

They slept side by side. When he put his arm round her to comfort her, she did not move away but it was as if her body was still in a trance. He dreamt of being back in the hut on the Saddle with Helen. Helen had a witch-doctor, an African with the face of John Redfern, who had ordered her to sleep only with black men.

Marie was up first next morning. While she prepared breakfast he heard her laughing and talking to the baby gorilla. She even went outside several times to play with it. Jean-Pierre was delighted. It was important that she took to the infant. Marie could do a great deal to help the baby over the crisis of its broken arm.

At last, when she brought the fresh fruit and coffee on a tray, her breasts were still covered. The night's rest seemed to have filled out her features. The beauty was already seeping back. Celibacy was going to be very hard for him. He must consult Veniard, though he thought he knew what the answer would be.

Marie bowed to him. He took her hand to reassure her and kissed it. When they had eaten he said, 'I am going to visit Dr Lawes at the Président.'

'May I please have the baby out of the cage while I do the housework?'

'Certainly, but she'll be an awful nuisance. She'll probably make a mess, too.'

'No matter. I can easily clear it up.'

Helen had breakfasted and was writing a letter to Redfern in her room.

'You ought to spend a few days down here getting acclimatised before you start rushing around in the forest.'

'I agree. It's going to take a little time getting used to Africa again. There's plenty we can do, if you've got the time. I've read all the notes you sent to John Redfern, but it

223

would help if you can bring me really up to date. I want to know all about the gorilla families you've studied. Is the Absolom I knew really still alive?'

'Not only that, he's back in charge of his group.'

'And his wound . . . the wound the tall, thin man. . . . Was it really him, Jean-Pierre?'

'Yes. The one they called General Patrice. It was him all right. I'm glad we came to that subject quickly. I must ask you: how do you really feel about returning here?'

'How should I feel? It's a unique scientific opportunity to continue my work.'

'But inside yourself. I must know so that I can help you in any way in my power.'

'I can cope with it. At least I think I can. Sometimes, like yesterday at the airfield, when I see an African who resembles one of the men who. . . .'

'Who raped you.' It was better said.

'Yes. I wanted to run back to the plane. But I managed to fight it. Back in the forest, when I'm working, I'll be all right. That's why I must stay in Baruva a little while, perhaps go round with you, until I get used to all these black faces.'

'There's one black face I'll never get out of my mind. If I ever meet him,' Jean-Pierre said unemotionally, 'I shall kill him.'

'Let's hope he's dead already. He and his kind killed something in me. Did you know that when I returned to the States the doctors told me I'd have to have a hysterectomy? Now, let's talk about something more constructive.'

So he spread out the maps and described the boundaries of the park. He pencilled in the home-range of those gorilla groups he had studied most closely. He showed her where the poaching was taking place and where he suspected there were undiscovered pockets of gorillas outside the park, on the far slopes of Vahinga. Then he told her about Chiribanda, everything about Chiribanda except what had happened to Marie. Why he kept that from her he could not be entirely sure. He expected her to be up in arms about Chiribanda's

224

campaign against himself and against the park. That would have been consistent with the Helen of four years ago.

'Well, of course,' she said at last, 'your friend Jacques Veniard is right. You've got to do a deal with him. As long as he's there, he's going to be a constant threat.'

'You're not serious, Helen?'

'Why not? Oh! I can see what you're thinking. When I was here before I'd have told you to see him in hell first. You'd be right about that. But three or four years spent in the world of American academics changes one's viewpoint a bit. You get to learn there's nothing done without a fair amount of wheeling and dealing.'

'What kind of deal would you suggest I make, then?' It wasn't a question so much as a comment of considerable sourness. Helen took it at face value.

'You won't know that until you've met this Chiribanda.'

They spent the rest of the morning going through Jean-Pierre's gorilla diaries and notes. Whatever else had changed in Helen Lawes, her utter absorption with the mountain gorilla had not. Frequently she exclaimed with delight over some item of behaviour he had observed.

'That's new, Jean-Pierre. I never saw them eat that. You're sure you've got the description right? At nine thousand feet, too. The tracing you made of the leaf fits exactly, though.'

Her enthusiasm began to rekindle the old pleasure he had always felt in her company. It was a pity she had to add, 'A qualified biologist couldn't have done better.'

When he returned alone that evening, Veniard's car was outside his office. Helen had decided to eat at the Président and go over his notes again. Understandably she was still tired after her flight and her first full day in Africa.

He heard laughter from the yard. Marie was holding Toto by her good arm and allowing her to swing to and fro.

Veniard caught sight of Jean-Pierre. 'I wish all my nurses were as good as Marie. Cut my work in half, a few more like her would.'

The baby gorilla grabbed Marie's dress with one leg. Marie supported it under its bottom and the baby immediately freed its hand and clasped the undamaged arm round the African girl's neck.

'She's beautiful, Jean-Pierre. I love her already.' She giggled delightfully. 'I'd far rather have her than a baby of my own.'

'Just as well,' Veniard said and winked lewdly, 'though from what I hear there's not much chance of that at the moment.'

Jean-Pierre snapped, 'You're never very careful what you say, are you, Jacques?'

'Marie's not offended, are you, Marie?' But the girl had turned away to play with the gorilla. Veniard went on, 'She's a realist, you see. Doesn't kid herself about what's happening to herself and others. Now, how about you, my friend? Are you prepared to be equally realistic or does permanent celibacy on the home front appeal to you?'

'Did you come here to examine the baby, to drink my Pernod, to needle me, or all three? Or is it just possible you wanted to talk seriously about something?'

'Sometimes,' said the doctor, his sallow, pinched features registering reflective doubt, 'I wonder how I dare risk rousing the black forces that I know lurk behind that bland, once-boyish face.'

'I'm a very mild man until pushed to a point at which something snaps. Perhaps we'd both better have a Pernod. I'd be obliged all the same if you would be more tactful in front of Marie. She's had . . . she's still having a hard time.'

'Ah yes — some more water please— Do you happen to know if your forest produces any woodworm? If so, we could make the true absinthe and perhaps go madder than we are.'

'I'm sure if it did, Mushi would already be making it. He's a willing victim of every other vile habit. He's steeped in all kinds of black arts.'

The doctor stared into the milky liquid in his glass.

'Talking of black arts, our friend Chiribanda is pretty steeped himself. Marie, I understand. . . .'

'I suppose you want another bloody goat or two, or is his price this time half Misoka Park?'

'I think you'll find him far more reasonable than that.'

'Who said I'd make a deal with the sod?' Helen's advice of that morning came back to him. 'I simply said I might be prepared to meet him.'

'Good. Then that's what I really came about. At my house at seven tomorrow evening. I'll pick you up here. . . . Don't you think Marie is getting on remarkably well? Of course, there's room for some improvement yet.'

It was quite a shock to realise that he'd never been to Jacques Veniard's bungalow along the south shore of the lake. When it had been necessary to visit the doctor professionally, he'd always called at the surgery in Baruva. That was where Veniard had lived before the civil war with his wife, Héloïse a faded and vitriolic Belgian beauty. Jean-Pierre had often wondered what sort of life those two could have had together. In terms of verbal asperity they must have been fairly equally matched. He'd heard one or two of their more blistering exchanges. Madame Veniard had suffered badly from malaria and had reputedly hit the bottle fairly hard. She had gone back to Europe after the *Fisi* rebellion and Veniard had never mentioned her since. Perhaps she was dead. Jean-Pierre hadn't cared to ask.

As they drove out along the red-dirt, south lake road Jean-Pierre became increasingly curious to see the Veniard establishment. He didn't know what to expect. Something pretty derelict, a compound of broken-down cane chairs and empty Pernod bottles, perhaps. A first glimpse of the exterior reinforced this notion, a typical, decaying, ex-colonial bungalow, creepers standing in for paint, a roof of unlovely corrugated iron the rusty red colour of a forest fungus which the building as a whole somewhat resembled. The setting was idyllic. The bungalow stood among a grove of yellow-barked

227

acacias, fever-trees, in the top of one of which a fish eagle perched and fluted its whistling territorial call.

'He's not here yet. Come in and have a drink.'

'I shan't wait long. If Chiribanda can't keep a simple appointment. . . .'

'Take it easy. I said seven o'clock. It's only ten minutes to the hour. Park your shooting irons on the verandah.' Veniard put on an excruciatingly bad Western accent for this last bit.

'Don't be bloody silly, Jacques. I don't go around armed all the time.'

'No? Well, that's an improvement.'

They crossed the verandah. So far it was much as Jean-Pierre expected. A broken-down cane lounging chair, buffalo horns on the wall, some crossed spears, a painted ritual mask of no particular distinction. The whole scene suggested a typical African bachelor's club-like semi-slum. But once inside the living-room, things changed. Hand-carved chairs were neatly arranged around a polished table of forest mahogany. One wall was filled with books, not textbooks but novels, biographies, classics. Having made these cultural declarations the room might have been expected to reinforce them with some prints, perhaps reproductions of the Impressionists. Pictures there were on every wall. Jean-Pierre saw that these were not prints. He knew little about art but on some he could see the paint standing out in relief where the light caught it. The pictures were painted as if a panga had slashed tubes of colour. One looked like a matting of vines and nettles caught by light through the forest canopy. He'd have liked to own that one. About others he was not so sure. One reminded him of a pattern of warriors' shields, another of linked animal horns, a third of flowers he had never seen in nature.

Veniard followed his glances.

'All local work. I doubt whether they'll ever be worth a fortune but at least they're originals. I believe in local talent.'

A handsome young African, perhaps sixteen years old, wearing a white robe and tarboosh came in and crossed his hands on his chest.

'Bring the refreshments now, please, Kiari, before we start.'

'Good God, Jacques. You amaze me. Quite an establishment.'

'I find life better ordered without women. I used to think they were essential, but now I almost prefer to have Kiari about the place. Nearly as decorative as your Marie, too, but then, I wouldn't like you to think there is anything like *that* about me. A queer doctor wouldn't really do, not with his women patients anyway. Still, if I ever did take it up again, perhaps Kiari. . . . After all the Arabs. . . . I've always rather admired the Arabs. Have some beer? No Pernod for you tonight. Must keep a cool head for Chiribanda. He's a hard bargainer, I'm told.'

Veniard had caught the sound of a car turning off the road. He was conscious of having ad-libbed to keep Jean-Pierre from looking at his watch and getting himself steamed up. Chiribanda was now five minutes late. Kiari brought in trays of peppers, grated onions, rice, sliced tomatoes, home-made bread, butter, cheese, mangoes, paw-paws, chutneys, dried tilapia, lake crayfish, and laid the plates on the mahogany table. He placed ice-cold beers, Pernod, whisky, gin and soft drinks on the sideboard and, bowing, withdrew just as the white Mercedes pulled up outside.

'About time,' Jean Pierre said.

'Now, promise me to behave youself. I will sit at the head of the table and act as chairman.'

Kama Chiribanda looked larger and hotter than ever. He held out his hand to Veniard, bowed stiffly to Jean-Pierre and sat down at once, helping himself to a handful of green peppers, the first bite of which caused him to sweat more generously even than before.

'I suggest the rest of us sit down, gentlemen.'

Chiribanda nodded vigorously in agreement and helped himself to a strip of dried fish. Jean-Pierre found him even less lovely than when they had last met in his office.

229

Veniard produced a piece of paper. 'I have here a rough agenda.'

Chiribanda got up and poured himself a stiffish whisky and water.

Veniard said: 'Since the first item concerns the boundary of the park with Mr Chiribanda's estates, perhaps you would kindly unroll the the maps you have brought with you, Monsieur Menant.'

Fascinated by the, to him, new role of cool, capable chairman in which the doctor had cast himself, Jean-Pierre did so without comment. Chiribanda sat down again, picked his nose with considerable thoroughness and then, with the same hand, selected a large green pepper from the dish, having turned over and rejected several smaller ones.

'As I understand it, Mr Chiribanda wishes to concede to the National Park the shaded area which he has clear-felled and planted with quinine, a total of 1,000 hectares.'

'Since it already belongs to the park he can hardly concede it.'

'He wishes to acknowledge the park's ownership.'

'Very kind of him, but since there aren't any trees left because he's chopped them all down it's not much use to the gorillas anyway. They don't eat quinine leaves.'

Chiribanda started on the nuts.

'He tells me,' Veniard went on, 'that he is quite willing for the park signs to be re-erected on his plantations.'

'So what does the *Sous-Commissaire* get out of it?'

'The right to continue farming his plantations.'

'Within the park?'

'Since, he maintains, this is an accomplished fact, why not recognise it as such?'

'And what does the park get out of it?'

Veniard turned to the big African, who was now spreading mango chutney on a piece of goat cheese and sprinkling the result with chopped onions. 'If I understand Mr Chiribanda correctly, he would, in exchange, guarantee the park's frontier at that point and protect it against intruders, including cattle. Since the quinine plantation appears to occupy a long, narrow strip which stands between the forest and a great deal of African cultivation, this could be a considerable asset to the park.'

'What about his own cattle?'

'They will be kept out of the forest. Furthermore, he will undertake not to make further encroachments.'

'That's what Hitler said.'

Chiribanda had either not heard of Hitler or just conceivably had heard of him and admired his technique greatly. He stopped chewing for a moment, grinned so that his gold tooth winked like a flashlight and said, '*Monsieur le Conservateur*, you are getting a very good deal, actually.'

'I demand complete protection of all gorillas by the *Sous-Commissaire* and those employed by him. A mature male has already been killed almost certainly at your orders, possibly even by your son.'

Chiribanda spread his large pink hands in an expression of infinite regret.

'One of my bulldozers was unfortunately assassinated also.'

Jean-Pierre couldn't bring himself to reply directly to Chiribanda. 'Tell him, bulldozers are replaceable: gorillas aren't.'

Chiribanda laughed loudly. 'Bulldozers are more expensive and more useful.'

'I think,' Veniard said, 'that we all need another drink.' He rang a bell and the white-robed Kiari appeared and filled the glasses. When Veniard had itemised the discussion to date, he asked, 'Monsieur Menant, what is your reaction to Mr Chiribanda's proposals?'

'He doesn't expect me to give him an answer here and now. I shall consider what he suggests carefully.'

'I know that he would like your reply as quickly as possible.'

'I may have to consult the appropriate minister in the capital.'

'That might take some time.'

'I doubt if you'll get an answer at all, actually,' Chiribanda put in. 'The *conservateur* knows as well as I do that decisions here on the spot are what count.'

'I've said I shall consider every aspect. . . . Is there anything else to be discussed? If not, I'd like to go back to town. . . .' For once, Jean-Pierre felt he was being outflanked. Oddly, his anger focused on Veniard for having put him in this position. Acting like the bloody chairman of a board of governers. Where did he get all this stuff from?

Chiribanda was whispering to Veniard.

'Ah, yes, he asks me to speak as his doctor and his son's doctor also. His son, as you know, has had a bad accident, but is fortunately recovering fast. He has heard, too, that you have had some domestic misfortune. Neither case, I have told him, can be considered to be entirely back to normal yet. As a doctor, it's my opinion that both patients would be helped a great deal with the right mental stimulus. One case might strangely enough be found to have a beneficial effect on the other. In the case of his son, Mr Chiribanda believes that he would make a most successful African warden in charge of your ranger force. He points out that as *Sous-Commissaire* he will, naturally, press for African representation on the park staff.'

Jean-Pierre's first feeling was that he should overturn the table and slam out of the room. Long training in the mechanics of personal survival, however, short-circuited this impulse.

'How old is he?'

'Nearly twenty-two.'

'Education?'

'Two years at Cairo University. Six months' military service.'

'Send him to the office to see me. I make no promises.'

Ever since the gazetting of Misoka Park, Jean-Pierre had known that the day would soon come when he would have to appoint an African warden. Perhaps better the devil you know even if the devil was called Chiribanda.

Nancy Genova had always hoped to find a specialised journalistic field in which she could graze without too much competition. Some might have added 'from the other cows'. Conservation now seemed to be it. Actually, she wasn't too fond of animals. Her knowledge of zoology didn't even extend to university level. She had majored in English Literature. What else? Nevertheless, she knew enough of ecology from high school to appreciate that one of the prerequisites of survival is that every single species finds an unoccupied niche and then exploits it. Thus the Galapagos woodpecker finch. Hence the giraffe and the kangaroo. Likewise Nancy Genova.

Protecting the environment was all the rage. She saw wild animals as not much more than a litmus paper which roughly indicated to the human race the state of the planet which it was so busy looting. Her skilled journalistic mind was as interested in this proposition as in boom or slump, white or black, war or peace. In fairness, she saw the environmental issue as basic to all the former and, in the long run, almost certainly more important. Wildlife was only a small part of it all yet she was shrewdly aware that it was the most instantly appealing part.

Nancy Genova was intensely ambitious. There were undoubtedly competitors in the field but she had been one of the first through the gate. Like many women journalists she was more concerned with people than with things. Inevitably, in view of her blue-stocking background, this usually meant People with a capital P rather than people as individuals. Nevertheless, as a series of perceptive profiles had proved, she could empathise enough with individuals to understand them, analyse them and set down what made them tick. Even her rivals liked her. As one older male colleague, who gratefully remembered the days when girls wore nylons, said, 'If Nancy's a blue-stocking, at least she's a fifteen denier blue-stocking.' Nor did anyone deny her sinewy, rawhide attractiveness, least of all Dr John Redfern.

In this department of her life Miss Genova now had something of a problem. Not in the matters of physical compatability or age differential. She could handle both of those. Even when she had admitted to herself that she had something of a father complex where Redfern was concerned, she still found him an extremely attractive and vital man whose demands — no, 'demands' was a horrible and inaccurate word — whose mutually enjoyable requests were by no means excessive and always flattering. Unless she became totally addicted to him, the years would, inevitably, gracefully fade out the importance of the gap in their ages. Moreover, she recognised in Redfern exactly the same limelight-seeking ambition she acknowledged in herself.

This was where her problem lay. It was a professional one. Redfern was a bright comet upon whose tail she had seized firm hold. His flair for headline-making would ensure that he flamed across the sky for quite a while yet. The launching of Ark International had made headlines round the world in a way which every other conservation body could only envy. In part this was due to that one stunning picture of the Intruder, but it was also due, in America at least, to Redfern himself. He had given endless interviews, appeared on every major TV chat show, managing to give out an aura that was a compound of the late Bertrand Russell at his most perceptive and waspish and Bing Crosby at the peak of his most relaxed, pipe-smoking charm. Having seen him on TV it was easy to see why he was often a fellow scientist's *bête noire*. He made it look too easy.

By pulling strings and twisting friends' arms, Nancy had arranged a good deal of this desirable publicity for him. Therein lay the danger. Her association with Redfern gave her the inside journalistic track on quite a few stories. But if she stayed on that track too long she was likely to find herself tagged as a publicist, a PRO for Ark International. This, undoubtedly, is what Redfern would have liked. It was her experience that self-determining journalists who crossed the

234

line into public relations very seldom made it back. They lost credibility with their peers and with the papers they had formerly served.

She met Redfern for lunch in the Cheval Blanc on 45th Street, between 3rd and Lexington. Today he looked nearer fifty than sixty-three. He kissed her on top of her hair, in a way that outsiders might construe as fatherly, and ordered a Campari. She could sense that he was crackling with excitement. She half expected to see a flash of static from his fingertips when he straightened the cutlery on the red-and-white chequered cloth. This straightening of eating equipment was his standard opening gambit in any restaurant they visited together. She had come to be both irritated and amused by it. It was as if he couldn't bring himself to release his thoughts until everything around him was ship-shape and to his satisfaction.

'Great news, Nancy. We've got our first hundred thousand bucks and without really trying.'

'Who hasn't been trying?'

'You have. I have. But the loot is just beginning to pour in. The trustees are soon going to be asking me what to do with it. Well, obviously, that's going to take a lot of serious discussion. We've a whole list of projects on the book for consideration, projects I agreed with the other wildlife organisations they'd leave to us. But Misoka's got to come first. That's what I pledged myself to do. . . .'

'You've already sent Menant his lady scientist and guaranteed funds for running costs and his ranger force.'

'Necessary but not very spectacular. I need something big as a gesture. Now we've got things rolling, we can't afford to let the momentum run down.'

He broke off to order a dozen oysters each, followed by tournedos Rossini and a bottle of Tokay. She smiled at the composition of the meal, noting that he had reached the time of life when he believed in the virility-reinforcing properties of traditional gastronomic specifics.

'Why don't you visit the president?'

'The White House?' he asked doubtfully.

'No, dear one. In Africa. Present his black excellency, President Olindo, in person with a cheque to run Misoka, to buy more land there, to buy the park an aeroplane. Whatever Menant needs most. It's Ark's agreed sphere of influence, isn't it? The British seem *persona non grata* there. Use the visit as a pretext for discussing the whole conservation scene in the country. It's a huge nation and it's had too many other troubles to worry much to date about its wildlife. Get a high level discussion going and it could be very fruitful, both from their point of view and from Ark's.'

'Yes, but could I get to him? You know what these black politicians are like.'

'He has an American counsellor. Name of Jack Wright. Used to be a lobby correspondent in Washington where I knew him pretty well. Did him a favour or two once. Wright met Olindo during his roughest time in the civil war. That's where the bond was established. He's one of the few guys, I understand, who has any clout with the president. Wright may just have too many other things on his mind but he'd be the first to see the propaganda value of his boss making a big play on the conservation front. After all, the country's miles behind all the other African nations in that respect.'

'Think you could pull it off?'

'I could at least try. Those guys are always ready to accept money. Besides, you got to the president once before. It's not as if you're unknown to him.'

The oysters were appearing over the kitchen horizon. Redfern waved at the wine waiter. 'Let's have half a bottle of Chablis as well to celebrate a great idea.'

'It's not very brilliant.'

'Nancy, why don't you come and join Ark full-time? I've asked you before. We could pay you the sort of money you need now.'

'Sorry, John. I have to stay outside your organisation to earn my living. If you get your meeting with the president I'll come to Africa with you. Since I invented the story, I might as well have the exclusive on it.'

'Is your photographer friend at home?'

'No. She's not back until tomorrow night. Why?'

'Oh, nothing.'

'I knew I shouldn't have let you order those damned oysters.'

'That's a very vulgar observation.'

'True, but perhaps you noticed I ordered them, too.'

On the fifth day after her arrival, Jean-Pierre agreed to take Helen into the forest. Mushi had reported that Absolom had brought his group well down the mountain to within half-a-mile of the park headquarters. Jean-Pierre hadn't visited the gorillas since he had brought in the orphaned Toto but Mushi had kept him in touch with events. The wandering Hepzibah had miraculously made contact with the family once again. Jean-Pierre was curious to see with his own eyes how they accepted her. In Helen he detected an excitement that almost amounted to jumpiness at the prospect of meeting wild gorillas again.

'What's Absolom like now? Does he still charge? Will he recognise me, do you think?'

'He may charge, but it's nothing to worry about. You've seen all that before. His wound hasn't made him any more irritable. He's certainly not dangerous.'

'Funny. I feel quite nervous about going into the forest again. I'll soon get used to it. You'll help me for a bit, won't you?'

He touched her arm in reassurance and felt her tighten her muscles as if trying to make herself smaller without wishing to be seen doing so. He felt a definite physical interest when he touched her and was disproportionately shocked to sense her almost indetectable gesture of withdrawal. Perhaps all that was gone for ever, on her side at least. For his part he couldn't be sure. Four years had passed. After all she had suffered, could she feel anything for anybody in that way? The sensation passed quickly. It was the first and only reaction of the kind he'd experienced since her return. Possibly it was no more than a nerve memory, tweaked by returning to the forest with her. What he'd felt was probably akin to the sensation a person who had lost a hand or foot is said to feel, a false message that it is still there.

He drove up the track towards the saw-mill before he realised where he was going and what he might be doing to her. A glance to his right in the pretence of pointing out where some trees had been felled registered a profile unmoved by the memory of the route they were travelling. Maybe she didn't recall that the saw-mill lay half-a-mile ahead. He hadn't intended to stop just yet but now he said, 'In another two hundred yards we must get out and take to our flat feet.'

She inhaled deeply and with pleasure. 'I'd almost forgotten what it smelt like. . . . Rotten, rich and musty. *Delicious!* I only hope I'm fit enough.'

'We'll take it easy. With luck the gorillas will be within a mile of here. Take your time about everything at first. Remember the altitude. You'll soon get used to it again.'

Their path lay upward through a part of the lower forest where the ground canopy was luxuriant. He could hear Helen panting. Once she pulled at his bush-shirt, urging him to halt for a while. The sweat was running down her forehead and dripping from the tip of her nose. He waited patiently and whispered, 'Not so far ahead now. You'll soon get fit again. Don't worry.'

Four years of campus-living had softened her. He guessed that part of her apparent exhaustion was due to nervousness. She was worried how she was going to make out when she had to stalk and observe on her own, as in the old days.

'I'll help you as much as you want until you get into the swing of things again.'

Mushi was pantomiming that they must push on. The gorillas, it seemed, were moving quickly towards a denser part of the forest where they would be impossible to observe.

It developed into one of those situations that had become

only too familiar to Jean-Pierre during his own four-year study of the Misoka gorillas. They were soon within thirty yards of the family. They could hear them only too well but could not see a single one of them. The heavy, nervous smell exuded by the males was thick on the air. Jean-Pierre coughed repeatedly to let them know who was approaching. Absolom answered once and then appeared to go into a sulk. Since his return to the family he had never been on quite such familiar terms with Jean-Pierre. Today it seemed possible that not only Absolom but the whole family sensed there was something unfamiliar in the forest. The unease communicated itself to the group in an increasing pattern of breast-beating and shrieking.

Jean-Pierre hurried Helen and Mushi on, taking a wide sweep round the downhill flank of the gorillas, aiming to get ahead of them. If his calculations were right, Absolom would have to bring the family across the track somewhere close to the spot at which they stood. He signalled Helen and Mushi to sit down in the grass at the track's far edge.

It was a full twenty minutes before they heard the group approaching, still a long way off. They were evidently finding interesting feeding along their route. Finally a branch swayed. Then a face appeared briefly, peering through the foliage at the far side of the track. A young male.

'Abraham,' Jean-Pierre whispered.

Abraham disappeared. A spasm of anxious breast-beating followed.

Helen was sweating hard again. She hadn't expected to feel fear like this.

Jean-Pierre was talking earnestly to Absolom, calling him by name, urging him to cross the track. 'It's me, Absolom! Come on, Absolom.'

Absolom's reply was to rush the bushes bordering his side of the track, tearing them apart violently like curtains on a stage. It was quite an entrance. He stood at his full height, bellowing.

'Come . . . come on, my old friend.'

Absolom came. He came at full charge. He came across the track, shrieking all the way, and he halted only a yard short of Jean-Pierre. He was so close that Jean-Pierre could see the scar over the bullet wound in his shoulder.

Jean-Pierre continued to talk to the furious male, softly, almost ingratiatingly. 'Absolom, my friend. Keep calm, Absolom.'

After perhaps thirty seconds, the great silver-back rushed back the way he had come. Jean-Pierre turned to speak to Helen only to find her no longer there. The full-blooded charge had been too much for her.

'Come back, Helen,' he said gently. 'He'll bring them across now. You'll be able to see them all.'

Ashamed of her panic, Helen crawled back in time to watch the whole group cross the track ten yards away.

First came Absolom, who stood on guard. Next Ahitabel, the old female, with Cain. Behind Ahitabel trailed Ahab and Abednego. At this point Abraham emerged and took over guard-duty from Absolom, who, satisfied that all was secure, shambled off into the bush. Now, for Jean-Pierre at least, came the surprise, two females with a half-grown male he had never seen before in his life, followed by the recently rejoined Hepzibah. When she was safely across, Abraham sauntered after her. He had grown greatly in stature but still lacked any sign of the silver hairs of maturity. Finally, a further surprise, a completely unknown silver-back bringing up the rear. It was obviously this male who had recently joined forces with the group, bringing the two females and young male with him. It was typical gorilla group behaviour.

He turned excitedly to Helen. 'There you are. All set up for you. Fantastic. Some new members. Ones I've never seen. An ideal situation for you to begin your study with.'

He could see she was still trembling, shattered by Absolom's charge yet absorbed and thrilled by what she had seen.

'I was stupid. I won't behave like that again.'

'Of course not. The first time after such a long interval. It's very unnerving. Don't worry, you'll soon be accepted by them again.'

Kama Chiribanda wasn't going to let the grass grow under his quinine bushes. Two days after the meeting engineered by Veniard, a tall, well-set-up young African knocked politely at the park office door in Baruva. One arm was bandaged and supported by a sling. Jean-Pierre didn't need any introductions.

'Sit down,' he said.

The boy remained standing. 'My father asked me to deliver this letter.'

'I see. Thank you. You're Francis Chiribanda.'

The young African smiled. He had a frank and engaging smile. Jean-Pierre slit open the note.

'*Monsieur le Conservateur*, this is to introduce my son, Francis, whom you said you would be good enough to interview for the post of head ranger. I have the honour to be, etc.'

Jean-Pierre allowed himself an inward smirk at the standard felicitations. He waved at the chair. This time young Chiribanda sat down.

'You're twenty-one?'

'Nearly twenty-two. I studied at Cairo University. I have a degree in economics. Last year I did six months' national service.'

'Why do you want to work for me?'

'I wish to work to preserve the natural resources of our country.'

'That is excellent, but you didn't answer my question. If I took you on, you would be working directly under my orders.'

'Monsieur Menant, I have done, as I told you, service in the army.'

'What do you think of wild animals?'

Chiribanda's answer impressed Jean-Pierre considerably. 'Until recently they were an expensive nuisance that raided

241

my father's crops. They may still continue to be that but they are also a natural resource, valuable to the nation.'

'So you would, if necessary, let gorillas eat your father's banana trees?'

'If I had the job to protect the gorillas, yes. My father would, of course, be right to claim compensation.'

'You can't be especially in sympathy with gorillas seeing that you killed a magnificent male with buckshot recently.'

Chiribanda didn't deny that he had shot the Intruder. 'Naturally, I have hunted them in the past. To an extent, a hunter has to be interested in his victims.'

'Most educated young men want a job in an office in town.'

'I was brought up in the forest. I understand the things of the forest.'

'But does such a job satisfy the ambitions you must have developed at university?'

'One day, after you. . . .'

'After I have gone?'

'I did not say that, but one day Africans must run all their own affairs, even national parks.'

Jean-Pierre said, 'You needn't sound so aggressive about it. What you say is almost certainly true. Now listen to what I say. If I think of *hiring* you' — he gave the word special emphasis — 'you will have one hell of a lot to learn before you're fit to take anything on.'

'You will' — slight hesitation — 'hire me, then?'

'I'll think about it. I will write to your father one way or the other within twenty-four hours.'

'He will hope to know something from me.'

'I am quite impressed by you. If I decide anything in your favour, then, tell him, he knows what I expect from him.'

Just as Chiribanda was about to leave, Helen Lawes drove up. Jean-Pierre had lent her his jeep.

'Wait a minute, there's someone I'd like you to meet. This is Dr Lawes. She's joined the park to make a scientific study of the gorillas.'

242

Helen held out her hand to Chiribanda. '*Continue* my study, actually. I began work here over four years ago, but it was interrupted by the war.'

'It must be very exciting to be back. There must be so much to find out.'

'I know all about *you*,' Helen said. 'You want a job with the park.'

'That is what I have been discussing with Monsieur Menant.'

'Oh, and what did he say?'

'Naturally, he didn't tell me. That is for him to decide. But he has promised to give me an answer very shortly. *Au revoir*, Dr Lawes. Thank you for your time, *Monsieur le Conservateur*.'

When Chiribanda junior had gone Helen asked, 'What did you think of him?'

'He's intelligent and ambitious.'

'And very well-mannered.'

'Perhaps a bit too damn smooth.'

'That's his university training.'

'Maybe. I'm more interested in his forest training.'

'And how was that?'

'He was brought up here. He's hunted a good deal.'

'You and I both agree, though many of those who give their dollars and dimes to conservation might not, that that's one of the best trainings of all.'

'Look at me, for example.'

'Yes, look at you. So what are you going to do about him?'

'What would you do? You're concerned to some degree, also.'

'I'd take him on.'

'He'll probably turn out to be a crook like his old man.'

'Probably, but then, haven't you always said that this country has a different morality and that, provided you know you're being taken for a small percentage, that's the best you can hope for?'

'Provided it *is* a small percentage.'

'You have more to gain than you can lose.'

'And supposing he turns out to be a disaster? What trouble do I have with his crook of a father then?'

'That's something you face when, and if, it happens.'

'That's what Veniard would say.'

'He's right. One thing that's certain is that you're in for a long war of attrition with Chiribanda senior if you turn the boy down.'

Outside, he heard Marie laughing as she played with the baby gorilla.

'O.K., I'll talk to Veniard.'

Helen looked through the window and saw Marie cradling the baby gorilla preparatory to giving her a bath in a tin bowl.

'Some day soon,' Helen said with unexpected sharpness, 'we're going to have to take that young animal away from your charming African friend and start rehabilitating her scientifically.'

Nancy Genova got her reply from President Olindo's American counsellor far more quickly than she expected. The cable said: 'If you arrive by fifteenth will try arrange audience stop President Olindo leaves following week visit Zaire stop No absolute guarantees but estimate chances good Regards Wright'

Nancy phoned Redfern and read it to him.

'What do you make of that?'

'When a man like Jack Wright says chances are good, he's being cautious. He knows he's encouraging you to travel half-way across the world, so he's simply covering himself. My bet is that he's already tried it on the president and got an affirmative reaction. It's the sort of propaganda exercise the president probably welcomes at this moment. Conservation is non-political, non-provocative and you *are* going to offer him a fair amount of money.'

'When can you leave?'

'Today's the eighth. That gives us a week. How about tomorrow? If I can get a flight?'

'Can't make it until the day after, I'm afraid. For once the darn university demands my services.'

'I wasn't talking about you. You asked me when *I* could leave.'

'Oh!' Obvious disappointment. 'I thought we were going together.'

'Not a good idea. For one thing, I'd like it to look as though I'd got wind of a story and am not travelling as your tame PRO. Second, I could use a day to try to get to Jack Wright and line the audience up.'

'O.K. Book both flights, honey, and some hotel accommodation, too, while you're at it.'

'Single rooms this trip.'

'But not too far apart. I get nervous in the tropics at night.'

'You must try to conquer it, John. With your willpower that should be easy.'

'It's not so much a question of willpower as of staying-power.'

He heard her laugh as she put the phone down.

Jean-Pierre had made up his mind about Francis Chiribanda even before Helen had walked in on their interview. He needed stability on his park boundary. Even more he needed Marie's return to his bed as wife, or whatever she was. He was amazed at the strength of the deprivation he felt, deprivation made stonger by Helen's presence and her reluctance even to be touched by him in the most casual and innocent way. What he expected after the long time-gap and all that had happened to them both he could not say. What he certainly had not expected was for her to return to Africa. This central fact had thrown him so badly. If Francis Chiribanda was the price he had to pay for re-establishing both professional and private peace, then perhaps the young man did not come too high.

He let two days pass, two days during which he constantly expected a visit from the doctor. None came. On the third evening he drove out to Veniard's lakeside bungalow. Veniard, naked from the waist up, the fold of an incipient pot-belly overflowing the rim of his kekoy, lay smoking a hand-rolled cigarette with whose smell Jean-Pierre was familiar. Veniard saw his visitor and wrinkled his nose.

'I forgot you don't smoke.'

'No, and certainly not that stuff.'

'It's far better quality than Mushi's rubbish.'

'No doubt.'

'Don't be such a prig.'

'It's your business, after all.'

'No harm in anything in moderation. An occasional reefer is more relaxing than Pernod and not nearly as bad for the system. But you didn't come here simply to disapprove of my ruinous and depraved habits.'

'I've been expecting you to call.'

'To hear what you've decided about young Francis? I've been away for a couple of days visiting patients up the lake.'

'I've decided to give him a trial.'

'Very sensible decision. Where do I come in?'

Jean-Pierre helped himself to a cold beer. 'Come in? Haven't you been in all the time?'

'In a way, yes. You could say that. More or less as medical adviser to all parties.'

'Precisely. So you can tell Chiribanda senior that the deal's on.'

'I don't think he'll accept it purely by word of mouth. Not from me, anyway.'

'Well, I'm not going round rubbing my nose in his murky pool like a warthog at a mud wallow.'

'I didn't suggest you should. But you are the head man. Kama Chiribanda will only take his son's appointment as a fact when he gets a letter to that effect on the park's paper, signed by you.'

'We haven't even got any park paper.'

'Any paper will do so long as it looks official. Don't muck around. Set out your conditions ... probationary period, appointment as head ranger ... park acceptance of Chiribanda quinine plantations ... absolute protection of the gorillas ... the lot. Include a map showing your boundary *outside* his plantations. State Chiribanda's right to continue farming, subject to the conditions laid down. Perhaps there should be two letters. Keep his son's appointment separate.'

'Think he'll sign?'

'Of course he'll sign. Look. Why don't you meet the bloody man and have it out round the table? I'll chair the meeting again.'

'Not everything can be resolved officially.'

'Oh, I see. You mean the hex on Marie's sex life. I suppose you could argue that that bit comes within my medical sphere of influence.'

'Tell him everything else is conditional on that.'

'I don't think he'll call off his spell-binder until he has your official assurance about Francis.'

Jean-Pierre shrugged. 'O.K. I'll type it in the morning. You can call a meeting when you like to regularise the matter of the plantations.'

Veniard offered the half-smoked reefer, saying, 'You really should have a puff occasionally. Makes life look rosier.'

To his surprise Jean-Pierre took it from him and had a quick drag.

'Tastes and smells disgusting. I'd rather be a gorilla any day.'

'Yes. I've often suspected that. That reminds me. Time I saw that young patient of yours again. Ought to look at how that pin is settling down.'

Africa seldom settles for half measures. If it ignores you, it ignores you completely. It is more than big enough to ignore anyone it pleases. On arrival in the capital, Nancy Genova fully expected to be ignored. To her total surprise there was an official Mercedes from the Ministry of Tourism and

247

Development to meet her at the airport. Her immediate reaction on seeing the welcoming smile beneath the driver's peaked, uniform cap was that somebody up there wanted something out of her. This was fine by Nancy Genova since the reverse was precisely true.

The driver took her to the newly-opened Africana Hotel. A big bunch of flowers lay on the dressing-table in her room and, buried in them, a letter from Jack Wright.

'Welcome! You came at a good time,' she read. 'Very hopeful I will be able to arrange meeting with the president the day after tomorrow. Presume Dr Redfern will be here by then. Can I meet with you ten o'clock tomorrow morning? The car will call for you at 9.45. Guess you need a nice rest right now. The hotel is pretty good but suggest you keep lid on loo at night. The sewage system in this town is still just short of perfection.'

Nancy kicked off her shoes, put the flowers in water, lifted the lid of the loo and sniffed apprehensively. There was just the faintest hint of bacteria hard at work somewhere close at hand. She took a shower, stretched herself naked on the bed and reached for the telephone. After thirty seconds the operator answered. She'd fared worse in New York. For a journalist, the efficiency of the telephone and cable service took priority far above that of the main drainage system. Better still, the operator expressed no surprise on being asked to send a cable to Berkeley University, California. Whether the wire got there or not was something Nancy did not propose to lose sleep over. She had done all that duty required by asking Redfern to hurry on down. This was Africa. Tomorrow she could find a news agency colleague and try to get a message out by more certain methods. She fell asleep.

When she awoke it was dark outside and tree-frogs were playing their little zithers in chorus beyond the window. She rang for room service and was amazed when a waiter in a neatly-tailored light-weight suit, patterned with bright leaves and flowers, brought the meal within ten minutes of her ordering it. She had brought *Through Darkest Africa* to read. What would her countryman, Henry Morton Stanley, have made of the Africana Hotel?

The car called for her promptly next morning and drove to the government building at a speed a Manhattan taxi-driver would have envied. The government building was not hard to find. It stood fifty feet taller than any other building in the city. Its architect had not intended it to do so. When it was half finished the president had learned that the proposed Africana Hotel would top his new government block by ten feet. The president had sent for the Swedish architect and ordered him to do better. The architect had been quite happy to do so, as had the contractors, but both were doubtful whether the foundations would stand the strain. Some clever and expensive work with glass and lightweight alloys on the topmost floor of all, subsequently used for official receptions, had ensured that the building obtained a fifty-foot superiority. The president had guaranteed it would keep its lead by issuing an edict limiting all future buildings to the height of the Africana.

Jack Wright had a large office on the tenth floor. He was something left over from the Jack Kennedy era of diplomatic whizz-kids. His crew-cut was grey but it was still a totally out-of-fashion crew-cut. He was tall, fit, athletic, a clean-cut, though ageing, all-American boy in a brand-new, rough-cut all-African state!

'Well,' he said, 'Nancy. And well again. Long time no see. So glad you could get here so quickly. . . .' Comically. 'You've got the cheque with you? Nothing talks like money in this place, you've got to believe me.'

She shook hands, wincing a little at the scratch-golfer's grip. 'Dr Redfern will be dealing with the financial angle.'

'Great! You got the flowers?'

'That was sweet of you. Thanks, too, for having me met at the airport.'

'Just part of the service. By the way, the car's at your disposal while you're here. If I can find an hour to two from my onerous duties, I'd like to show you round myself. Plenty to show you. These boys mean to go places, I'll tell you. How did you find the Africana?'

'Unbelievably good.'

'American money, of course.'

'But the service is good. The African staff. . . .'

'If I tell you a secret, you'll promise not to print it? O.K. then. You know the way they got those waiters and receptionists so good so quickly? They trained them on a machine that rewarded them with banana-flavoured pellets. You know . . . serve a gin and tonic without lemon, a mild electric shock . . . add lemon and ice, a banana candy comes down the shoot and yummie!'

Nancy laughed dutifully. She'd heard from Redfern about similar experiments in educating chimpanzees. She was beginning to get the measure of Jack Wright. He aimed to be a great little kidder about the locals to strangers, particularly, perhaps, to Americans. It was his way of excusing the fact that he had become, in effect, a diplomatic mercenary. Just the same, she'd bet he was one hundred per cent the servant of his new employer. It might not do to kid back at him.

'Whatever method they used to train that staff,' she said, 'it certainly worked.'

'You could have been lucky. The other day a guy phoned room service at the Africana and ordered breakfast. "Send me a raw egg, toast burned on both sides, some cold coffee slopped on the tray and some milk mixed with orange juice.' "I'm sorry," says room service, "we don't serve breakfast like that." "Well," says this guy, "you sure did yesterday." '

Nancy smiled. It was the best she could do. She'd already heard slightly different versions of the same story about four new hotels in four capital cities.

The kidding was temporarily over. Wright had put on his sincere look. He produced a whole file of cuttings featuring the Intruder's picture.

'This couldn't have come at a better time. This country has had so many things on its mind that conservation and the

250

environment have hardly rated an any-other-business heading on its national agenda. Things are changing. President Olindo is very much aware of the natural wonders his country contains. Now understand, Nancy. This is classified information, off the record at this moment, but he's prepared to make a declaration that ten per cent of his country will be devoted to national parks.'

'That's a lot of territory.'

'It is precisely one hundred and twenty thousand square miles of territory. Have a look at this.' Wright pressed a button and two polished, wooden wall-panels slid back to reveal a relief map, illuminated from behind. 'Those dark-green areas,' he indicated them with stabbing and not very precise gestures, 'are all untouched forest. God knows what natural treasures they contain. Peacocks, okapi, some say even a link between man and gorilla. All that the president is prepared to give to nature conservation.'

'That's a tremendous gesture and it raises tremendous problems of control, policing, research.'

'Easy there. Step by step. The first thing, surely, is the will to succeed and that this country has in large measure.'

Miss Genova was not prepared just to sit there and swallow the official hand-out. 'Of course, there is the point that there probably isn't much else you can do, anyway, with one hundred thousand square miles of dense rain-forest.'

'You're so right, but what other African ruler can you name who's prepared to come right out and say that he's going to hand it over to the birds and the bees?'

'What other African ruler do you know who's got that much rain-forest?'

'*Touché*, but it's still not a bad offer. We could find we had a lot more gorillas among all those trees, for one thing.'

'No, it's not a bad offer, counsellor.'

'Call me Jack. I have no official title.'

'Maybe, but they say you have more influence than anyone else with the president.'

'Let's say *some* influence and, talking of influence, let's

251

come right out and ask what Redfern wants.'

'You've heard of Ark International?'

Wright tapped a thick folder of cuttings.

Nancy said, 'Your Misoka—Vahinga National Park for mountain gorillas is Ark's major project. He's coming here to present President Olindo with a cheque for one hundred thousand dollars to increase the services in Misoka Park.'

'Great. So what's *he* want?'

'Publicity for Ark. Your country is one of its agreed spheres of influence in the conservation world.'

'And you're here just for the story?'

'Just that.'

'And to do a little advance fixing?'

'If possible.'

'Fixing is something we're pretty good at — if the price is right.'

For the first time she warmed to Wright. He had spoken nothing but the literal truth and he knew that she knew it.

'One hundred thousand bucks is not a bad price.'

'I'd rather it went almost anywhere else than Misoka.'

'Why the hell? Misoka's damned important.'

'But it's one heck of a long way from here.'

'So? What's distance to the outside world?'

'Not a damn thing, but it's a hell of a lot to the world's Press when they have to travel there.'

'What alternative do you suggest?'

'Olindo Park, right here, twenty-five miles from where we're sitting.'

'What kind of a park is that, counsellor? I've never even heard of it.'

'The president has only just gazetted it.'

'How big?'

'Roughly fifty square miles, much of it lake. Lake Olindo.'

'Animals?'

'Mostly water birds. A few antelope.' Wright consulted his notes. 'Waterbuck, bushbuck, impala, kob.'

'How many?'

'A hundred or so at present. We're going to bring in some rhino and giraffe.'

'Sounds like the president's private zoo. You want Redfern to pour his hard-won dollars into that?'

'Some dollars, maybe. He'll see the advantage.'

'That could be quite a story. How to waste international conservation funds.'

'You're quite the complete little independent journalist, aren't you?'

'I take this ecological thing fairly seriously.'

'And Redfern?'

'I take him seriously, too.'

'So I hear.' A cutting edge to the observation?

'There are obviously angles for all of us here, if we play it right. I'm sure you'd like to have the exclusive on the president's statement. I *could* let all the other Press boys and girls in on it. Look, I have a pretty full day. Why don't I pick you up for dinner? Use the car meantime. The driver will take you wherever you like. Lake Olindo, for instance.'

'O.K. But about dinner, don't expect any favours outside the line of duty.'

'That Redfern,' Wright said admiringly. 'He must be quite a ball of fire. Pick you up around seven-thirty, then?'

Nancy asked the driver to take her straight to Lake Olindo. The road was one of the tarmacadam radii that centred on the capital. Most of these petered out after ten miles. This one was a bit better than most. It lasted for fifteen increasingly pot-holed miles and then relapsed into the familiar rutted, red, dusty track. Before it did so it passed through the usual depressing collection of mud and corrugated-iron shanties. The driver hooted continually to blast a way through the press of people; women driving goats with a stick, but more often boys or girls driving goats with a stick; women carrying great bunches of green bananas on their heads; women carrying miraculously-stacked piles of sugar-cane and oc-casionally firewood on their heads. There were throngs of men, too, but mostly they were doing nothing except

253

watching the women do all this, just as they might have watched ants busily at work and with about as much interest. The men had made a life-study of doing nothing.

Further out of town they came to farming country, but not farming as Nancy Genova or any Westerner knew it. Here the small farmers were literally scratching a living from soil that got no rest, no encouragement, in fact no husbandry at all. The trees had long since been chopped down to make charcoal, which, further along the road, men sold in sacks. With the trees gone, the grass-roots chewed away by goats and continual ploughing by oxen dragging tree-trunks as primitive ploughs, the soil had lost its grip on the face of the earth. When the inevitable heavy rains came and the strong winds blew, that soil took off for places elsewhere. It was washed down the little watercourses into the great rivers and the thin skin of fertility by which men live departed with it.

Nancy recalled the words of a famous agriculturist with whom she had toured a similarly over-populated, over-farmed area in another part of Africa. The expert, an irascible Scot who dearly loved Africa, its people and the principles of good farming in equal proportions, had sourly regarded the milling locals bouncing off the wings of his Land Rover as he jostled his way through a village. 'Look at them,' he had screamed in fury, 'the whole damn lot of them are only good for fucking bone-meal.' It was the cry of a humanitarian driven beyond endurance. Nancy understood it now as the red dust clouds swirled around her. She did not expect any more from Lake Olindo than from the *shambas* that bordered it, and was consequently not disappointed.

Lake Olindo was salmon-pink. It was not pink with flamingoes as were many of the African lakes she had seen. This was reasonable enough. It was not a soda lake and therefore had nothing to offer flamingoes. It was pink with the topsoil the wind had blown into it. It had once, no doubt, been a beautiful place. It still had the bones of beauty in its features. The flesh, however, had shrunk and shrivelled. *Shambas* stretched practically all along the near shore, leaving

254

only a narrow band of lacustrine vegetation. Dense stands of fever-trees had once occupied the shoreline. Only remnants remained. Most of the trees had already fallen to the charcoal-burners.

The lake was seldom more than a mile wide. Steep hills fell abruptly to the further shore. The habitat there looked more promising for wild animals but the slopes of the hills showed the familiar scars of subsistence farming. The run-off into the lake from those hills must contain not only red topsoil but anything toxic used in local agriculture. No, the prospect was not promising. A newly-erected and decidedly flimsy scaffolding arch bore the sign 'Lake Olindo National Park'. Beside this stood a portable aluminium hut. An African in khaki uniform came out as he heard the car and held up his hand. When he saw the official badge on the door of the Mercedes he waved them past.

Nancy Genova did not claim to be an expert on African animals. She had visited a number of African national parks, however, including some like Nakuru and Manyara whose central feature was a lake. What she saw did not excite her greatly. Human habitation was far too close. At some points the villagers even came down to the lakeside to wash themselves and their clothes. The mud flats attracted fair numbers of small, brownish birds that scuttled about like large insects with long, probing beaks. These she took to be waders. There was little sign of the larger and more spectacular waterbirds. She spotted a solitary fish eagle, which suggested that the lake was not over-supplied with fish. She looked in vain for mammals. Giving Lake Olindo the benefit of the doubt, she put this down to the nearness of humans.

The chauffeur was reluctant to drive his already dust-covered limousine further along the shore in case he got bogged down on the rapidly deteriorating track, but Nancy insisted. She could see some woodland and scrub about a mile ahead. When they at last reached this she was rewarded by finding four waterbuck. Where the trees still stood, progress had not quite caught up with Lake Olindo and it was possible to see what it had once been.

Miss Genova was not impressed. She drove back to the city in a state of gloom. While it was admirable to try to save or restore any wild place of beauty or value, Lake Olindo plainly did not deserve to come high on the list of anyone's priorities. It would take a great deal of money to make anything of it, even if the problems posed by too adjacent humanity could be solved by presidential edict. That funds needed to secure Misoka might be diverted to it made her want to go straight home and write a knocking story. She could hardly wait until John Redfern got there.

At dinner that night Jack Wright didn't push Lake Olindo. He didn't push his luck with her, either. Nancy found his views about his adopted country interesting and fairly convincing. He agreed that in many ways the administration was a shambles but argued that it had achieved a lot in the four years since the *Fisi* uprising. Yes, it was often dishonest — by Western standards of dishonesty, at least — but what African state was not? What had happened to all the *Fisi*? Well, yesterday's rebel was often today's patriot. The big boys had been bumped off, naturally, simply because they were big and couldn't be allowed to stick around. Some medium-sized and smaller fish had survived and slid quietly back into different ponds. He himself knew three or four businessmen who had fought on the wrong side. The rank and file? They'd just gone back to their *shambas*, got de-oathed or de-magicked and taken to chopping down sugar-cane with their pangas again instead of chopping off human heads.

Then it was his turn to ask the questions. He wanted to know all about Jean-Pierre Menant, his park, his aspirations, the importance of a handful of mountain gorillas to the rest of the world. When she had replied as objectively as she could he said, 'Well, I'll probably have to divide all that by two.'

'Probably,' she agreed. 'But then, I already divided your load of inspired garbage by three.'

He took this good-humouredly. 'Talking of garbage, you visited Lake Olindo? What did you think of it?'

'You've just described it. Why your president should want to attach his good name to that. . . .'

'My idea.'

'You're capable of better thinking than that.'

'I'm not so sure. It has a lot to commend it. Other African rulers renamed the Great Rift Valley lakes after themselves. Lake Idi Amin . . . Lake Mobutu Sese Seko. Nothing much wrong with those lakes from a conservation point of view. My motto is: if you want to make a splash that everyone will notice, jump in a sewer. Lake Olindo's not quite that, but supposing my boy restored it to its pristine beauty? Great propaganda stuff, you'll agree?'

'Not if it means ditching something really worthwhile.'

'Who talked about ditching anything?'

'Sorry, I couldn't have heard you right.'

'Conservation at African government level, my dear Nancy, is just another arm of politics. Who's being so high and mighty, anyway? Aren't you and the good Dr Redfern hoping for a useful plug for Ark International?'

'I'll admit that much. But Ark's aims are sound conservation ones.'

'And no kudos for Redfern attached to them? Don't give me that. No inside stories for you?'

'O.K., wait until Redfern arrives before you jump to conclusions.'

'Sure. Now let's just enjoy ourselves. We've got at least one good night-club in this town.'

Jack Wright put no more pressure on her during the rest of the evening. At the end of it he saw her back to the Africana. Unexpectedly, he did not even make a ritual ploy to come up and have a nightcap. She was glad about that. He was the sort of man who might take a rebuff, however skilfully handled, as a short, sharp slap in the ego.

She took a shower and then sat before the open, screened window in her house-coat, jotting, as was her invariable custom, notes and impressions in a large diary.

Against Jack Wright's name she recorded: 'Distrustful of

257

his ambivalent view of his masters. Joked about their short-comings too much but also obviously admires their success. Perhaps he only does this for visiting American firemen, to underline the fact that, under the burned cork, he's still a white American boy. Wonder what his African colleagues think of him and what would happen if a coup deposed Olindo? Has two-faced Jack got a secret underground passage to the American Embassy? In such circumstances, he'd probably need one. One thing for sure: his loyalty to the president is real enough and, it would seem, the reverse is also true. Conclusion: feel we are in for some real horse − or should it be zebra − trading with honest Jack. How will John react? I *think* he's dedicated to the Misoka gorilla project. Anyway, much of the money's dedicated to it by the *Paris-Match* commitment. If we have to accommodate Wright's crazy lake scheme, what do we ask for in return? Must sleep on that one.'

Nancy placed the quarto-sized diary under her pillow. Things got stolen in the best regulated hotels. Someday she planned to make a book of those jottings. Then would be time enough for Wright and everyone else mentioned therein to read about themselves.

Before she fell asleep she remembered to close the lid of the loo. Her last wakeful thought was that if President Olindo wanted to spend money clearing up open sewers, he couldn't do better than start with the capital's main drainage. She'd heard somewhere − or was she now dreaming it? − that an American overseas-aid envoy had offered funds to do just that. Olindo's government had turned the proposal down and built a grandiose post office with the money instead. A post office, they'd said, you could see. Sewers were underground so no one noticed them. Whether she made the story up or not she could no longer tell but she did know that she was smiling in her sleep at the Alice in Wonderland quality of it all.

Redfern flew in at noon the next day, only an hour after

Nancy received the cable announcing his arrival. Nancy's call to Wright's office got tangled up in the Africana's exchange with one he was already making to her. That took five valuable minutes to sort out. Things were happening fast. President Olindo had agreed to give Redfern an audience on the one condition that he receive the presentation cheque Redfern was bringing by the waterside at Lake Olindo. The presentation had to happen the following day to fit the President's schedule. Wright's call had been to know whether Redfern would be there in time. Well, great, now he would be. He'd send the official car round right away. He guessed it would be better if Nancy met the great man at the airport. They must have a lot to discuss, Wright said. If Nancy would look after the good doctor for lunch, he and Redfern could get together to go over final details in his office at the government building at four that afternoon. Before she could say that she expected to be included in this meeting, either Wright or the switchboard operator had cut off. This time she had a feeling it was Wright.

So she reached the airport ten minutes after Redfern had cleared customs. There he stood, bow-tied, lightweight-suited, outwardly, and, no doubt, inwardly, cool. He kissed her on the cheek in parental manner and whistled at the government crest on the ministry Mercedes.

'All seems to progress smoothly.'

'So—so, John. There's a good deal of wheeler-dealing in the air.'

'Never forget that the barter system has long prevailed in these parts.'

'Let's get out of this concrete and glass oven and find a cool drink. You could probably do with a shower and a lie down.'

'Invitations already?'

'I told you. We're in well-separated rooms.'

'It's too hot for an old man, anyway.'

'Or even for a not-too-decrepit lady.'

'I suppose they've got air-conditioning in the hotel?'

'Yes, but it's largely cancelled out by the smell of drains.'

259

'Remind me to tell you sometime what happened when the American aid envoy. . . .'

'What a pity. I thought I'd made that story up in a dream.'

But he wasn't listening. Instead, he kept up a joyously enthusiastic commentary on everything he saw on the drive to the hotel. 'Look at that woman with that sack of melons on her head. If only you Western gals would walk around like that, you wouldn't have any slipped disc problems. . . .' He watched a man in a long robe squatting on a vacant lot to relieve himself. 'Maybe main drainage *would* be a waste. Better to put the money into wildlife conservation.'

'Wait until you hear,' she warned him.

Over lunch she told him Olindo was going to demand half of the Misoka money for Lake Olindo. When he didn't jump out of his chair she snapped at him, 'Why aren't you hopping mad?'

'I can even see his point of view. It's damn good presidential propaganda, a lake right on his own front doorstep.'

'He'll need far more than fifty thousand bucks to put that particular show back on the road.'

'Far more than twenty-five thousand bucks, you mean.'

'Good for you. You'll only agree to half?'

'Not necessarily. I was counting on him keeping half for himself.'

'That's pretty cynical.'

'Pretty realistic. Mind you, it depends what we get in exchange.'

'Now I can see why other scientists don't always care for you. You should have been on Wall Street.'

'That's a very nice compliment. Thank you, Nancy.'

'You're an old bastard.'

Redfern smiled with pleasure. 'A legitimate negotiator wouldn't get far with these babies. I'll repeat my original question: what do we get from His Excellency in return?'

'Wright says he'll give a pledge to turn ten per cent of the country over to national parks.'

Redfern skewered a piece of Parma ham and melon. 'Wow!

260

That's worth fifty thousand bucks of any man's money, especially since this country's Ark's zone of responsibility. If I, on behalf of Ark International, could announce that, this trip would have achieved a great deal.'

'What about Misoka? I thought you were a dedicated primate man, that you regarded the mountain gorilla as the most important. . . .'

'I do. Of course, it's the biggest thing this country has. But does Olindo think so?'

'He thought enough of it once to gazette Misoka as a park. *You* persuaded him, if I remember.'

'You mustn't get things out of proportion. I've never seen you angry with me before. I'm not sure that I like it.'

'And I'm not sure if I like to see that remarkable man Menant let down just for some grubby political game.'

'I'm afraid it's all of that. But who said Ark would let him down? The rest of the hundred thousand dollars, plus a lot of the loot Ark will collect as a result of a diplomatic success with Olindo, will go to Misoka.'

'How can you tell it won't get intercepted on the way? If the president or his ministers expect to steal half of everything, what hope has conservation got in this benighted country?'

'As much as it has in East Africa or in Zaire. Those countries have all got off to a fairly good start. Some of them make a lot of tourist revenue out of wildlife, too.'

'Some day I'll write the real conservation story.'

'I'm sure you will, too.'

'How about right now? I could go back to the States and pull the plug straight out of little old Lake Olindo — just wait until you see it, by the way.'

'I saw it last time I was here. The president even told me about his hopes for saving it.'

'And you didn't discourage him?'

'No. And if I had discouraged him, it would be Olindo who was doing the plug-pulling out of Ark, out of Misoka, out of everything.'

'O.K. Supposing in your aged wisdom you are guilefully right. There's still one thing I have to know because, strangely enough, I have a high regard for your scientific integrity. I don't want all my girlish dreams shattered at once. Are you, John, really committed to saving what's left of the mountain gorilla and the Misoka gorillas in particular?'

He took her hand across the table. 'I still haven't forgotten I did all my best work on primates.' He could feel her hand trembling. 'Hey,' he said, 'you journalists are not as tough as you make out.'

She laughed, feeling that uncontrollable prickling at the corners of her eyes.

'Either that,' he said, 'or you're fonder of me than I thought. Either explanation is one I find pretty nice.'

Redfern turned his back to reach for the wine in its ice bucket, pausing long enough for her to dab her eyes with her serviette.

'Well, now,' he said, 'I can tell you that I'm going to do a little bartering on the gorillas' account. I've got a great idea to put them, and Misoka, on the map. I'm not going to tell you what it is yet. Anyway, let's drink to it.'

While they finished the wine the manager brought a letter addressed to Redfern. Nancy spotted the official crest.

'A welcoming note from Wright?'

'Yes. He's sending a car for me at a quarter to four.'

'I'll be ready and waiting.'

'Sorry, honey. Press excluded from this one. He specifically asks for that.'

'The bastard.'

'Oh, I dunno. He probably just wants to give me the run-down on the meeting with the president tomorrow.'

'The run-around is more like it.'

'Trust me. I'm a big boy. I can look after myself.'

'I'll expect to hear all about it when you get back.'

'Sure. Unless, of course, he puts an embargo on my aspect of the news until after the meeting tomorrow.'

'If you'll excuse me, John. I've got a splitting head. I'm

going to lie down.'

She showered, wrote up some caustic diary notes and, about the time Redfern left for the ministry, fell asleep. It was seven-thirty when she woke. She rang Redfern's room but got no reply. The desk hadn't seen him since he left in mid-afternoon. She dined miserably by herself, sat in the garden under the stars hoping he'd return and find her. At ten she went to bed, took a sleeping pill and had a bad night. There were no jokes in her sleep this time.

Redfern rang her before she was up.

'Sorry, honey. Did I wake you?'

'I guess so. I took a sleeping pill.'

'I called to apologise for not contacting you last night.'

'That's O.K., John. I had an article to get started.'

'I feel really awful about it. I was so looking forward to dinner together.'

'Forget it. I wasn't much company. That darn headache wouldn't let go of me.'

'That darn Jack Wright wouldn't let go of me. Insisted I go out to his place. Had to meet a lot of people at the ministry.'

Despite her pique she was professionally interested. 'Oh! Who?'

'Forestry men, drainage engineers, a mining man. The mining guy was a tough nut. I've seldom seen such a tall African. He must be a Watutsi. Aren't they supposed to be seven feet tall?'

'Apart from the forestry department they don't sound much like conservation experts to me.'

'That was the whole point. They're not. Wright's smart enough to see theirs are the conflicting interests we've got to win over, or at least do a deal with.'

'Does that mean more bribes?'

'You sound a little rough this morning, Nancy. Why don't we have breakfast together on my balcony?'

'Is that proper?'

'It's got a nice view.'

'Over the cess-pit drainage?'

263

'In forty minutes. That leaves us an hour to talk before the car comes to take us out to meet the president at Lake Olindo.'

'Oh, am I invited this time?'

'Stop playing hurt, Nancy. You're too big a girl for that. Besides, we've both got work to do.'

'Papa's getting cross.'

'Oh, bullshit,' the great man said. 'See you in forty minutes.'

Over breakfast Redfern spread charm and concern thicker than he plastered maple syrup on to the excellent American-style waffles.

'Olindo's going to make his pledge to me personally.'

'Great. Who's going to be there?'

'Ministers. Half the cabinet. Wright, of course. Some of the guys I met last night. What Wright calls a cross-section of the conservation scene.'

'Who else?'

'Oh, you mean Press? No one except the official government photographers. You can have the story exclusively. From me. I'll give you the written text.'

'What about Misoka?'

'Half the dough.'

'And your great ploy to put it on the map?'

'I'll announce that in my speech.'

'It had better be good.'

'Wright says that, once I've made my suggestion in front of all those dignitaries, Olindo will more or less have to go along with it. Besides, he'll see it as another useful piece of conservation propaganda.'

Half the populace on the road out to the lake must have been working all night. Flags sagged in the lifeless air all along the route. Two triumphal arches of rusty scaffolding had been heaved across the road with 'Welcome to our President' draped over them on a banner whose background was an unhappy blend of the national colours. One or two of the larger pot-holes on the tarmac part of the road were no longer waiting to test the suspension of the official cars. Nancy noted that they had been hastily filled in with what looked like mud. Where these lightning repairs coincided with a white line, the latter had been painted over the surface of the mud. The repair gangs must have known that at this season of the year rain was unlikely.

Beyond three rows of chairs, a dais with microphone had been erected at the lakeside. The dais, too, was draped with 'Welcome to our President' banners. Nancy had the cynical thought that this simple sentiment could be used on behalf of any president. It was therefore coup-proof. She had to admit that what she had seen of the country so far suggested that no coup was imminent. Olindo seemed firmly in control.

Olindo's arrival at the lakeside partially belied this fact. First came six motor-cycle outriders in white, American-steel helmets and with sirens screaming. When the cortège was still only a red dust-cloud no bigger than a policeman's truncheon, the noise of these sirens put the only wildlife in the vicinity, a party of reeves and sandpipers probing in the mud not far from the dais, hysterically on the wing. Behind the outriders, who silenced their sirens as they approached the scaffolding arch, drove four cars filled with civilian dignitaries and a scattering of generals and colonels. Finally, like a great white shark surrounded by a school of pilot fish, came the presidential Mercedes, escorted by eight more motor-cyclists.

The president's car was of the ultra-lengthy sort that looks as long as a cricket pitch and has almost as many doors as a railway carriage. The outriders fell back at the archway to let the great car pass through first. The riders saluted more or less in unison as they passed under the arch. Unfortunately, the right-hand motor-cyclist hit a jackal hole at the precise moment he snapped his hand up to the salute. The resulting loss of control swerved him sideways into his nearest companion, who cannoned off to unseat the motor-cyclist on his immediate left. Had the entire escort been dressed by the right as had originally been intended, this would have resulted in the sort of military chain reaction only usually observed among lead soldiers. Amidst a yowling of open throttles, the three machines gave the appearance of actually fighting their fallen masters as they rolled in the dust. Mercifully, the dust-cloud raised by the cortège that had now swept on towards the dais concealed the worst humiliations of this minor disaster.

Jack Wright rode with an aide in the car immediately preceding the president's. While the aide led Olindo to the dais, Wright strode over to greet Redfern, helped him from his car and shook him warmly by the hand. He winked at Nancy, muttering out of the side of his mouth, 'There's a Press seat for you, the only Press seat, honey, in the centre of the third row of chairs. Wait until the mob is seated and then grab it.'

While the military and civilian big-shots sorted themselves out, Nancy took a good look at Olindo. So this was the strong man. The president stood only five foot six, despite all that platform-heeled boots could do for him. The face behind the gold-rimmed glasses was chubby and almost benign. It was hard to imagine this man giving orders for the extermination of rivals. Certainly, in the months following the civil war he had done so on a scale Hitler might have admired.

In one of the cars someone switched on a tape machine. The national anthem shattered the composure of a single pair of great white pelicans far out in the lake. The flag was hoisted up a pole whose last-minute erection had left it at an aggravating slant. Nancy remembered the advice given her the previous day by Jack Wright. 'If ever you see the flag unfurled, or hear what you suspect may be the national anthem, for God's sake freeze. Foreigners have been put in gaol for less.'

She froze, as did everyone else including the president, who turned towards the flag and saluted.

The ceremony that followed was brief, commendably brief. Dr Redfern handed over Ark International's cheque for one hundred thousand dollars.

The president's speech was long, almost unendurably long. She'd been promised a text, so Nancy concentrated on excavating the nuggets from the vast piles of verbal spoil in which Olindo buried his captive audience '. . . A great new drive towards conserving the natural wonders of the nation which the rest of the world will both admire and envy . . . starting at the very spot where we now stand which the nation has asked me to name Lake Olindo. . . .'

The president made a gesture as if to embrace the reed-beds around him. The official photographers worked over-time. He gazed out over the pinkish waters, hand shading the eyes as if dazzled by the flashing wings of a great gathering of water birds. To the photographers' delight a bird did fly behind the president at this moment. They were not to know it was that omnipresent scavenger, found even on city refuse heaps, a yellow-billed kite.

He was into the second ten minutes of his speech. 'The country's first national park will therefore be called Lake Olindo National Park.' At this, Nancy made a furious note. What about Misoka? Had the president forgotten about that?

Olindo was developing his theme. His name was proudly dedicated to the restoration of this beautiful lake right on the outskirts of the capital city. Before long millions of tourists would visit it just as they came to see the lions in Nairobi National Park or the pelicans — he meant flamingoes, of course — at Lake Nakuru in Kenya. But this was only the start. He was marking this historic occasion by announcing to the world that his nation intended to designate ten per cent of its entire territory, nearly two hundred thousand square kilometres, as national parks. President Olindo consulted the notes Jack Wright had prepared for him. He began to list the rare species this huge area of rain-forest might contain. At last, nearly at the end, came mention of the mountain gorilla and a reserve already established on the slopes of Mount Misoka.

Nancy felt let down. Her instincts told her to go back home and write a blistering piece about Olindo and conservation. The disadvantage of being close to Redfern seemed at that moment as real as though she were his tame, salaried PRO. She had reckoned without the old man, though. Whether he was intended to say a few closing words of thanks, or not, she couldn't say. As soon as the president sat down to prolonged clapping, Redfern was at the microphone. He stood waiting for the applause to die away with the professional aplomb of a host on a network TV show. What a performer! First in English and then each thought repeated in pedantic though intelligible French, he paid gracious compliments to Olindo and his ministers for their thought for future generations. Without wasting more time than necessary, he said how honoured Ark International was to assist in the restoration of this once beautiful lake. As quickly as was decent, he came to the president's remarks about the Misoka gorillas. Despite all the other natural glories of the country, he pointed out, these magnificent animals were the ones the scientists of the world most hoped to see preserved and studied. Ark International was itself pledged to give every assistance in this. He knew that the world's Press who, he understood, were represented here today by a distinguished lady journalist, would give full credit to the president's magnificent gesture. He felt confident that President Olindo would wish the international importance of the gorillas to be given full prominence in any report on the nation's conservation plans. Half of the sum which Ark International had this day presented — and President Olindo had graciously accepted it for the purpose — was covenanted to the Misoka sanctuary for mountain gorillas.

Nancy noted that Redfern was astute enough not to refer to Misoka as a national park. How could it be since Olindo had just declared Lake Olindo to be the country's *first* national park? Conveniently, Olindo had momentarily overlooked Misoka for propaganda purposes.

'I will just add this to everything the president has said and promised here today. My scientific colleagues all over the world see the survival of the mountain gorilla and the forests in which it lives as being of such paramount importance that Ark International will pledge itself to call, and partly finance, a world conference of experts on gorillas and their ecology at Misoka one year from today. It will be a conference that will truly put this nation in the vanguard of African conservation.'

So that was it. The cunning old bastard. Great publicity for Ark, for Redfern and for Olindo, too. Olindo was smiling and applauding even though he had plainly never heard of such a world conference before that moment. It would be hard for even him to back out of it now.

Nancy caught a look of complicity between Redfern and Wright. The American counsellor had known what the old man was going to suggest, had plainly been in league with him. They must have discussed the manoeuvre last night. But, if so, what else had they discussed? What other bargains had been struck?

Nancy drove back alone. Redfern had been invited to join Olindo and Wright.

A flight for Nairobi left at three in the afternoon, arriving there at five. She could file her story much more easily from Kenya. A note at the desk told her Redfern had been held up for further talks at the ministry and was having lunch with the president. The Africana found her a seat on the afternoon flight. She decided to preserve her independent journalistic status by catching it.

Two nights after Francis Chiribanda received the letter appointing him as head ranger to Misoka Park, Marie came to bed topless in her kekoy and immediately moulded herself to Jean-Pierre. It was as if there had never been any break in their love-making. She offered no explanation, made no comment. She was warm, affectionate and enthusiastic but no more so than on normal occasions. Not so Jean-Pierre. The embargo had lasted too long for that. They made love twice within the first hour. As they lay together afterwards he planned to wake her in the early hours hoping for a

269

response. He never did so. His mood changed as they lay, fingertips touching. It was not because he felt any less desire for her. His Western mind was simply blocked by the fact that she had returned to full normality without any apparent physical or psychological memory of the blank that had gone before. It had been almost the same when she had first emerged from the witch-doctor's hypnotically induced coma. She had never referred to the weeks in which she had lived as a vegetable. Her mental pattern was uniquely African. He found that, though this enhanced her fascination for him as a person, it did not further excite his desire. Rather, he preferred to fall in with her rhythm. His final thought as he fell asleep was that he was more deeply involved with Marie Maputa than he had ever thought possible.

She was up when he woke soon after dawn. He heard her laughing and calling to the baby gorilla as she lit the stove that provided the house with hot water. When she finally appeared he expected her to be carrying the breakfast tray. Instead she cradled Toto.

'Isn't she lovely? So much better behaved than a child.' She prised the baby loose and dropped it in Jean-Pierre's lap.

'I hope you're right. She's not exactly house-trained.'

'Don't you like her?'

'The most important thing to me is that you like her. She lacks a mother.'

'But, Jean-Pierre, you must like her also.'

'I do. Of course I do. But I have to harden my heart and remember that one day she must go back to the forest. You can play a very important part while she's getting over her wound. But she mustn't become too much of a pet, so take her back now and put her into her enclosure.'

Breakfast was only just out of the way when Francis Chiribanda knocked on the office door.

'Reporting for duty, *Monsieur le Conservateur*.'

'Begin by being less formal. Let's settle for Monsieur Menant.'

'If that is what you wish, Monsieur Menant.'

'I do.'

Was there a hint of send-up or was Francis Chiribanda just trying hard from the outset to please? His expression seemed respectful enough.

'What do you wish me to do?'

'Do? I wasn't even expecting you so soon.'

Jean-Pierre was so unused to having a subordinate that he was caught completely flat-footed by the young man's arrival.

'Shall I sit in the car until you're ready for me?'

'No. There's plenty to learn. Start by studying the boundaries of the park. Make sure you know them precisely. Later I'll want you to accompany me on my rounds.'

Ten minutes later Veniard dropped in. He nodded to Chiribanda. 'Good morning, Francis. I see your arm is now sufficiently recovered for you to start work. Congratulations on your appointment, by the way. Roll up your sleeve. Let's look at those stitches. Good. Good. It's knitted up beautifully but I didn't really come to see you. My visit concerns my other patient.'

Veniard crossed to the window and looked out towards Toto's pen where Marie was giving the baby her morning feed.

'Good morning, Marie. You're looking positively blooming. Something must be agreeing with you.' He winked lewdly at Jean-Pierre, who said acidly, 'All right. You're a bloody marvellous physician. Cures for everyone and everything. Now do you mind doing what you came to do? I've got a full morning ahead.'

'Quite right,' Veniard said good-humouredly. 'I came to take the pin out of your gorilla's arm.'

'You think she's ready for it?'

'Of course. Otherwise I wouldn't propose it.'

'You want help?'

'Marie can hold her. She's obviously a born nurse.'

'And the anaesthetic?'

'A simple shot in the backside. She may struggle a bit.

271

How strong is she?'

Jean-Pierre said, 'I'd like Chiribanda to assist you. It can be his first official job for the national park.'

'O.K. Good idea. Marie can get some boiling water to sterilise things. Like in the Westerns. The doctor always calls for plenty of boiling water. God knows what they do with it. Make coffee, probably.'

Veniard went into action at once. He loaded his syringe, laid out his instruments. Then he told Marie to bring the baby into the house. Once she was inside he ordered Chiribanda to take the gorilla and hold her tightly, bottom uppermost. At once Toto squealed and struggled. Chiribanda hung on. The baby bit him in the wrist as the needle went home. Chiribanda laughed and maintained his grip while the hypodermic did its job. Jean-Pierre noted all this but made no comment. In seconds the baby gorilla was unconscious. Veniard went to work on the pin and soon had it out. He flexed the elbow joint very gently.

'She'll have forgotten how to use it for a bit but don't worry. She'll soon find out again.' He looked at Chiribanda's arm. 'Here, swab it with this spirit. You won't need a tetanus shot. I put enough into you the other day to last a lifetime.'

Veniard called Marie over. 'When our young friend wakes up, give her all the mother love you've got. She's going to need a lot of reassurance for a day to two.'

Helen Lawes had walked in during the last minutes of the operation.

'But only for a day or two,' she said. 'If you're not careful you're going to imprint that young gorilla with the belief that it's a man, or' — she looked at Marie — 'perhaps a woman.'

'What you all do with her after she's well,' Veniard said tactfully, 'is your business. Mine is to get her arm working again.'

'I'm a scientist, doctor.'

'Fine, my dear. Well, you take over when this poor old quack has finished.'

Jean-Pierre said, 'It's good of you to call so early, Helen.

I'd no idea Jacques was going to operate this morning. You came to tell me something?'

'Yes. I'm ready to go back to the Saddle and start work.'

'When do you want to leave?'

'As soon as you can get all the supplies up there.'

'O.K. We'll go to work at once. Chiribanda, you know the hut Dr Lawes is talking about?'

'Sure, Monsieur Menant. I've been up there many times.'

'Good. This afternoon you can take up a detail with all the stores. Right now you'd better come and take over your ranger force. See if you can get a little parade ground smartness into them.'

At the park's headquarters the ranger force — Loti, Ndungu, Marema and Jahazi — received their new commander without marked enthusiasm but also without noticeable resentment. While Jean-Pierre checked and assembled the stores Helen would need taken up to the Saddle, he watched Chiribanda's progress with his troops, at first with tolerant amusement and then with grudging approval. The young man kept them at drill far longer than Jean-Pierre would have bothered to do. He barked commands at them in a most competent military manner. When Ndungu made a greater mess than usual of porting arms for inspection — not only did he get the rifle in his wrong hand but also held it upside down — Chiribanda took it from him and gave a copybook demonstration of the drill, correcting each movement crisply in drill-sergeant style. Ndungu was enchanted with the demonstration and grinned broadly to show his appreciation.

'Stupidity is nothing to laugh at.'

Ndungu's grin vanished like a half-moon hiding behind a black cloud. When the weapon was returned to him he managed to complete the evolution with only two minor errors.

'Far better, Ndungu.'

The moon popped out again. It was a full one, full with pleasure. This time Chiribanda did not admonish him. When

Chiribanda at last dismissed his sweating squad, Jean-Pierre told him, 'Quite a good start. Make an impression on them but don't try to overdo it.'

Jean-Pierre admitted to himself that the young man had made quite an impression on him also. But it would be unwise to praise too much in the early stages of their relationship. So much could go wrong.

Just before mid-day he left Chiribanda with orders to take the four rangers and carry the supplies up to the hut. As an afterthought he told Mushi to go with them. With the little tracker's help, Chiribanda could find out what gorillas were in the immediate area. Mushi, he knew, would gleefully tell him how Chiribanda had made out in the forest.

Francis Chiribanda, as Mushi later reported, had made out all right. Six weeks later he was still making out all right, in fact he was making out better and better. Jean-Pierre had hoped that the arrival of a second-in-command would leave him free to spend more time in the forest helping Helen Lawes with her gorilla study. Quite the opposite was the case. Administration seemed to pile up. Nancy Genova had sent him all the cuttings reporting Redfern's visit to President Olindo. He had snorted loudly when he had read about the proposed world conference on gorillas at Misoka.

'Where the hell do they think we'd hold it?' he asked Veniard one evening. 'Up in the trees with the apes, maybe.'

'It's all hot air,' Veniard had agreed. 'The sort of thing that sounds good to the outside world. They'll never do anything about it.'

They had both been wrong. The internal airways Dakota even took to turning up regularly and, when it did, it brought official letters demanding to know what accommodation there was in Baruva for visiting scientists; how many the Hôtel du Président could put up; the number of serviceable rooms existing at the park's headquarters. This last had caused the usually bland and controlled *conservateur* to shout out loud with laughter. He had written: 'Rooms at park HQ consist of one oil store (roofless); one office two metres by four metres; one ammunition store shared with a large python. The rest of the building is open to the sky having been gutted by fire.'

The next week's Dakota brought a senior official from the Ministry of Tourism and Development who surveyed the derelict building, filled pages of a note-book with figures and, having inspected the Hôtel du Président and other possible sources of temporary residence, caught the plane — which had been ordered to wait for him — back that afternoon.

Jean-Pierre was impressed, not to say flabbergasted, at this semblance of efficiency. Nevertheless, he expected to hear no more of it. Someone was just going through the motions. Jean-Pierre had had more than enough of bureaucracy for one day. Next morning, he told Marie, he would leave for the forest.

Even Marie had changed in some subtle way. No doubt this was a natural development helped by his own enriched feelings for her. Though she still accepted his decisions to come and go without question, it was clear that, on the increasingly rare occasions he was away for several days at a time, she missed him. He did not know whether he liked this or not. On balance, he thought he did not. It made her somehow less African, more like a European woman. He resolved to be away more in order to make it clear that he did not expect this reaction. From Helen Lawes, yes. Not the old Helen but the one who had returned — was it only a couple of months ago? This Helen, changed by the terror of her experiences but changed, too, by the cosseting effect of American academic life, was prickly about almost everything. He was glad that she had recently moved up on to the Saddle and had thrown herself so wholeheartedly into her work once again. It kept her out of Baruva where the causes for friction were many, not the least of them being Marie Maputa. The last thing Helen showed was a wish to reawaken her old affair with him. This did not in the least prevent her from expressing deep resentment at his relationship with Marie. Strangely enough, this manifested itself through the baby

275

gorilla. On several occasions Helen had practically snatched Toto out of Marie's arms and bundled her back into her enclosure. The pretext had always been a scientific one, namely, that the young gorilla was in danger of losing its identity, of becoming too dependant on humans. Jean-Pierre had never intervened during these scenes but he had noticed the protective clasp with which Helen had cradled the baby, her obvious desire for close contact with it, her eventual reluctance to let go once the enclosure was reached. The pauses, the lingerings, the claspings could be measured only in seconds yet they were long enough to betray motive.

Though he was not a trained scientist, Jean-Pierre had studied behaviour in primates intensively for four years. He had received his initial grounding from no less a person than the subject of his present observations. Shrewdly, then, he knew what to look for and he did not overlook much. He could hardly blame any woman for feeling warmly maternal towards the baby. If he doubted the total purity of Helen Lawes's self-declared scientific interest, it was perhaps because she had told him that she could never now have children herself.

He had anticipated great pleasure from Helen's return, not, as he quickly came to accept, pleasure in any romantic sense, but pleasure in introducing her to the forest once more, in passing on for her scientific appraisal the store of intelligent observation which he, the layman, had accumulated. Her initial reaction to the gorillas, one of apprehension if not fear, had seemed to be to his advantage. She would need his guidance, assurance and comradeship for some time. Here, too, he had been disappointed. To her credit, Helen had quickly overcome her early fears. It was too much to suppose that Absolom and his group remembered her. They had, however, become so conditioned to Jean-Pierre's presence that they rapidly accepted Helen's. Absolom occasionally charged her but in a half-hearted manner.

She had begun her reacclimatisation to the forest by following Absolom's group. Armed with Jean-Pierre's notes she had confined her early researches to confirming or modifying his observations. In this respect she was extremely generous. She told him on several occasions that a trained behaviourist might have been more cautious in his conclusions but on the whole his study was of doctorate standard. Jean-Pierre did not take offence at this summation nor was he unduly flattered. He merely smiled charmingly and observed that he frequently found points of value in the papers produced by qualified scientists.

Helen did not smile back as she once would have done. Helen, he admitted to himself, had become a bit of a prig. Nevertheless, he still got pleasure, albeit diminishing, from guiding her in the forest. Latterly he had had less and less time to do so. The duty had fallen increasingly to Francis Chiribanda.

It was natural that this should have been the case. After a month of Helen's acclimatisation in which Jean-Pierre had played his part, administration, greatly increased by the sudden interest in Misoka on the part of officialdom in the capital, had taken more and more of his time. Consequently, Chiribanda spent many more days on the mountain now than Jean-Pierre did. One of the main reasons he had wanted a competent African head ranger was to keep down poaching around the park's borders. This job alone kept Chiribanda on patrol in the forest. Mushi's early reports on the young African's skill in tracking and living in the forest, in approaching gorillas and reacting to the charges of irate males, were full of the expected mockery and criticism, often conveyed in comic and sometimes ribald mime. But then, Mushi criticised everyone in much the same way, including Jean-Pierre whom he loved dearly. Underneath the little man's performance Jean-Pierre could detect a grudging and surprised respect. Translated freely, Mushi's remarks and gestures meant: 'Though totally ignorant and lacking the lion-hearted courage which you and I possess, Jean-Pierre, this man is not entirely hopeless and can be taught. However, why an African should wish to walk through the forest simply to look at gorillas defeats me. Such lunacy is for white men and at least one white woman. Perhaps after all,' Mushi had added hopefully, 'he is simply selecting the best ones for us to eat.'

So Jean-Pierre had gone to see Francis Chiribanda in action for himself. In general, Mushi's summary was an accurate one. Chiribanda's fieldcraft was far better than average. He had clearly learned to approach animals as a hunter, just as he had claimed. He did not run from the gorillas, even though Absolom appeared particularly to dislike and distrust him and charged within feet every time they met. According to Mushi this irascibility on the part of the great silver-back did not decrease, as it might reasonably have been expected to do, as the acquaintanceship increased. Absolom continued to charge Chiribanda with undiminished enthusiasm.

Why this should be, Jean-Pierre could only guess. Chiribanda stood all of six feet tall. He was thus a good six inches shorter than the tall *Fisi* who had wounded Absolom with the pistol over four years previously. Some reflex of memory might still be at work. More likely, Absolom merely associated Chiribanda with the tall race of farmers who tended the plantations at the edge of the forest. Possibly he had suffered a frightening experience at their hands. Jean-Pierre knew that Francis Chiribanda had killed the Intruder. Had Absolom been a witness to that murder?

All these thoughts passed through Jean-Pierre's mind as he climbed up through the forest the day after the ministry official departed for the capital. That morning's mail had brought him other food for thought. The post flown in by the Dakota usually took anything from two to three days to travel the nine miles from the airstrip to its several destinations in Baruva. It wasn't mere distance which slowed it up but the speed, or, rather, lack of it, with which the clerks at the Baruva post office sorted and dispatched the letters. This day they had beaten all previous records. Jean-Pierre rather wished they hadn't. The mail had brought him yet another official envelope. This one, from the office of the president of the republic, confirmed that the sum of 50,000 dollars had been paid to the account of a fund set up in the name of Misoka Park. It went on to say that the *conservateur*, M. Menant, was to create forthwith a park's board of whom at least two members were to be Africans. This board would be required to approve all expenditure between 1,000 and 5,000 dollars. Above that, all sums drawn from the fund must be approved by the office of the signatory. The letter was signed 'Jack Wright, Counsellor to His Excellency the President of the Republic.'

When he read this Jean-Pierre swore fluently and obscenely, a thing he seldom did mainly because he did not approve of losing his cool. His independence was disappearing fast. Soon he'd be no more than a paid civil servant. Was this what conservation ventures like his own became? He'd known the answer to that question long, long ago. Now it was all happening fast, far too fast.

This morning not even the balm of the forest was entirely able to push these thoughts out of his mind. A park's board with a minimum of four directors, two of them African! He'd have to talk to Jacques Veniard about it. Would Veniard himself agree to serve? The doctor always appeared to have his finger on the pulse not only of his patients but on that of Baruva and half Kenanja Province as well. Jean-Pierre brightened at the thought. Between them, Veniard and he ought to be able to water down the wilder proposals of the two obligatory African representatives. But who were they to be? He'd have to talk to Veniard about that also. Strange how much he had come to rely on the doctor's judgement.

Two thousand feet above him the Saddle was still covered in mist. The sun was only just forcing its way round Misoka's false peak to thin and drive it away. Somewhere up there, in the mist-dripping trees, Absolom and his family were warming their immense bodies by cramming in vegetation as if stoking fuel into a series of all-consuming, fur-covered boilers. He smiled at the ridiculous nature of the comparison, hearing as he did so those imaginary boilers bubbling and

279

rumbling. His sheer affection for those monstrous animals was reflected by the fact that the worry lines were slowly smoothing out of his face. Easy to overlook that the protection of the gorillas and their forests was what the whole increasingly complicated manoeuvering was about.

Helen Lawes started from the hut about the same time that Jean-Pierre began his climb. Francis Chiribanda had returned from an anti-poaching patrol with Loti and Jahazi at dusk the previous evening. He had reported that Absolom and the whole group had moved down the slope on the nearside of the lava field where Toto had fallen and broken her arm. They were feeding in a comparatively open area of low scrub where the trees had recently been killed by volcanic activity. It was a first-class place for observation. Helen had been frustrated in her attempts to get close pictures of the newly-joined members of the group by the dense nature of the woodland in which they had recently been feeding. She did not want to spend more time than was strictly necessary studying this group since Jean-Pierre had already supplied most of the basic information about its members. Her main objective during her first year back at Misoka was to come up with a population and density study. Only when this was accurately compiled could the park know how many gorillas lived within its boundaries and how many more in the adjacent forest, notably on Mount Vahinga.

Year Two would be devoted to population dynamics, to learning the ages, sexes and, especially, the fertility rate of the Misoka—Vahinga gorillas. When all these things were known, then would be the time to formulate a management plan on which the future of the park could be based and, more important, secured. Three years for such a programme might seem a long time to a layman. To a scientist it was decidedly rushing things. She was sufficiently a realist, however, to know that she would be very lucky to get three uninterrupted years of research. Anything could happen, politically or financially, to wreck the scheme. She could even find herself thrown out or replaced by an African. All this she knew and accepted.

Nevertheless, the opportunity was good. It must be seized for the preservation and furtherance of her own career as well as for the preservation of the mountain gorillas. Naturally, she hoped it would work out for both. But the job for which Redfern had selected her put her within reach of the plums of her profession. If this particular plum fell off the tree, then the chances were that she could move on to other equally fruitful scientific orchards. There were always other countries, other endangered species to study. Such a realistic appraisal was one she would have been shocked to acknowledge four short years ago.

She had expected to feel total repugnance at being alone for long periods with an African man in an exposed and vulnerable situation. The upper slopes of Misoka were certainly that. The initial terrors she had experienced during her first days in Baruva had largely subsided. She had never registered the slightest anxiety with Francis Chiribanda. Quite the contrary. Most of the time she found him an agreeable companion. He had an attractive, intelligent face with high cheek-bones and fine features which suggested Arab or Hamitic blood. In this he was quite unlike his rotund, sweating father whom Jean-Pierre had described to her as a fat slob. He had never once suggested that he might take advantage of his position as guide and escort. Once or twice she had had to force herself to suppress a fantasy that he was about to do just that so that she could put him in his place, of course.

When it came to fieldcraft in approaching gorillas he was not in the same league as Jean-Pierre. His skill was sufficient, though, especially when backed up by that of one of the pygmy trackers. Often, when Francis was away on poaching patrol, she went alone with Mushi or the second tracker, Musharamena. She had gradually overcome her early nervousness with the gorillas, but she had to admit that it was a comfort to have Francis Chiribanda around whenever he was available. This morning she was delighted that he had found Absolom's group on such favourable ground and had volunteered to guide her to them.

Absolom had intended to start moving the whole group down the mountain towards the cyperus swamp that morning. The mist had hung around far longer than it had any business to do and this in itself had made him miserable. From the huddled attitude of the older females, Ahitabel, Abigail and Hepzibah, he could tell that the other members of the family felt as morose as he did. This, however, was not what was urging him to lead them to lower altitudes. His built-in time-clock told him that the season had arrived when the young shoots at the base of the cyperus clumps in the swamp would be green and succulent. It was the time of year for yet another cyperus binge.

Try as he would to urge the group down the mountain to where not only the weather but also the feeding was more attractive, he sensed a quite unaccustomed hanging back among the females and on the part of one female in particular. This animal was one of the two brought in by the young silver-back who had joined the group soon after Adam had disappeared along with Aquila and the New Arrival. Absolom was simply aware that the components of his group changed from time to time and, provided all concerned accepted his dominance, he was not particularly worried by these alterations. At first he had eyed the incoming silver-back with suspicion and even hostility. But when this virile young male had reacted in a gratifyingly submissive manner to Absolom's ritualised threats, the older male treated him as his second-in-command and ceased to be concerned about him.

Already made irritable by the drizzling mist, Absolom this morning was in no mood to put up with delays. He barked and growled at the females to get a move on. Soon the young silver-back and even the junior Abraham caught his mood and joined in the chorus of chivvying and cajolement.

Gradually the family responded. Even so, the two most recently joined females hung back, one more so than the other. When at last Absolom led the group down below the line of the mist, one of the pair was a good fifty yards behind the rest. The reason for her tardiness was a sopping wet bundle which she carried for a while and then put down, only to cradle it in her arms before picking it up once again to carry it a few more yards before the next halt.

Jean-Pierre would undoubtedly have guessed where Absolom was heading and planned his approach to intercept his line of march towards the cyperus swamp. Chiribanda did not yet possess such intimate knowledge of gorilla behaviour nor the intuition that grew from experience. So he headed directly for the spot at which he had found the family the night before, meaning to track them from that point. As a theory there was nothing wrong with this. In practice it was simply time-consuming. The mist didn't help and he hadn't realised that the swamp must be Absolom's eventual destination. He had left the pygmies at the hut, something that even Jean-Pierre wouldn't have done in the prevailing weather conditions. In the mist he hit a wrong trail. Before he realised it he was back-tracking the group up the mountain. In so doing he hit the fresh tracks of a different group of gorillas. After three exhausting hours Helen hadn't come within sight or sound of a single gorilla.

'It's no good, Chiribanda. You've lost them.' The use of the word 'you' riled Chiribanda. She had gone along with all his moves. She was supposed to know something about gorilla movements, too. She couldn't simply blame him.

'We'll find them soon. I know it.'

'Nonsense. We're just wasting time. Getting wet through for nothing. Besides, if we actually do catch up with them, I can't see much, let alone take photographs in this stuff.'

'I say we look a little longer, Dr Lawes.'

'And I'm telling you we've had enough for today.'

'May I remind you, Dr Lawes, that I am supposed to be

responsible for you.'

'I'm not going to stand on this damned mountain arguing with you. Let me just remind *you* of one thing. This is my scientific programme and you're detailed to help me carry it out.'

Chiribanda looked as though he was about to lose his temper. Then the tenseness went out of him and he smiled.

'It's a question of who's in charge, Dr Lawes, isn't it? I think that Monsieur Menant would uphold the authority of the head ranger as a representative of the park. Still, if the weather is too disagreeable. . . .'

Helen forced herself to remain calm. Besides, she didn't really want a show-down with Chiribanda. It would be both unpleasant and counter-productive.

'Good. Let's agree to call it a day, then.'

'Back to the hut?'

'Yes, please.'

'If it's all right with you, Dr Lawes, I'll see you safely on to the track until you know where you are and then I'll come back and carry on with the search by myself.'

'That'll be fine. You do that.' Cocky bastard. He was determined to be right. Here was something that would have to be sorted out before it went any further.

Jean-Pierre picked Mushi up at the hut. He and Musharamena, Ndungu too, were all pretty high on pot. It was clear that both the pygmy trackers were piqued because Chiribanda had decided to leave them behind. Well, that was his business. The two little men had decided to fill their unexpected day off with their favourite relaxation, sitting in the smoke of a wood fire and rolling themselves the occasional joint.

Mushi was glad to see Jean-Pierre nevertheless. He filled in the details of Helen's and Francis Chiribanda's excursion with elaborate pantomime which included a hilarious imitation of Chiribanda stalking gorillas. Not until Mushi pointed it out with body caricature had he noticed that the tall Chiribanda

284

used a kind of half stoop which appeared to reassure him that he was totally invisible to the animals.

Jean-Pierre hid his smile, saying, 'If you can still see enough not to trip over every gorilla dropping you'd better come with me.' Jean-Pierre hadn't met Absolom for some time. Besides, he'd like to get a look at his head ranger in action, preferably unobserved. It would be useful but it would also provide the kind of challenge he enjoyed since they would have to approach, unsuspected, not only Chiribanda and Helen but the gorilla group, too. Spook one and he would certainly spook the other.

The situation never arose. Helen was already on her way back to the hut, while Francis Chiribanda was wandering about in the clouds five hundred feet above the apes.

Guided by Mushi's description of Absolom's recent movements, Jean-Pierre guessed the silver-back's intention correctly. Once round the shoulder of Misoka, Jean-Pierre set off downhill through an area of breast-high scrub. He planned to cut across the path the animals used when they were headed for the swamp. He would come in below them and then lie up in cover until they passed. With luck, Chiribanda and Helen would be following.

In mid-afternoon he reached a suitable vantage point and sat down to wait. The gorillas hadn't yet passed. There were no droppings, no torn or chewed vegetation. After half an hour Mushi began to get restless but Jean-Pierre pointed to the trees that began two hundred feet below them. He mimed sleeping and the pygmy nodded. Jean-Pierre was sure that the group would go as far as those trees to rest for the night and that this meant they still had to pass.

They hadn't been in position more than an hour when Mushi nudged him with the handle of his panga and gestured by rolling the brown whites of his bloodshot eyes in an uphill direction. It was a full minute before Jean-Pierre caught the sound the pygmy had detected. Far off a branch was being wrenched from a tree. Five minutes later the family came into view, fanned out in open feeding order, the two silver-backs on the flanks, Abraham at the point, the youngsters and females towards the centre. It was clear that Jean-Pierre's guess had been right on target. The family would pass within twenty yards. If Chiribanda and Helen were following them they must be doing so with great skill. Every member of the group appeared relaxed.

He counted and identified them. First he spotted Absolom; then the new, young silver-back whom he'd persuaded Helen to christen Ammon; Abraham next (he'd soon be feeling the wanderlust that went with approaching maturity); the old faithfuls with their gaggle of familiar young — Abigail with Ahab and Abednego, Ahitabel and Cain, not to mention Abel. Now, where were the two recently-arrived females and the young male attached to the one he'd called Rachel? He'd run out of feminine Biblical names beginning with A by now. The second new female had become Rebecca for the same reason. Here came Rebecca at last, far behind the rest.

As Absolom drew abreast, Jean-Pierre coughed and called softly to him. Absolom stopped, stared in the direction of Jean-Pierre's hiding-place and roared briefly. Then, having almost disdainfully identified the intruder, he passed on. The others strolled along behind Abigail, passing within ten feet, all of them heading for their night's stop in the trees.

Jean-Pierre had already decided that Chiribanda and Helen were not in contact with the animals — their progress was too calm for that — when he detected a movement higher up the slope. He thought at first that he had been wrong, that Chiribanda was bringing up the rear after all. The branches of a young tree moved. A man wouldn't have done that. Of course, Rachel!

When the missing female appeared in the open she was moving very slowly. Jean-Pierre saw that she was carrying her baby, carrying him in a most unusual way, cuddled close to her chest. She put him down twice so that she could eat. After a few seconds she picked the baby up and carried slowly on. When she stopped for the third time in one hundred yards she was directly opposite Jean-Pierre.

The male infant she carried was a soggy bundle of matted hair. When the head turned towards Jean-Pierre he saw that the open eyes were glazed and covered with dirt as the result of many lowerings to the ground. The mouth gaped, the surprisingly white teeth of the baby set in a sad caricature of a snarl. The baby had been dead for some time. The rigor had gone out of it and it was as limp as a soft toy from which much of the sawdust has leaked. Rachel must have been carrying the dead infant for at least twenty-four hours. Her teats were swollen with accumulated milk. Perhaps it was the discomfort of her distended breasts that drove her to continue mothering the dead baby. Jean-Pierre preferred to think it was an excess of mother-love. Whatever the reason, such devotion could not last much longer. From where he crouched he could smell that the little body was already putrefying. The fact that the family had allowed Rachel to lag so far behind showed their reaction to a hopeless and unnatural situation. Soon, tomorrow at the latest, the pull of the group would prove the stronger force. Rachel would abandon the corpse, perhaps leave it at the nest site when she rose with the rest to start foraging.

Rachel started at the click of Jean-Pierre's camera shutter and shambled on in the wake of the disappearing family.

Helen was back at the hut when Jean-Pierre returned just before dusk. He was looking forward to an evening on the mountain with her, the first since that fatal night when they had woken to the glare of the burning stores hut and felt the *Fisi* pangas at their throats. Tonight there would be no question of sleeping-bags laid together outside under Misoka's moon. Still, it would be pleasant to be able to relax on the balcony until the mountain chill drove them inside, to eat together in the snug security of the hut, to discuss plans for the park and for Helen's work. They had hardly talked about her work since she had returned. This was another way in which she had altered. She had become more self-contained, almost secretive, as if the scientific aspect of the park was her private preserve. Maybe it was, but, after all, he had started the park and he *was* the *conservateur*. He felt just the slightest sense of irritation at her attitude but quickly suppressed it, reminding himself that it was not his style to let his personal temperature rise by so much as half a degree until a situation called for instant heat. It was certainly a very long way from that at the moment. So they would have a pleasant evening together. Perhaps, under the benign influence of the mountain, they would be able to discuss these minor differences openly.

He was excited about the photographs he had taken of Rachel carrying the dead baby and wanted to tell her all about it. Maybe under Chiribanda's guidance she had seen the situation for herself, earlier in the day. She was writing up notes in the hut and turned to face him.

'Jean-Pierre. I want to tell you about something that happened today.'

'So you saw it, too?'

'Saw what? I saw nothing. Chiribanda kept me wandering round in the clouds all morning. A total waste of a day.'

'Bad luck. But then, those things happen. He's not all that experienced yet awhile.'

'That's what I want to talk to you about. As you know, I've nothing against him. In fact, I rather like him, and the fact that I can bear to be alone with an African man at all must say quite a lot for master Francis.'

He waited, thinking, 'Oh God, I hope the bastard's been keeping his hands to himself.' Jean-Pierre could see the whole ghastly chain-reaction that would result had young Chiribanda put one foot, or even one finger, out of line. He'd have to sack him. There'd be open warfare with Chiribanda senior again. It was the sort of impossible situation he had warned Veniard about.

'Do you know what he had the darn nerve to do today? He refused to take instructions from me. He insisted that he was in charge. That was how we came to miss making contact with the gorillas altogether.'

Jean-Pierre felt intense relief. He could already see a way through the political undergrowth, even though it meant opposing Helen. Far better that than have half of black Africa round his neck.

'Tell me all about it,' he said gently. 'Meantime, how about offering me a drink? I brought a couple of bottles of wine up to celebrate your return. It's in the paraffin fridge.'

She told him about the incident with Chiribanda, emphasising that she had remained polite and had parted on good terms. Jean-Pierre sipped his wine and said nothing.

'Well?'

'It seems to me you handled it very well.'

'That's nice to know. But what about him? I can't have him telling me what to do. It's my research project.'

'Ark International's, actually.'

'All the more reason for him to co-operate since Ark's putting up the money for his wages.'

'Yes, I can see that. But Chiribanda *does* work for Misoka Park. He's head ranger.'

'I can see from your expression what you think of that title. Even your famous enigmatic calm can't hide your feelings there.'

'He's got a lot to learn. You have to give him his due. He's learning fast.'

'Not learning fast enough who's in charge up here.'

He put his hand out to touch hers. Calm her. She let her hand lie inert until he removed his.

'I'll speak to him, Helen, and tell him to be more tactful. But we must all be clear about one thing. The park is responsible for your safety. Francis Chiribanda was told by me to look after you. So, when he's out with you, he represents the park and myself. I'm afraid you'll have to listen to him.'

'You're taking his side against mine.'

'It shouldn't be a question of sides. Any scientist working in this park comes under park authority. But, as I say, I'll talk to him.'

'You accused me of changing the other day. Your attitude towards Africans seems to have changed somewhat.'

'It's their country now,' he said. 'But I'd have to back Chiribanda up, whatever the colour of his skin. Look, we're making far too much of a very small incident. Let me tell you what I saw today while you two were wandering about in the clouds.'

So he told her about Rachel and the dead baby; about how the mother repeatedly put her bundle down; how she seemed willing to sacrifice her solidarity with the group, for a time at least, to the stronger pull of mother-love. Helen made him describe every detail and, for a time, their common enthusiasm made them seem as close as they had once been. The illusion that the clock had been turned back was strengthened when Helen asked if she could develop the pictures he had taken. He put on a thick sweater against the mountain air and sat out on the verandah while she worked in the dark-room. The moon would soon be up round Misoka just as it had been that other night. There the similarity ended. He was both disappointed and relieved to discover that the fact that there would be no double sleeping-bags out there in front of the hut tonight did not greatly trouble him. Helen had gone back to the States as a lover and returned as a colleague. The warmth they had both felt as he told and retold the events of the day was no more than friendship strengthened by a common cause. At least her passion for the gorillas seemed as strong as ever. That they could still share.

She called him to come in. Four wet prints lay on the table. The light had not been good on the mountain. Rachel had not been obliging in her poses, seeming always to place some piece of vegetation between herself and the lens. There was one in which she had been caught in the open, though, with a dark bush as background into which she disobligingly merged. The baby was visible as no more than a shapeless lump.

Helen said, 'If I take more care with the printing I'm sure I can get more out of it. There's no doubt at all what the female's carrying. It's a unique record and it gives us such an opportunity.'

'Opportunity?' he said. 'I'm sorry I didn't make more of it.'

'I did not mean it like that. Besides, in those conditions no one could have done better. That's not what I'm talking about. That female, Rachel, is going to have milk for quite a while. On your evidence she's not only bursting with milk but also with frustrated maternalism. It's possibly one and the same thing in any case.'

A small alarm-bell rang in Jean-Pierre's head.

'Meantime, she's in a perfect state to accept an orphaned baby like the one you've got down in Baruva.'

'How do you know wild gorillas will accept a strange infant?'

'I don't. That's just the point. It's a unique chance to find out.'

'Over my dead body, Helen.'

'Nonsense. You're just being emotional, treating that small animal as a pet.'

'And you, my dear, are being non-scientific, wanting to treat her as the subject of an experiment on which you have done absolutely no work.'

'Work! How can I have done any work? There's never been a chance to observe such a situation before.'

'Precisely. In my view, Helen, what you suggest is on about the same level as totally unjustified vivisection.'

'Now that *is* an emotional attitude.'

'Maybe. But it's my attitude. I hate to pull rank but I do have to point out that I am the *conservateur*. My letter of appointment makes it clear that all mountain gorillas in the *région* are my direct responsibility.'

'Then you never contemplated trying to return the orphan to the wild?'

'I didn't say that. I do say that she isn't ready yet.'

'Then, Jean-Pierre, it's high time her preparation for the

great day began. She ought to be moved up here for a start.'

'She's not ready to be moved anywhere.'

'Because Marie Maputa enjoys having her around as a household pet?'

Jean-Pierre shrugged. 'I'm bored. Let's change the subject and have a pleasant dinner together. Like in the old days. We used to see eye to eye, then.'

Helen did her best to meet him, drinking half a bottle of wine while she supervised the goat-meat steaks cooked in garlic and tomato purée. After dinner, while he quite un-usually drank half the second bottle alone, she returned to the dark-room and tried to get clearer prints of the baby in Rachel's arms. He was in his sleeping bag, dozing, when she at last produced one to her satisfaction. The last thing he remembered was her saying, 'You must promise to take me out to see Rachel with the dead baby tomorrow.'

He nodded and fell asleep.

They found Absolom's family at mid-day, half way down the watercourse that led to the cyperus swamp. They found the baby, too. By then Rachel had abandoned it. The dead infant lay two hundred yards beyond the trees in which the gorillas had built their nests. Jean-Pierre had been wrong about one thing. Rachel had started the day by trying to carry her dead child.

Veniard accepted chairmanship of the Misoka Park Board without a struggle. 'Someone,' he said, 'has got to keep you out of trouble with the locals and the politicians and it might as well be me. Sometimes I wonder whether I shouldn't have been a politician myself.'

'Richelieu or Machiavelli?'

'Either. I have many of the talents of both though, since I have never inclined towards the church, I can hardly pretend to have all the Cardinal's cunning. Now the court of the Borgias. . . .'

'Never mind your historical reminiscences. I have to appoint at least two African board members.'

292

'One is blissfully obvious. Kama Chiribanda.'

'Are you mad?'

'Let me ask the same question of you. No, let me ask a different question. Have you had the least trouble from that direction since you got him on your side? It's the classic opportunity to turn poacher into gamekeeper. He'll be greatly flattered, especially since his son's appointment. Most important, you can keep a beady eye on him.'

'No. To have his son under my control is one thing: to have him on the park board, possibly voting against me—'

'Approach him. Take it from Machiavelli. You can't go wrong.'

'Suppose I go along with your crazy idea. I've still got to find a second African.'

'I know just the man.'

'I was afraid you might.'

'Do you know Daudi Mahoja?'

'That crook.'

'I see you do know him.'

'He made a fortune out of repairing the civil buildings in Baruva — not that you'd notice it — after the civil war.'

'Exactly. A building contractor. Respected African businessman. From what I hear you're going to need some repair work done yourself. You'll need someone with business sense. African-type business sense, that is.'

'How does Mahoja get on with Chiribanda?'

'Like the true brother-in-law he is.'

'That is practically condoning crookery on a large scale. They'll gang up against us.'

'Why should they? There's me to back you up and you'll have a casting vote.'

'Aren't you forgetting this fellow Jack Wright, counsellor to our beloved president?'

'Ah, the American *éminence grise*.'

'Whoever it is his office nominates, you can bet your sweet life it will be an *éminence noire*.'

'I'm inclined to agree with you, but it could be the

counsellor himself.'

'Very unlikely. Anyway, he'd act blacker than all the rest of them put together.'

'Wright's office will only vote when it's a matter of state policy. It's not likely to happen very often. And when it does it'll be just as if you'd got a vote directly from the president. So there's nothing you'll be able to do about it. . . . On the other hand, our President Olindo appears to be very conservation-minded at present. So his personal representative could be a very useful man to have on your park board.'

'I'll believe it when I see it,' Jean-Pierre said gloomily. 'Now, if you insist, you'd better issue invitations to Chiribanda and Mahoja.'

'No. You must do that. I've one further suggestion. Let's at least have one straightforward and disinterested African on the board.'

'Wright's office only insisted on two. Now you want three.'

'Why not? What's wrong with one good man of our own choosing?'

'Who?'

'Joshua Ndesi, the schoolmaster. He's honest, progressive and highly intelligent. Besides, he's one of my patients. You simply mustn't get into the state of mind where you believe all the locals are Chiribandas or Mahojas.'

'O.K. I don't like the idea. But if you say so. . . .'

When the DC3 flopped in over the mountains next day it brought a letter from Jack Wright's office addressed to the *conservateur*. This was delivered by the hand of a special messenger. The letter set an official date for the world conference on gorillas, now only ten months away. It was a formal though friendly letter, emphasising the importance which the president attached to conservation in general and to the world conference in particular. It requested the names of the members of the Misoka Park Board by return. It ended by saying that Counsellor Wright would greatly appreciate meeting M. Menant. Circumstances made it impossible for him to leave the capital just at the moment. However, if convenient, he would send an official aircraft at 1400 hours in three days' time. Please inform the messenger accordingly.

Jean-Pierre experienced a growing sense of unease. Recognition by the government was what he'd always hoped for, recognition that would provide him with the funds and authority to carry on the park as *he* thought best, not as some bureaucrat, no matter how high-powered, thought best. In the early days the president's letter had given him all the authority he felt he needed. Ark had produced a substantial amount of the essential funds. There had been no strings to either of these originally desirable situations. Or had there? Had the strings been there all the time, just waiting to tighten if he showed signs of wanting to pull in his own direction?

To hell with Counsellor Jack Wright. Jean-Pierre hadn't yet made up his mind whether to accept Veniard's proposed African members for the park board. Perhaps it would be more accurate to say that he hadn't yet invited them to serve. Chiribanda and Mahoja might even refuse. What a hope! What disturbed him most was the degree of annoyance — no, anger was a more honest word — he was allowing himself to feel. He must control it.

He sat down and wrote a courteous note to Jack Wright. He'd be delighted to accept the invitation to visit him in the capital. He regretted that his selection of board members was not yet finished but that he hoped to bring the names with him.

When he had handed his reply to the messenger — the DC3 was kept waiting by official order — he sat down and wrote formal notes to Kama Chiribanda and Daudi Mahoja and a more friendly one to the schoolmaster, whom he knew and liked. As he finished Francis Chiribanda walked in and saluted.

'Ah, Chiribanda. I've been wanting to have a word with you about Dr Lawes.'

'She's complained about me?'

'In a way, yes.'

'She wouldn't take instructions from me, Monsieur Menant.'

'So I heard. You get on all right with her?'

'Normally, Monsieur Menant, very well. But on this occasion. . . .'

'Quite. I know all about it.'

He expected the young man to burst out with self-justification and counter-complaints. Instead, Chiribanda stood clamly waiting.

'She's a very distinguished scientist. You must remember that.'

'May I ask just one question, Monsieur Menant?'

'By all means.'

'As head ranger, am I not responsible for her safety?'

'You most certainly are.'

'Then if I direct a course of action when she is in my care, should she not listen?'

'I have made that point with her myself on your behalf.'

'Thank you, Monsieur Menant.'

'However, like many people of character and great ability, she has a will of her own and a viewpoint that is certainly worth listening to.'

'I think I understand.'

'Good. It is all a question of tact.'

How Veniard would have laughed to hear his friend advising the use of such a quality.

'One more thing. Will you please see that this letter reaches your father as soon as possible?'

'I will take it myself. I must go home and get some clothing. Dr Lawes wishes me to accompany her on a two-day safari around the far side of Vahinga. She is beginning a survey there.'

'Good. Handle her with tact, Chiribanda.'

Chiribanda saluted, turned smartly about and walked out with the suggestion of a smile.

*

On the third day after receiving Jack Wright's letter, Jean-Pierre was at the airstrip half-an-hour early. Two o'clock in the afternoon was leaving things a shade late in the cloud conditions prevailing at that time of year. He hoped the pilot would know this and get in ahead of time. If not, it could be a bumpy and roundabout flight to the capital. At ten to two there was still no sign of the aircraft. He strained his ears for the familiar beat of a Dakota's or perhaps a Cessna's or Piper's twin engines bouncing off the mountains. Nothing. He strained his eyes in case the pilot had decided to approach up the lake.

At three minutes to two he heard engines with a different sound. Now he knew why the pilot hadn't hurried. A Dassault Falcon executive jet dropped out of the clouds like an assegai, made a wide circle of the field and landed precisely at 1400 hours. It shone blue and white in the brilliant sunshine, managing to look like some exquisitely painted toy, newly unwrapped. When it taxied up it was no longer a toy but nearly a million dollars' worth of beautifully maintained personal hardware. The badge on the nose showed whose. The Falcon was part of the president's personal flight.

The pilot wore air-force uniform with yellow and hot orange colour flashes. It was the first time Jean-Pierre had been aware that the country possessed an air force. He saluted. 'Hi. You Jean-Pierre Menant?' The pilot was black, all right, but his accent revealed where he had learned his flying. In the United States Air Force. No doubt about that.

'Ready to go?'

'Yes. Completely.'

'You a flier?'

'No, I'm afraid not, though I'll have to learn some day. We need a light aircraft to watch for poachers.'

The co-pilot, an African this time, strolled over to what passed for a control tower to file the return flight plan.

'Like to sit up front, Monsieur Menant? You can have your first lesson on jets. My old buddy can have a sleep in the back.'

The African co-pilot grinned.

A minute later they were airborne with an acceleration that pinned Jean-Pierre against his seat. The nose of the Falcon pointed steeply upwards at the cloud base. For half a minute they were enveloped in grey gloom. Then the little jet burst out into a world of sun and light. The mountains might not have existed except for one peak well to the east, obstinately puncturing the sea of cloud foam — Misoka. He'd have liked to have asked the pilot to turn back and fly low over the crater but Misoka was being snatched away from him at four hundred miles per hour. Three hours later they let down through a grey rain squall to find the white buildings of the capital laid out below them.

'Painless, huh?' the pilot said.

'Yes. I really must get one of these.'

'Ask the head man. He's got two.'

When they taxied in to a reserved parking area at the new airport building an African in a tattered cellular vest and khaki shorts, one leg of which was practically missing, wheeled up the ladder for them to disembark.

'One of our smartest men,' the pilot said. 'Have a nice stay. There'll be someone to meet you.'

Jean-Pierre was given the full VIP treatment, just like that accorded to Nancy Genova and John Redfern some months before. Despite this, he was ill at ease. Used to the hard springing of his jeep, he felt almost seasick in the official Mercedes. He had very seldom been driven by anyone else, let alone an African chauffeur he neither knew nor trusted. The experience rattled him far more than being charged by an unknown solitary male gorilla would have done. Conditioned to the minimal traffic problems in Baruva, he found the cut-and-thrust driving of both Africans and whites on the busy streets of the capital frankly terrifying. He now knew what a newcomer to the forest must feel when confronted at close quarters by a gorilla group. He had not been in a large city since his parents had taken him to Europe as a small boy and his first reaction was one previously unknown to him.

Something close to panic. It was almost like standing on a cliff edge and knowing one had lost one's sense of balance.

The Mercedes put him down at the Africana and a porter seized his rucksack, the only baggage he had brought apart from a brief-case borrowed from Veniard. He thought that he would feel better once he was out of the car and on to his own two feet, but the immediate impact of the Africana only aggravated his attack of temporary agoraphobia. The foyer was full of guests coming and going, demanding, requiring, requesting, complaining. An African businessmen's convention had just debouched from a conference salon. A Sabena air crew was checking out and a KLM one checking in. Jean-Pierre wanted to run, a thing he had never done in his life before. The moment of revelation that this could happen steadied him. He forced his brain into neutral with all the will-power he could exert. The shallow band of calm he managed to wrap around himself lasted long enough to allow the porter to steer him to the reception desk. He leaned against it like an exhausted man reaching a rock at the edge of a cataract. And there, while the reception clerk checked the reservation made for him by the ministry, he began to master the fear which had nearly devastated him simply because it was absurd and beyond reason. He knew that he would get it beaten now but that the city had very nearly beaten him.

A porter took him up on the escalator to his room. Once there he leaned against the door sweating. Slowly he crossed to the windows leading on to the small balcony. Below, the city assumed its true size, shrunken, manageable and filled with more people, more vehicles, more noise than he had seen for many, many years. Yet looked down upon, what did it add up to? Just people, cars, noise in larger quantities. He knew he wasn't going to enjoy it but he knew that he had it in proportion now. The shock passed. He'd been too long in a backwater, too long in the forest. How many days or hours would it be before he could return to the forest and the backwater once again?

The phone rang. It was Counsellor Jack Wright's office. The counsellor was unexpectedly out of town until next morning. Was there anything Monsieur Menant would like arranged for the evening? No? In that case Counsellor Wright would send a car for him at nine-thirty the following morning.

Jean-Pierre was suddenly very tired. Whatever other failings civilisation might have, the bed it provided was superbly comfortable. He lay down and slept. When he awoke it was dark. He undressed, crawled under the covers and slept again.

If Jack Wright impressed Jean-Pierre Menant, the reverse was also true. Each recognised in the other a vein of extremely durable metal. Jean-Pierre did not find the counsellor an instantly likable personality, nor even a distantly likable one. Jack Wright put Jean-Pierre in mind of a bullet. Even the rounded dome of his greying crew-cut added to the illusion. Bullets, in certain circumstances, were useful objects. No one knew this better than Jean-Pierre. Pointed in the right direction they went on until they hit things, whereupon they penetrated them. This only ceased to be true when they met something harder than themselves, whereupon they flattened, exploded, stopped dead, or were deflected on to an unwanted course. Jean-Pierre found it hard to imagine any of these things happening to Jack Wright.

To Wright, Menant was a strange animal indeed. He didn't know quite what he had expected. He'd met park wardens and game biologists in other African countries. They had varied enormously, of course, but the range had been roughly between the hearty, enthusiastic white hunter turned conservationist and the introverted, scientific type who tended to regard wildlife as something created expressly for him to study. Menant fitted nowhere in this range of stereotypes. He was quiet, modest and self-contained and this last, mark you, after a fairly shattering drive through the streets that had so disturbed him the day before, though Wright did not know this and would have been quick to try and

300

exploit it if he had.

They exchanged courtesies according to the styles of their nationalities. They discussed the amazing qualities of the Falcon jet in perhaps a dozen sentences. After that Wright saw no sense in hanging about and felt sure his guest would feel the same.

'The president is a great admirer of what you've achieved almost single-handed, Monsieur Menant.'

'That is very generous of him.'

'He intends that this country should give a world lead where conservation is concerned.'

'I shan't forget that he made Misoka his first national park.'

'*Second*,' Wright corrected gently.

'I didn't know there was another park.'

'There is now. Lake Olindo. Right outside the capital.'

'Oh. I hadn't heard of that.'

'Nor had anyone else until a few weeks ago.'

'But Misoka. . . .'

'Is several months old? Quite. But what's a few months? It's simply a question of. . . .'

'Politics?' Jean-Pierre asked politely.

'Ah. I see you're ahead of me. You catch on fast.'

'Yes, but it doesn't mean that I like that kind of manoeuvring. As a matter of fact, I hate the very word politics.'

'But you recognise that politics are an essential ingredient of survival.' A faint emphasis on the last word, perhaps?

'I imagine, counsellor,' Jean-Pierre said politely, 'that you would be the first to recognise that fact.'

'You're darn right,' Wright said with engaging frankness. 'And if you want what I think you want for Misoka, and possibly for other wildlife in this country, you'll be wise to take cognisance of that fact also.'

'You didn't get me here just to give me a little lecture, counsellor.'

'You're absolutely correct. I got you here partly because I

301

wanted to see whether you were all the man Redfern and others said you were.'

'And?'

'Because, I guess, you couldn't care less what answer I gave to that question, I reckon you're all they said — apart from your distrust of politics.'

'Was that all you wanted?'

'Hell, no. I wanted your advice.'

'About?'

'Lake Olindo among other things. I imagine you don't care for cities too much. Why don't you accompany me to nature's paradise right on our doorstep?'

Jack Wright drove Jean-Pierre out to the lake. When they had bumped slowly up the shore Wright asked, 'Well, what do you think of our *first* national park?'

'It's a dump.'

'A garbage dump?'

'If you insist.'

'Could it be made beautiful again?'

'I imagine so.'

'What would you need to do it?'

'Power and money. Power to move all these people away first and then resettle them. Power to prevent pollution, not only from garbage and sewage but also from agricultural chemicals from the hills on the far side. You'd need money to do all this, money to pay scientists to do the right kind of surveys before you did anything else.'

'And then?'

'Then you could build up, restock with fish that would bring the bigger waterbirds, storks, pelicans, fish eagles. Oh yes, it could be done. It would never be a grand spectacle but it could be beautiful enough.'

'How do you know all this? I thought you were a gorilla man?'

'All conservation problems are basically the same. All you need are the right experts, the right advice.'

On the drive back Wright said, 'You realise Lake Olindo is

mainly a shop window. For this reason we shall put it right, whatever the cost.'

'Even at the expense of parks that matter far more?'

'No. We shall tackle those, too. One at a time.'

'That will need a lot of money.'

'Don't worry, if the president wants it done, we'll find the money even if it comes from something else. Besides, there's Ark International. Redfern has come up with a daring concept. The World Wildlife Fund spreads its effort around the world. Redfern's outfit is thinking of adopting us exclusively for a period of five years.'

'Doesn't sound very international.'

'After five years he can switch his attention somewhere else. Besides, Ark International can still make a few small bequests to other nations to keep up appearances.'

'And the subscribers?'

'They may find it rather attractive. It means they'll be able to watch results in one area. We'll even work out a scheme by which donors can make cheap tours to see where their money's going.'

'To Lake Olindo?'

'By then we'll have made some progress even here.'

'I bet the donors won't be shown where *all* of their money's going.'

'Ah. I see you *do* understand something of African politics. Nevertheless, you'd better keep such opinions to yourself.' There was a touch of the file and rasp in Wright's voice.

Over lunch, served in a room on the glass penthouse floor of the government building, Wright expanded. 'Misoka's of vital importance. You and I know that. President Olindo knows that. In the mountain gorilla you've got something there that scientists and naturalists all over the world revere and envy. Other governments, too. Redfern's world conference is a brilliant idea. What a publicist that man is! Now he's suggested that we widen the scope. It's to be a conference on protection of the larger primates with gorillas as the focal

303

point, of course. We'll have the Americans, British, Germans, West Africans, even Indonesians there. The best men and women in the world on orang-utans, chimpanzees, lowland gorillas. And as host, you, Jean-Pierre — you don't mind me calling you that, do you?'

'That's what my pygmies call me.'

'Eh? Oh, I see. You, Jean-Pierre, as *conservateur*, will be the central figure.'

Jean-Pierre experienced his second moment of genuine horror since he had arrived in the capital.

'I would be most reluctant to take charge of such an eminent gathering.'

'You would be required to do nothing out of the ordinary. To give a talk or two. To conduct parties into the forest. We will send conference organisers.'

'How many people will be attending?'

'One hundred at the most. Perhaps fewer. I realise you are not a man to seek the limelight but just consider the benefits such a conference can bring to Misoka and to conservation in this country in general.'

After lunch Wright sent for two bright, young, African under-secretaries. They produced lists of experts and Press invited to the four-day conference. There was a suggested lecture schedule devised by Redfern.

Jean-Pierre noted that he was down to speak on the first and second days. On the third and fourth he was to show selected delegates groups of gorillas in the forest. In addition, plans had been drawn up for rebuilding his old plantation house not only to accommodate some of the guests but also to include a large, thatched, lean-to area that would serve as an open-air lecture hall.

'Afterwards,' explained one young under-secretary, 'the space can be used for storage or for transport.'

They had certainly been thorough. What was more, the proposed building was of the kind African workmen did quickly and extremely well.

'Who's going to carry out all the work?'

'I'm sure you won't have any trouble there. We're sending an architect next week. You'll find a local contractor easily enough.'

No doubt about that. Daudi Mahoja, the park's board member and Kama Chiribanda's brother-in-law. Wright would have been proud of the *conservateur's* grasp of local African politics. Jean-Pierre felt no pride at all, just a stale taste of the city in his mouth.

Wright entertained him to dinner in his bachelor apartment one floor below the penthouse. Though the president was not in residence, Jean-Pierre gathered that he had a large suite next door. The meal was simple but well-chosen and could only have been produced by Africa. The same went for the view over the capital. In the foreground blazed the lighted windows of any modern city. Far beyond, where the horizon grew inky blue, small red pinpoints of light winked, the night-eyes of an older Africa, the flames of bush fires.

Jack Wright was a good host. He knew how far to go in telling amusing and mildly scandalous stories about his adopted masters. He even named the well-known politician who had publicly announced that the nation was about to launch into the technological age with its first home-built aeroplane. For 'home-built' the politician should have said 'home-made'. This creation, the product of a mechanic at the capital's airfield, was built entirely of corrugated-iron beaten flat with a hammer. The inventor had mounted the monster, complete with engine, on the edge of a high cliff for its maiden flight. Undoubtedly, he had never meant to launch it, but the publicity attracted by the enthusiastic politician's speeches had made a ceremonial launching inescapable.

White-faced and shaking, the designer eventually climbed into the cockpit, surrounded by Press, politicians and public, to dive to what he saw as inevitable death. Fortunately, when the order was given to start the engine the wooden propeller flew to pieces. Delivered from destruction by a miracle, the aviator climbed gratefully out of the cockpit and announced that, as the nation's first aircraft was too precious to risk in flight, he proposed to dedicate it, where it stood on the cliff top, as a national monument.

Jean-Pierre enjoyed the story, especially as it had all the hallmarks of truth.

'A resourceful fellow, eh?' Wright said.

'He deserved to survive.'

'You strike me as equally resourceful and certainly you've survived. I admire survival qualities above all else. Jean-Pierre, I want to put an idea in your head. When the president implements his wish to make ten per cent of this country into national parks, those parks will need a strong and resourceful man as their director. You're my idea of such a man. Would you be willing to take the job on? It's a hell of a big job.'

'I'm essentially a retiring man, counsellor. I'm very happy with the gorillas in my own forest.'

'I expected you to say something like that. Don't worry about it. Just think it over for a while. Say until after the world conference. But no longer than that. Will you do that for me?'

'I'll think it over, but you heard my first reaction. I don't expect it to change.'

'O.K. Let's leave it right there.'

Over the brandies Wright said, 'I've checked out your list of Misoka Board members. They seem a very wise choice to me. My office will nominate a sixth when necessary. On high days and holidays it might just turn out to be me. When you need some presidential clout, that is. For the sake of appearances I'm nominating a man called Varuti.'

'Do I know him?'

'No. He's a mining engineer and all-round development man who's an adviser to my department.'

'Doesn't sound too much like a wildlife enthusiast to me, counsellor.'

'What about your own nominations? A local plantation owner, a building contractor, a school teacher, a European doctor.'

'Touché?'

'Then why did you pick them?'

Jean-Pierre smiled faintly. 'Local politics, I suppose.'

'Exactly. And you were quite right. But Misoka *is* a national park and national politics come into it somewhere. Besides, Varuti's an excellent businessman. Even gorillas need a good business head on their hairy shoulders.'

'The words "mining" and "development" worry me a little.'

'Yes. I can see that they might do. Well, all I can say is that a developing country has many needs. They all have to be dove-tailed, reconciled, and given priorities. In politics most things are a compromise. It's my job to decide the balance of that compromise; Varuti's to advise me on certain aspects of such compromises. His judgement is good. That's why I want him as my representative on your board. I don't suppose he'll ever actually attend. He's my nominee. It's just a formality.'

'When can I meet him? We'll be having a first board meeting very shortly.'

'Can't say for sure. Possibly not before the world conference. He's very tied up on a mining survey right now. As I said: my department won't interfere. We'll just keep an eye on things in the background. We're here to help if needed. You guys are more than capable of running things at your end.'

'What's this Varuti fellow like?'

'Intelligent. Sharp. Gets things done. Redfern met him. I remember he asked whether he was a Watutsi.'

The Falcon jet flew Jean-Pierre back next morning. This time the clouds had cleared over Misoka and Vahinga. The black American pilot was only too happy to fly round Misoka's ancient volcanic peak. Beyond lay the crater itself, a saucepan one mile across in the bottom of which a rich, black broth, shot with cherry-red seethings, boiled at more than one thousand degrees centigrade beneath a haze of brownish-yellow smoke.

'Stay out of that stuff. It's as deadly as cyanide,' Jean-Pierre warned.

307

The pilot banked steeply, making as tight a turn as he dared to stay within the rim of the cauldron.

'Christ,' he said. 'I'm glad we're up here and it's down there.'

'I've camped inside that crater,' Jean-Pierre told him. 'It's all right just as long as you stay upwind of the fumes.'

'Hear that, birdman?' the American asked the African co-pilot. 'Stick to something safe like flying the president's private jet.'

The co-pilot rolled his eyes.

'He's a little nervous,' the American explained. 'Someone tried to put a bomb on board this crate last week.'

'Bombs are one thing,' said the co-pilot. 'We get paid for bombs but no one told me about flying inside volcanoes. Let's get out of here.'

The pilot made one low pass over the crater, keeping well to the side of the smoke pall and aiming directly at the far wall. He pulled up with a G-force that felt as though it was going to push Jean-Pierre through his seat. A split-second later Misoka's peak flashed by seemingly only yards to port. Then they were over the lake for a gentle touch-down at Baruva.

His home-coming was not quite as smooth as that landing. After her fashion, Marie was never effusive on his return. She used that most charming of African greetings, taking his hand and kissing it and then remaining, hand clasped, while he took her hand to his lips. Today she waited in the kitchen, eyes downcast. He called her softly, and when she turned he could see that she had been crying. Without moving towards her he held out his arms. She did not rush to accept his invitation to be comforted as a European woman might have done. Instead, she walked slowly across the room and stood close to him. At first he had feared that the spell-makers had been at work again but now he saw that her face and eyes were unclouded by magic. He lifted her chin and asked quietly, 'What is it? What happened?'

She took him by the hand and led him into the yard and he saw at once what had happened. The enclosure door was open, the enclosure empty. The baby gorilla had gone.

'How? She escaped? When? She can't have gone far. We'll soon find her.' The terrible thought occurred that Toto was dead.

'Tell me how it happened.' He understood why Marie was so downcast. She was afraid he would be angry. He began to reassure her.

There was anger in the situation, a great deal of anger, but it was all bottled up inside Marie Maputa and now the anger broke out. It burst in a volcanic display of fury. Most of this was in her tribal tongue, some of which even Jean-Pierre did not understand; some in mission French, a good deal in French which the good fathers had certainly never taught her. There were even a few oaths and obscenities in English, one of the milder of which, namely, 'American bastard', gave Jean-Pierre his first clue to what it was all about.

He waited for the tropical storm to pass. 'What happened?' he asked again, even more gently this time.

'That American woman. She came a day after you left. She brought Loti with her. Loti was unhappy. He did not wish to do what she said without hearing you give the order. She told Loti to take the baby. She said it was bad for me to have it any longer. She said you knew this and that you agreed. Did you? Did you agree, Jean-Pierre?'

'I said that eventually we would have to try to return the baby gorilla to the forest.'

'But did you tell her to take it now?'

'No. I did not. Soon, yes. It will need scientific preparation for its return.'

Now she blazed at him. 'Scientific preparation. That's what *she* pretended. But she couldn't fool me. I could see what that barren American bastard wanted. She wanted the gorilla to treat it as a child. Just because she can't have one of her own. I know all about it. She's dried up like an old gourd and she's about as empty.'

309

'And what did you want the baby for, Marie? For scientific purposes also?'

'No. I treated it like a child, too.' Now she was shouting at him, beating at his chest with her fists. 'But I'll tell you this. There's one difference between me and that female baboon. I can have a real child and she can't.'

'And is that what you want, Marie?'

'Never mind what I want or don't want. You make that American bastard bring that baby gorilla back until you say the word that she can have it.'

'You're behaving like a hysterical American woman yourself, Marie.'

'Am I? Perhaps I should never have had anything to do with white people like you or her.'

'But you like having things to do with me, don't you, Marie?'

'I used to until you started breaking your word.'

'I see. Then I'd better leave straight away and go up into the forest. I wasn't intending to leave until tomorrow or the day after.'

'You want to go and see that American bastard, I suppose.'

She was sobbing, so this time he took her in his arms. She didn't, as he had expected, struggle. Instead, she went to work on him straight away, undoing the front of his bush-shirt, sliding her snake-smooth hands round his rib-cage until they found and began to knead his shoulder blades. If she'd been a wheedling Western woman she might at that moment have begun to bargain again about the return of Toto. Marie simply withdrew her hands from his shoulders and undid his belt. From first to last — and there was less than three minutes separating those two points — Jean-Pierre wasn't aware of being in control of the situation once. She pushed him back on the bed and then sat astride him. For the first time her love-making had a functional efficiency about it. *She* was possessing him, almost using him. At the end he felt as though she were seizing him with her womb as if forcing him to impregnate her. Not a chance! He knew she took a dark brew her tribal doctor gave her as a specific against unwanted pregnancy. At last she became calm and loving again. When she had finished she lay beside him, kissing his eyes as though she were reassuring him. He dozed off but, before he did so, he saw that she was at peace and smiling to herself.

Early next morning he left for the Saddle. He made the climb in record time. If there was a disagreeable situation to be sorted out, he wanted to get it over and done with as quickly as possible. When he reached the Saddle, he made a slight flanking detour so that he could approach the hut from above and to one side. He emerged from the hypericum bushes at much the same point from which the gorilla group had once watched his own rangers clearing the four-year growth of scrub to make the place habitable again. Now he looked down on the present occupant and the small gorilla who, when living wild with her family, must have watched the clearing operations on that day. Probably the youngster had huddled close to her natural mother, demanding reassurance at the presence of strange and noisy humans. Now, ironically, she was huddled close to a substitute human mother.

Both parties were obviously deriving a great deal of pleasure from the proximity. Helen, he saw, was laughing and talking to the baby in almost exactly the same way that Marie had done. He sat watching the pair play together for five minutes. Was this, he wondered, what the increasingly austere Dr Lawes had meant by a scientific approach to eventual rehabilitation? This looked like fun and games in the children's zoo. It most certainly gave some point to Marie's tirade concerning Helen's motives for taking the little gorilla.

At last Helen had had enough of the game. She picked the baby up and carried it to the large, wired-in pen at the back of the hut, a pen that enclosed several small trees, trees for nesting and climbing. Jean-Pierre rose and walked down the slope.

311

Helen spotted him far off and shouted, 'Oh, I guessed you'd be up here almost as soon as you got back.'

'I like to see what's going on in my park.' He said this carefully, trying not to stress the 'my' unduly. 'I wish you'd asked about taking the baby.'

'I suppose the Maputa girl made a scene.'

'What did you expect? But let's leave Marie out of it for the moment. The point is, I would have expected you to ask me, Helen.'

'I apologise for that.'

'Well, that's something.'

'You said yourself that the baby offered unique opportunities for study and that it would need to be scientifically prepared before rehabilitation in the forest.'

'So I did.'

'My dear Jean-Pierre.' Helen was getting more confident. 'Surely you don't deny that I'm the scientific officer appointed to this park?'

'Not in the least. But we've had this sort of discussion before over Francis Chiribanda. While you're working in the park, Helen, you're under park jurisdiction.'

'And if I cut a corner or two to get my job done?'

'Never mind about cutting a corner or two. I'm talking about taking a different route entirely.'

'Like taking the baby gorilla.'

'Yes, like taking the baby gorilla.'

'I took her because I regard her education as being much more within my competence than that of your African lady.'

Jean-Pierre allowed himself a half-smile. 'Yes, Helen. I saw you being very scientific with her when I arrived.'

'She still needs affection. . . . Anyway, you must have been spying on me.'

'Observing. Part of my job is observing gorilla behaviour. You yourself taught me quite a lot about that.'

'Now that you've made it clear that you run things including, it seems, my programme, what do you propose to do about it? Take the baby back to Baruva as your black girlfriend's plaything?'

Jean-Pierre looked at her calmly and said almost conversationally, 'No. I propose to leave Toto here as the plaything of science but I shall require to know in detail your plans and time-table for rehabilitating her and returning her to the forest.'

'That's reasonable enough.'

'So is this. Next time, Helen, you deliberately ignore the authority of the park I shall ask that you be found a subject for study somewhere else. Now, if you've got Mushi handy, I want to borrow him. As a change from everything that's happened during the last few days, I'd like to go into the forest and say hello to a few gorillas.'

By then Helen had gone back into the hut.

Three days later, under Veniard's chairmanship, the park board held its first meeting. Jean-Pierre's principal reaction was amazement that he could find himself sitting down with two such notable crooks. Kama Chiribanda, gold tooth aglint, customary beads of sweat glistening on his brow, shook him warmly by the hand. Daudi Mahoja was more diffident. He was a complete physical contrast to Chiribanda, a little stick of a man, dried up, a sort of African version of Gandhi but without the saintly look. When he bowed formally by way of greeting, Jean-Pierre half expected him to crack and break in the middle.

Jean-Pierre looked at Joshua Ndesi with relief and gratitude. He knew him as a man who would take his own line if necessary and was not afraid to speak his mind. He wore his best suit for the occasion, was obviously flattered to be included and shook hands with everyone twice.

Veniard conducted the meeting at a pace that would have done credit to the chairman of a large international company. A phrase of welcome; a quick but not too detailed outline of the park's finances left reasonably vague ('Otherwise,' Veniard had said at his pre-meeting meeting with Jean-Pierre, 'those two monsters will begin by plotting how much of the annual budget they can get their hands on.'); a review of staff; a word about the valuable scientific programme conducted by Dr Lawes and financed by Ark International. Ndesi asked some sensible, informed questions about this while Chiribanda picked his nose. Then to the main business of the day: the world conference on primates.

Veniard went straight to the heart of the matter — the rebuilding of the park headquarters as the focal point of the conference. There was a need to find a building contractor in view of the fact that time was short and an architect was due from the capital at any moment. Of course, in more leisurely times it would be proper to put the work out to tender. The board had a duty to get the lowest possible quotation consistent with good workmanship. However, in the circumstances, the board might wish to consider the fact that it had among its members a well-known local builder who had been asked to prepare in advance some provisional estimates for the work. Perhaps the board might be prepared to consider them?

With becoming reluctance, Daudi Mahoja circulated some single sheets of paper on which there was a rough break-down into materials and labour for the reconstruction work, including the lean-to conference room. Jean-Pierre was surprised to see that the total only came to 25,000 dollars. Allowing for fifty per cent profit, Mahoja was doing the work reasonably cheaply. No doubt, if he had not been a member of the board he could have been beaten down by at least 5,000 dollars. But then, Chiribanda would have lost his share of the profit also.

Mahoja naturally abstained from voting. The tender was accepted unanimously, though Jean-Pierre fancied he felt his fingertips burning when he held up his hand to vote. Damned African politics again!

He heard himself saying, 'One thing, Mr Chairman. We've agreed to accept this tender but we must insist on the work being completed to park board satisfaction at least a month before the conference date.'

'Don't worry, *Monsieur le Conservateur*, I guarantee the job will be done three months before the conference starts.'

The schoolmaster suggested that he include this guarantee in the minutes which, unbidden, he had been keeping.

To his surprise, Marie never referred to the baby gorilla again. She did not even ask Jean-Pierre what he had said to Helen about its abduction. As the weeks went by she became more and more relaxed, more and more loving. It was two months after his return from the capital that she said one night in bed, 'Put your hand on my belly.'

It was an unusually direct phrase for her to use and, since they had not made love and he knew from her manner that she was expecting it, he imagined that this was some new love-game. He gladly did as he was bidden.

'Can you feel it yet?'

'What?'

'The baby.'

He withdrew his hand as if he had put it down on a red-hot plate.

'Can you feel its heartbeat?'

He lay there, saying nothing.

'You're not pleased.'

'You didn't tell me.'

'I didn't know for certain until now.'

'But you take something your doctor gives you. You always told me it was safe.'

'It was but I stopped taking it.'

'When? For God's sake, when?'

'When that American bastard stole the baby gorilla.'

'I see.' He did see, too. He saw it all.

'Now I have a baby of my own, something that she can never have.'

'Yes, I understand.'

'And you're angry. You're not glad?'

'Give me a little while to get used to the idea.' He put his hand back on her lower belly. 'You don't know anything

315

about babies,' he said. 'It's far too early to feel its heartbeat.'

As the weeks went by, Helen Lawes spent more and more time away from the hut on the Saddle, more and more time on the unexplored slopes of Vahinga. At first her expeditions were made within several hours' march of the hut so that, by starting at first light, she could cover her chosen ground and still get back by nightfall. On these early trips she took either Mushi or the second tracker as guide and escort. During these absences she was surprised to find how much she missed the company of the baby gorilla. She persuaded herself that the periods when she was absent were all part of the independence training of Toto. So, no doubt, they were. Left to its own devices, the infant certainly did learn to climb trees and feed itself on wild banana leaves, herbs and vines dumped wholesale into its pen. When Helen returned, however, she over-compensated for its periods of aloneness by smothering it with affection, even though affection took the guise of crawling with it through the undergrowth as its mother might have done, perching it on the branches of trees to see how it would cope, facing it with its future forest familiars, non-poisonous snakes, chameleons, tree-frogs and a selection of large insects such as crickets and mantids.

Helen's first researches into the gorilla population of Vahinga were far more encouraging than she had dared to hope. She had already pinpointed and identified four families new to her whose home-range lay within five hours' travel of the hut.

Six weeks were taken up by these short-range excursions. The time had come to survey the unknown ground on the far slopes of Vahinga. She had been almost dreading the moment because she knew she would need a guide more confident and reassuring than either of the pygmies. Jean-Pierre was the obvious choice. However, she had persuaded herself that he was far too involved with the park administration in general and with the forthcoming conference in particular. This was only partly true. Since the incident of the baby gorilla she had found it increasingly hard to make contact with their older, easy relationship or even with their newer, more distant one. She had turned to Francis Chiribanda despite, or, if she were entirely honest with herself, because of her former friction with him. It amazed her that after her civil war experiences she could bear the solitary companionship of an African man.

She could not explain it to herself but she found Francis both attractive and disagreeable. At first it was a toss-up which side of his personality made the stronger impression on her. Gradually this doubt resolved itself in his favour. After their differences on the mountain that morning in the mist, Francis had certainly learned some tact. He never now openly opposed her. He suggested rather than ordered. She responded to this by avoiding any high-handedness, by wheedling and bargaining whenever their views clashed. Francis did not possess Jean-Pierre's great store of fieldcraft and instinctive anticipation of how a gorilla group would behave in any given situation, but he was skilful enough. Between them they made few serious mistakes and caused no dangerous confrontations. Thus, a working relationship was built up.

Between safaris Francis Chiribanda went down to Baruva, to the park's headquarters to report to Jean-Pierre and to carry out his more routine duties. Sometimes he was away for three or four days at a time. Helen found herself increasingly looking forward to his return. He was always so cheerful when he arrived at the hut. These days, the extrovert side of his nature was uppermost. He acted as though he had the best job in the world with everything going just right for him. His tendency to sulkiness disappeared in direct ratio to his growing confidence. This confidence showed pleasantly in his handsome young face, a face so different from the African faces Helen still saw in occasional nightmares.

They were to be away this time for four days. Helen planned to travel to the furthest limits of Vahinga, searching for signs of gorillas in that so far unexplored region. Nothing very thorough could be accomplished in the time, but it would at least be possible to form an idea of the suitability of the habitat. They could obtain from tracks and signs an idea of how heavily the area was populated by the great apes. It was not even known what human presence, if any, existed on the far side of the mountain. Were there, for instance, pygmies living there and, if so, how many?

Francis Chiribanda was at his most helpful and companionable. They cooked and shared their first evening meal. Afterwards, he set up her mosquito net, hanging it from a branch.

'Animals are frightened of mosquito nets,' he assured her. 'They won't come near such a strange creature.'

'What about you? You haven't got a net.'

'Insects never bite me. I'm too thick-skinned. As for the gorillas, they've all gone to bed, too.'

She enjoyed his talk. As they sat by the fire he told her stories of his childhood in the forest, of tribal rites and ceremonies, of spells and witchcraft.

'You don't believe in such things?'

'Most certainly I do. Quite recently I was the victim of such sorcery myself.' He showed her the still-livid scar on his arm where the saw-blade had bitten.

She felt the little dots that were the stitch-marks and instantly wished she hadn't. She was conscious of a powerful physical charge. When she was safely zipped up in her sleeping-bag and he in his, she lay looking at the Southern Cross and thought about that moment of contact with confusion, shame and excitement. She ought to have felt revulsion at the mere idea of touching, or being touched by, a black man. Instead, she'd felt a strong, physical attraction.

Ought to have felt revulsion? This was not entirely consistent with the facts. Being raped and nearly killed by two Africans might well have put her off sex for life. It had come close to doing exactly that. Her sex-life after her return to the States had been almost non-existent. She had tried to establish normal relationships with lecturers and even students. She had found it impossible except in one brief instance, and that had been with a black American teacher in a Monterey motel. It had been far less than satisfactory. The teacher had turned out to be inconsiderate, almost brutal, in his approach. She had needed something gentle, less reminiscent, even in the mildest degree, of that other awful experience.

When she had been invited by Redfern to return to Misoka her heart had leapt, not only at the scientific opportunity but also because it offered a chance to meet again her first lover, the man whom she perhaps admired most in life — Jean-Pierre. But somehow that had gone wrong, too. She still admired him. Greatly. All other feeling had disappeared, though. She had searched for an explanation. Sheer passing of time. Inevitable changes in both of them. The fact that he had seen the two *Fisi* do *that* to her. The fact that he had chosen an African woman to live with him. Any, or all, of these would serve. Probably no single reason would suffice.

Nor did any of this explain what she had been forced to acknowledge as a strong and growing sexual attraction for Francis Chiribanda. Subconsciously, perhaps, she wished to even the score with Jean-Pierre. You sleep with a black woman, I'll take a black man as my lover. O.K., so why not get it over and done with and simply invite Francis over? He'd be a fool to refuse, but what a fool she would look if he did.

All next day she avoided touching him. If he was aware of any development in their relationship, he gave no sign. It was a long, exhausting day with many ravines to cross and hidden streams to ford. It was also a rewarding day. They made contact with two entirely new gorilla groups and found clear indications of a third. When they had eaten they were both too tired to do anything but crawl into their sleeping-bags. A mist had crept down off the peaks. Helen pulled the flap of the sleeping bag over her head and escaped from fatigue and the dourness of the weather into deep sleep.

*

By twelve noon next day they'd reached the limit of Helen's survey. At that point the furthest face of Vahinga was a vast lava-scar from one of its more recent eruptions. Only sparse vegetation grew on it. It was certainly not gorilla country and it formed an obvious boundary on this one flank to any future enlargement of the park. Below stretched miles of forest so thick that it seemed you could walk to the horizon on the roof of its canopy. If Misoka—Vahinga Park was to be extended, then this was the obvious direction in which it must spread. Reconnaissance of even the fringe of that forest would have to wait for future safaris.

Helen now suggested that they route their return journey round the base of the mountain. This would not add more than a day to their safari and would at least enable them to form some idea of whether gorillas were living in any numbers on the lower slopes. A week or two ago Francis might have been expected to oppose such a change of plan on principle. He might have given almost any reason; because he was expected back by Jean-Pierre; because the territory was unknown to him and he therefore felt he could not guarantee her safety there; because he had not left word at head-quarters that they might be operating in that area. If anything happened, Jean-Pierre would not know where to search for them. Now he simply smiled and said seriously, 'Yes, I think that would be well worth doing now we've come this far, but it may mean spending another night on the mountain.'

'How about food?'

Francis tapped his rifle. 'This is as good as a store cupboard.'

Before they had walked more than three hours in the new direction it was clear that this region, rich in vines and herbs, was much frequented by gorillas. In early afternoon they picked up the trail of one large party and were able to get close enough to learn that there were nineteen animals in the group, including two silver-backs and, far more exciting, three very small babies. The group as a whole was shy and the

320

two males nervously aggressive. Despite this they got within fifty yards of them, having to face in their final approach two flat-out charges from the silver-backs. Francis was justifiably pleased with his fieldcraft, Helen elated at her ability to stand fast in the face of those charges.

When they camped for the night the sense of excitement and joint achievement stayed with them. To eke out their rations Francis had shot a duiker. He roasted the little antelope, not much bigger than a hare, over a wood fire on an improvised spit. The smell of the meat mingled agreeably with the night scents of the forest. It was far warmer and more congenial at this lower altitude. The thick forest canopy seemed to hold the warmth for a long while after sundown. After the meal there was no immediate need to escape the mountain chill in their sleeping-bags.

Knowing perfectly well where she was heading, Helen lay three feet from Francis looking up at the stars caught like fireflies in a spider's web of interlacing branches.

'Today was marvellous. You never made a wrong move with that big family, Francis.'

'You weren't at all afraid this time when they charged?'

'I had complete confidence in you, like I used to have with Monsieur Menant.'

'Ah!' He was delighted.

'I have to be honest. I never thought I would get my confidence back with anyone else.'

'Especially with an African?'

'Oh, I didn't say that. There are plenty of. . . .'

'Of bright, intelligent, brave Africans?'

'Don't be so touchy.'

'Touchy?'

'Sensitive. What I meant was, I never thought I'd be willing to trust myself alone with an African again.'

'But you aren't scared of me?'

'I'm not scared *with* you. Quite the reverse, in fact.'

'Perhaps you should be.'

'Well I'm not.'

'Are you ever afraid that here, alone in the forest, I might behave to you as those others did?'

'Never. Besides,' she said, trying to turn it aside at the last instant, 'you'd lose your job.'

'It might be worth it.' It was the nearest he had come to familiarity. She didn't like it but was thrilled by the implication and the fact that he had considered the situation and its possible outcome.

Later, when she was in her sleeping-bag, she called out, 'I'm cold.'

'It's warmer tonight.'

'Not where I am.'

A pause, then, deliberately, he said, 'I have to be quite sure. Don't be offended, but are you issuing me an invitation?'

'Yes,' she said, scarcely believing she had said it. And then, jokingly but with a shake in her voice, 'Somehow I have to overcome my fear of Africans.'

Francis was amazingly gentle with her. It was quite different from that time with the American negro teacher at Monterey. This time she was able to relax and to forget completely what had happened in the saw-mill and afterwards, to acknowledge frankly to herself that what had happened there had, by some strange somersault of the libido, made it possible for only a man with a black skin, but the right man inside that black skin, to turn her on sexually.

Francis asked, 'Will I lose my job now?'

'Not if I say nothing.'

'You may find that impossible. There are other ways than talking by which such secrets become common property.'

'Not if it never happens again.'

'And won't it?'

'I don't know. Perhaps tonight was just very special and very unexpected.'

'For me too, Dr Lawes.'

She laughed. 'Mind you keep up the formality.' Afterwards, when he had gone back to his own sleeping-bag, she

322

knew she should have reproached herself for making their entire future relationship impossible. As she fell asleep she felt nothing but liberation and contentment.

For the first few hours next morning they saw further signs of gorillas as they traversed the lower shoulder of Vahinga. Then, unmistakably, the signs petered out. Shortly after noon the reason for their absence became clear. Men had been working recently in the forest. At regular intervals they found small clearings. In one they came across surveyor's poles, in another the place where a small hut had been set up and recently dismantled. Limited excavations had been made at each site.

'What do you make of it, Dr Lawes?' Francis had been meticulously formal ever since the moment at which they might have been said to have started the day's work again. At breakfast he had called her 'Helen', using the christian name as though it might sting his tongue.

'I know what I make of it. I've seen the same sort of thing in America, in Alaska to be precise. Someone is doing some mineral prospecting. See where the earth has been scooped away? It's the same at each site. See that rock cracked open with a geologist's hammer? Volcanoes usually don't produce any worthwhile minerals but here we're on lower ground. There's been some faulting. The earth's crust has lifted in some places, sunk at others, probably as the result of volcanic activity higher up. No, wait a minute. I'm no geologist but surely it should be the other way round? The faulting is probably part of the process that gave rise to the volcanoes. However it happened, it's apparently left something near the surface that is commercially worth looking for.'

Francis turned the broken rock slowly in his hand.

'What is it, then? Uranium perhaps?' And then, hopefully, 'Gold?'

'Probably something much less glamorous, but that's not the point. What matters is that it obviously occurs right here, just where we might be wanting to extend Misoka—Vahinga Park. If anyone did start mining here, they'd cut right across

323

the gorilla trails to the forests down below. They'd put in roads. They'd wreck the whole delicate habitat. It could be the end of the gorillas in these mountains. Jean-Pierre must be told all about this at once.'

The joy had gone out of the day. They hurried now, instinctively striking uphill away from the contamination with which the chain of prospecting sites seemed to affront their own special world. They climbed two thousand feet into the region of recent vulcanism again. As they sat resting on an exposed lava-scar in late afternoon, Francis caught a glint of sunlight on a bright, moving object far below. Borrowing Helen's binoculars, he searched the forest for the source of that reflected beam. At last he found it in a forest clearing.

'There it is. There are men actually at work down there.'

'Here, give me the glasses.'

'No, just a minute. Something's happening. That flash. It's a helicopter. It's just starting up.'

Helen snatched the glasses. 'I've got to see.'

'There. You're looking too much to the right. Give them back to me.'

'I've got it. There are two men getting aboard. One's tiny, almost like a pygmy. Either that or the other one's ridiculously tall. Yes, that's it. He had practically to double himself up to climb aboard.'

'Let me look, please. I should know all about this to make my report. After all,' almost petulantly, 'I am the head ranger.'

Helen brushed his hand aside. 'Shut up or neither of us will see anything.'

'Too late now. It's taking off.'

Far, far below a blue and white helicopter cleared the tree-tops, turned steeply and headed away. Half a minute later the sound of its engine reached them.

They were silent as they set up camp that evening. They ate the cold remains of the duiker and turned in early. The love-making was as if it had never happened.

Where Jean-Pierre was concerned, Helen was right about one thing. The preparations for the world conference were taking more and more of his time. He seemed to spend most of the day arranging accommodation for the delegates, answering correspondence and keeping his eye on the rebuilding work at headquarters. None of this made him happy. Much of it was the sort of thing he knew he should have delegated to Francis Chiribanda. And yet, the thought of the two Chiribandas having their fingers in the till already occupied by the rapacious brown digits of Daudi Mahoja filled him with horror. The alternative, which he did not like very much better, was to detail Francis for extended duty with Helen Lawes.

Jean-Pierre's path had not crossed Francis Chiribanda's for over a fortnight since Helen and he had come upon the activities of the prospecting-team working on the distant lower slopes of Vahinga. Francis had been down to headquarters several times. He had even reported to the Baruva office on two occasions. Each time Jean-Pierre had missed him. Jean-Pierre had twice been on the point of visiting Helen at the hut, but each time routine and administration had got in the way.

One thing he was forced to admit: the choice of Daudi Mahoja as building contractor had been an effective selection if not the most economical one. Work on rebuilding park headquarters was going on at a great pace. Mahoja had demanded, and got, three extra lorries. These had had to be hired at some cost from (Guess who?) Kama Chiribanda. The understanding was that these trucks, two Mercedes five-tonners and a three-ton Chevrolet, would be useful when not required to carry building materials for the reconstruction of park tracks, a sorely needed service.

One evening Jean-Pierre decided to drive out to see how the work at park headquarters was progressing. He was surprised to find how much pleasure he got from watching his old family home being brought back to life. Darkness was falling. The workmen had long since returned to their homes.

325

He was, therefore, surprised to see the headlights of a truck flickering down the park track towards him. He pulled off into the bush and killed his own lights. As the truck drew level he saw it was the hired Chevrolet with Loti at the wheel. The truck passed within ten feet of him. As it did so it hit a bump, throwing its load around under the tarpaulin cover. The sound was not one he associated with building materials. It could only have been made by a great many bottles bouncing inside their crates.

Jean-Pierre gave the truck a good start and then turned back and followed it. At the main road it turned left, northward along the lake shore. Two miles later it pulled off into an African village. Jean-Pierre parked his jeep and moved in through the banana trees on foot until he could see clearly what was going on. By then the lorry was being unloaded by Ndungu and Jahazi. Only Marema was missing, presumably — though how could one be sure of anything? — because he was on duty at headquarters. That was something that could be checked on later.

Loti was now collecting money for the merchandise. There was no longer any doubt what that merchandise consisted of. Loti and the village headman were sampling a specimen apiece. Jean-Pierre even recognised the label on the bottles — the local Simba beer. Someone had got a nice little racket going, using park transport to collect the stuff wholesale from the Baruva brewery and then selling it at night, at considerable profit, around the village. Someone had to be the organising brain.

It would certainly not be Loti, Marema, Ndungu or Jahazi. Everything suggested the sharp-witted Francis Chiribanda. Once he had got the thing going, the others would be quite capable of operating it.

Jean-Pierre drove back to town, worrying. One more problem to solve. The obvious solution was to find out whether Francis was at the back of it and, if he was, to fire him. Perhaps too obvious a solution. He'd have to talk to Veniard about it.

When he told Veniard the story next morning, the doctor laughed.

'What the devil is so funny about it?'

'It doesn't sound very serious to me.'

'It's a question of discipline. Let young Chiribanda get away with this and God knows what racket he'll organise next. Selling baby gorillas, perhaps.'

'Ah, now that would be something you'd have to stamp on.'

'And you don't think I should stamp on this?'

'My dear chap, it's typically African. They're simply getting the most out of that hired transport.'

'And who hired it? You did, indirectly, Jacques, as a member of the park board. They're using our petrol, our time, our labour. . . .'

'They're working after hours, aren't they?'

'They aren't picking the stuff up from the brewery after hours. They must do that during the daytime.'

'So what? The lorries go down into Baruva for building materials quite a lot. They aren't always fully loaded when they come back. Besides, they have to pass the brewery on the way.'

'That doesn't excuse it.'

'So, what are you going to do about it?'

'I'd like to shoot young Chiribanda for a start.'

'Come on. That's the old Jean-Pierre. The man of action. What about the new one, the manipulator of African politics?'

'You know how I hate politics of any sort.'

'Maybe, but it's the game you've got to play if, in the long run, you want to save your precious gorillas.'

'O.K. You win. If I fire young Chiribanda, his father will probably resign from the park board, or, more likely, stay put and make life bloody impossible for me. He might even go back to chopping down trees again. I could give master Francis a warning, let him know that I know what he's up to. But that would look as if I approve. He'd see that as weakness. I could insist that all transport keys are brought down to Baruva every night but then they'd probably just make duplicates. I suppose I could ignore the whole thing and only thump Chiribanda if he does something really criminal. . . .'

'That last suggestion would have been my advice precisely. You'll make a politician yet. Here, split a Simba beer with me. Of course, there's no telling where I got it from.'

Helen walked into his office in late afternoon, the first time he had seen her since the row over the baby gorilla. He stood up courteously and reached for her hand in order to kiss it.

'Is that just Continental good manners or are you offering me the pipe of peace?'

'Both, I hope.'

'You were very angry about the baby gorilla.'

'Yes, I was. But that's over and done with.'

'I'm sorry if I upset your domestic life.'

'Shall we leave that subject?' Why did the silly bitch have to drag Marie into it again? 'Tell me what's happening on the mountain.'

'That's exactly what I came to tell you about. I should have got to you several days ago but we wanted to get more positive information.'

'We?'

'Francis and I.'

'Oh, of course.' A subtle shift here? Things must be settling down between them. Before, she had always called him plain Chiribanda.

'Something pretty worrying is happening on the far side of Vahinga.'

'Tree-felling? Poaching?'

'No. There's a prospecting-team at work, taking rock samples all the way round the foot of the south-east slope.'

'But it's all volcanic. What could they be looking for?'

'It's not all volcanic. Let's have a look at your map. Most of this area here is heavily faulted and only lightly covered

328

with volcanic ash. I'm not a geologist, but any kind of mineral could be lying beneath the surface.'

'How big are the test sites?'

'Very small, as yet, but just imagine what it could be like if they really started surface mining there.'

'It could be the beginning of the end for the gorillas.'

'The line of test sites cuts right across the access routes to the very areas I'm starting to survey. They're the precise parts we're hoping will soon become an extension to the park. But just imagine what will happen to the central gorilla range if they get started.'

'I must come and see for myself.'

'The sooner the better.'

'Tomorrow morning?'

'Suits me fine. Just gives me enough time to order some stores. Francis can take them up for me later.'

Since her return to America Nancy Genova had become increasingly worried about John Redfern. He seemed to take more and more for granted that she was willing to act as his personal PRO. These days it was about the only personal thing they shared. The success of Ark International had filled John Redfern's life completely. Phenomenal as his energies were, they were bound, at his age, to be a strictly limited resource. Ark drained this resource dry. Redfern seemed always to be travelling; to Europe to raise funds; the length and breadth of America to cajole and wheedle industry into giving conscience-money for use abroad so that it might continue to pollute the planet nearer home.

Though it always seemed to Nancy that the idea of devoting all Ark International's funds to conservation in one country might come grievously unstuck, she had to admit that, so far, she'd been wrong. It had succeeded out of all proportion. People actually liked the idea of knowing where their dollars, pounds or Deutschmarks were going, of being able to see, or anyway be told about, tangible results. The gorillas had helped immeasurably. The stories and pictures

329

Nancy had willingly produced had done a great propaganda job. The crucified Intruder had, arguably, become the most famous ape of all time. She had even managed to make Lake Olindo look good. She had done all this, in the first instance, out of affection and admiration for Redfern and because she passionately believed his cause was worthwhile even if supporting it did, to some extent, compromise her reputation for professional detachment.

As the world conference drew nearer, Redfern increasingly involved her in its organisation and advance publicity. When she was in New York she was expected to be in attendance on Redfern, even to the detriment of other assignments. Their love-making became rarer and after a few months ceased altogether. At first Nancy was sad about this. After a time she felt only relief. It had to stop sometime, so why not now? Ark International had supplanted all other drives in the old man.

Nancy felt less happy about other aspects of their changing relationship. As Redfern's confidante and publicist she saw more and more behind the scenes of world conservation. She quickly discovered that many conservation organisations, both government and free enterprise, were pretty much of a jungle in themselves, their human denizens as red in tooth and claw as anything living out there amid the forests, savannahs and deserts they sought to preserve. This should have come as no surprise to a journalist of Nancy Genova's experience. Surprise, no: shock, yes. In this one field of human activity she was still something of an idealist. She had been badly shaken by the Lake Olindo business, by the fact that Redfern was willing to throw, almost literally down the drain, fifty thousand dollars that should have gone to Misoka. Once she had learned about Lake Olindo she had tended to distrust his entire performance in the capital that time. What other wheeler-dealing had he been up to with Jack Wright?

Six weeks before the world conference was due to start in Baruva she found out. Redfern called her at her flat and asked if she could lunch with him. He'd just flown in from

Africa the previous day and had something big to tell her.

The old man was waiting at the table looking as patrician as ever. He wore a tailored suit, cut like a bush-jacket, that would have been great on a man of thirty-five and looked even better on Dr Redfern. He was, perhaps, a trifle jaded by travel but still seemed good for fifty thousand miles without a rebore. As always, the charm was there, including the hand-kissing. He had a large Campari ready for her. She noticed the orchid by her plate — typical touch, it was an African one flown over specially, no doubt, in the plane that had brought him. She alerted herself that she was about to be sold a gallon of snake oil by one of the finest vendors of oleaginous reptilian by-products in the business. It would be at least one hundred proof python oil, or maybe mamba.

Over the smoked Atlantic salmon he said, 'Nancy, we have a very delicate conservation situation to handle. I'm not going to pretend it will be easy. That's why I want your advice.'

'Here it comes,' she said to herself. 'Please, Nancy dear, keep a tight hold on the thought that you already have shelves groaning under jars of snake oil bought under similar circumstances all over the world.' She waited for him to warm up.

'I've just made a special trip to Africa to confer with the president's personal counsellor.'

'Good old Jack Wright,' she translated, just to remind him to cut the bullshit.

'Exactly! He's as disturbed as I am at what, quite un-expectedly, has come about.'

'O.K.,' she thought, refusing to make it easy for him by asking, 'Just you go ahead and tell me what *has* come about.'

'A developing country, Nancy, has all sorts of needs. We international conservationists can't expect to have everything our own way. We've got to be realistic.'

She mocked him gently. 'You've been reading my articles, John.'

'Oh yes,' he said, 'and you were paying close attention to

331

me, no doubt, before you wrote them, so I don't have to explain any of this to you.'

'Right on! So why not give it to me straight before I start on the tournedos Rossini you're about to order for me.'

'The point is, Nancy, we have to balance up the importance to the country of, say, gorillas against vital economic developments.'

'*Gorillas!*' She shouted the word so loudly that a Cuban-looking diner two tables away spilled his wine. 'Importance to the country! I thought your belief was that gorillas are so important that they are world property.'

'*Du calme*, as Jean-Pierre Menant might say — you see, I do read your articles, Nancy — *du calme*. You can't expect President Olindo to see it quite that way when his mining people come up with the information that there's a rich, though limited, vein of bauxite right on the gorillas' back doorstep.'

'Where? Not in Misoka Park, for Christ Jesu's sake.'

'No, luckily. Not inside the park. Across the lower southern slopes of Vahinga, just where Helen Lawes is carrying out her survey.'

'Perhaps there aren't any gorillas there.'

'Unfortunately, her first reports suggest that there are a good many. Alas, the vein seems to cut right across the corridor which she believes connects the Misoka—Vahinga gorillas with those at lower altitudes.'

'You've got to stop it. Ark is pledged to protect and develop Misoka.'

'Misoka, yes. The extension of the park to those lower forests was something we hoped we might achieve in the future.'

'*Was*? You're already talking in the past tense.'

'No conservation organisation in the world can tell an African government what to do. You know that as well as I do.'

'No, but it can damn well try. It can rouse would opinion. If it had the guts, it might even succeed. What the hell did you put Helen Lawes into Misoka for unless it was to help get the present area of the park extended?'

'Easy,' he said, 'easy! That bauxite represents an awful lot of hard currency. A country that is poor can't afford to put conservation at the top of its list.'

'Maybe. But do you mean to say that you're willing to set up a world conference on primates when all the time you're prepared to sell the damn gorillas down the river?'

'Now you're letting your emotions cloud your judgement. Who said I'd sold anything down the river?'

'Well, haven't you? First Lake Olindo and now carving up Misoka for a short-term financial gain. The goddamn bauxite can't last forever.'

'No, it's a finite resource, all right. From four to five years at the most.'

'By which time the forest will have been wrecked. People will have swarmed into the area. The gorilla's range will have shrunk even more.'

The tournedos arrived, with them a bottle of Château Latour. They were Nancy's favourites. She treated the wine as if it was Coca Cola and barely touched the succulent medallion of steak on its bed of pâté. Redfern touched her hand as she reached for her glass. She lifted the glass to drink in order to break the contact as quickly as possible.

'You have to trust my judgement, Nancy.'

'Do I? I'm not so sure this time.'

'If I told you that Olindo intended to go ahead and scratch that bauxite out anyway. If I said that I had got certain concessions in exchange.'

'What, for instance?'

'Well, for a start, a whole new government department with a large budget largely derived from the bauxite royalties to be entirely devoted to conservation. A European director of conservation is proposed for the whole country, none other than your friend Jean-Pierre Menant.'

Nancy choked on her wine. 'That's hilarious. Has anyone asked *him* yet?'

'No. And I must ask you to keep all this secret.'

'Then why tell me, a mere journalist?'

'Oh, come on,' he said mildly. 'As a journalist you'd be the first to respect classified information. As a friend. . . .'

'You said you wanted my advice. I doubt that. You and Wright seem already to have made all the decisions.'

'Perhaps I should have said that I wanted your help.'

She resisted asking him how she was expected to help. For one thing, she already knew. For another, she decided to let him wriggle a bit.

John Redfern was no wriggler. She should have known that. The snake oil was slurping seductively in its barrels. He smiled his most disarming smile, the one that said: 'You and I know that I've got the most outrageous gall to ask this but, if nothing else, you'll enjoy the sheer bloody nerve of it.'

'I want you to do everything you can to put the mining proposition across as essential and not in itself damaging to the Misoka gorillas, who will, after all, be left untouched by it.'

She looked at his unabashed, smiling face. Then she laughed out of sheer relief, knowing that this time the super hustler hadn't made a sale.

'You can't possibly believe they'll be untouched. I'm not your official PRO, John. Thank God I turned the job down. I don't have to write anything I don't want to write or don't believe in.'

'You're acting emotionally. That's very understandable. But you're too practical when it comes down to it not to see that the Vahinga deal is the best one for the country's economy and for the future of conservation there.'

'Am I? So what do you expect me to do? Agree with you?'

'I wouldn't expect you to do that entirely, you can't say anything for a while. The news won't be available for release until a fortnight before the world conference.'

'Soon enough for the delegates to get used to the idea and recover from any legitimately outraged feelings?'

'Most of them will fully understand the problems because

they've got similar ones themselves back home. The Indonesians, for instance, with their orangs. They're chopping down their rain-forests as hard as they can go.'

'Let me ask you something. What on earth do you think this is going to do for Ark's image?'

'Ark will come out just fine. It will have persuaded President Olindo to take conservation seriously at a government level.'

'Yeah! And what about Jean-Pierre?'

'He'll be happy in the end. The offer to take over direction of conservation in a country that's prepared to give ten per cent of its land to national parks is a pretty hard one to refuse.'

'Just try him.'

'We will. He'll take it.'

'Then you don't know him very well. And what about Helen Lawes?'

'She's pretty ambitious. Supposing she gets to control research programmes in all those parks?'

'She's dedicated to mountain gorillas.'

'Then you don't know scientists as well as I do.'

'All I know, John, is that your approach is entirely cynical.'

'*Practical*. We have that quality in common.'

Over the liqueurs that he insisted on buying, but which she didn't really want, he said, 'I'll get in touch with you directly all the details are available for you to consider objectively.'

'There's only one place to consider the details objectively and that's in Africa. I'll go see for myself and then I'll write the story as I see it, with or without the official hand-out.'

'You do that, honey. Ark will pay your fare.'

'Thanks, John, but if I'm to keep a clear eye I'd better pay my way for myself.'

When a severe electric storm comes to the peaks and the high forests it is often heard first, far off, grumbling and growling like a huge animal that means to take a bite out of the mountains. Then, as if the animal has snorted in anger, it breathes out a draught of air from a great distance which riffles the highest leaves in the forest canopy. Sometimes a pause follows, sometimes not. The sky darkens and then, lower this time, the wind bends the middle leaves and branches. This is the last moment at which to take cover, though even then it may be too late. Within minutes the storm takes possession of the forest, the wind ripping at gale force through the trees, tearing off leaves and branches, moaning through the trunks, playing them like giant Pan pipes. With the gale comes the rain, or sometimes hail, in slanting, stinging, grey, nearly horizontal lines. Just occasionally it is as if a whole cloud has been emptied, like a huge bucket, in one wild throw.

Jean-Pierre had heard the first tiny rumblings of the storm that was slowly gathering about Misoka. For a time the lightning had played far off in small, flickering, seemingly inconsequential flashes.

The beer-running night operations with the hired transport had been one such inconsiderable glimmer of sheet lightning. Helen Lawes's report on the mining survey resembled a vicious, forked shaft that had struck far too close for comfort. Lately there had been more or less continuous mumblings and grumblings of distant thunder. Daudi Mahoja had suddenly announced that the construction of the lecture hall for the conference was more difficult than he had anticipated. The architect sent by Jack Wright's department had returned to the capital so there was no way of checking whether Mahoja was right, whether he did actually need the extra labour he was demanding. The lorries would now have to be hired for an additional period. All this confirmed Jean-Pierre's suspicion that it was not only the local Simba beer that was being taken for a ride at the park's expense; the *conservateur* was being given the run-around also.

In the spreading swamp of frustration and helplessness in which he felt himself to be floundering, he found only two pieces of solid ground. The first somewhat surprised him.

With the coming of the baby and the dignity and reserves of strength she had previously shown, Marie Maputa had grown in stature sexually and domestically; she now began to emerge as someone he could turn to and rely on. Perhaps he should have guessed that these qualities lay in her from the way she had handled everyday affairs in the park's office from the very beginning.

The second solid rock was Jacques Veniard.

'You, my friend,' he said one evening when Jean-Pierre was recounting his problems, 'are like an insect caught at a moment of metamorphosis. You are either half-way between being a caterpillar and a chrysalis or maybe at mid-point between chrysalis and butterfly. I rather think the latter. . . .'

'I don't see the slightest resemblance.'

'You haven't yet made your mind up which stage of development you've reached. Being between stages, you're at your most vulnerable. You would still like to be your old man-of-action, settle-it-with-a-well-placed-bullet self. That's the caterpillar stage, creeping about the forest, relying on protective colouring and stinging hairs to survive. Stage two is the chrysalis, lying dormant while subtle changes take place within you. My guess is that you're coming to the end of that phase in your evolution as founder of Misoka Park.'

'O.K., so what are these subtle changes that have taken place?'

'You haven't noticed them? No more, I suppose, does the caterpillar as wings form and false legs drop away.'

'I didn't know you were an entomologist, Jacques.'

'I have a modest collection of forest lepidoptera. But you wanted to know about those changes. Very well. Inside your chrysalis you've learned to play the game the African way and — I know how you hate the thought — you're finding out how important local and even national politics are.'

'And what do I become next?'

'A beautiful butterfly, my friend — if you make it out of the chrysalis, that is.'

'How will I recognise myself *if* I make it?'

'You will need strong wings like many of the forest species. You will need to be powerful and fast to avoid predators, great and small.'

'And where does the beauty come in?'

'That is represented by the effectiveness and aplomb with which you flit from flower to flower, fertilising here, extracting goodness there.'

'You're talking balls, Jacques. Just say in words of one syllable what you mean.'

'I mean simply this: this country is going to play conservation for all it's worth, for a time anyway. For propaganda purposes? Of course! To attract tourists? Fair enough. Just possibly because it means it. Whatever the reasons, it's going to need a strong, knowledgeable conservationist to run its affairs. You could be that man.'

'You're out of your mind. All I'm interested in is Misoka and my gorillas.'

'That's the caterpillar speaking.'

'Maybe, but what am I supposed to do about it?'

'Ah, that's the question. You have to develop power, real power, and for you that means that you have got the state behind you. That's where the real and only power lies. Africans only understand that kind of power.'

'And if I want it, how do I get it?'

'That's your problem. That's for you to find out.'

'Thanks very much. You've been most helpful, as usual.'

The coming storm next blew with the strong breeze that ruffled the highest leaves in the forest canopy. Nancy Genova flew in to find out just what was going on with those mining sites on Vahinga.

Jean-Pierre met her at the airstrip. He was glad to see her after all this time. He thanked her gravely for the marvellous propaganda use she had made of his picture of the dead Intruder. She surprised him by saying, 'I've got a great fat cheque for you in my bank account. That picture's earned you a lot of money. At the last count it was around eleven thousand dollars.'

'Good God, I never expected anything from it. It had better go to Ark International.'

'I'm not sure that's the wisest course.'

'How do you mean? Dr Redfern has done everything for Misoka.'

'Well, not quite everything.'

She told him about Lake Olindo. At the end of her account he said, 'I'm not denying we could have done with the money, but I suppose it is up to Dr Redfern to decide exactly how Ark International allots its funds.'

'Sure. All I'm saying is that, if you paid your eleven thousand bucks into Ark's coffers, Misoka might not see it all or, just possibly, might see none of it. So keep it yourself. If you want to spend it on the park, that's your affair.'

He looked closely at her. 'This doesn't sound quite like you. Why are you so disillusioned?'

'I didn't say that I was. I believe Ark to be one hundred per cent pro conservation in this country.'

'But?'

'I didn't say there were any "buts".'

'I'm glad about that. You haven't yet told me why you're paying us this visit.'

'I want to see things for myself before the world conference gets going. I understand you've got some mining operations on your doorstep that could prove a nuisance.'

'Dr Redfern sent you to find out what it's all about?'

'No. He doesn't send me anywhere. I came to see for myself and form my own opinions.'

'And to write about them. That might not do us any good.'

'You trusted me before, didn't you? Can't you trust me again?'

'Yes,' he said, 'I think I can.'

That pre-storm wind was riffling through the roof of the forest. The second blast of wind, the one that rips through the

339

lower branches and gives warning that the gathering storm means business, arrived twenty-four hours later.

Jean-Pierre took Nancy to see for herself. They started just after first light the next morning. Nancy's sinewy physique served her well on the mountain. Jean-Pierre was impressed by the fact that, as a city girl, she didn't tire easily or grow short of breath at altitude. They skirted the Saddle and took the shortest route to the far face of Vahinga. By two in the afternoon they had reached a vantage-point on a lava up-welling from which it was possible to look down on three of the test sites that the mining prospectors had cut out in the forest below. Jean-Pierre put the glasses on each site in turn.

'They're all old sites. At least no one's actually working on them. Here, look for yourself.'

At first Nancy had difficulty in picking out the small clearings. She found the first two and then swept the glasses in vain over the area Jean-Pierre had indicated. She stopped suddenly and began to fine-focus the binoculars.

'I thought you said there was no one working them.'

'You're looking in the wrong place.'

'Am I? Hey, wait a minute.'

'You're miles out. The third site's much further down the mountain.'

Nancy whistled.

'What have you found? Gorillas?'

'Gorillas nothing. People!'

'People! Let me look. People have no right to be there. They must be poachers.' He held out his hand for the glasses.

'I'm not sure you ought to see this.'

Jean-Pierre took the glasses gently but firmly. This time it was he who had difficulty in finding the target. At last he focused on it. A small, dark-green tent stood in a clearing. He recognised the tent as the one issued to Helen. It was too far to identify the faces of the two figures who lay on the outside. He could, however, make out that one was an African, the other white. Even at that distance their move-ments were unambiguous. Francis Chiribanda was right about

340

one thing. There are other ways such secrets become common property other than by talking about them.

When the wind rips through the lower branches of the forest it is the last moment to take cover from the coming mountain storm. Jean-Pierre doubted whether it would make much difference now even if he tried.

He needed time to think. His first reaction was, as usual, that he should consult Jacques Veniard. What Helen Lawes did was her business. What Chiribanda did, however, was very much his business, park business; nothing personal, he told himself, nothing to do with jealousy or dislike of Chiribanda. In the ordinary way there was no reason why Chiribanda shouldn't have an affair with a white woman. But this wasn't the ordinary way. This was undermining discipline. He just couldn't be allowed to get away with this.

By the time Nancy and Jean-Pierre had made a wide detour to avoid attracting the attention of the figures below them — not that there seemed much chance of that — it was too late to get off the mountain. There was no apparent danger of Helen and Chiribanda returning to the hut that night. They were obviously happy enough to camp where they were. Jean-Pierre and Nancy arrived at the hut just before nightfall.

Nancy Genova was thrilled to spend a night on the mountain. Jean-Pierre cooked some bushbuck meat he found in the freezer-compartment of the paraffin fridge. There was even a bottle of wine. He did not feel in the least guilty about cutting into Helen's precious supplies. Serve her damn well right. Over the meal, Nancy said, 'I'm sorry if I was responsible for turning over a stone and showing you something nasty.'

'I'd have seen it sooner or later.'

'What will you do about it? Not that it's my business . . . but off the record.'

'Probably sack young Chiribanda.'

'Why? Because he's black?'

'Nothing to do with it. This is an African state. Anyway,

341

mixed relationships were accepted even in colonial days.'

'But usually the other way round. White man taking black woman.'

'Sometimes.'

'If you do sack Chiribanda, won't that cause a whole lot of trouble?'

'Yes.'

'What kind of trouble?'

'His crook of a father will resign from the park board and start a war against me. Everything seems to be getting hopelessly screwed up all at once.'

'Can you sort it out?'

'Only if I have complete power, which I don't. Only two forms of power count here. One is this.' He tapped the stock of the hunting rifle on the wall-rack.

'And the other?'

'The sort of power Africans understand. Being head man in a way that everyone recognises. That's purely tribal.'

'I see. And you don't have that?'

'How could I? I'm a European.'

'Jack Wright has it.'

'That's only because the president has said he has it and made everyone understand the fact.'

'And if the president said the same sort of thing about you?'

'Why should he?'

'What you've done is not unrecognised in the capital.'

'Hooray! So they send me a bloody conference I could well do without.'

'But if you were given the power to sort all these people out?'

'I'd turn it down flat. I was happy before I got this place made into a national park. Since then everything has been self-defeating. In those days the survival of the gorillas was all that mattered to me.'

'Isn't that still true?'

'Think so? You saw that line of damned mining sites.'

342

'Are they that serious a threat?'

'To the long-term prospects of the whole park they're almost certainly fatal. If they find whatever they're after and start digging it up, just think of the weight of humanity it will bring into the area. That alone is the biggest threat the Misoka gorillas could face.'

'Is that what I should write when I get back to the States?'

'It's the truth.'

They left the hut early next morning. Jean-Pierre wished to avoid an immediate confrontation with Chiribanda or with Helen. He had already decided to choose his own time and place. Nancy had hoped to get Helen's views about the mining encroachment but agreed in the circumstances to settle for Jean-Pierre's. In any case, Jean-Pierre had all the facts and figures she could possibly need. That evening, while Marie served the dinner in the house in Baruva, Nancy asked, 'Are there any circumstances in which the mining on Vahinga could be justified?'

'In terms of the gorillas, as I've told you, it's an outright disaster.'

'In any other terms?'

'If there's enough of what they're after, I can imagine the government saying "to hell with gorillas".'

'You'd fight that?'

'Fight? You can't beat odds like that. I can't even beat the local African problems I've got here at the moment.'

'For lack of that power you were talking about?'

'Just that.'

Nancy left next morning. She knew exactly the kind of story she would write. It would be a dead factual one, but not at all the kind of hand-out John Redfern would have prepared.

Jacques Veniard's advice was as predictable and inevitable as the storm about to break.

'Don't!' he said.

'I can't let Chiribanda get away with this one.'

'Jealous?'

'Don't be bloody silly. All that was over a long time ago. It's purely a matter of discipline.'

'You'll have to fire him.'

'There's no other choice this time.'

'I can't think of a worse disaster with this bloody world conference rushing down on us. Chiribanda and Mahoja would see that your buildings never got finished. You'd have a fight on your hands.'

'Maybe it's about time I did.'

'Wait until the damned conference is over. If that turns out to be a shambles, you could lose government support for good.'

'Not sure if I'd mind that.'

'And if you personally lost Olindo's support as well?'

'I might like that, too.'

'Bide your time. There's only a month to go. Get the conference over first.'

Shock-waves from the coming storm had radiated far out from Baruva. Nancy Genova phoned John Redfern as soon as she got back to the States.

'John, I've been and I've seen.'

'You have?' he said cautiously.

'John, I'm convinced that if you allow them to start digging up Mount Vahinga it will be a calamity.'

'For whom?'

'For you personally, for the reputation of Ark International and, most important, for the future of the mountain gorilla.'

'I can take care of myself, dear.'

'I'm afraid that's only too evident.'

A silence, then, 'So what are you going to do about it?'

'I'm going to write a perfectly fair article, or articles, giving the situation as I see it.'

'Perfectly fair?' the old man repeated slowly. 'I wonder. You won't be putting the other side of the case, I suppose?

How Ark has got a new deal for conservation throughout the country?'

'Make the facts available and I'll use them.'

'I can't. You know that. There's an embargo on it all still.'

'Sorry, John. I feel this is one story that can't wait.'

'O.K.,' he said sadly, 'then I guess we'll just have to make *your* story look bit sick when all the facts do come out.'

'John, I truly am sorry to have to disagree with you.'

'Perhaps we could get together and talk it over?'

'Dear John. I don't think that's a good idea. That famous charm of yours. It's proved my undoing a few times before.'

'I fear all that ended for some reason when we made that trip to Africa together.'

'Just because I don't happen to see eye to eye with you on this issue doesn't mean that I don't admire you and what you're doing.'

'I wasn't exactly talking about conservation, Nancy.'

'I know that, John.' This time it was her voice that had a note of sadness in it.

By some incredible freak of communication and the goodwill of a Pan-Am captain who owed her a favour, Nancy Genova managed to get photocopies of her syndicated piece to Jean-Pierre within a week of publication. The headlines said:

MINING THREAT TO MOUNTAIN GORILLAS
Rare Species in Danger.

The story, under Nancy's by-line, kept, as she had promised, to the facts. She'd managed to get quotes from a number of world authorities. These did not include John Redfern. Though she'd approached him the old man had declined, saying artfully that he was keeping his views for his own Press release. The story ended with the words: 'World conservationists feel that any country that threatens the existence of one of the few remaining large pockets of mountain gorillas had better have a good reason for doing so. They also ask: does this country have such reason?'

Just a week after Jean-Pierre received Nancy's cuttings, John Redfern's views received front-page coverage in the government's own newspaper, *La République*. Jack Wright had really gone to town. Besides a front-page lead about setting up a new government conservation department with a director in charge of all national parks, the issue included a four-page supplement in honour of the coming world conference. In this appeared a complete list of delegates attending, the countries they came from, potted biographies of the most famous and a whole column on John Redfern and Ark International. There were pictures of rain-forests, pygmies, gorillas and, of course, a flattering, wide-angle shot of Lake Olindo across four columns. To Jean-Pierre's utter surprise there was also a picture of himself and a fulsome account of his work at Misoka.

The mining project was described vaguely as being in Baruva District, Kenanja Province. The story tucked away down the page read: 'When, and if, surface mining of bauxite commences, the operations will provide royalties to finance new conservation measures which will be announced at the world conference. This has been decreed at the direct orders of President Olindo, who insists that the country's industry should play its part in protecting the environment, an aspect that is far too often overlooked in modern industrial countries until it is too late.'

'Hooray,' Jean-Pierre said bitterly when he read the last paragraph.

Four days before the first delegates were due to arrive in Baruva, the storm broke directly overhead. The first clap of thunder was loud enough. By comparison with what was to follow, it was merely a warning pistol-shot.

Jack Wright's ministry had sent two efficient African clerks to handle last-minute arrangements for accommodating and feeding the delegates. Once again Marie had shown herself to be invaluable in running the routine affairs of the park office and in bridging the gap between the temporarily attached clerks and local procedures. Despite this assistance, Jean-Pierre found his days completely occupied with chivvying Mahoja and his workmen, chasing Francis Chiribanda and his rangers, back-stopping almost everything that did or, more likely, did not happen.

As far as young Chiribanda was concerned, Jean-Pierre had forced himself to take Veniard's advice once more. He found this a severe strain. Every time he saw Chiribanda he longed to hit him in his handsome, smiling face. Whether this was pure jealousy, part jealousy, or anger at being made use of, he could not tell. He simply knew that he would like to give this apparently admirable young African the sack but dare not because of the immediate consequences.

The warning clap of thunder took the unexpected form of the frightened face of Loti as he knocked at the window just after midnight. For several minutes after Jean-Pierre had let him in Loti was too scared to speak. When he finally became convinced that Jean-Pierre was not about to kill him, he got it out. One of the lorries was upside down in a ditch. What was the lorry doing? Jean-Pierre demanded, although he was perfectly well aware of the answer. Loti became speechless with terror again. He had been driving the vehicle and, having miraculously escaped with his life once that night, was unwilling to put his personal survival at hazard a second time. Loti remembered his chief shooting Kama Chiribanda's prize cows. At that moment he thought it likely that Jean-Pierre would regard himself as less deserving of mercy than a trespassing cow. Why, then, had he come to bring the news of the disaster in person? This was a complicated question to which he did not really know the answer.

After he had discovered himself alive in the overturned cab of the three-ton Chevrolet, he had considered flight until he had realised that there was nowhere to flee to. Jean-Pierre would find him anywhere he went. Better to risk all now, to make some case for leniency by reporting the accident. Even in his state of extreme fear Loti sensed that Jean-Pierre was a hard but fair man. Besides, he could always claim that he was under orders. Loti's panic abated a little when Jean-Pierre did not reach for the Walther automatic that was seldom far from his reach but simply ordered him to wait outside in the jeep.

Ten minutes later they were bowling along the north lake road. The lorry did not take much finding. The tail-lights were still on. They were unnaturally high above the ground and at a crazy angle. A strong smell of bottled beer hung over the scene. Much of it was now unbottled by the crash. A carpet of smashed glass glittered in the headlights of the jeep. Figures caught in those same beams scuttled away into the bush like cockroaches disturbed pilfering a darkened kitchen. Fortunately for the bootleggers, two-thirds of the load had been delivered by the time Loti made his fatal steering error. Of the remaining third well over half had been smashed, the rest having vanished into the bush with the cockroaches. There would be some sore heads in the villages tomorrow.

By the time Jean-Pierre drew up there might not have been a living soul within miles. He walked round the wreck. The damage, except to the upperworks, did not seem to be severe. Amused at the futility of the gesture, he switched off the lights. Then, finding a single bottle the looters had overlooked, he wrenched the cap off in the hinge of the upturned driver's door. Loti watched all this, the whites of his eyes seemingly large enough to illuminate the whole scene. Perhaps Jean-Pierre would shoot him now. His chief drank the beer slowly and then ordered Loti to remain on guard by the lorry for the rest of the night. Loti saluted gratefully. Where one bottle had survived, there might be others.

Jean-Pierre's first reaction was to drive to Chiribanda's house and make Francis start salvaging the lorry. Then he remembered he had ordered him to set out at dawn to fetch Toto from the Saddle. He had decided to bring the baby gorilla down to Baruva for the conference. Once again, the reckoning would have to wait.

The plan had been urged on him by Marie, though the idea

348

had been lurking in the back of his mind for some time. Marie wanted to see the baby again. She also undoubtedly wished to see it taken away from Helen for no matter how short a period. Jean-Pierre was well aware what a focus of interest the baby would be for the delegates if housed for the duration of the conference at park headquarters. It could be kept in the old pen at the house for forty-eight hours until Mahoja's workmen had constructed a new enclosure close to the conference hall. And so he had ordered Francis Chiribanda to set off for the Saddle at dawn, armed with written instructions to Helen to send Toto down with Francis and two porters the following day. Helen would not like this but she could hardly ignore a written order. She would, no doubt, console herself with the thought that she would be following herself within a couple of days and so the baby would continue to be, as it were, her own prize exhibit.

Francis Chiribanda was extremely thankful he was going. The news of the accident had reached him about the same time as Jean-Pierre reached the scene of the disaster. There was no immediate way of connecting him with the bootleg operations of his rangers but this by no means reassured him. Jean-Pierre would start by demanding to know how he came to be so ignorant of the activities of his ranger force. He had little doubt that, when questioned separately, one of his faithful followers would give him away. So Francis woke his father and told him the bad news. For one thing, as a senior partner in the beer business, he had a right to know. For another, Francis needed his support and advice.

Kama Chiribanda fell out of a deep sleep and hit the ground running. He had appreciated the situation almost before his eyes were fully open and the bad news fully told. His advice was very much to the point. His son must set off for the Saddle even before it was light. If Monsieur Menant came before then he would swear Francis had already left. When Menant did come he would make it very clear what the consequences of any severe action against his son, such as dismissal, would be. He himself would be forced to resign from the board immediately. Mahoja would have to do the same. Victimisation of an African head ranger would not look good to officials from the capital attending the conference. Come to that, an unfinished conference hall would not look good either. There was still at least two full days' work to be done on the roof. No, by the time Francis returned the day after tomorrow, there would be little for him to fear. Kama Chiribanda would see to that.

Having pronounced this verdict, Kama fell back into the sleep of a man whose conscience is utterly clear. He might not have slept so well had he realised he had made one important miscalculation, namely, that the officials from the capital would automatically support an African against a white man. The most important visiting official was a white man himself and one of enormous power — Jack Wright, *éminence grise*, or perhaps, more correctly, *éminence blanche*.

With such an early start Francis was at the hut well before mid-day. Helen read Jean-Pierre's note with prinked-mouth disapproval. Then she smiled. She was always careful to observe the proprieties where Jean-Pierre was concerned.

'Oh well, if *Monsieur le Conservateur* doesn't mind interrupting the baby's rehabilitation programme for a few days. It's a nuisance, to say the least. I was planning to conduct an important part of her training today or tomorrow.'

'Perhaps there is time. So long as we return by tomorrow night or even the next morning. . . .' Francis could see at least two possible advantages to this situation. One was that it would give his father maximum time to put pressure on Jean-Pierre.

'All right, I'll stick to my plan. But we'll do it tomorrow morning.'

'Do what, Helen?'

'Absolom and the whole family are quite near by. I'm going to take Toto close to them, to get her used to the idea of wild gorillas again. Her reactions should be very interesting.'

'And theirs, too, perhaps? It could be dangerous. Since I'm

responsible for your safety perhaps I ought to forbid it?'

'There are several things, Francis, I should forbid.'

'Yes, Dr Lawes.'

Next morning they set out with Musharamena, the second pygmy tracker. Very soon they came upon Absolom and the whole group feeding among some dense undergrowth. Francis was uneasy and told Helen so twice. He knew he should have insisted that they wait for a better moment and meeting place. A month ago he would have opposed Helen, largely to rile her, but not any more. The cover was so dense that they could only spot half the gorilla family.

If Helen wanted reactions she certainly got them, and from the baby first of all. Toto began to cry louder than she had ever done in captivity. Almost at once the males in the group answered, barking, coughing and screaming. Abraham, the young male, made the first overt demonstration, standing upright, barking and opening his mouth wide to show his yellowed teeth. Helen now realised that the gorillas were all around them. Even if she'd wanted to she couldn't retreat. She saw from Francis's face that he was badly frightened. He stood directly behind and almost touching her while Musharamena crouched behind him. Arranged in single file they should have presented the least disturbing appearance to the gorillas. Normally the pygmies, who were perpetually terrified by gorillas at close range, were in the safest position when kept to the rear. Nothing about this encounter was normal and it was becoming less so at every second.

The baby in Helen's arms relieved herself all over her shirt. She struggled violently and cried out louder than ever. Her cries triggered off a pandemonium of barking, shrieking and beating of breasts and bushes. Abraham made several darts forward as if to charge but he was obviously waiting for a lead. Suddenly he got one. Everything happened at once. Absolom burst through the bushes six feet from Helen, standing tall and shrieking with mouth wide open. He paused long enough for Helen to become convinced that in a few seconds she would be dead. He came straight for her in a

351

roaring charge, looking so immense that she felt that a great wall of brown earth was about to fall on her. Earth may bury you, crush you, suffocate you, but it does not have flailing arms that can strike like a steel bar, or hands that can tear you in half.

Helen felt the wind displaced by one of those arms as it passed inches from her face. In that instant she instinctively half turned away and dropped Toto on the ground. Absolom scooped the baby up and, lifting her, backed away fast.

It was at the moment of that final charge that the small, dark heart of Musharamena found it had taken all it could stand. He broke and ran, ran back to where safety should have lain. Instead, he blundered straight into the young silver-back, Ammon, who caught him round the neck as he passed, hurling him high into the air. He flew in a short, straight trajectory until he hit a tree. When he fell to the ground he did not move.

For a full three minutes after Absolom had taken the baby neither Helen nor Francis realised that the pygmy had gone. Both sensed that the moment of danger had passed yet they stood where they were, too shocked to move. The bushes all around them shook as the entire family converged on Absolom as if to examine the baby. Helen was sobbing from reaction. For once, all his easy confidence had deserted Francis Chiribanda. He shook as if in fever. He shook even more when he eventually found Musharamena. The little man was breathing but only faintly. His one thought was, 'If he dies. . . .' Overturned trucks were one thing and could be, as his father had suggested, dealt with. He knew, without any argument, that he was responsible for Helen and Musharamena's safety. Not even his father would be able to gloss over what had just happened.

Jean-Pierre had done nothing, precisely nothing, about the beer truck, or, rather, nothing in terms of the Chiribandas. He knew that lack of action in that direction was the right course for the moment yet he hated and despised himself for

it. Jean-Pierre, the so-called man of action! He had questioned the rangers and had no doubt that they were all
implicated in the beer-running. He had doubled their duties
and stopped their pay until after the conference but this was
no better than firing the office boy when the firm was going
broke. Once the bloody conference was over he would blow
the whole thing sky-high, the Chiribandas, Mahoja, Redfern,
the lot. Or he would chuck the job in. Or both.

His resolve not to declare open war on the Chiribandas
nearly broke when Francis did not arrive next day with the
baby gorilla. The bastard was disobeying orders once again.
He would give him until mid-day tomorrow. But next
morning, early, he had other things on his mind. A plane had
brought in the delegates from P.P.A., the Indonesian government's conservation organisation. They were a day early and
requested to be taken out into the forest immediately. If
Francis had been on hand, as ordered, he could have
conducted them. This would have given Jean-Pierre time to
bully Mahoja's men into putting the finishing touches to the
Indonesians' accommodation at park headquarters. As it was,
he had to drive them quickly up to the saw-mill himself to
show them something of the lower hagenia woodland while
the clerks frenziedly switched their rooms to the Hôtel du
Président. Now the Cameroons delegates would have to stay
at the headquarters instead.

When he arrived, hot and furious, at his office at lunch-
time, Francis Chiribanda was there. He jumped to his feet
and saluted.

'Where the hell have you been?'
'There's been an accident, *Monsieur le Conservateur*.'
'Oh, so you've decided to report it?'
'I thought it my duty to do so as soon as possible.'
'Is this what you call as soon as possible? That bloody
truck has been a write-off for three days now.'
'I do not speak of any truck, *Monsieur le Conservateur*.'
'Well, I do. You can have it with both barrels, right now,
between the eyes. I've known about your little beer-running

353

racket for quite some time now.'

Francis was badly rattled by the attack from this direction. Any calm he had had now deserted him.

'It's not the truck,' he blurted. 'It's the pygmy, Musharamena. I think he's dying. The second silver-back in Absolom's group clawed and threw him. . . . I couldn't come down until we'd spent the night with him to be sure he'd live through it. Helen . . . Dr Lawes. . . .'

'Don't say that she's involved.'

'No, she's all right, but the baby. . . .' Chiribanda was incapable of going on. Jean-Pierre took a step towards him and grabbed him by the front of his jacket.

'I don't think it would be wise for a white man to strike an African in his service.'

'In my service! In my *service*! You twisting, two-timing bastard.' Jean-Pierre let go of Chiribanda and pushed him down into a chair. 'Now you will tell me exactly what happened up there, and what part you played in it, from beginning to end. Don't attempt to hide anything from me because I shall find out.'

'Who from?' A hint of defiance had crept back.

'From Dr Lawes.'

'She will confirm everything I tell you.'

'I've no doubt. Her present partiality to you hasn't escaped me either.'

'I do not know what you are suggesting.'

'Oh yes, you damn well do.'

Francis shrugged. 'What you are suggesting is not a crime.'

'It is in my eyes.'

'That is understandable.'

Jean-Pierre held on to himself tightly. Chiribanda had been right about one thing. If he hit him now, he was lost.

'Crime is perhaps too strong a word for your relationship with Dr Lawes. By any reckoning it's a gross breach of discipline for which you should be fired.'

'I don't think my father would care for that.'

'I don't give a warthog's arse what your father would or

354

would not like. You were in charge up there, responsible for the safety of everyone concerned, not least for that young ape. And if Musharamena dies. . . .'

'I must let my father know about everything at once.'

'Don't worry about that. I shall be doing the telling. At a special meeting of the park board. I'd like to kick you out this very moment but right now you'll take two rangers and bring that little man down off the mountain. I want him in Dr Veniard's surgery by noon tomorrow. I hope for your sake he's alive when he reaches it. And tell Dr Lawes I want her down here at the same time.'

This time Jean-Pierre didn't take Jacques Veniard's advice.

'I want that bastard out and I want the board to know why he's going.'

'With less than two days before the conference starts?'

'Right!'

'Wait.'

'Not this time. I've called a special meeting of the board for eleven tomorrow. You'll attend?'

'You know I will, but will the others? Anyway, if you're so set on giving dear Francis the boot, why not do it yourself? You're fully entitled to.'

'Not a hope. I've had it up to here.'

'Oh well. At least it will be an interesting meeting.'

The meeting was short and to the point. There was only one item on the agenda: the conduct of Head Ranger F. Chiribanda.

Veniard called the meeting to order and asked Monsieur Menant to explain his reason for summoning them all. Jean-Pierre wisely left out the whole question of the beer truck. That would need detailed supporting evidence. Instead, he described the incident involving Dr Lawes and Musharamena. Veniard noticed Kama Chiribanda's mouth fall open. It was the first he had heard of the accident and he was badly shaken. He interrupted. 'Obviously Dr Lawes was to blame. She insisted. . . .'

355

'Observations, please, only when Monsieur Menant has finished his statement.'

'But this is not justice,' Daudi Mahoja yapped. 'It is plain and typical victimisation of an African.'

'I must ask you to reserve your comments.'

Jean-Pierre finished his statement quickly. 'Head Ranger Chiribanda disobeyed orders in at least two respects. He was ordered to tell Dr Lawes to hand over the baby gorilla to him and had those orders in writing from me. Second, he was directly responsible for the safety of Dr Lawes and by disobeying those written orders he put her in a position of great danger. As it is, one of the park staff is likely to lose his life because of the head ranger's irresponsibility. There may be charges concerning other matters later. For the moment, therefore, I suspend Francis Chiribanda from further duty and all pay and allowances cease as from this moment.'

'A vote,' shrieked Kama Chiribanda. 'You must put it to the vote.'

'As a matter of procedure, I don't think a vote is necessary.' It was the first time Joshua Ndesi had spoken.

'You keep out of it,' Chiribanda shouted. 'You must put it to the vote.'

'I have no need to do so. I have called you to let you know my decision.'

'Then hear mine.' Kama banged the table. 'I resign from the park board and you must take the consequences.'

'I wish to resign also,' Mahoja echoed dutifully.

'I shall record both your resignations.' Veniard made a note.

'We will wait and see what happens when the ministry's representatives get here,' Kama shouted.

Jean-Pierre said, 'We will also wait and see whether Musharamena is alive when he comes down the mountain.'

'I declare the meeting closed,' Veniard said ceremoniously but quite unnecessarily since the two Africans were already half-way to their cars.

'It's going to be a great conference, Jean-Pierre.'

'I'm past caring what the hell they all do. They can chop all the trees down and sell the whole bloody place as a bauxite mine for all I care.'

Veniard looked at him narrowly. 'Yes, for the first time I believe you mean it.'

'I do.'

He meant it even more when, an hour later, he heard that Mahoja's men had been sent home without putting the final section of roofing on the conference hall and without attempting to clear up the inevitable builders' chaos of bricks, planks, timber and tools.

When Francis Chiribanda eventually brought Musharamena to Veniard's surgery the doctor pronounced the little man had no more than a fifty per cent chance of living. His skull was cracked. This was the first shock for the head ranger. The other was to learn that he could go home and take his uniform off.

Now that the storm had truly burst the gale ripped the leaves and branches off the trees, moaning through the bending trunks as if they were Pan pipes. With the gale had come the rain in grey, slanting, stinging, horizontal lines and Jean-Pierre was caught in it.

At first he couldn't bring himself to meet Helen. Finally he gave in when she repeatedly requested to see him. He admired her because she looked him straight in the eye with a look he used to know well.

'It was my responsibility. I made him take me to Absolom with the baby.'

'I'm afraid that doesn't make any difference. His orders were quite clear. Besides, there are other things.' He meant the beer lorry.

She had jumped to another conclusion. She dropped her eyes. 'Oh, you know about that, too.' She was crying. 'I'm not going to attempt to explain or justify. These things happen.'

'Perhaps, as you suggested, you shouldn't try to explain.

You're right when you say that these things happen but not, perhaps, with a park employee.'

Her chin was up again. 'I have to explain that much, at least. In some strange way Francis was a method for getting over my terror of that other time. He was kind. I can't tell you why, but being with him has helped to release me. Perhaps I can be normal about sex, about love even, again.'

Jean-Pierre, remembering what they had once had together, remained silent.

'What will you do to Francis?'

'I've suspended him until after the conference and then someone will have to hold an inquiry.'

He saw tears in her eyes again.

'Will I . . . will he and I come into it?'

'I see no need. But there are minor matters of corruption that will come out. Using park transport to sell beer illegally. Causing a hired truck to be wrecked.'

'After the inquiry, what?'

'He'll go.'

'You realise I shall have to ask Redfern for a transfer, too. After what's happened, I can't stay on either.'

'No reason for that. I shall be the one who's quitting. I've got tired of trying to sort out the whole bloody awful mess. Let's just get this conference over first. That's all I ask now.'

During the next forty-eight hours the delegates streamed in. Redfern held court in the master-suite of the Président. The British party, a spry and aged Scottish primatologist and a bright, young behaviourist from Oxford, was housed there, too. To balance things up the Americans, a Fulbright Scholar who had worked in Sumatra on gibbons and a fearsome little girl from Cornell whose speciality was brachiation and loco-motion among the great apes, were lodged at park head-quarters. Tanzanians, Kenyans, Zairois, West Africans, Malaysians, Rwandans, Dutch, Germans, Swiss, Swedes, French — they had been bedded and boarded in a sincere and painstaking attempt to ensure that no person or nation felt that he, she, or it had been treated less prestigiously than any other. Not that this was even remotely possible.

The Press was there in surprising force, mostly writers from specialist papers but also some science correspondents from national newspapers and one international news agency. Redfern had done his job well. Sadly, and even he felt sad about it, there was one notable exception — Nancy Genova. Her articles about the proposed mining activities on Vahinga had become more and more strident after Redfern had launched his inevitable counter-attack. The authorities in the capital had refused to issue Nancy with a Press visa. Although Redfern could have intervened on her behalf, he hadn't done so.

Redfern opened the conference, introducing the main speakers, outlining the programme, using just the right degree of lightness to explain the partly-unfinished state of the conference hall. 'These folks here,' he said, 'worked out their own air-conditioning system long before we got around to it and I think you'll find it pretty effective.' Only at the end of the speech did he touch upon the issue which was in the Pressmen's minds.

'You've no doubt heard that there is a proposal to mine bauxite outside the boundaries of the park. I stress the phrase *outside the boundaries*. There'll be plenty of time to discuss this matter more fully. I understand that, on the final day of the conference, the mining expert responsible for the survey will be available for your questions. I would just say this: gorillas may live on herbs and vines but young nations that have to pay their way in this world cannot. Only if they *can* pay their way in the world will conservation receive the funds and attention it deserves. Conservation in this case means saving one of the rarest and most impressive creatures on the face of this earth — the mountain gorilla.'

He had them. He'd crossed the first hurdle. Then it was Jean-Pierre's turn. He spoke almost mechanically. His heart and mind weren't in it. The shaft of sunlight blazing down through the unfinished roof certainly wasn't living up to

John Redfern's light-hearted description. The heat was making even the Kenyan delegates squirm in their seats with discomfort. The gap in the roof reminded him of the whole untidy mess that was Misoka at this moment.

Helen followed Jean-Pierre. She was good. He admired the way she presented her material on the family structure of the gorilla groups. The afternoon was filled with papers read by lowland gorilla experts from the Cameroons, the American girl on aspects of brachiation and pipedal locomotion. At other times Jean-Pierre would have found it all interesting if not absorbing. He was glad he was scheduled to take a party of botanists into the forest. In the forest he could recapture something of what Misoka had always been about.

The presidential jet flew in with Jack Wright the next day. He timed his arrival at the Hôtel du Président to coincide with the start of the conference's two-hour mid-day siesta break. The first hour he was closeted with Redfern in his suite. The second hour he had reserved for Jean-Pierre.

'Can we go somewhere private?'

'My house? I've got my jeep outside.'

'Great!' Jack Wright vaulted over the side and put a large, twisted, silver-knobbed stick beside him. As he did so he knocked the catch of the dashboard compartment, making it fly open. The Walther automatic and two spare, loaded magazines were clipped, almost out of sight, to the roof of the compartment.

'Are you always armed, Monsieur Menant?'

Jean-Pierre pointed to the heavy stick. 'Aren't you?'

Wright laughed. 'You could say that.'

Marie was in the office, elegant in glowing African cottons that hid her pregnancy. Wright bowed in a most un-American way. Jean-Pierre introduced her.

'Could you prepare some cold food for us in the office?'

Now it was Marie's turn to bow. In doing so, the robe fell away to reveal her swollen belly. When she had left the room, Wright said, 'You've got yourself a beauty. Your wife?'

'It's never been formalised. Now, perhaps, I think we may

360

do so.'

'Because of the child?'

'Only in part.'

'As I said: she's lovely.'

'Marie is a great help to me in every way. She runs this office when I'm away.'

'A great asset in an African country.'

'She's far more than that . . . but you didn't just want to talk about my domestic life.' He indicated the chair opposite his own. Jack Wright sat as he was bidden. Though he found it strange not to be in the commanding position behind the desk, he counted it greatly in Jean-Pierre's favour that he did not intend to be overshadowed in his own office.

Jean-Pierre regarded him calmly and politely, waiting for him to come to the point. Wright instincitvely felt for an opening that would give him an advantage.

'I heard you've had a whole mess of trouble up here in Misoka Park.'

Now, how the hell had he heard any such thing? Of course, Chiribanda! He would have sent notice of the resignations out on one of the planes that had been flying in regularly for the past week. No doubt the report had been as highly spiced as a plate of his favourite peppers.

Jean-Pierre said, 'I've suspended my African head ranger. There'll have to be a full inquiry. Two African members of the board have resigned. Apart from that,' he added drily, 'everything is fine.'

'Huh. Yeah. Well, I guess you can handle all that.'

'Unfortunately, no. At least, I no longer intend to try.'

'Doesn't sound like you.'

'Maybe. Once you gave me a lecture on playing African politics. Unfortunately, I'm not an African.'

'Neither am I.'

'No.' Jean-Pierre pointed at the twisted, silver-knobbed cane. 'But you carry a big stick.'

'Ah, you've noticed it. The president's personal cane, or rather' — Wright smiled slightly — 'a smaller version of the

361

president's cane. Everyone recognises it and what it stands for.'

'Precisely. It stands for authority. What's more, the kind of authority which every African acknowledges. The big stick wielded by the tribal leader. The reason my job has become impossible is that I do not even wield the smallest twig.'

'You could be given a big stick.'

'How?'

'You could become director of all our national parks. We are prepared to offer you the job.'

'Pardon my asking, counsellor, but what national parks besides Misoka? Lake Olindo?'

'Ten per cent of the whole country. The president's promise will be implemented. I have been instructed to set up an entire conservation department.'

'As I have observed before: most of that ten per cent is impenetrable rain-forest.'

'But rain-forest that may contain more gorillas than Misoka and Vahinga put together.'

'*May*. But that's very doubtful. It's mostly lowland forest and unsuitable.'

'You sound very disillusioned.'

'What else am I supposed to be when you're preparing to wreck the only tract of gorilla habitat worth talking about just for a short-term mineral gain?'

'It won't affect the park.'

'You know the answer to that as well as I do. All the people it will bring in for a start.'

'You're completely overlooking the advantages. A large percentage of the mining profits will go towards conservation.'

'So it's all settled, then? Didn't even Redfern oppose you? If I'd been him, I'd have withdrawn Ark International's support.'

'Perhaps John Redfern is more realistic.'

'That word again!'

'You're too wound up to see it clearly. It's understandable.

362

You've had a rough ride up here recently. Think about it. You could set up your headquarters in Baruva. We could fly you in to the capital in the Falcon whenever it was necessary. I hear you want to fly. You could learn and have your own parks' plane.'

'I'm not very bribable.'

'Of course not. Well, think about it. Remember the big stick. Chiribanda and the rest. They're small fry. Once they've been shown that you carry this' — he held up the replica of the president's cane — 'they'll come running.'

'Thank you, counsellor. If you could see your way to calling off your mining engineers, I might at least consider it. But mining is the last totally unacceptable straw.'

'Remember your beloved gorillas. You're the best chance, possibly the only real chance, they've got. Look, I have to return to the capital after I've said a few words at the conference this afternoon. But I'll be back on the final day, for the winding-up party. Let me have your answer then.'

'You can have it right now.'

'Wait until then. By the way, if you want to reassure yourself about the bauxite operations, our chief mining surveyor is flying in tomorrow. Redfern has already had long discussions with him, a tall, thin guy called Varuti.'

That afternoon Jean-Pierre took six of the fitter and younger delegates into the forest. Mushi had reported that a silver-back with two females was within an hour of head-quarters. The big male had obligingly charged and caused two of the scientists to run. Jean-Pierre certainly didn't blame them. If anything, the incident somewhat restored his faith not only in the frailty of human nature but in the predictable magnificence of gorillas. When the delegates met for the pre-dinner cocktail in Redfern's suite at the Président the six scientists were still breathless from the encounter.

Jacques Veniard had the first good news for days. 'I think the pygmy Musharamena is going to make it,' he said.

The Falcon came in over the town early next morning.

Jean-Pierre paused outside his office to look up at its lovely shark shape and retaste the beauty of flying in it. Redfern drew up alongside in a conference Mercedes.

'Say, Jean-Pierre. Introduce the first speaker for me. It's the Frenchman on lowland gorilla habitat.' He handed over some brief biographical notes. 'That jet has just brought in this mining guy, Varuti. Guess I have to meet him at the strip.'

The Mercedes spurted off. Since when, Jean-Pierre wondered, had conservationists of John Redfern's stature played eager host to the spoilers of the earth?

Jean-Pierre introduced the French speaker and then moved sideways off the stage and sat down at ground level, to one side, in the open where it was fairly cool. From this vantage point he could hear perfectly well though he could only see the lower half of the speaker's body. The Frenchman had an exceedingly monotonous delivery, so that, despite the comfort of his chosen position, Jean-Pierre dozed off.

He awoke with a start to realise that John Redfern was finishing his introduction to a new speaker. The latter now advanced to the microphone. Jean-Pierre saw only his legs. They were long and exceedingly thin with a thinness which showed even through the neat khaki-drill trousers. Perhaps it was the angle from which Jean-Pierre viewed those legs that plucked a chord. But lots of tall men had thin legs.

The notes struck in memory might have died away but for the voice that now reached him, trebled by the amplifiers of the public address system. The voice was high-pitched and intense and became more so as the speaker warmed to his theme — that of the vital national necessity of extracting the bauxite and the benefits the venture would bring to wildlife projects all over the country.

Jean-Pierre was sitting bolt upright now. He would never forget a very similar voice, the voice of the man in the saw-mill, the man whose features he had never seen closely enough to identify.

Jean-Pierre eased himself to his feet. From where he stood

all he could see was the back of an immensely tall man, a man whose build fitted John Redfern's description of the mining expert he had met in the capital as a 'Watutsi; a man whose outline fitted the long-range glimpses Jean-Pierre himself had obtained during the chase of the fleeing *Fisi* across the mountains five years earlier; a man who matched the description given by Helen of a tall figure seen through binoculars bending to climb into a helicopter at the mining site. But to match the *Fisi* leader of the saw-mill massacre exactly, the so-called General Patrice, the man he had vowed one day to kill, one important detail was missing. The speaker had no stammer. He was speaking in French without a trace of impediment.

Jean-Pierre searched for Helen Lawes in the audience and found her at last, white-faced and open-mouthed, in the back row. Though she could not have had the advantage of his own low-angle view, plainly the same terrifying thought had struck her.

Jean-Pierre slipped quietly out of his place and moved round outside the conference hall until he reached the empty row behind Helen. He could feel her trembling. French-speaking delegates were starting to ask the tall man some highly critical questions. The speaker's voice rose half an octave as he countered these conservationists' objections to the mining proposals. On the stage Redfern sat smiling benignly. He had judged the exchange correctly as a useful way of blowing off righteous steam. The newspapermen were loving it. This is what they had come for.

Under cover of the first questioner's indignation, Helen hissed, 'It's him, isn't it?'

'You were certain, too. I saw your face.'

The American girl behaviourist from Cornell was now having a go. The tall man parried her objections in passable English.

'Jean-Pierre. Perhaps we're wrong. It's not the *Fisi*. Where's the stammer?'

'I had the same doubts. He speaks perfectly freely.'

'The resemblance to that other voice is too horrible. It all comes back.'

'I know, but a resemblance is not enough.'

'Enough! Enough for what?'

'You know what I've always sworn. To kill a man one has to be utterly sure.'

'You'd do that? Even now?'

'Somehow. But I'd have to be so totally sure. . . .'

Then suddenly the last piece fell into place.

One of the Africans asked a question in his own language. Varuti, the mining expert, answered excitedly in the same tribal tongue and this time he tripped over a word in every other sentence.

It was partly in the language of his own country that the tall *Fisi* leader had directed the massacre that night in the saw-mill. It was in that language that the stammer had occurred.

Jean-Pierre dragged Helen away from the conference hall. He had to get away from the sight and sound of the tall man. Now he knew how fanatics, religious and political assassins, felt at their first close glimpse of the victim. But at least they were sure they had got the right man. The Walther was still clipped to the roof of the dashboard compartment in the jeep. It would be simple to shoot the man down now. To his previous crimes of rape and murder Varuti was now proposing to add the rape and murder of Jean-Pierre's beloved Vahinga. To five years of hatred was added this new loathing. It was as if Varuti, with his almost hysterical defence of the bauxite project, summed up in one appalling personality all the ills with which Jean-Pierre had been beset during the past few weeks.

Slowly calmness returned and, with it, doubt. Could he be sure? If he was sure, wasn't the right thing to do to report his findings to Jack Wright? He recalled Wright's words about former *Fisi* leaders when they had discussed the question during his visit to the capital. 'Some of the small and medium-sized fish slipped through the net. Some are doing useful jobs as businessmen and technicians. It doesn't always do to inquire too closely.' Jean-Pierre couldn't imagine Wright inquiring too closely into Varuti's past. He was too useful to him for that.

Helen was tugging his sleeve. 'What are you going to do?'

'If I'm right, I shall kill him.'

She knew him too well to oppose him directly. 'There's no longer a civil war, Jean-Pierre. It will be murder. They'll hang you. What good will it do now?'

'Accidents aren't unknown in the forest ... a poacher's bullet. I've been shot at several times. If I could get him there.... Besides, he must have a number of enemies. Someone who recognised him from the civil war.'

'If you succeed, you won't stop the mining development, Jean-Pierre. It's your life I'm thinking of.'

He looked at her and saw, perhaps for the first time since her return, that she really was concerned for him. 'I have to be certain,' was all he said, and then, 'How long is he staying?'

'Until tomorrow morning.'

Jean-Pierre kept away from the conference hall for the rest of the morning but, just before lunch, John Redfern found him.

'I thought Varuti did very well to answer all those hard-nosed scientists and newspapermen this morning. Of course, they're not persuaded but at least they understand the realities of the situation now. I gather you're by no means convinced.'

'Correct, Dr Redfern.'

'Jack Wright outlined an interesting proposition to you, I understand.'

'I turned it down.'

'A tragedy if you do, but I believe the matter is still open until he returns.'

'Hardly. I told him to stop the miners and then I might

listen to him.'

'Have you talked to Varuti himself?'

Jean-Pierre waited until he had control of his voice and said, 'I see no point.'

'I don't entirely agree. There's always something in the other fellow's point of view. Would you do something for me?'

Jean-Pierre was listening hard now.

'Take Varuti up into the forest this afternoon. He's free until the reception I'm organising for him tonight. Tell him how you feel about things. Hear his point of view. . . .'

This was it. The opportunity on a plate. But total proof of identity? How did he achieve that? Then Redfern gave him a clue.

'To save time, why not take him in the jeep up the saw-mill track?'

Jean-Pierre looked at his watch. Two-and-a-half hours. 'I'll pick him up at the Président at two, Dr Redfern. Not that I expect much to come out of it.'

'That's my boy.' Redfern smiled delightedly at having achieved even this mild diplomatic success.

Now Jean-Pierre knew how he would establish identity beyond all doubt.

'Get in the jeep,' he told Helen. 'We've got some calls to make.' They drove first to Baruva's only clothing store. Jean-Pierre had known the European proprietor since he was a boy.

'I want to borrow three or four tailors' dummies.'

'Good God! What for? For your gorillas to play with?'

'Something like that. For the conference. It's a joke.'

The proprietor shrugged. 'There are some old-fashioned white ones in the store-room. These days all the dummies have to be black.'

'White ones are just right.'

They drove next to the town abbatoir. There, they were about to slaughter some pigs.

'I want some pigs' blood. A lot of it. A five-gallon drum full of it.'

'You're just in time. You'll have to pay. We make sausages from it.'

'That's all right. I'll pay so long as you're quick.'

'Ten minutes?'

'Make it five.'

'Pigs don't bleed to order,' the slaughterman said.

They sat outside while the drum was filled. Even the distant smell of animal blood made Helen fight to keep her stomach contents. A skyful of kites circled like the elements of a mobile and four white-backed vultures fought over a pile of bones.

Jean-Pierre told Helen, 'When we've got the blood, we'll stop at my house for some old clothing. Then we'll go straight to the saw-mill and set the scene. That will leave me just enough time to go back and pick up Varuti at the Président.

'What do I do?'

'I want you to stay at the saw-mill.'

'I haven't been there since. . . .'

'I realise that. Think you can face it?'

'There'll be someone else there?'

'No, they've shut down the mill during the conference. We've borrowed their workmen.'

'I'll try, though the thought of going inside that place again makes me want to scream.'

'It's going to be tough on you, but it's the only way to make sure of our man.'

They pulled up outside Jean-Pierre's house. 'Marie,' he shouted as he ran in. 'Quickly! I want those old brown blankets and a pair of my slacks and a shirt.'

'Jean-Pierre, what's wrong?' She was acutely sensitive to his moods these days. She seemed to know that something unusual or hazardous was about to happen.

'Nothing. Give me those old blankets and the clothes. Bring them out to the jeep. Three or four blankets will do.

The old army ones.'

Minutes later Marie rushed out of the house, a blanket under each arm, one balanced on her swollen stomach together with slacks and shirt. She saw Helen in the jeep. Instead of showing resentment, she said, 'He's doing something dangerous. I know it. Make him take care.'

As the tyres bit into the pot-holes of Baruva's main street, Helen asked, 'How does she know?'

Jean-Pierre gave his famous shrug. 'That's Africa.'

'I'll never understand it.'

'That's because you have a rational, scientific mind. Now listen. . . .'

As they turned on to the saw-mill track he began to explain his plan.

The saw-mill was deserted and the power for the saw-bench turned off. He found the main switch and flicked it down just as the *Fisi* had done on that terrible night. He heard Helen catch her breath.

'Hang on to yourself tight.'

He clothed two of the tailors' dummies in the brown blankets so that they bore an extraordinary resemblance to the priests murdered at the orders of the tall *Fisi*. Slacks and shirt he pulled roughly on to the third dummy. This one he laid on the saw-bench, its head inches from the blade. The fourth figure, a badly smashed one, he broke into component parts, hands, legs, head, torso. These he scattered about in the sawdust. Then he began on the blood, spattering it over the dummies representing the dead priests, broadcasting it in gouts across the floor, soaking the sawdust with it, daubing the severed imitation limbs. The result was hideously death-like. He heard Helen throw up. The smell of fresh blood in the resinous sawdust brought it all back so that even he could hardly stand it.

He found Helen and put his arm round her to comfort her. 'I realise this is terrible for you. If it is the *Fisi*, he must give himself away.'

'I can't wait inside here alone.'

'You don't have to. Helen, here's what you do. You stay outside until you hear me coming back with him in the jeep. Then you go inside. I'll bring Varuti into the mill on the pretext of meeting the head forester.'

'And if he refuses?'

'Why should he? He only came here once before and that was in the dark. If he does refuse it's as good as an admission of guilt.'

'Not quite. In fact, not by a long chalk.'

'Don't worry, he won't refuse.' Jean-Pierre tapped his waistband. She saw the butt of the Walther automatic there.

'All right. I think I can face the place again once you're here.'

'Good. When you hear me struggling to open the door, spill the remains of the blood in that drum, hit the red button that starts the saw and duck out of sight behind those logs. I've set the bench so that it'll feed the tailor's dummy, head-first, into the blade. If that doesn't get some reaction. . . .'

'What will your reaction be, Jean-Pierre?'

'To be honest, I don't know. I've rather lost my taste for shooting people in cold blood — even him. I'd rather he made a fight of it.'

It was only forty minutes before she heard the jeep grinding its way up the steep forest track but it was the longest wait Helen remembered since the night of the massacre when she and Jean-Pierre had lain, hoping they would be overlooked, behind the log-pile. The cicadas ticked away around her like the mechanism of a time-bomb. She heard Jean-Pierre change down for the sharp corner below the mill. The engine revved as the wheels spun in the soft patch where a stream ran down through the forest. In thirty seconds the jeep would be visible as it came out of the final bend. Time to be going.

The heat inside the mill had made the stench of pigs' blood even more nauseatingly reminiscent. She gagged again as she sloshed the remainder of the blood in the drum over the saw-bench, forcing herself to pour the last pint or so over the bald skull of the dummy whose eyes seemed to look up at her in china-blue terror.

Jean-Pierre was making a great business of getting the door open. She pressed the red button and heard the great toothed wheel of the saw start to pick up speed. She darted out of sight as the saw-bench table moved to feed the dummy's head towards the singing blade.

At first Jean-Pierre thought he had failed. Varuti, walking a yard in front of him into the mill, appeared either not to notice or not to be impressed by the Grand Guignol tableau arranged for his benefit.

'Is this a practical joke?' he asked calmly.

He took a pace forward as if to examine the figure under the saw whose head the blade had now revealed to be ridiculously hollow and empty. That took him towards an iron bar lying on the side of the bench. The tall man picked it up and in one slashing movement crashed it across Jean-Pierre's stomach. Jean-Pierre's last thought as he saw that bar coming was: So this is what I've come to. A tabby cat where once walked a leopard. A hundred-watt bulb appeared to explode inside each eye. Red-hot metal poured into his chest as he gulped and gulped for air.

By the time he could breathe again the sound of the jeep's engine was dying away as Varuti drove it high up into the forest, as high as a derelict track and four-wheel drive would take him.

Jean-Pierre lay on his stomach while Helen pumped his back, forcing air back into his lungs. Where does a hunted animal go, he asked himself, when it realises that it's in bad trouble? Answer: it uses the runs and bolt-holes it knows best. Varuti would know the lower slopes of Vahinga from his mining surveys. Yet escape in that direction would be of little use to him. He would still be in the country where his crimes had been committed. Surely he would wish to cross a more friendly, or at least neutral, frontier? The betting was that he would follow the route he had taken to escape from Jean-Pierre five years before. The trouble was, he already had a fair start. Against this Jean-Pierre knew every foot of the country. Varuti's memory of it must, at best, be hazy.

Jean-Pierre sat up and felt in his belt for the Walther. It must have taken much of the force of that blow, otherwise he himself would have been in worse shape. The automatic had gone. He searched the floor. It was not there in the sawdust, either. If the blow had dislodged it, then the tall man must have picked it up. Helen said, 'He stooped for something just before he ran for it. He's got the gun, hasn't he?'

'Looks like it.' All he had now was his hunting-knife. 'Helen, go back down the track. Rejoin the conference as if nothing had happened. Cover for me, if necessary. Say Varuti wanted to see the Saddle, anything.'

'I can't let you go after him alone.'

'Do what I tell you. I'll move faster on my own. Besides, I can go via the Saddle. There's a rifle in the hut.'

'Promise you'll get it?'

'I promise.'

'Jean-Pierre.'

'Yes?'

'I'm sorry about us, truly sorry.'

'These things change.'

'Yes, but in there, in the saw-mill, I remembered how it was.'

He was impatient to be off. He kissed her lightly on the mouth but it was a gesture of thanks for what she had just said. He felt nothing stir. 'Get going now, Helen. It will take you an hour to reach headquarters. When you arrive, try to act normally.'

'What will you do if you catch up with him?'

'I *will* catch up with him. I know the way he's travelling.'

Half-a-mile up the mountain he found the jeep. It had been driven into a bog and had sunk axle-deep. Varuti hadn't wasted much time trying to drive it out. He had set off into

373

the forest almost at once. Proof that he had his wits about him was that he had either taken the ignition key or thrown it away. If he was taking the escape-route he and his party of *Fisi* had used before, he would strike up directly towards the Saddle and then swing away right-handed round Misoka's southern face.

At first his spoor was easy to follow. The tall man was in a hurry as sliding footmarks and broken fronds showed. But hurry is not the best climbing aid to use in the thick forests of Misoka. It leads to falls and slides which in turn lead to breathlessness and exhaustion. There was ample evidence that Varuti was making all these mistakes. In the normal way, Jean-Pierre would have expected to overhaul him long before nightfall, but the blow to his guts had hurt him more than he had imagined and had slowed him considerably.

It was now half-past-three. It would be getting dark by the time he reached the hut. Varuti, he was certain, would not try to move towards the border in the dark. He would hole up somewhere and build a fire as he must have done numerous times during *Fisi* operations. Jean-Pierre decided he could afford to visit the hut for the rifle, some food and a blanket, and then push on for an hour or so in early darkness so that he was as close as possible to Varuti when daylight came. What happened when he caught up with him was still not clear in his mind. On that southern face of Misoka poachers were fairly common. A poacher's bullet would be relatively easy to explain. Other questions might be harder to answer. Why should Varuti be so far afield? Why had he stayed the night on the mountain? He could say that the tall man had asked to see the entire range of the park. That was plausible enough.

Jean-Pierre was so deep in these calculations that he nearly overlooked the signs that showed his quarry had changed direction. In a clearing, deep-covered with moist leaves, there were footmarks leading in two directions and then a centre ground where a man had wandered as if trying to make up his mind. The footsteps leading upwards towards the Saddle ran out after a few yards. The second set of tracks that headed directly round the shoulder of the mountain, climbing only slightly, were the ones that continued on until they hit harder ground and became more difficult to follow.

Varuti knew what he was up to. He had decided to hold to the more difficult lower ground and take a short-cut to the border. For Jean-Pierre there could now be no question of taking time to visit the hut for arms, food or blankets. For both of them now it meant a cold night on the mountain.

Jean-Pierre moved more cautiously. His enemy had ample experience of guerilla tactics. It would be a simple thing for him to set an ambush provided, of course, that he knew he was being closely followed. There was no reason to suppose that he did.

Just before darkness fell, Jean-Pierre hit a set of tracks whose message was completely familiar to him. A large group of gorillas had passed this way about two days before. The state of the droppings told him this. The gorillas appeared to be travelling in much the same direction as himself and Varuti. Almost certainly they were heading for the *bwamba* trees that grew lower down Misoka on the southern border of the park. Jean-Pierre toyed with the idea of pushing on, trying to spot any fire Varuti made in order to jump him with the knife in the dark. Well as he knew the forest, even he could wander far off course at night. Better to make a start before dawn and try to catch him unprepared in the half-light.

It was going to be cold but Jean-Pierre had spent nights in the forest without warm clothing before. The pygmies sometimes built themselves shelters from the giant leaf that grew on parts of the forest floor. He pressed on slowly until he found a dense bed of these leaves. Behind a low bank, well hidden from view, he made a tent-like structure of leaves. In the mouth of the shelter he lit a small fire, making sure that its glow would not be reflected on the branches above. Somewhere not far ahead Varuti must be doing the same kind of thing. Jean-Pierre hoped that he was. A comparatively warm night might make him less inclined to start out too early in the morning. If he was freezing he would be likely to move to get some warmth back in his bones as soon as there was a crack of light.

Jean-Pierre built up the fire as much as he dared. Then he allowed himself a doze, knowing from long habit that he would wake as soon as the fire began to lose its heat. He would replenish the fire several times during the night. Thus the night would be broken into watches, each affording him the chance of sleep if he wished to take it. The last watch of all, the one before dawn, he would not attempt to sleep but would key himself up, ready to move at the first possible moment. He laid the hunting-knife at his side, freeing the thong that held the hilt. Then, satisfied that he had done all he could for the moment, he closed his eyes.

He woke several times during the night to rebuild the fire. An hour before dawn he was fully awake. He felt rested enough and wanted to keep his limbs as supple as possible. In the morning a lot would depend on swift and silent movement. There was, he realised, only an outside chance of jumping Varuti but, if he could spot him or work out his route, he had every chance of out-flanking him as he might have done a group of gorillas.

The tall man spent a bad night. He, too, had contrived some form of shelter but it had not been nearly so skilfully constructed as Jean-Pierre's. It had leaked badly. He had not doubted for a minute that the man who had so elaborately laid the trap in the saw-mill would follow him. And, since that man knew these forests like his own backyard, he would follow and travel fast. But how closely on his heels? How the man, Menant, had known of his civil war record was something he could not figure out. There had been no survivors from the saw-mill to recognise him. It was possible that Menant had guided the mercenaries who had pursued him across the border after the final battle in Baruva. To Varuti's certain knowledge the pursuers had never come close enough to make individual identification possible. Exceptional height could easily have been spotted, must have been spotted, but there are plenty of exceptionally tall men. Somehow, Menant must have been at the saw-mill that night. Somehow, he must have overlooked his presence.

Varuti knew he had been one of the few medium-sized fish not only to swim through the net but to pass back through its meshes when the time was right and safe. For two years he had lain low across the border, working for a mining company who needed skilled men. He had posed as a refugee, applied for, and obtained, new documents and, when the same company had started work on a contract in his own country, had simply returned there. His skill had quickly been appreciated, right up to ministry level. Even had any suspicion attached to him, it was by then highly unlikely that anyone would take action against him. By that time disclosures and reprisals were invariably the result of personal enemies paying off old or new scores. As far as he knew, Varuti had no such enemies. Those whom he had injured were white, dead, or both. So why had he panicked during the charade at the saw-mill yesterday? Why had he not assumed an amused or angry bafflement? He could not give himself a satisfactory answer beyond the fact that he had panicked, and the realisation was bitter.

He stretched his long, thin legs. They were sodden with rain and had stiffened. In half-an-hour he must be moving. Normally a gun gave a man some confidence, even if the enemy was armed, too. The gun he now possessed failed to do so. The blow he had given Menant had caught the Walther automatic, which had been stuck in Jean-Pierre's belt, across the slide, just to the rear of the ejector slot, its weakest point, bending it slightly. The bend was sufficient to ensure that, on firing, the slide would not move fully to the rear, ejecting the spent cartridge-case and feeding another cartridge from the magazine into the chamber on its forward journey. Varuti had been able to pull the slide far enough back to discover that Menant had already fed one round into the breach. It would therefore fire just once. That was all. What he had, therefore, was no better than a single-shot pistol with one round of ammunition.

He put the Walther into his pocket, rose and stood over the fire, stamping his feet and swinging his arms. In ten minutes he should be able to detect individual leaves on a tree twenty yards away. When that happened, he would move.

Six hundred yards to Varuti's rear, and half-an-hour earlier, Jean-Pierre had kicked out his fire. He had done this so that his eyes could become accustomed to the darkness. Even the faint, pink glow of the wood embers might impair his night vision. He eventually began moving, some fifteen minutes earlier than his quarry. Movement was only a relative term. In the tangle of the forest it was impossible to maintain constant direction in pitch darkness. All he could do was to creep across the slope, trying to keep to the same contour line, neither ascending nor descending. In this way he gained perhaps one hundred yards on Varuti before the tall man felt confident enough to start out. It was a valuable one hundred yards but his slender chance of jumping his quarry had gone. As soon as it was light enough he knew that he would have to cast about, wasting the time he had gained, in order to pick up the spoor again.

Varuti hit it lucky almost as soon as he got moving. The trees above him were relatively short and bushy so that little sunlight penetrated to promote impeding undergrowth. He soon made up the one hundred yards Jean-Pierre had gained on him. Several times he stopped and listened for sounds of pursuit. He heard none but he was not especially encouraged by this. If Menant was behind him he did not expect him to announce his presence.

With full daylight, his confidence grew fast. Ahead he could see the last buttress of Misoka he had to cross. Beyond lay the relatively flat and easy country to the border. That country contained one last threat to him — the death-breathing gas vent, the *musuku*, where most of his men had died that time before. On this occasion he would be sure to make a wide detour to avoid it.

Shortly after it became light a third being emerged from sleep on the southern face of Misoka. Absolom had passed the sort of night he liked least, drizzling wet and with no decent trees around for the family to build nests. His old shoulder-wound ached. He was in a foul temper and went around barking and growling and hustling the rest of the family out of their sodden ground-nests. He harried the younger silver-back, bullied the females so that the lactating Rebecca, who was mothering the recently returned Toto, had to knock her own baby off her teat. Only the thought of the *bwambas* within a day's march sustained Absolom.

He had the family moving off in single file in a very short time. They would just have to restrain their urge to eat everything along the route for a while. He knew just where he was taking them. It was close to a place he had been unable to make himself approach for some time, a narrow defile where clumps of succulent bedstraw grew. It was close to the spot at which he had once received his great hurt.

Jean-Pierre picked up the tall man's spoor ten minutes after full daylight. He knew then that he had a great deal of ground to make up. These were still yesterday's tracks. He soon hit fresh ones and, like Varuti, began to make good time. He caught his first glimpse of him half-an-hour later, fully five hundred yards ahead, moving fast and about to make the slight climb to traverse that last buttress thrown out by Misoka. Jean-Pierre bitterly regretted that he had not taken the chance of fetching the rifle from the hut. By doing so he might never had caught up with Varuti but now he had little chance of doing so anyway. The delay might have put him one thousand, instead of five hundred, yards behind, but at least he would have had a faint chance of stopping him or harrying him, even at that range. As Varuti laboured up the slope five hundred yards away, he knew that with the rifle he could have broken his thin body like a clay pipe in a sideshow.

Varuti topped the buttress. He was out of breath. He looked briefly behind but saw no pursuit. Jean-Pierre had anticipated that a man topping a last commanding rise might do exactly that, He crouched, hidden, in the scrub, waiting for Varuti to move on. Instead, his quarry was so sure of himself that he threw himself down to recover his breath. There was nothing to be lost now if the tall man did see him. It might even panic him into doing something foolish, like running into another *musuku*. There were many of them in the border country. Jean-Pierre broke cover, running whenever the ground allowed.

By the time he reached the point at which Varuti had briefly rested, the tall man was barely three hundred yards ahead.

Jean-Pierre saw everything that happened next as if watching an event in an arena. He was about to start downhill in pursuit when his eyes took in that, beyond Varuti's hurrying figure, though not far beyond, other movement was taking place in the scrub. A group of gorillas was about to cross the track from the direction of the high ground. He knew them at once. The young silver-back, Ammon, came out first, then two or three females. Even without glasses Jean-Pierre recognised them all. Varuti had no idea of their presence yet. He was loping on at a carefree half-run, still hidden from the apes by a bend in the track. Jean-Pierre watched Abraham cross next, then Abigail with Cain and Abel.

For the moment he was so absorbed by the gorillas that he almost forgot Varuti. The tall man had rounded the corner and had seen Cain and Abel crossing. He stopped irresolutely, no doubt badly disturbed by memories of a previous, similar encounter. Suddenly he decided to rush on, as if to pass the danger-point as quickly as possible. It was the worst decision he could have made. At that moment, barely twenty yards ahead of him, the lactating female with her own young and Toto at heel decided to make a dash for it.

Toto, perhaps because she was used to human beings, stopped in the middle of the track and found herself behind and on her own. Varuti now had gorillas all round him, barking and shrieking with anger and distress and calling for the baby to join them in the safety of the bush.

Then Jean-Pierre saw Absolom. He rose and stood tall, fifteen yards behind Varuti. Varuti heard him scream and turned.

The tall man stood in the middle of the track, much as he had once stood facing Absolom before. And, as before, he raised his automatic and aimed.

Absolom would have charged anyway but it is probable that something in the combination of circumstances — the tall figure, the place, the raised arm that held a thing that had once hurt him so badly — made him press home his charge as ferociously as he did now.

Jean-Pierre heard the single shot as it went high, humming like a hornet over Absolom's unwounded shoulder, and this time a hornet that failed to sting. Jean-Pierre expected at least two more shots in the ten yards Absolom had to cover to reach Varuti. No shots came.

Absolom caught Varuti with a swinging right claw, tore his throat open, clutched him before he fell and, with both hands, tore his head from his body. The great silver-back stood looking down at the corpse and then, almost casually, dropped to all fours and sauntered off after the rest of the family.

Jean-Pierre didn't bother to move or cover Varuti's remains. Ants, ravens, vultures would do the cleaning up. He recovered his damaged Walther because he was fond of it and because it had served him well. The fact that it was now irreparably damaged seemed significant to him. He took Varuti's blood-soaked jacket because he would have to report how he had died, though that report would be made privately and in confidence to Jack Wright.

For the next hour he sat quietly on the mountainside, watching his favourite gorilla family dine on what Helen insisted on calling *galium* but which he still liked to think of by its common name — bedstraw.

So there they were, feeding as peacefully as if nothing had happened. For him they would always be the most magnificent animals on earth. Abraham, Abigail, Ahab and Abednego, Ahitabel, Cain and Abel with the new, young silver-back, Ammon, eating slightly apart from the others. At any moment now Ammon would be feeling his oats and making his bid for leadership and freedom. Close by munched the two females that Ammon had brought with him to join the group, Rachel and Rebecca. The most exciting thing of all was that one of this pair, Rebecca, allowed Toto an occasional suck at her breasts.

And there, presiding over them all, Absolom, the great leader, whose dominance was still supreme but which must one day, in the not too distant future, pass from him.

Anyone, even a stranger who didn't much care for wild animals, seeing gorillas in the wild must surely be overwhelmed by their size and dignity. But Jean-Pierre had known them as familiars, day in, day out, year after year, not only this group, but many others. The Misoka gorillas could not, must not, be left to take their chance with any guardian who did not feel their unique quality as he did. They were on the retreat, no doubt about that, but someone with the real power to do so had to fight their rearguard action for them, even if it ended in defeat. Varuti had been killed but someone else would come to get the bauxite. Jean-Pierre had no illusions about that. And, after the bauxite? There would be other threats — from foresters, farmers, local politicians after a fast buck, from developers of all kinds. All these would have to be held at bay if the gorillas were to have the faintest chance of survival.

Jean-Pierre looked at Absolom peacefully eating and felt an overwhelming and proprietary affection for him. It was almost as if the great ape, in killing the monstrous Varuti, had put Jean-Pierre for ever in his debt.

Jean-Pierre watched Absolom and his relatives going about their ponderous business. He had no urge to move from the scene. It was a full hour before Absolom decided that it was time his family moved on in search of yet more food. In the course of that hour Jean-Pierre's mind was made up for him.

When the last ape had disappeared into the scrub, Jean-Pierre rose to his feet and began the long trek back to Baruva. As he walked he tried to work out how precisely he would explain to Jack Wright that he had, after all that he had said and all that had passed, decided to take up the president's offer: that he would agree to become Director of National Parks because, in the end, it was the only hope he had not only of controlling the Chiribandas, and Mahojas, even scientists like Helen Lawes, but the even more powerful pressure-groups who would undoubtedly follow. To give the gorillas even an outside chance of surviving he would have to be able to wield President Olindo's big stick.

But then, he reflected, Jack Wright, to whom personal power was everything, would simply have assumed that Jean-Pierre would take the job all along. Jean-Pierre's consolation would have to be that Jack Wright would almost certainly have come to this conclusion for all the wrong reasons.

Far behind him now he heard Absolom bark.